MY BIG FAT
Supernatural
HONEYMOON

ALSO EDITED BY P. N. ELROD

My Big Fat Supernatural Wedding

MY BIG FAT
Supernatural
HONEYMOON

Edited by

P. N. ELROD

ST. MARTIN'S GRIFFIN

NEW YORK

www.stmartins.com

Book design by Spring Hoteling

ISBN-13: 978-0-312-37504-1
ISBN-10: 0-312-37504-2

First Edition: January 2008

10 9 8 7 6 5 4 3 2 1

CONTENTS

MY BIG FAT Supernatural HONEYMOON

Stalked

KELLEY ARMSTRONG

Werewolves Elena Michaels and Clayton Danvers are the protagonists of the first two novels in the Women of the Otherworld *series, and appear as major characters in succeeding books.*

I HAD TO GET RID OF THE MUTT.

Killing him would be easiest but, unfortunately, out of the question. If Elena found out, she'd be pissed. Ten years from now, I'd still be hearing about it: "Clay couldn't even get through our honeymoon without killing someone."

She'd laugh when she said it . . . in ten years. Right now, she'd be furious.

She'd argue there were better ways to handle the situation. I disagreed. The mutt knew we were in town and that by sticking around, he was taking his life into his hands. If he'd skittered into the shadows and stayed out of our way, I'd have said, "Fuck it," and pretended not to notice. After all, it was my honeymoon.

Even if he'd just stood his ground and refused to hide, I

wouldn't have made a big deal of it. Beaten the crap out of him, yes. Had to. The Law was the Law, and it stated that a non-Pack werewolf had to cede territory to a Pack one. Unfair, maybe, but if you let one mutt break the rules, the next thing you knew, they'd be camping out back at Stonehaven, knocking on the door, asking if they could use the facilities.

But this mutt wasn't hiding or defending his territory. He was stalking Elena. He'd been following us all morning and was now sitting across the restaurant, gaze glued to her ass as she bent over the buffet table.

When your mate is the only female werewolf, you get used to other wolves sniffing around. I'd spent the last eighteen years dealing with it or, more often, watching her deal with it. With Elena, interference is not appreciated. She can fight her own fights, and gets snippy if I rob her of the chance. But this was our honeymoon, and damned if I was going to let this mutt spoil it. He had to be dealt with before Elena realized he was stalking her. The question was how.

When Elena walked back to the table, the mutt had the sense to busy himself gnawing on a sparerib.

"You okay?" she asked as she slid into her seat. "You've been quiet since the Arch."

The mutt had started following us there.

"Just hungry. I'm fine now."

"I should hope so. After three plates." She buttered her bread, then studied me. "Are you sure you're okay?"

"I don't know. . . ." I shrugged and pretended to ease back in my chair, then lunged and snagged bacon from her plate. I folded it into my mouth. "Nope, still hungry."

She brandished her fork. "Then get your own or—"

I snatched another slice, too slow this time, and she stabbed the back of my hand. I yelped.

"I warned you," she laughed.

The women at the next table stared in horror. Elena glanced their way. Five years ago, she would have blushed. Ten years ago, she would have found an excuse to leave. Today, she just murmured a rueful "whoops," and dug into her potatoes.

I got another plate of food, avoiding the temptation to pass the mutt's table. He'd made a point of staying downwind outside and now sat partially obscured by a pillar, too far away for his scent to carry. For now, I'd let him think he was safe, undetected.

When I came back, Elena said, "I think I have an outing idea for us. Someone behind me in line was talking about a state park. Could be fun." Her blue eyes glittered. "Of course, we shouldn't go during the day when there are people around."

"Nope, we shouldn't." I speared a ham slab. "This afternoon, then?"

She grinned. "Perfect."

WHEN YOU RESORT TO EVERYDAY ACTIVITIES ON YOUR honeymoon, you know it's not going well. Planning our second run in as many days meant Elena was bored and trying very hard not to let me know it.

The first couple of days had been great. With two-year-old twins at home, the only time we normally got away was when our Alpha, Jeremy, sent us to track down a misbehaving mutt. Being on a mission doesn't mean we can't enjoy ourselves. There's nothing like celebrating a successful hunt with sex. Or working out the frustration of a failed hunt with sex. Or dulling that edge of pre-hunt excitement with sex.

But there was also something to be said for skipping the whole "track, capture, and maim" part and being able to go straight to a hotel room, and lock the door. Still, we could stay in there for only so long before we got restless, and when we came out, we'd discovered a problem with our honeymoon destination: there wasn't a helluva lot to do.

BACK AT THE HOTEL, WE CALLED HOME AND talked to the kids. Or they listened as we talked, and had their answers interpreted by Jeremy. As much as we loved our daily call, we spent most of it braced for the inevitable "Momma? Daddy? Home?" or in Kate's case: "Momma! Daddy! Home!" Jeremy managed to spare us this time, stopping as soon as Logan asked "Momma where?" and bustling them off with his visiting girlfriend, Jaime.

Next Jeremy and Elena would talk about the kids and discuss any new Pack or council business. Normally, I'd listen in and offer my opinion—whether they wanted it or not—but today I told Elena I was going downstairs to grab a map and a bottle of water, and took off.

I WAS REASONABLY SURE THE MUTT HADN'T FOLLOWED us from the restaurant, but wanted to scout to be absolutely certain. We'd walked to the Arch and then to the restaurant, meaning we'd had to walk back, which gave him the opportunity to follow. A cab would have solved that, but if I'd voluntarily offered to spend time trapped in a vehicle with a stranger, Elena would have been on the phone to Jeremy, panicked that my arm was reinfected and I was sliding into delirium.

So I'd suggested we take the long route back. The mutt hadn't followed. Maybe he'd had second thoughts. If he'd heard the rumors about me, he'd know he could be setting himself up for a long and painful death. But if he'd believed that, he should have hightailed it the moment he crossed our path. So while I hoped, I didn't trust.

I grabbed a brochure on state parks, stuffed it into my back pocket, then headed out the front door to circle the hotel. I got five steps before his scent hit me. I stopped to retie my sneaker and snuck a look around.

The bastard was right across the street. He sat on a bench facing the hotel, reading a newspaper. Cocky? Or just too young and inexperienced to know I could smell him from here?

I straightened and shielded my eyes, as if scanning the storefronts. When I turned his way, he lifted the paper to hide his face, but slowly. Cocky. Shit.

Normally, I'm happy to show a cocky young mutt how I earned my reputation. At that age, one good thrashing is all it takes. But damn it, this was my honeymoon.

I crossed the road and headed into the first alley.

THERE WERE TWO WAYS THE MUTT COULD PLAY this, depending on why he was stalking Elena. It could be his misguided way of challenging me. Stupid—any wolf knew his mate wouldn't lift her tail for the first younger male who sauntered her way. Only a human would fly into a jealous rage and call a man out for it. But if challenging me was his goal, he'd follow me into the alley.

Or he might really be after Elena. He wouldn't be the first mutt to think she might not object to a new mate.

I walked far enough into the alley to disappear, then crept back along the wall, lost in its shadow, stopping when I could see the hotel door. After a few minutes, a car horn blasted and a figure darted through the heavy traffic. It was the mutt, heading straight for the hotel.

I circled around the block, then came in the hotel side entrance, beside the check-in desk. I stopped there, partially hidden by a huge fake plant. The stink of the plastic fern overpowered everything else.

I peered through the fronds. There he was, hovering at the other end of the desk, sizing up the staff. Hoping to get our room number? I stepped out. Just as he turned, a pale blond ponytail bounced past on the other side of the lobby. Elena.

I turned away from the mutt before he realized I'd made him. I opened my mouth to hail Elena, then stopped. If she saw me, she'd head over here. Better for her to keep walking and I'd catch up outside the front doors—

Shit. He'd walked *in* the front doors. His scent would still linger there, and Elena had a better sense of smell than any werewolf I knew. I started walking fast to cut her off. She caught sight of the brochure rack and veered that way.

"Elena!"

I yanked the park guide from my back pocket and waved it. I moved to the left, blocking her view of the mutt. She couldn't smell him from here, but she was in charge of the Pack's mutt dossiers and might recognize him.

"Got the maps," I said. "I was looking for water. I can't find a damn machine—"

She directed my attention to the gift shop.

"Shit. Okay, let's grab one and go."

Out of the corner of my eye, I saw the mutt watching us. Elena's gaze traveled across the lobby, as if sensing something. I took her elbow and wheeled her toward the gift shop.

She peeled my fingers from her arm. "I'm looking—"

"The gift shop's behind you."

"Where I just pointed. No kidding. I'm looking for the parking garage exit. I was going to say we can get a drink on the way. It's too expensive here."

"Good. I mean, right. The stairs are back there, by the elevators."

She nodded and let me lead the way.

THE PARK WASN'T BUSY, SO AVOIDING HUMANS WAS easy. That took some of the challenge out of it, but a new place to run is always good.

We spent most of the afternoon as wolves, exploring and playing, working up a sharp hunger for the hunt. We'd found a few deer trails, but all our tearing around scared the small herd into hiding. Probably just as well—in places like this, people pay attention to ripped-apart deer carcasses, and we'd have felt guilty later, knowing we'd nudged the line between acceptable and unacceptable risk. We settled for rabbits, the fat dull-witted sort you find in preserves with few natural predators.

The snack was enough to still the hunger pangs without making us sleepy, so we followed it up with more games, these ones taking on an edge, the snarls sharper, the nips harder, fangs drawing blood, working up to the inevitable conclusion—a fast Change back and hard, raw sex that left us scratched and bruised, happy and drowsy, stretched on the forest floor, bodies apart, feet entwined.

I was on my back, shielding my eyes from the sun shifting through the trees, too lazy to move out of its way. Elena lay on her stomach, watching an ant crawl across her open palm.

"What about a second stop for our honeymoon?" I asked.

Her nose scrunched in an unspoken "What?"

"Well, I know this isn't shaping up to be everything you'd hoped. . . ."

"This afternoon was." She grinned and rubbed her foot against mine. "I'm having a good time, but if you're not . . ."

How the hell was I supposed to answer that? *No, darling, our honeymoon sucks. I'm bored and I want to go somewhere else.*

If it was true, I wouldn't have minded saying so, though I supposed, being a romantic getaway, I'd have to phrase it more carefully. Walking away from a threat set my teeth on edge, but it was better than having this mutt ruin our honeymoon. Still, given the choice between staying and making Elena think I was having a shitty time, something told me option one—even if it meant fighting a bigger, younger werewolf—was a whole lot safer.

"I'm fine," I said. "You just seemed a little . . . bored earlier."

Alarm brightened her eyes and she hurried to assure me she was, most certainly, not bored. I should have known. Any other time, Elena would have no problem admitting it. But a honeymoon was different. It was a ritual and, as such, came with rules, and saying she was bored broke them all.

Shortly after I met Elena, I'd realized that while she squirmed and chafed under the weight of human rules and expectations, there was one aspect of them she embraced almost to the point of worship. Rituals. Like Christmas. Ask Elena to bring cookies for the parent-and-tot picnic and she'll buy them at the bakery, then dump them into a plastic container so they'd look homemade. But come mid-December, she'll whip herself into a frenzy of baking, loving every minute because that's part of Christmas.

When the subject of "making it official for the kids' sake" came up, I knew she'd want the ritual—a real wedding, the kind she'd dreamed of eighteen years ago when we'd bought the rings, her face lit up with dreams of a white dress and a new life and happily ever after.

Instead of the happily ever after, she got a bite on the hand

and the kind of new life that had once existed only in her night-mares.

I won't make excuses for what I did. The truth is that your whole life can change with one split-second decision and it doesn't matter if you told yourself you'd never do it, or if you stepped into that moment with no thought of doing it. All it takes is that one second of absolute panic when the solution shines in front of you, and you grab it . . . only to have it turn to ash in your hand. There is no excuse for what I did.

After I bit Elena, it took eleven years for her to forgive me. Forgetting what I'd done to her, though, was impossible. It was al-ways there, lurking in the background.

When Elena vetoed a wedding, I thought it was just the weight of human mores again—that it didn't feel right when we already had kids. So I'd decided I'd give her one, as a surprise. Jeremy talked me out of it and it was then, as he waffled and circled the subject of "why not" that I finally understood. There could be no wedding because every step—from sending invitations to walking down the aisle—would only remind her of the one she'd planned all those years ago, and the hell she'd gone through when it fell apart.

But the honeymoon was one part of the ritual we hadn't dis-cussed. So, if a wedding was out, the least I could do was give her that.

I'd made all the arrangements, trying to create the perfect honeymoon. My way of saying that I'd screwed up eighteen years ago and I was damned lucky we'd ever reached the stage where a honeymoon was even a possibility.

THE MUTT RESURFACED AT DINNER, SPOILING MY SECOND meal in a day. Not just any meal this time, but a special one at a place so exclusive that I—well, Jeremy—had to reserve our table weeks ago. It was one of those restaurants where the lighting is so dim, I don't know how humans can see what they're eating or *find* what they're eating—the tiny portions lost on a plate filled with inedible decorations. But it was romantic. At least, that's what the guidebook said.

It matched Elena's expectations, and that was all that mattered. She'd enjoy the fussy little portions, the fancy wines, the fawning waitstaff, then fill up on pizza in our room later. Which was fine by me . . . until the mutt showed up.

As I was returning from the bathroom, he stepped into the lobby to ask the maître d' for directions. Our eyes met. He smiled, turned, and sauntered out.

I knew I should walk away. Take care of him later. But there was no way I could enjoy my dinner knowing he was prowling outside. And if I didn't enjoy it, Elena wouldn't enjoy it, and we'd get into a fight about why I'd take her someplace I'd hate only to sulk through the meal. I was determined to make it through this trip without any knock-down, drag-out fights . . . or, at least, not to cause any myself.

I waited until the maître d' escorted a couple into the dining room, then took off after the mutt.

I FOUND HIM WAITING FOR ME IN THE lane behind the restaurant. He was leaning against the wall, ankles crossed, eyes closed.

Who raises their kids like this? That was the problem with mutts. Not all mutts—I'll give them that. Some teach their sons basic survival and a few do as good a job as any Pack wolf, but there are far too many who just don't give a damn. At least in a Pack, if your father doesn't teach you properly, someone else will.

Here stood a perfect example of poor mutt-parenting skills— a kid stupid enough not only to challenge me, but to feign confi-

dence to the point of boredom, lowering his guard in the hopes
of looking "cool." Now I had to teach him a lesson, all because his
father couldn't be bothered telling him I wasn't someone to fuck
with.

Werewolves earn their reputations through endless challenges.
Twenty-seven years ago, when I'd wanted to protect Jeremy on his
rise to Alphahood, I didn't have time for that. So I'd sealed my reputation with a single decisive act, one guaranteed to convince every
mutt on the continent that the infamous child werewolf had grown
into a raging lunatic. To get to Jeremy, they had to go through me,
and after what I did, few dared try.

I could only hope this mutt just didn't realize whom he'd
challenged and, once he did, a few abject apologies and a brief
trouncing would set the matter straight and I could get back to my
honeymoon.

I walked over and planted myself in front of him.

He opened his eyes, stretched, and faked a yawn. "Clayton
Danvers, I presume?"

So much for that idea. . . .

I studied him. After a moment, he straightened, shifting his
weight and squirming like a freshman caught napping during my
lectures.

"What?" he said.

I examined him head to foot, eyes narrowing.

"What?" he said again.

"I'm trying to figure out what you've got."

His broad face screwed up, lips pulling back, giving me a shot
of breath that smelled like it'd never been introduced to mouth-
wash.

"So what is it?" I asked. "Cancer, hemorrhagic fever, rabies . . ."

"What the hell are you talking about?"

"You do have a fatal disease, right? In horrible agony? 'Cause that's the only reason any mutt barely past his first Change would call me out. Looking for a quick end to an unbearable existence."

He let out a wheezing laugh. "Oh, that's a good one. Does that line usually work? Scare us off before you have to fight? Because *that's* the only reason a runt like you would have the reputation of a psycho killer."

He stepped closer, pulling himself up straight, just to prove, in case I hadn't noticed, that he had a good five inches and fifty pounds on me. Which did *not* make me a runt. I'd spent my childhood being small for my age, but I'd caught up to an average size. Still, mutts like to point out that I'm not as big as my reputation, as if I've disappointed them.

"You do have a daddy, right?" I asked.

His face screwed up again. "What?"

"You have a father, don't you?"

"Is that some kind of Pack insult? Of course, I have a father. Theo Cain. Maybe you've heard of him."

I knew the Cains. Killed one of them a few years ago in an uprising against the Pack. "And your daddy warned you about me? Told you about the pictures?"

"Pfft." He rolled his eyes. "Yeah, I've heard about those. Photos of some dude you carved up with a hatchet."

"Chain saw."

"Whatever. It's bullshit."

I eased to the side, getting my nose away from his mouth. "And the witness? He's still alive, last I heard."

"Some guy you paid off."

"The pictures?"

"Photoshopped."

"It was almost thirty years ago."

"So?"

I shook my head. The problem with stupid people is you can't reason with them. Waste of my time, while my meal was getting cold and Elena was spending our romantic dinner alone.

Screw this.

I surveyed the dark service lane. There was never a convenient Dumpster when you needed one. I eyed the garbage cans, eyed Cain, sizing him up. . . .

"So when do we fight?" he asked.

"What?"

"You know. Go mano a mano. Fight to the death. Your death, of course. I'm looking forward to enjoying the spoils." His tongue slid between his teeth. "Mmm. I gotta thing for blondes with tight little asses, and your girl is fine. Bet she'll fix up real nice."

"Fix up?"

"You know. Get some makeup on. Get rid of that ponytail. Trade the jeans for a nice miniskirt to show off those long legs. You gotta keep after chicks about things like that or they get comfortable, let it slide. Not that she isn't damned sweet right now, but with a little extra effort, she'd be hot."

I shook my head.

"What?" he said. "You've never tried?"

"Why would I?"

"Why *wouldn't* you?"

I opened my mouth, then shut it. Another waste of time. He wouldn't understand my point of view, no more than I understood his. "So you think if you kill me, you get Elena?"

"Sure, why not?"

"If it didn't require my death, I'd be tempted to go along with it, just to watch you tell her that."

"Whatever." He rolled on his heels. "Let's get this over with.

I'm hoping you brought your chain saw, 'cause otherwise, this fight isn't going to be nearly as much fun as I was hoping, with your fucked-up arm and all."

I stopped, then slowly looked up, meeting his gaze. "My arm?"

"Yeah, Brian McKay said you busted his balls last year for having some sport with a whore. He said something was wrong with your arm. You kept using your other one. Tyler Lake says he did it, as payback for what you did to his brother."

"Yeah? Did he mention which arm it was? This one?"

I grabbed him by the throat and pinned him to the wall, hand tightening until his face purpled and his eyes bulged.

"Or was it this one?"

I slammed my fist into his jaw. Teeth and bone crackled. He tried to scream, but my hand against his windpipe stifled it to a whimper.

I dragged him down the wall until his face was level with mine, and leaned in, nose to nose. "I'd say that will teach you not to listen to rumors, but you're a bit thick, aren't you? I'm going to have to—"

A thump to my left stopped me short. I glanced over as the restaurant rear door swung open. We were behind it, a dozen feet away, out of sight. I held Cain still as I watched and listened, ready to drag him into the alley if a foot appeared under that door.

Garbage can lids clattered. They were right next to the door. No need to step outside. Just dump the trash—

Cain let out a high-pitched squeal—the loudest noise he could manage. Then he started banging at the boarded-up window beside him. I tightened my grip, my glower warning him to stop. A foot appeared under that door, someone stepping out. I dropped the mutt and dove around the corner.

"Hey! Hey, you there!"

I pressed up against the wall. Footsteps sounded. A man yelled at Cain, mistaking him for a drunk. The mutt mumbled something about being jumped, struggling to talk with a broken jaw.

I gritted my teeth. Ending a fight by alerting humans was bad enough. Trying to set them on my trail? That toppled into full-blown cowardice.

I shook it off and retreated before someone came looking for the "mugger."

BACK IN THE RESTAURANT, I LONGED TO VISIT the washroom and scrub Cain's stink off me. But I'd been gone too long already. So I grabbed a linen napkin from a wait station, wiped the blood from my hands as I strode through the dining room, and tossed the cloth onto an uncleared table.

Elena looked up from the last bites of her meal.

"Hey, there," she said, smiling. "Thought you'd made a fast food run on me."

"Nah." I took my suit coat from the chair and slipped it on, blocking the mutt's smell and covering the blood splatter. "Something didn't agree with me."

"Lunch, I bet. That's the thing about buffets—lots of food, none of it very good. So, is dessert out of the question?"

I shook my head. "Just give me a second to finish dinner."

OUR HOTEL WAS A FEW BLOCKS FROM THE restaurant, so we'd walked. Heading back, I had to switch sides every time we turned a corner, staying downwind from Elena and keeping a foot's gap between us. She didn't notice the extra distance. Neither of us was much for public displays of affection, so walking hand-in-hand wasn't expected.

That worked only until we got to our room. She leaned against me as she pulled off her heels, then ran her hand up the back of my leg, grinning upside down, hair fanning the floor. She swept it back as she stood, her hand sliding up my leg and into my back pocket.

"Pizza now?" she asked. "Or after we work up an appetite?"

I tugged her hand out, lacing my fingers with hers, elbow locked to keep her from getting close enough to smell Cain.

"Hold that thought," I said. "I'm going to grab a shower."

Her brows shot up. "Now?"

"That problem in the restaurant? I'm thinking it might be something I rolled in this afternoon. My leg's itching like mad. Let me scrub it off before I pass it along."

Her head tilted, the freckles across her nose bunching as she studied me, her bullshit meter wavering. Normal-Elena would have called me on it, but honeymoon-Elena was struggling to avoid confrontations just as much as I was, so after a moment, she shrugged.

"Take your time. I'll catch the news."

I RAN MY HANDS THROUGH MY HAIR AND lifted my face into the spray. My forearm throbbed as the hot water hit it. Tomorrow I'd pay for overworking the damaged muscle, but it was worth it if Cain took home proof that Clayton Danvers's arm was definitely *not* "fucked-up."

For two years, I'd been so careful in every fight, convinced no one would notice I was favoring my left. I should have known better. Like scavengers, mutts could sense weakness.

Damn Brian McKay. If Elena had listened to me, we wouldn't have had to worry about him talking to anyone. When he'd killed a prostitute in El Paso, Jeremy sent us after him, but left his punishment up to Elena, as he often did these days. To me, the answer was simple. McKay was a vicious thug and we should eliminate the threat while we had the excuse. Elena had disagreed and we'd let him off with a beating. Let him return home to spread his story about my arm.

I squeezed the water from my hair as I moved out of the spray and looked down at the pitted rut of scar tissue. All these years of fighting without a permanent injury and what finally does it? One little scratch from a rotting zombie. At the worst of the infection, I'd been in danger of losing my arm, so I couldn't complain about some muscle damage.

But if rumors were already circulating, I had to squelch them. And maybe even that wouldn't be enough. Was Theo Cain's son only the first in a new generation of mutts who'd heard the stories about me and fluffed them off as urban legends or, at least, ancient history?

I'd first cemented my reputation to protect Jeremy. Now I had fresh concerns—a mate, kids . . . and a fucked-up arm that was never going to get any better. So how was I going to convince this generation of mutts that Clayton Danvers really was the raging psychopath their fathers warned them about?

I rubbed the face cloth over my chest, hard and brisk enough to burn. I didn't want to go through that shit again. What the hell would I do for an encore? What *could* I do that wouldn't have Elena bustling the twins off to a motel while she reconsidered whether I was the guy she wanted raising her kids?

Elena understood why I'd taken a chain saw to that mutt. If pressed, she might even grudgingly admit it had been a good idea. Anesthetic ensured the guy hadn't suffered much—the point was only to make others think he had. Still, only in the last few years had she stopped twitching every time someone mentioned the photos. Admitting I might have been right didn't mean she wanted to *think* about what I'd done. And she sure as hell wouldn't want me doing it again.

I shut the taps and toweled off, scrubbing away any remaining trace of Cain.

As I got out, I could hear the television from the next room. So the news wasn't over. Good. I had no interest in local or world events—human concerns—but Elena would be engrossed in them. Distracting her was always a challenge . . . and a sure way to clear my head of thoughts that didn't belong on a honeymoon.

I draped the towel around my shoulders, then eased open the door to get a peek at the playing field. Through the mirror, I could see the bed. An empty bed, the spread gathered and wrinkled where Elena had sprawled to watch the news.

A sportscaster was running through scores. Shit.

I tried to see the sitting area through the mirror, but the angle was wrong. It didn't matter. If she was finished with the news, I'd lost my chance to play. I gave my dripping hair one last swipe, tossed the towel on the bathroom floor, walked into the suite, and thumped onto the bed, springs squealing.

"All done. Still ready to work up that—?"

The room was empty.

I strode to the door, heart thudding as I sniffed for Cain. I knew my fears were unfounded. No way could he get Elena out of this room . . . not without blood spattered on the walls and carpet.

But what if he'd been lurking outside the door? If she'd heard him? Peeked out and he bolted? She'd give chase.

I opened the door and was crouching at the entrance when a yelp made me jump. Down the hall, a middle-aged woman stumbled back into her room, chirping to her husband. For a moment,

I thought "Hell, I wasn't even sniffing the carpet yet." Then I remembered I was naked.

I slammed the door and stalked into the bathroom for a towel. Humans and their screwed-up sensibilities. If that woman saw Elena dragged down the hall kicking and clawing, she'd tell herself it was none of her business. But God forbid she should catch a glimpse of a naked man. Probably on the phone to security right now.

Towel in place, I cracked open the door. When I was certain it was clear, I crouched, smelling the carpet. No trace of Cain. A quick glance around, then, holding the door open with my foot, I leaned into the hall for another sniff. Nothing.

I paused for a few deep breaths, sloughing off the fear, then strode into the room to search for clues. The answer was right there, on the desk. A page ripped off the notepad, Elena's looping handwriting: *salty crab + no water = beverage run.*

Shit.

As I pulled on a T-shirt, I told myself Cain was long gone. I'd had him in a death-hold before he could lay a finger on me. A sensible mutt would take it as a lesson in arrogance, swallow the humiliation, get out of town, and find a doctor to set his jaw before he was permanently disfigured. But a sensible mutt wouldn't have gotten himself into that scrape in the first place.

Cain would back off only long enough to pop painkillers. Then the humiliation would crystallize into rage. Too cowardly to come after me, he'd aim a sucker punch where he thought I was most vulnerable: Elena, who'd just strolled out alone into the night, having no idea that a mutt had been stalking her all day because I hadn't bothered to tell her.

Shit.

As I tugged on my jeans with one hand, I dialed Elena's cell phone with the other. Elena's dress, discarded on the chair, began to vibrate. Beneath lay it the purse she'd taken to dinner, open, where she'd grabbed her wallet, leaving the purse—and her cell phone—behind.

I grabbed my sneakers and raced out the door.

I DIDN'T BOTHER CHECKING THE GIFT SHOP. ELENA had already decreed the water there too expensive. Jeremy and I might have had some lean times during my childhood, but Elena knew what it was like to wear three sweaters all winter because you couldn't afford a coat. Even if she could now buy the whole damned gift shop, she wouldn't give them three bucks for water that cost a dollar down the block.

Normally, I respect that, but this was one time when I wished to hell she'd just spend the damned money.

I strode out the front doors, stopped and inhaled. A couple glowered when they had to drop hands to walk around me. I scanned the road, sampling the air. Finally it came. Elena's faint scent on the wind. I hurried down the steps.

THERE WAS A CONVENIENCE STORE ON THE CORNER, but Elena's trail crossed the road and headed down the very alley where I'd lain in wait for Cain that afternoon. What the hell was wrong with the shop on the corner? Was the water ten cents cheaper three blocks away? Goddamn it, Elena!

Even as I cursed her, I knew I was really angry with myself. I should have warned her about the mutt. If I'd honestly believed I could keep her in my sights twenty-four hours a day, then I was deluded. Elena would see no reason why she shouldn't run out at night for water. She was a werewolf; she didn't need to worry about muggers and rapists. But a pissed-off mutt twice her size?

I broke into a jog.

THE MOMENT I STEPPED INTO THE ALLEY, I smelled him. He must have been lying in wait outside the hotel, formulating a plan. Then his quarry had sailed out the front doors . . . and waltzed straight into the nearest dark alley.

By the time he got over the shock at his good fortune, he'd lost his chance to catch her in the alley. She'd exited, walked a block then . . . cut through another alley.

Goddamn it!

I raced to that alley, then pulled up short. Cain stood at the far end, his back to me, gaze fixed on something across the road. Elena.

I could drive him toward her . . . if she'd known he was coming. I circled to the next side road, hoping to cut him off. As I approached the end, I moved into the shadows.

Elena was still there. I could sense her, that gut level calm that says she's near.

The streets and sidewalks were empty. Our hotel was in a business section of town. That had looked good when I'd picked it online—surrounded by restaurants and other conveniences. But we arrived to discover those conveniences weren't nearly so convenient when they closed at five, as the offices emptied.

Around the corner, I saw yet another quiet street, vacant except for a lone shopper gazing at the display of a closed clothing store. I had to do a double-take to make sure it was Elena. It certainly looked like her—a tall, slender woman in jeans and sneakers, her pale blond hair hanging loose down the back of her denim jacket. But window-shopping? At a display of women's business suits? This honeymoon was boring her even more than I thought.

As she studied the display, her gaze kept sliding to the right. I squinted to see what was drawing her attention, but the streetlights turned the glass into a mirror, reflecting . . . Reflecting Cain across the road behind her.

She knew he was there. I exhaled in relief. The sound couldn't have been loud enough for Elena to hear, but she went still, then pivoted just enough to see me.

She grinned. Then her smile vanished as she jerked her attention back to the window and motioned, palm out, for me to stay put.

A quick sequence of charade moves as she kept her gaze on the display. Nose lifting to inhale, fingers gesturing to the alley to her right, the stop signal again—warning me there was a mutt in that alley.

Another flurry of gestures to say she'd handle it and I could settle into backup mode. Then, midmotion, she stopped. A slow smile, teeth glinting in the darkness. Seeing that smile, I knew what she was thinking before she glanced over, lips forming the word.

"Play?"

My grin answered.

NO GAME IS FAIR—OR MUCH FUN—WHEN one of the parties doesn't realize he's playing. So Elena took care of that first. She started by drumming her fingers against her leg, her head twisting his way, a subtle hint that she knew Cain was there and was growing impatient waiting for his next move.

While I couldn't see the mutt, I could picture him, poised at the end of the alley, rocking on the balls for his feet, seeing Elena's signals but afraid to misinterpret.

She glanced over her right shoulder, hair sweeping back as her face tilted his way, and I didn't need to see her expression to imagine that too. I'd seen it often enough. Lips parted, eyes glittering beneath arched brows, a look that translated, in human or wolf, into "Well, are you going to come get me or not?"

Cain shot from the alley so fast, he stumbled. Elena laughed, a husky growl that made me lock my knees to keep from answering it myself. As Cain recovered, she turned my way with a grin. Then she took off, in a sprint, hair flashing behind her.

Cain teetered on the curb and stared after her in confusion and disappointment, the human telling him that a woman running in the other direction wasn't a good sign. She stopped at the next corner and turned to face him.

He stepped off the curb. She took a slow stride back. Another forward, another back, and it wasn't until the dance had gone on for five paces that the wolf instinct finally clicked on and he realized that to her, running away meant not "I'm trying to escape" but "catch me if you can."

His broad face split into a grin. He winced, slapping a hand to his broken jaw. When he looked up, Elena was gone. One panicked glance around, then he started to run.

HAD ELENA BEEN A WOLF PLAYING THIS MATING ritual for real, she'd have ditched Cain after five minutes, deciding he either wasn't interested enough or competent enough to track her and, either way, wasn't worthy of her attention.

He kept losing her trail and backtracking. Or he'd glimpse a pedestrian down another road and take off that way before his nose finally told him it wasn't her. Without a Pack, a werewolf grows up immersed in human society, feeling the instincts of a wolf, but not trusting them, not knowing what to do with them.

Cain seemed to be running on pure lust and enthusiasm which, while amusing, wasn't much of a challenge . . . or much fun.

After he backtracked over my trail twice—thankfully not noticing—Elena decided it was time to end this segment of the game before Cain realized there was a third player. She'd intended to take it to the next level anyway. Hunting in human form was like playing "catch me" with this mutt—not very challenging . . . and not much fun.

She led him to a park down by the river, then darted into a cluster of shrubs to Change. Cain caught up quickly—Elena had made sure he'd been right behind her. This time, once he realized what she was doing, there'd been no indecision. After a few seconds of trying unsuccessfully to see her naked through the bushes, he tore off to find a Changing spot of his own.

I guarded Elena until I heard Cain's first grunt, assuring me he wasn't about to change his mind. Then I ducked into a hiding place and undressed.

WHEN I CAME OUT, ELENA WAS ALREADY LYING in the shadows, tail flicking against the ground, eager to be off. Seeing me a dozen feet away, she let out a soft chuff, her blue eyes rolling, saying, "Settle in—this could take a while."

I was looking around when Cain's bushes erupted in a flurry of rustling, punctuated by very human grunts. He'd barely begun.

Elena's head slumped forward, muzzle resting on her forelegs as a sigh rippled through her flanks. I growled a laugh and loped off to set up the playing field.

I LAY ON A FLAT ROCK OVERLOOKING THE path, nose twitching as the river scents wafted past, making me salivate at the smell of fish. I hooked my forepaws over the rock and stretched, back arching, nails extending, foot pads scraping against the rough broken edge. I'd been waiting a while, and I could feel the ache in my muscles, urging me to get up, get moving, get running.

I stretched again and peered over the edge. The perfect launch-pad. Elena would lead Cain along the path, and with one leap, I'd have my workout. The chase, the hunt, the takedown—all more satisfying than the actual fight.

A low whine cut through the night. I lifted my head, ears swiveling as they tracked the sound to a brown wolf a hundred feet away. Cain, whining for Elena, probably worried she'd given up and taken off.

After a moment, she appeared, a pale wraith sliding silently from the shadows. Cain let out a sharper whine and danced in place like a domestic dog seeing his master come home.

Elena continued toward him, taking her time, tail down, head high. She stopped about six feet away, making him come to her, gaze straight ahead, a queen granting her subject permission to approach.

Cain paced, keeping his distance. Her body language was perfectly clear—she was establishing hierarchy—but he didn't know what to make of it, and kept pacing.

When he didn't accept the invitation to approach and sniff her, Elena started turning away. Again, clear wolf behavior, not snubbing him, just coquettishly saying "Well, if you aren't inter-ested. . . ."

Cain went still. As she presented him with her flank, his head lowered, hackles rising. I leapt to my feet, nails scrabbling against the rock, a warning bark in my throat, but before it could escape, he sprang.

Cain grabbed Elena's shoulder, teeth sinking in, whipping her off her feet. I raced down the slope as he threw her in the air. She hit the ground, spun, and dove at him, snarls slicing through the night. Cain let out a yelp of surprise and pain as she ripped into him.

I skidded to a stop fifty feet away, still unseen. Ears forward, eyes straining, sight now the most critical sense as I watched and evaluated.

After a moment, I retreated to my perch, my gaze fixed on them, ready to fly back down if the battle turned against Elena.

They continued to fight, a rolling ball of growls and fur and blood. I could smell that blood, his and hers, the latter making a whimper shudder up from my gut. I shook it off and locked my legs, standing my ground.

Finally, Elena backed away, snarling, head down, hackles up. Cain got to his feet, shaking his head, blood spraying. As he recovered, Elena glanced in my direction, wondering whether she should finish this herself or follow through on the plan.

My muscles coiled and uncoiled, as my gaze fixed on him, twice her size, too much for her to handle if she didn't have to, praying she made the right choice, the safe choice. Of course she did. With Elena, common sense always wins over ego. With one final, lip-curling snarl, she ran for the path.

She'd covered half the distance when her muzzle jerked up and she swerved, circling an oak tree and going back the other way. I was scrambling up when I caught the scents: dog and human. I followed the smell and saw a man walking a terrier, heading this way.

Elena looped back, darting a weaving path around every obstacle she could find, trying to buy time. I glanced at the dog walker. An elderly man and an old dog, creeping along, oblivious and unhurried.

As Elena circled a small outbuilding, she dipped, paw probably catching a rodent hole, not enough to make her stumble, but slowing her down. Cain lunged. He caught only a mouthful of tail hair. As his snarl of frustration reverberated through the park, the old dog lifted his muzzle in a lazy sniff, then went back to dawdling along beside his master.

Elena disappeared behind the building. A yelp, loud enough even to make the man look up. Elena's yelp. I sprang to my feet. She shot from behind the building, a pale streak, low to the ground, running full out now, Cain on her heels.

A third shape raced from behind the building, larger than the first two. *That* was Cain—I could make out the odd drop of his jaw. My gaze swung to Elena and the new mutt behind her. Cain had brought backup.

I crouched, ready to leap from the rock. The man and dog rounded the corner, bringing them right into my path below. I looked over my shoulder, at the long route, then at Elena, now tearing across the park, heading for the river, getting farther from me with each stride.

A split second of hesitation and then I leapt, sailing over the man and dog and hitting the ground hard on the other side. The little dog started yelping, a high-pitched *aii-aii-aii*. The old man wheezed and sputtered, his gasps echoing the pound of my paws as I raced away.

With my first sprint, I started closing in on Cain. But he wasn't the one I was worried about. I recognized the other mutt's scent now. Brian McKay. The mutt who'd spread the rumor of my injured arm.

McKay wasn't an arrogant kid like Cain. He was an experienced mutt with a deadly reputation. And he was right on Elena's tail, the gap between us only getting larger.

Come on, circle around! Bring him back to me!

I knew she couldn't. She finally began to veer, but east, toward the river, heading up an embankment to a set of train tracks. At the top, she started to run back down, then sheered again, staying the course. McKay bought the fake-out, turning to race down the hill, probably hoping to cut her off in descent. When she swerved back, he tried to stop himself, but spun too sharp, losing his footing and tumbling down the embankment.

I adjusted my course, heading straight for McKay. He saw me bearing down on him and found an extra spurt of energy, flying to his feet, bruises forgotten as he bolted after Elena.

The clatter of nails on wood told me she was on the train tracks. As we crested the embankment, I saw her tearing along the railway bridge, Cain a half dozen strides behind.

I caught up with McKay at the bridge's edge. I launched myself and landed on him. We went down fighting, rolling and biting, ripping out fur and flesh.

Last year, fighting in human form, McKay had pushed me closer to my limits than I'd been in years. He was a first-rate fighter and a decade my junior. I'd reached the age where those extra years were starting to make a difference and my arm hadn't made it any easier. In wolf form, though, it was all about teeth and claws. There I had the advantage, understood how to use the wolf, how to *be* the wolf better than anyone else, mutt or Pack.

That didn't make it an easy fight. McKay had a score to settle. I'd sent him packing from El Paso with broken bones and a bloodied face. The worst, though, were the bruises . . . the ones on his ego. When he took home the story of my "fucked-up" arm, the obvious question would be, "If his arm's in such bad shape, why couldn't you take him?" I'm sure McKay came up with a reasonable story—in his version, I'd probably had every Pack brother at my side—but that wouldn't stop the cut from stinging. He'd had a chance to beat me and he'd blown it.

We rolled, struggling for a hold, fangs slashing, aiming for that critical throat bite. I managed to get close, but ended up with a mouthful of fur. When I drew back, he butted his head against the bottom of my muzzle. Pain blinded me. I staggered, head shaking.

McKay let out a snort of a laugh and charged. I kept shaking my head, acting disoriented, until the last moment. Then I side-stepped. He swung around. In midturn, when he was off-balance, I dove, hitting his side. I knocked him off his feet and we skidded over the grass, plowing through a small bush, twigs crackling.

He yanked his head down, instinctively covering his throat. I slashed at his belly instead. A yelp of surprise and pain as my fangs ripped through flesh. He tried to scramble up, legs kicking, claws scratching any surface they could reach, tearing through my coat, scraping the skin beneath. His teeth clamped down on my hind leg, chomping through to bone. A gasp burbled up, but I pushed it back before it reached my throat. If I let go, he'd run. Here was my chance to prove I wasn't growing old or soft, wasn't crippled with a fucked-up arm. My chance to squelch the rumors by taking out the very mutt who'd started them.

I bit down on his belly, ignoring the pain as he chewed on my leg. When I had the best grip I could manage, I ripped back with everything I had, eyes shut against the flood of hot blood as his stomach tore open, intestines spilling out.

He let go of my leg then. He twisted around, as if he could still escape. I grabbed him by the throat and whipped him into a bridge girder. A huge chunk of flesh came free, filling my mouth with blood. I dropped him. He fell, shuddering, dying. I bit the back of his neck, swung him up, and pitched him into the river below.

A quick kill, but during those few minutes, the blood pounding in my ears blocked everything else and it was only as McKay's body splashed into the water that I finally heard Elena's snarls. I started running. My hind leg throbbed from the bite, but it wasn't broken or gushing blood. Good enough.

Halfway down the bridge, she'd stopped and was facing off with Cain, head down, ears back, fur on end. At first, the mutt seemed uncertain, prancing forward, then back, like a boxer bouncing on his heels waiting for the signal. As I rocketed down the tracks, paws pounding the railway ties, he dropped into fighting position, as if hearing the sound he'd been waiting for: the arrival of his backup.

I slowed, rolling my paws, footfalls going silent. Then, right behind him, I hunkered down and let out a low growl. He turned, and had he been in human form, he would have fallen over backward. On four legs, he did an odd little stumble, paws scrabbling against the gravel as he veered toward me.

I snarled, teeth flashing, blood flecks spraying as I shook my head. He glanced over my shoulder, probably praying the blood came from some bird or rabbit. Seeing no sign of McKay, he knew, and swerved back, in flight before he'd finished his turn. He made it two strides before Elena landed in his path, snapping and snarling.

I backed up two steps and sat. He looked from Elena to me, the challenger and the road block. Confused, he kept glancing back as if to say, "You're going to jump me, aren't you?"

Elena gave up and rushed him. She caught him in the chest, knocking him backward. They went down fighting.

It didn't last long. Cain was spooked and distracted, knowing his buddy was dead and the killer sat five feet away, waiting to do the same to him. He managed to do little more than rip out tufts of fur while Elena sank her teeth into his flank, his shoulder, his belly.

Finally, when one bite got too close to his throat, the coward kicked in. He threw himself from her and tried to make a run for it. Elena flew onto his back. She grabbed his ear between her teeth, chomped down hard enough to make him yelp, then yanked, leaving tatters. He howled and bucked. She leapt off the other side, putting him between us again.

He flipped around and took a few running strides my way. I growled. He looked from Elena to me, hesitated only a moment, then flung himself between the girders and plummeted into the river.

As Elena leaned through the metal bars to watch him, I circled her, inventorying her injuries. A nasty gash on her side was the worst of it. A lick to wipe away the dirt. When I tried to do a more thorough job, she nudged me aside, then checked me out, nosing and licking my back leg, before deciding the bite wasn't fatal and moving up beside me.

We watched Cain flail in the water below.

She glanced at me. "Good enough?" her eyes asked.

I studied him for a moment, then grunted, not quite willing to commit yet. An answering chuff and she loped off across the bridge. I went the other way.

WE TOYED WITH CAIN FOR A WHILE, RUNNING along the banks, lunging at him every time he tried to make it to shore. When he finally showed signs of exhaustion, Elena gave the signal and we left him there.

A lesson learned? Probably not. Give him a year or two and he'd be back, but in the meantime, he'd have to return to his buddies with a shredded ear and without McKay, and no matter what slant he put on the story, the meaning would be clear: situation normal. I wasn't suffering from a debilitating injury or settling into comfortable retirement with my family. I'd bought myself a little more time.

ELENA LIFTED HER HEAD, PEERING INTO THE BUSHES that surrounded us.

"Don't worry," I said. "No one can see."

"Something I really should have checked about ten minutes ago."

She pushed up from my chest, skin shimmering in the dark. She sampled the air for any sign of Cain.

"All clear." A slow stretch as she snarled a yawn. "One of these days, we're actually going to *complete* an escape before we have sex."

"Why?"

She laughed. "Why, indeed."

She started to slide off me, but I held her still, hands around her waist.

"Not yet."

"Hmm." Another stretch, her toes tickling my legs. "So when are you going to blast me?"

"For taking off and running down alleys at midnight?"

"Unless you slipped something past me in the wedding vows, I think I'm still entitled to go where I want, when I want. But do you really think I'd go traipsing down dark alleys in a strange city for a bottle of water? Why not just stick a flashing 'mug me' sign on my back?"

"Well, you did seem a bit bored. . . ."

"Please. That mutt's been following us since this morning. I was trying to get rid of him."

"What?"

"Yes, I know, I should have warned you. I realized that later, but you worked so hard to plan our honeymoon and I didn't want this mutt ruining it. I thought I'd give him a good scare and send him packing before you noticed him sniffing around."

"Huh."

I tried to sound surprised. Tried to look surprised. But her gaze swung to mine, eyes narrowing.

"You knew he was following us."

I shrugged, hoping for noncommittal.

She smacked my arm. "You were just going to let me take the blame and keep your mouth shut, weren't you?"

"Hell, yeah."

Another smack. "That's what you were doing at dinner, wasn't it? Breaking his jaw. I thought it looked off, and I could swear I smelled blood when we were walking back from the restaurant." She shook her head. "Communication. We should try it sometime."

I shifted, putting my arm under my head. "How about now? About this trip. You're bored." When she opened her mouth to protest, I put my hand over it. "There's not a damned thing to do except hole up in our hotel room, run in the forest, and hunt mutts—which, while fun, we could do anywhere. So I'm thinking, maybe it's time to consider a second honeymoon."

She sputtered a laugh. "Already?"

"I think we're due for one. So how's this? We pack, head home, see the kids for a couple of days, then take off again. Someplace where we can hole up, run in the forest and *not* have to worry about tripping over mutts. A cabin in Algonquin . . ."

She leaned over me, hair fanning a curtain around us. "Wasn't that where I suggested we go when you first asked?"

"I thought you were just trying to make it easy on me. We can rent a cabin anytime. I wanted this to be different, special."

"It was special. I was stalked, chased, attacked . . . and I got to beat the crap out of a mutt twice my size." She bent further, lips brushing mine. "A truly unique honeymoon from a truly unique husband."

She put her arms around my neck, rolled over, and pulled me on top of her.

KELLEY ARMSTRONG is the author of the Otherworld paranormal suspense series. She grew up in Ontario, Canada, where she still lives with her family. Her Web site is www.KelleyArmstrong.com.

Heorot

JIM BUTCHER

Jim Butcher's bestselling Dresden Files (now a Sci Fi Channel series) chronicles the life of modern-day Chicago's only professional wizard, Harry Dresden.

I WAS SITTING IN MY OFFICE, SORTING THROUGH my bills, when Mac called and said, "I need your help."

It was the first time I'd heard him use four whole words all together like that.

"Okay," I said. "Where?" I'd out-tersed him. Another first.

"Loon Island pub," Mac said. "Wrigleyville."

"On the way." I hung up, stood up, put on my black leather duster, and said, to my dog, "We're on the job. Let's go."

My dog, Mouse, who outweighs most European cars, bounced up eagerly from where he dozed near my office's single heating vent. He shook out his thick gray fur, especially the shaggy, almost leonine ruff growing heavy on his neck and shoulders, and we set out to help a friend.

October had brought in more rain and more cold than usual,

and that day we had both of them, plus wind. I found parking for my battered old Volkswagen Bug, hunched my shoulders under my leather duster, and walked north along Clark, into the wind, Mouse keeping pace at my side.

Loon Island Pub was in sight of Wrigley Field, and a popular hangout before and after games. It was bigger than most such businesses, and could host several hundred people throughout its various rooms and levels. Outside, large posters had been plastered to the brick siding of the building. Though the posters were soaked with rain, you could still read CHICAGO BEER ASSOCIATION and NIGHT OF THE LIVING BREWS, followed by an announcement of a home-brewed beer festival and competition, with today's date on it. There was a lot of foot traffic going in and out.

"Ah-hah," I told Mouse. "Explains why Mac is here, instead of at his own place. He's finally unleashed the new dark on the unsuspecting public."

Mouse glanced up at me rather reproachfully from under his shaggy brows, and then lowered his head, sighed, and continued plodding against the rain until we gained the pub. Mac was waiting for us at the front door, a sinewy, bald man dressed in dark slacks and a white shirt, somewhere between the ages of thirty and fifty. He had a very average, unremarkable face, one that usually wore a steady expression of patience and contemplation.

Today, though, it was what I could only describe as "grim."

I came in out of the rain, and passed off my six-foot oak staff to Mac to hold for me as I shrugged out of my duster. I shook the garment thoroughly, sending raindrops sheeting from it, and promptly put it back on.

Mac runs the pub where the supernatural community of Chicago does most of its hanging out. His place has seen more than its share of paranormal nasties, and if Mac looked that worried, I wanted the spell-reinforced leather of the duster between my tender skin and the source of his concern. I took the staff back from Mac, who nodded to me and then crouched down to Mouse, who had gravely offered a paw to shake. Mac shook, ruffled Mouse's ears, and said, "Missing girl."

I nodded, scarcely noticing the odd looks I was getting from several of the people inside. That was par for the course. "What do we know?"

"Husband," Mac said. He jerked his head at me, and I followed him deeper into the pub. Mouse stayed pressed against my side, his tail wagging in a friendly fashion. I suspected that the gesture was an affectation. Mouse is an awful lot of dog, and people get nervous if he doesn't act overtly friendly.

Mac led me through a couple of rooms where each table and booth had been claimed by a different brewer. Homemade signs bearing a gratuitous number of exclamation points touted the various concoctions, except for the one Mac stopped at. There, a card-stock table tent was neatly lettered, simply reading MCANALLY'S DARK.

At the booth next to Mac's, a young man, good-looking in a reedy, librarian-esque kind of way, was talking to a police officer while wringing his hands.

"But you don't get it," the young man said. "She wouldn't just leave. Not today. We start our honeymoon tonight."

The cop, a stocky, balding fellow whose nose was perhaps more red than warranted by the weather outside, shook his head. "Sir, I'm sorry, but she's been gone for what? An hour or two? We don't even start to look until twenty-four hours have passed."

"She wouldn't just *leave*," the young man half shouted.

"Look, kid," the cop said. "It wouldn't be the first time some guy's new wife panicked and ran off. You want my advice? Start calling up her old boyfriends."

"But—"

The cop thumped a finger into the young man's chest. "Get over it, buddy. Come back in twenty-four hours." He turned to walk away from the young man and almost bumped into me. He took a step back and scowled up at me. "You want something?"

"Just basking in the glow of your compassion, Officer," I replied.

His face darkened into a scowl, but before he could take a deep breath and start throwing his weight around, Mac pushed a mug of his dark ale into the cop's hand. The cop slugged it back immediately. He swished the last gulp around in his mouth, purely for form, and then tossed the mug back at McAnally, belched, and went on his way.

"Mr. McAnally," the young man said, turning to Mac. "Thank goodness. I still haven't seen her." He looked at me. "Is this him?"

Mac nodded.

I stuck out my hand. "Harry Dresden."

"Roger Braddock," the anxious young man said. "Someone has abducted my wife."

He gripped too hard and his fingers were cold and a little clammy. I wasn't sure what was going on here, but Braddock was genuinely afraid. "Abducted her? Did you see it happen?"

"Well," he said, "no. Not really. No one did. But she *wouldn't* just walk out. Not today. We got married this morning, and we're leaving on our honeymoon tonight, soon as the festival is over."

I arched an eyebrow. "You put your honeymoon on hold to go to a beer festival."

"I'm opening my own place," Braddock said. "Mr. McAnally has been giving me advice. Sort of mentoring me. This was . . . I mean, I've been here every year, and it's only once a year, and the prestige from a win is . . . the networking and . . ." His voice trailed off as he looked around him.

Yeah. The looming specter of sudden loss has a way of making you reevaluate things. Sometimes it's tough to know what's really important until you realize it might be gone.

"You two were at this booth?" I prompted.

"Yes," he said. He licked his lips. "She went to pick up some napkins from the bar, right over there. She wasn't twenty feet away and somehow she just vanished."

Personally, I was more inclined to go with the cop's line of reasoning than the kid's. People in general tend to be selfish, greedy, and unreliable. There are individual exceptions, of course, but no one ever wants to believe that the petty portions of human nature might have come between themselves and someone they care about.

The kid seemed awfully sincere. While endearing, awfully sincere people whose decisions are driven mostly by their emotions are capable of being mistaken on an epic scale. The worse the situation looks, the harder they'll search for reasons not to believe it. It seemed more likely that his girl left him than that someone took her away.

On the other hand, likely isn't the same as true—and Mac isn't the kind to cry wolf.

"How long you two been together?" I asked Braddock.

"Since we were fifteen," he replied. An anemic smile fluttered around his mouth. "Almost ten years."

"Making it official, eh?"

"We both knew when it was right," he replied. He lost the smile. "Just like I know that she didn't walk away. Not unless someone made her do it."

I stepped around Braddock and studied the high-backed

booth for a moment. A keg sat on the table, next to a little card-stock sign that had a cartoon bee decked out with a Viking-style helmet, a baldric, and a greatsword. Words beneath the bee proclaimed BRADDOCK'S MIDNIGHT SUN CINNAMON.

I grunted and reached down and pulled a simple black leather ladies' purse from beneath the bench seating. Not an expensive purse, either. "Not much chance she'd walk without taking her bag," I said. "That's for damned sure."

Braddock bit his lip, closed his eyes, and said, "Elizabeth."

I sighed.

Well, dammit.

Now she had a name.

Elizabeth Braddock, newlywed. Maybe she'd just run off. But maybe she hadn't, and I didn't think I would like myself very much if I walked and it turned out that she really was in danger, and really did get hurt.

What the hell. No harm in looking around.

"I guess the game's afoot," I said. I gestured vaguely with the purse. "May I?"

"Sure," Braddock said. "Sure, sure."

I dumped Elizabeth's purse out on the booth's table, behind the beer keg, and began rummaging through it. The usual. Wallet, some makeup, a cell phone, Kleenex, some feminine sanitary sundries, one of those plastic birth control pill holders with a folded piece of paper taped to it.

And there was a hairbrush, an antique-looking thing with a long, pointy silver handle.

I plucked several strands of dark wavy hair from the brush. "Is this your wife's hair?"

Braddock blinked at me for a second, then nodded. "Yes. Of course."

"Mind if I borrow this?"

He didn't. I pocketed the brush for the moment, and glanced at the birth control pill case. I opened it. Only the first several slots were empty. I untaped the folded paper and opened it, finding instructions for the medicine's use.

Who keeps the instructions sheet, for crying out loud?

While I pondered it, a shadow fell across Braddock and a beefy, heavily tattooed arm shoved him back against the spine of the partition between booths.

I looked up the arm to the beefy, heavily tattooed bruiser attached to it. He was only a couple of inches shorter than me, and layered with muscle gone to seed. He was bald and sported a bristling beard. Scar tissue around his eyes told me he'd been a fighter, and a lumpy, often-broken nose suggested that he might not have been much good at it. He wore black leather and rings heavy enough to serve as passable brass knuckles on every finger of his right hand. His voice was like the rest of him—thick and dull. He flung a little triangle of folded cardstock at Braddock. "Where's my keg, Braddock?"

"Caine," Braddock stammered. "What are you talking about?"

"My keg, bitch," the big man snarled. A couple of guys who wished they were more like Caine lurked behind him, propping up his ego. "It's gone. You figure you couldn't take the competition this year?"

I glanced at the fallen table tent. It also had a little Wagnerian cartoon bee on it, and the lettering read CAINE'S KICKASS.

"I don't have time for this," Braddock said.

Caine shoved him back against the booth again, harder. "We ain't done. Stay put, bitch, unless you want me to feed you your ass."

I glanced at Mac, who stared at Caine, frowning, but not doing anything. Mac doesn't like to get involved.

He's smarter than I am.

I stepped forward, seized Caine's hand in mine, and pumped it enthusiastically. "Hi, there. Harry Dresden, PI. How you doing?" I nodded at him, smiling, and smiled at his friends too. "Hey, are you allergic to dogs?"

Caine was so startled that he almost forgot to try crushing my hand in his. When he got around to it, it hurt enough that I had to work not to wince. I'm not heavily built, but I'm more than six and a half feet tall, and it takes more strength than most have got to make me feel it.

"What?" he said wittily. "Dog, what?"

"Allergic to dogs," I clarified, and nodded down at Mouse. "Occasionally someone has a bad reaction to my dog, and I'd hate that to happen here."

The biker scowled at me and then looked down.

Two hundred pounds of Mouse, not acting at *all* friendly now, stared steadily at Caine. Mouse didn't show any teeth or growl. He didn't need to. He just stared.

Caine lifted his lips up from his teeth in an ugly little smile. But he released my hand with a jerk, and then sneered at Braddock. "Say, where's that pretty little piece of yours? She run off to find a real man?"

Braddock might have been a sliver over half of Caine's size, but he went after the biker with complete sincerity and without a second thought.

This time Mac moved, interposing himself between Braddock and Caine, getting his shoulder against Braddock's chest. The older man braced himself and shoved Braddock back from the brink of a beating, though the younger man cursed and struggled against him.

Caine let out an ugly laugh and stepped forward, his big hands closing into fists. I leaned my staff so that he stepped into it, the blunt tip of the wood thrusting solidly against the hollow of his throat. He made a noise that sounded like, "glurk," and stepped back, scowling ferociously at me.

I tugged my staff back against my chest so that I could hold up both hands, palms out, just as the dumpy cop, attracted by Braddock's thumping and cursing, came into the room with one hand on his nightstick. "Easy there, big guy," I said, loud enough to make sure the cop heard. "The kid's just upset on account of his wife. He doesn't mean anything by it."

The bruiser lifted one closed fist as if he meant to drive it at my noggin, but one of his two buddies said urgently, "Cop."

Caine froze and glanced back over his shoulder. The officer might have been overweight, but he looked like he knew how to throw it around, and he had a club and a gun besides. Never mind all the other uniforms theoretically behind him.

Caine opened his fist, showing an empty hand, and lowered it again. "Sure," he said. "Sure. Misunderstanding. Happen to anybody."

"You want to walk away," the cop told Caine, "do it now. Otherwise you get a ride."

Caine and company departed in sullen silence, glaring daggers at me. Well. Glaring letter openers, anyway. Caine didn't seem real sharp.

The cop stalked over to me more lightly than he should have been able to—no question about it, the man knew how to play rough. He looked at me, then at my staff, and kept his nightstick in his hand. "You Dresden?"

"Uh-huh," I said.

"Heard of you. Work for Special Investigations sometimes. Call yourself a wizard."

"That's right."

"You know Rawlins?"

"Good man," I said.

The cop grunted. He jerked his head toward the departing Caine as he put the stick away. "Guy's a con. A hard case too. Likes hurting people. You keep your eyes open, Mr. Wizard, or he'll make some of your teeth disappear."

"Yeah," I said. "Golly, he's scary."

The cop eyed me, then snorted and said, "Your dentures." He nodded, and walked out again, probably tailing Caine to make sure he left.

The cop and Caine weren't all that different, in some ways. The cop would have loved to take his stick to Caine's head as much as Caine had wanted to swat mine. They were both damned near equally sensitive about Braddock's missing wife too. But at least the cop had channeled his inner thug into something that helped out the people around him—as long as he didn't have to run up too many stairs, I guess.

I turned back to Mac and found him still standing between the kid and the door. Mac nodded his thanks to me. Braddock looked like he might be about to start crying, or maybe screaming.

"No love lost there, eh?" I said to Braddock.

The kid snarled at the empty space where Caine had been. "Elizabeth embarrassed him once. He doesn't take rejection well and he never forgets. Do you think he did it?"

"Not really. Mac," I asked. "Something tipped you off that this was from the spooky side. Lights flicker?"

Mac grunted. "Twice."

Braddock stared at Mac and then at me. "What does that have to do with anything?"

"Active magic tends to interfere with electrical systems," I said. "It'll disrupt cell phones, screw up computers. Simpler things, like the lights, usually just flicker a bit."

Braddock had a look somewhere between uncertainty and nausea on his face. "Magic? You're kidding, right?"

"I'm tired of having this conversation," I said. I reached into my pocket for Elizabeth Braddock's fallen hairs. "This joint got a back door?"

Mac pointed silently.

"Thanks," I said. "Come on, Mouse."

THE BACK DOOR OPENED INTO A LONG, NARROW, dirty alley running parallel to Clark. The wind had picked up, which meant that the cold rain was mostly striking the upper portion of one wall of the alley. Good for me. It's tough to get a solid spell put together under even a moderate rain. When it's really coming down, it's all but impossible, even for a relatively simple working—such as a tracking spell.

I'd done this hundreds of times, and by now it was pretty routine. I found a clear spot of concrete in the lee of the sheltering wall and sketched a quick circle around me with a piece of chalk, investing the motion with a deliberate effort of will.

As I completed the circle, I felt the immediate result—a screen of energy that rose up from the circle, enfolding me and warding out any random energy that might skew the spell. I took off my necklace, a silver chain with a battered old silver pentacle hanging from it, murmuring quietly, and tied several of Elizabeth's hairs through the center of the pentacle. After that, I gathered up my will, feeling the energy focused by the circle into something almost tangible, whispered in faux-Latin, and released the gathered magic into the pentacle.

The silver five-pointed star flickered once, a dozen tiny sparks of static electricity fluttering over the metal surface and the hairs bound inside it. I grimaced. I'd been sloppy, to let some of the energy convert itself into static. And I'd been harping on my apprentice about the need for precision for a week.

I broke the circle by smudging the chalk with one foot, and glanced at Mouse, who sat patiently, mouth open in a doggy grin. Mouse had been there for some of those lessons, and he was smarter than the average dog. How much smarter remained to be seen, but I got the distinct impression that he was laughing at me.

"It was the rain," I told him.

Mouse sneezed, tail wagging.

I glowered at him. I'm not sure I could take if it my dog was smarter than me.

The falling rain would wash away the spell on the amulet if I left it out in the open, so I shielded it as carefully as I could with the building and my hand. A hat would have come in handy for that purpose, actually. Maybe I should get one.

I held up the amulet, focusing on the spell. It quivered on the end of its chain, and then swung toward the far end of the alley, a sharp, sudden motion.

I drew my hand and the amulet back up into the sleeve of my duster, whistling. "She came right down this alley. And judging by the strength of the reaction, she was scared bad. Left a really big trail."

At that, Mouse made a chuffing sound and started down the alley, snuffling. The end of his short lead, mostly there for appearance' sake, dragged the ground. I kept pace, and by the time Mouse was twenty yards down the alley, he had begun growling low in his throat.

That was an occasion worth a raised eyebrow. Mouse didn't

make noise unless there was Something Bad around. He increased his pace and I lengthened my stride to keep up.

I found myself growling along with him. I'd gotten sick of Bad Things visiting themselves upon people in my town a long time ago.

When we hit the open street, Mouse slowed. Magic wasn't the only thing that a steady rain could screw up. He growled again and looked over his shoulder at me, tail drooping.

"I got your back," I told him. I lifted a section of my long leather duster with my staff, so that I could hold the amulet in the shelter it offered. I looked only moderately ridiculous while doing so.

I'm going to get a hat one of these days. I swear.

The tracking spell held, and the amulet led me down the street, toward Wrigley. The silent stadium loomed in the cold gray rain. Mouse, still snuffling dutifully, abruptly turned down another alley, his steps hurrying to a lope. I propped up my coat again and consulted the amulet again.

I was so busy feeling damp and cold and self-conscious that I forgot to feel paranoid, and Caine came out of nowhere and swung something hard at my skull.

I turned my head and twitched sideways at the last second, and took the blow just to one side of the center of my forehead. There was a flash of light and my legs went wobbly. I had time to watch Caine wind up again and saw that he was swinging a long, white, dirty athletic sock at me. He'd weighted one end with something, and created an improvised flail.

My hips bounced off a municipal trash can, and I got one arm between the flail and my face. The protective spells on my coat are good, but they're intended to protect me against gunfire and sharp, pointy things. The flail smashed into my right forearm. It went numb.

"So what, you steal my keg for Braddock, so his homo-bee cinnamon crap would win the division? I'm gonna take it out of your ass."

And with that pleasant mental image, Caine wound up again with that flail.

He'd made a mistake, though, pausing to get in a little dialogue like that. If he'd hit me again, immediately, he probably could have beaten me unconscious in short order. He hadn't hesitated long—but it had been long enough for me to pull my thoughts together. As he came in swinging, I snapped the lower end of my heavy staff into a rising quarter-spin, right into his testicles. The thug's eyes snapped wide open and his mouth locked into an open, silent scream.

It's the little things in life you treasure.

Caine staggered and fell to one side, but one of the Cainettes came in hard behind him and pasted me in the mouth. By itself, I might have shrugged it off, but Caine had already rung my bells once. I went down to one knee and tried to figure out what was going on. Someone with big motorcycle boots kicked me in the guts. I fell to my back and drove a heel into his kneecap. There was a crackle and a pop, and he fell, howling.

The third guy had a tire iron. No time for magic—my damned eyes wouldn't focus, much less my thoughts. By some minor miracle, I caught the first two-handed swing on my staff.

And then two hundred pounds of wet dog slammed into Cainette Number Two's chest. Mouse didn't bite, presumably because there are some things even dogs won't put in their mouths. He just overbore the thug and smashed him to the ground, pinning him there. The two of them flailed around.

I got up just as Caine came back in, swinging his flail.

I don't think Caine knew much about quarterstaff fighting. Murphy had been teaching it to me, however, for almost four years. I got the staff up as Caine swung and intercepted the sock. The weighted end wrapped around my staff, and I jerked the weapon out of his hands with a sweeping twist. With the same motion, I brought the other end of the staff around and popped him in the noggin.

Caine flopped to the ground.

I stood there panting and leaning on my staff. Hey, I'd won a brawl. That generally didn't happen when I wasn't using magic. Mouse seemed fine, if occupied holding his thug down.

"Jerk," I muttered to the unconscious Caine, and kicked him lightly in the ribs. "I have no idea what happened to your freaking keg."

"Oh my," said a woman's voice from behind me. She spoke perfectly clear English, marked with an accent that sounded vaguely Germanic or maybe Scandinavian. "I have to admit, I didn't expect you'd do that well against them."

I turned slightly, so that I could keep the thugs in my peripheral vision, and shifted my grip on the staff as I faced the speaker.

She was tall blonde, six feet or so, even in flat, practical shoes. Her tailored gray suit didn't quite hide an athlete's body, nor did it make her look any less feminine. She had ice-blue eyes, a stark, attractive face, and she carried a duffel bag in her right hand. I recognized her. She was the supernatural security consultant to John Marcone, the kingpin of Chicago crime.

"Miss Gard, isn't it?" I asked her, panting.

She nodded. "Mr. Dresden."

My arm throbbed and my ears were still ringing. I'd have a lovely goose egg right in the middle of my forehead in an hour.

"Glad I could entertain you," I said. "Now if you'll excuse me, I'm working."

"I need to speak to you," she said.

"Call during office hours." Caine lay senseless, groaning. The guy I'd kicked in the knee whimpered and rocked mindlessly back and forth. I glared at the thug Mouse had pinned down.

He flinched. There wasn't any fight left in him. Thank God. There wasn't much left in me, either.

"Mouse," I said, and started down the alley.

Mouse rose up off the man, who said, "Oof!" as the dog planted both paws in the man's belly as he pushed up. Mouse followed me.

"I'm serious, Mr. Dresden," Gard said to my back, following us.

"Marcone is only a king in his own mind," I said without stopping. "He wants to send me a message, he can wait. I've got important things to do."

"I know," Gard said. "The girl. She's a brunette, maybe five foot five, brown eyes, green golf shirt, blue jeans, and scared half out of her mind."

I stopped and turned to bare my teeth at Gard. "Marcone is behind this? That son of a bitch is going to be sorry he ever *looked* at that—"

"No," Gard said sharply. "Look, Dresden, forget Marcone. This has nothing to do with Marcone. Today's my day off."

I stared at her for a moment, and only partly because the rain had begun to make the white shirt she wore beneath the suit jacket become transparent. She sounded sincere—which meant nothing. I've learned better than to trust my judgment when there's a blonde involved. Or a brunette. Or a redhead.

"What do you want?" I asked her.

"Almost the same thing you do," she replied. "You want the girl. I want the thing that took her."

"Why?"

"The girl doesn't have enough time for you to play twenty questions, Dresden. We can help each other and save her, or she can die."

I took a deep breath and then nodded once. "I'm listening."

"I lost the trail at the far end of this alley," she said. "Clearly, you haven't."

"Yeah," I said. "Skip to the part where you tell me how you can help me."

Wordlessly, she opened up the duffel bag and drew out—I kid you not—a double-bitted battle-ax that must have weighed fifteen pounds. She rested it on one shoulder. "If you can take me to the grendelkin, I'll deal with it while you get the girl out."

Grendelkin? What the hell was a grendelkin?

Don't get me wrong—I'm a wizard. I know about the supernatural. I could fill up a couple of loose-leaf notebooks with the names of various entities and creatures I recognized. That's the thing about knowledge, though. The more you learn, the more you realize how much there *is* to learn. The supernatural realms are bigger, far bigger, than the material world, and humanity is grossly outnumbered. I could learn about new beasties until I dropped dead of old age a few centuries from now and still not know a quarter of them.

This one was new on me.

"Dresden, seconds could matter, here," Gard said. Beneath the calm mask of her lovely face, I could sense a shadow of anxiety, of urgency.

As I absorbed that, there was a sharp clicking sound as a piece of broken brick, or a small stone from roofing material fell to the ground farther down the alley.

Gard whirled, dropping instantly into a fighting crouch, both hands on her ax, holding it in a defensive position across the front of her body.

Yikes.

I'd seen Gard square off against a world-class necromancer and her pet ghoul without batting a golden eyelash. What the hell had her so spooked?

She came back out of her stance warily, then shook her head and muttered something under her breath before turning to me again. "What's going to happen to that girl . . . You have no idea. It shouldn't happen to anyone. So I'm begging you. Please help me."

I sighed.

Well, dammit.

She said please.

THE RAIN WAS WEAKENING THE TRACKING SPELL ON my amulet and washing away both the scent of the grendelkin and the psychic trail left by the terrified Elizabeth, but between me and Mouse we managed to find where the bad guy had, literally, gone to earth. The trail ended at an old storm-cellar-style door in back of the buildings on the east side of Wrigley Field, under the tracks of the El, near Addison Station. The doors were ancient and looked like they were rusted shut—though they couldn't have been, if the trail went through them. They were surrounded by a gateless metal fence. A sign on the fence declared the area dangerous and to keep out—you know, the usual sound advice that thrill-seeking blockheads and softhearted wizards with nagging headaches always ignore.

"You sure?" I asked Mouse. "It went in there?"

Mouse circled the fence, snuffling at the dry ground protected from the rain by the El track overhead. Then he focused intently on the doors and growled.

The amulet bobbed weakly, less definitely than it had a few minutes before. I grimaced and said, "It went down here, but it traveled north after that."

Gard grunted. "Crap."

"Crap," I concurred.

The grendelkin had fled into Undertown.

Chicago is an old city—at least by American standards. It's been flooded, burned down several times, been constructed and re-constructed ad nauseum. Large sections of the city have been built up as high as ten and twelve feet off the original ground level, while other buildings have settled into the swampy muck around Lake Michigan. Dozens and dozens of tunnel systems wind beneath its surface. No one knows exactly how many different tunnels and chambers people have created intentionally or by happenstance. And since most people regard the supernatural as one big scam, no one has noticed all the additional work done by not-people in the meantime.

Undertown begins somewhere just out of the usual traffic in the commuter and utility tunnels, where sections of wall and roof regularly collapse, and where people with good sense just aren't willing to go. From there, it gets dark, cold, treacherous, and jeal-ously inhabited, increasingly so the farther you go.

Things live down there. All kinds of things.

A visit to Undertown bears more resemblance to suicide than exploration, and those who do it are begging to be Darwined out of the gene pool. Smart people don't go down there.

Gard slashed a long opening in the fence with her ax, and we descended crumbling old concrete steps into the darkness.

I murmured a word and made a small effort of will, and my

amulet began to glow with a gentle blue-white light, illuminating the tunnel only dimly—enough, I hoped, to see by while still not giving away our approach. Gard produced a small red-filtered flashlight from her duffel bag, a backup light source. It made me feel better. When you're underground, making sure you have light is almost as important as making sure you have air. It meant that she knew what she was doing.

The utility tunnel we entered gave way to a ramshackle series of chambers, the spaces between what were now basements and the raised wall of the road that had been built up off the original ground level. Mouse went first, with me and my staff and my amulet right behind him. Gard brought up the rear, walking lightly and warily.

We went on for maybe ten minutes, through difficult-to-spot doorways and at one point through a tunnel flooded with a foot and a half of icy stagnant water. Twice, we descended deeper into the earth, and I began getting antsy about finding my way back. Spelunking is dangerous enough without adding in anything that could be described with the word "ravening."

"This grendelkin," I said. "Tell me about it."

"You don't need to know."

"Like hell I don't," I said. "You want me to help you, you gotta help me. Tell me how we beat this thing."

"We don't," she said. "I do. That's all you need to know."

That sort of offended me, being so casually kept ignorant. Granted, I'd done it to people myself about a million times, mostly to protect them, but that didn't make it any less frustrating. Just ironic.

"And if it offs you instead?" I said. "I'd rather not be totally clueless when he's charging after me and the girl and I have to turn and fight."

"It shouldn't be a problem."

I stopped in my tracks, and turned to regard her.

She stared back at me, eyebrows lifted. Water dripped somewhere nearby. There was a faint rumbling above us, maybe the El going by somewhere overhead.

She pressed her lips together and nodded, a gesture of concession. "It's a scion of Grendel."

I started walking again. "Whoah. Like, *the* Grendel?"

"Obviously," Gard sighed. "Before Beowulf faced him in Heorot—"

"*The* Grendel?" I asked. "*The* Beowulf?"

"Yes."

"And it actually happened like in the story?" I demanded.

"It isn't far wrong," Gard replied, an impatient note in her voice. "Before Beowulf faced him, Grendel had already taken a number of women on his previous visits. He got spawn upon them."

"Ick," I said. "But I think they make a cream for that now."

Gard gave me a flat look. "You have no idea what you're talking about."

"No kidding," I said. "That's the point of asking."

"You know all you need."

I ignored the statement, and the sentiment behind it to boot. A good private investigator is essentially a professional asker of questions. If I kept them coming, eventually I'd get some kind of answer. "Back at the pub, there was an electrical disruption. Does this thing use magic?"

"Not the way you do," Gard said.

See there? An answer. A vague answer, but an answer. I pressed ahead. "Then how?"

"Grendelkin are strong," Gard said. "Fast. And they can bend minds in an area around them."

"Bend how?"

"It can make people not notice it, or to notice only dimly. Disguise itself, sometimes. It's how they get close. Sometimes it can cause malfunctions in technology."

"Veiling magic," I said. "Illusion. Been there, done that." I mused. "Mac said there were two disruptions. Is there any reason it would want to steal a keg from the beer festival?"

Gard shot me a sharp look. "Keg?"

"That's what those yahoos in the alley were upset about," I said. "Someone swiped their keg."

Gard spat out a word that would probably have gotten bleeped out had she said it on some kind of Scandinavian talk show. "What brew?"

"Eh?" I said.

"What kind of liquor was in the keg?" she demanded.

"How the hell should I know?" I asked. "I never even saw it."

"Dammit."

"But . . ." I scrunched up my nose, thinking. "The sign from his table had a drawing of a little Viking bee on it, and it was called Caine's Kickass."

"A bee," she said, her eyes glittering. "You're sure?"

"Yeah."

She swore again. "Mead."

I blinked at her. "This thing ripped off a keg of mead and a girl? Is she supposed to be its . . . bowl of bar nuts or something?"

"It isn't going to eat her," Gard said. "It wants the mead for the same reason it wants the girl."

I waited a beat for her to elaborate. She didn't. "I'm rapidly running out of willingness to keep playing along," I told her, "but I'll ask it—why does it want the girl?"

"Procreation," she said.

"Thank you, now I get it," I said. "The thing figures she'll need a good set of beer goggles before the deed."

"No," Gard said.

"Oh, right, because it isn't human. The *thing* is going to need the beer goggles."

"No," Gard said, harder.

"I understand. Just setting the mood, then," I said. "Maybe it picked up some lounge music CDs too."

"Dresden," Gard growled.

"Everybody needs somebody sometime," I sang. Badly.

Gard stopped in her tracks and faced me, her pale blue eyes frozen with glacial rage. Her voice turned harsh. "But not everybody impregnates women with spawn that will rip its own way out of its mother's womb, killing her in the process."

See, another answer. It was harsher than I would have preferred.

I stopped singing and felt sort of insensitive.

"They're solitary," Gard continued in a voice made more terrible for its uninflected calm. "Most of the time, they abduct a victim, rape her, rip her to shreds and eat her. This one has more in mind. There's something in mead that makes it fertile. It's going to impregnate her. Create another of its kind."

A thought occurred to me. "That's what kind of person still has her instructions taped to her birth control medication. Someone who's never taken it until very recently."

"She's a virgin," Gard confirmed. "Grendelkin need virgins to reproduce."

"Kind of a scarce commodity these days," I said.

Gard snapped out a bitter bark of laughter. "Take it from me, Dresden. Teenagers have always been teenagers. Hormone-ridden, curious, and generally ignorant of the consequences of their actions. There's never been a glut on the virgin market. Not in Victorian times, not in the Renaissance, not at Hastings, and not now. But even if they were ten times as rare in the modern age, there would still be more virgins to choose from than at any other point in history." She shook her head. "There are so *many* people, now."

We walked along for several paces.

"Interesting inflection, there," I said. "Speaking about those times as if you'd seen them firsthand. You expect me to believe you're better than a thousand years old?"

"Would it be so incredible?" she asked.

She had me there. Lots of supernatural critters were immortal, or the next best thing to it. Even mortal wizards could hang around for three or four centuries. On the other hand, I'd rarely run into an immortal who felt so human to my wizard's senses.

I stared at her for a second and then said, "You wear it pretty well, if it's true. I would have guessed you were about thirty."

Her teeth flashed in the dim light. "I believe it's currently considered more polite to guess twenty-nine."

"Me and polite have never been on close terms."

Gard nodded. "I like that about you. You say what you think. You act. It's rare in this age."

I kept on the trail, quiet for a time, until Mouse stopped in his tracks and made an almost inaudible sound in his chest. I held up a hand, halting. Gard went silent and still.

I knelt down by the dog and whispered, "What is it, boy?"

Mouse stared intently ahead, his nose quivering. Then he paced forward, uncertainly, and pawed at the floor near the wall.

I followed him, light in hand. On the wet stone floor were a few tufts of grayish hair. I chewed my lip and lifted the light to examine the wall. There were long scratches in the stone—not much wider than a thumbnail, but they were deep. You couldn't easily see the bottom of the scratch marks.

Gard came up and peered over my shoulder. Amidst the scents of lime and mildew, her perfume, something floral I didn't recognize, was a pleasant distraction. "Something sharp made those," she murmured.

"Yeah," I said, collecting the hairs. "Hold up your ax."

She did. I touched the hairs to the edge of the blade. They curled away from it as they touched it, blackening and shriveling, adding the scent of burnt hair to the mix.

"Wonderful," I sighed.

Gard lifted her eyebrows and glanced at me. "Faeries?"

I nodded. "Malks, almost certainly."

"Malks?"

"Winterfae," I said. "Felines. About the size of a bobcat."

"Nothing steel can't handle, then," she said, rising briskly.

"Yeah," I said. "You could probably handle half a dozen."

She nodded once, brandished the ax, and turned to continue down the tunnel.

"Which is why they tend to run in packs of twenty," I added, a couple of steps later.

Gard stopped and gave me a glare.

"That's called sharing information," I said. I gestured at the wall. "These are territorial markings for the local pack. Malks are stronger than natural animals, quick, almost invisible when they want to be, and their claws are sharper and harder than surgical steel. I once saw a malk shred an aluminum baseball bat to slivers. And if that wasn't enough, they're sentient. Smarter than some people I know."

"Od's bodkin," Gard swore quietly. "Can you handle them?"

"They don't like fire," I said. "But in an enclosed space like this, I don't like it much, either."

Gard nodded once. "Can we treat with them?" she asked. "Buy passage?"

"They'll keep their word, like any fae," I said. "If you can get them to give it in the first place. But think of how cats enjoy hunting, even when they aren't hungry. Think about how they toy with their prey sometimes. Then distill that joyful little killer instinct out of every cat in Chicago and pour it all into one malk. They're to cats what Hannibal Lecter is to people."

"Negotiation isn't an option, then."

I shook my head. "I don't think we have anything to offer them that they'll want more than our screams and meat, no."

Gard nodded, frowning. "Best if they never notice us at all, then."

"Nice thought," I said. "But these things have a cat's senses. I could probably hide us from their sight or hearing, but not both. And they could still smell us."

Gard frowned. She reached into her coat pocket and drew out a slim box of aged, pale ivory. She opened it and began gingerly sorting through a number of small ivory squares.

"Scrabble tiles?" I asked. "I don't want to play with malks. They're really bad about using plurals and proper names."

"They're runes," Gard said quietly. She found the one she was after, took a steadying breath, and then removed a single square from the ivory box with the same cautious reverence I'd seen soldiers use with military explosives. She closed the box and put it back in her pocket, holding the single ivory chit carefully in front of her on her palm.

I was familiar with Norse runes. The rune on the ivory square in her hand was totally unknown to me. "Um. What's that?" I asked.

"A rune of Routine," she said quietly. "You said you were skilled with illusion magic. If you can make us look like them, even for a few moments, it should allow us to pass through them unnoticed, as if we were a normal part of their day."

Technically, I had told Gard that I was *familiar* with illusion magic, not skilled. Truth be told, it was probably my weakest skill set. Nobody's good at everything, right? I'm good with the ka-boom magic. My actual use of illusion hadn't passed much beyond the craft's equivalent of painting a few portraits of fruit bowls.

But I'd just have to hope that what Gard didn't know wouldn't get us both killed. Elizabeth didn't have much time, and I didn't have many options. Besides, what did we have to lose? If the bid to sneak by failed, we could always fall back on negotiating or slugging it out.

Mouse gave me a sober look.

"Groovy," I said. "Let's do it."

A GOOD ILLUSION IS ALL ABOUT IMAGINATION. YOU create a picture in your mind, imagining every detail, imagining so hard that the image in your head becomes nearly tangible, almost real. You have to be able to see it, hear it, touch it, taste it, smell it, to engage all your senses in its (theoretical) reality. If you can do that, if you can really believe in your fake version of reality, then you can pour energy into it and create it in the minds and senses of everyone looking at it.

For the record, it's also how all the best liars do business—by making their imagined version of things so coherent that they almost believe it themselves.

I'm not a terribly good liar, but I knew the basics of how to make an illusion work, and I had two secret weapons. The first was the tuft of hair from an actual malk, which I could use to aid in the accuracy of my illusion. The second was a buddy of mine, a big gray tomcat named Mister who deigned to share his apartment with Mouse and me. Mister didn't come with me on cases, being above such trivial matters, but he found me pleasant company when I was at home and not moving around too much, except when he didn't, in which case he went rambling.

I closed my eyes once I'd drawn my chalk circle, gripped the malk hair in my hand, started my image on a model of Mister. I'd seen malks a couple of times, and most of them bore the same kinds of battle scars Mister proudly wore. They didn't look exactly like cats, though. Their heads were shaped differently, and their fur was rougher, stiffer. The paws had one too many digits on them too, and were wider than a cat's—but the motion as they moved was precisely the same.

"Noctus ex illuminus," I murmured, once the image was firmly fixed in my thoughts, that of three ugly, lean, battle-marked malks walking through on their own calm business. I sent out the energy that would power the glamour and broke the circle with a slow, careful motion.

"Is it working?" Gard asked quietly.

"Yeah," I said, my eyes still closed, focused on the illusion. I fumbled about until I found Mouse's broad back, and rested one hand on his fur. "Stop distracting me. Walk."

"Very well." She drew in a short breath, said something, and then there was a snapping sound and a flash of light. "The rune is active," she said. She put her hand on my shoulder. The malks weren't using any light sources, and if a group of apparent-malks tried to walk through with one, it would kind of spoil the effect we were trying to achieve. So we'd have to make the walk in the dark. "We have perhaps five minutes."

I grunted, touched my dog, and we all started walking, trusting Mouse to guide our steps. Even though it was dark, I didn't dare open my eyes. Any distraction from the image in my head would cause it to disintegrate like toilet paper in a hurricane. So I walked, concentrating, and hoped like hell it worked.

I couldn't spare any brain-time for counting, but we walked for what felt like half an hour, and I was getting set to ask Gard if we were through yet when an inhuman voice not a foot from my left ear said, in plain English, "More of these new claws arrive every day. We are hungry. We should shred the ape and have done."

I nearly fell on my ass, it startled me so much, but I held on to the image in my head. I'd heard malks speak before, with their odd inflections and unsettling intonations, and the sound only reinforced the image in my head.

A round of both supporting and disparaging comments rose from all around me, all in lazy, malk-inflected English. There were more than twenty of them. There was a small horde.

"Patience," said another malk. The tone of its voice somehow suggested that this was a conversation that had repeated itself a million times. "Let the ape think it has cowed us into acting as its door wardens. It hunts in the wizard's territory. The wizard will come to face it. The Erlking will give us great favor when we bring the wizard's head."

Gosh. I felt famous.

"I'm weary of waiting," said another malk. "Let us kill the ape and its prey and then hunt the wizard down."

"Patience, hunters. He will come to us," the first one said. "The ape's turn will come, after we have brought down the wizard." There was an unmistakable note of pleasure in its voice. "And his little dog too."

Mouse made another subvocal rumble in his chest. I could, just barely, feel it in his back. He kept walking, though, and we passed through the stretch of tunnel occupied by the malks. It was another endless stretch of minutes and several turns before Gard let out her breath between her teeth and said, "There were more than twenty."

"Yeah, I kind of noticed that."

"I think we are past them."

I sighed and released the image I'd been holding in my head, calling forth dim light from my amulet. Or tried to release the image, at any rate. I opened my eyes and blinked several times, but my head was like one of those TVs at the department store, when one image has been burned into it for too long. I looked at Mouse and Gard, and had trouble shaking the picture of the savage, squash-headed malks I'd been imagining around them with such intensity.

"Do you have another of those rune things?" I asked her.

"No," Gard said.

"We'll have to get creative on the way out," I said.

"There's no need to worry about that yet," she said, and started walking forward again.

"Sure there is. Once we get the girl, we have to get *back* with her. Christ, haven't you read any Joseph Campbell at all?"

She shrugged one shoulder. "Grendelkin are difficult opponents. Either we'll die, or it will. So there's only a fifty-fifty chance that we'll need to worry about the malks on the way out. Why waste the effort until we know if it will be necessary?"

"Call me crazy, but I find that if I plan for the big things, like how to get back to the surface, it makes it a little simpler to manage the little things. Like how to keep on breathing."

She held up a hand and said, "Wait."

I stopped in my tracks, listening. Mouse came to a halt, snuffling at the air, his ears twitching around like little radar dishes, but he gave no sign that he'd detected lurking danger.

"We're close to its lair," she murmured.

I arched an eyebrow. The tunnel looked exactly the same as it had for several moments now. "How do you know?"

"I can feel it," she said.

"You can *do* that?"

She started forward. "Yes. It's how I knew it was moving in the city to begin with."

I ground my teeth. "It might be nice if you considered *sharing* that kind of information."

"It isn't far," she said. "We might be in time. Come on."

I felt my eyebrows go up. Mouse had us both beat when it came to purely physical sensory input, and he'd given no indication of a hostile presence ahead. My own senses were attuned to all kinds of supernatural energies, and I'd kept them focused ever since we'd entered Undertown. I hadn't sensed any stirring of any kind that would indicate some kind of malevolent presence.

If knowledge is power, then it follows that ignorance is weakness. In my line of work, ignorance can get you killed. Gard hadn't said anything about any kind of mystic connection between herself and this beastie, but it was the most likely explanation for how she could sense its presence when I couldn't.

The problem with that was that those kinds of connections generally didn't flow one-way. If she could sense the grendelkin, odds were that it could sense her right back.

"Whoah, wait," I said. "If this thing might know we're coming, we don't want to go rushing in blind."

"There's no time. It's almost ready to breed." There was hint of a snarl in her words as the ax came down off her shoulder. Gard pulled what looked like a road flare out of her duffel bag and tossed the bag aside.

Then she threw back her head and let out a scream of pure, unholy defiance. The sound was so loud, so raw, so primal that it hardly seemed human. It wasn't a word, but that didn't stop her howl from eloquently declaring Gard's rage, her utter contempt for danger, for life—and for death. That battle cry scared the living snot out of me, and it wasn't even aimed in my direction.

Gard struck the flare to life with a flick of a wrist and shot me a glance over her shoulder. Eerie green light played up over her face, casting bizarre shadows, and her icy eyes were very wide and white-rimmed above a smile stretched so tightly that the blood had drained from her lips. Her voice quavered disconcertingly. "Enough talk."

Holy Schwarzenegger.

Gard had lost it.

This wasn't the reaction of the cool, reasoning professional I'd seen working for Marcone. I'd never actually *seen* anyone go truly, old-school *berserkergang,* but that scream . . . It was like hearing an echo rolling down through the centuries from an ancient world, a more savage world, now lost to the mists of time.

And suddenly I had no trouble at all believing her age.

She charged forward, whipping her ax lightly around with her right hand, holding the blazing star of the flare in her left. Gard let out another banshee shriek as she went, a wordless cry of challenge to the grendelkin that declared her intent as clearly as any horde of phonemes: *I am coming to kill you.*

And ahead of us in the tunnels, something much, much bigger than Gard answered her, a deep-chested, basso bellow that shook the walls of the tunnel in answer: *Bring it on.*

My knees turned shaky. Hell, even Mouse stood with his ears

pressed against his skull, tail held low, body set in a slight crouch. I doubt I looked any more courageous than he did, but I kicked my brain into gear, spat out a nervous curse, and hurried after her.

Charging in headlong might be a really stupid idea, but it would be an even *worse* idea to stand around doing nothing, throwing away the only help I was likely to get. Besides. For better or worse, I'd agreed to work with Gard, and I wasn't going to let her go in without covering her back.

So I charged headlong down the tunnel toward the source of the terrifying bellow. Mouse, perhaps wiser than I, hesitated a few seconds longer, then made up for it on the way down the tunnel, until he was running a pace in front of me, matching my stride. We'd gone maybe twenty yards before his breath began to rumble out in a growl of pure hostility, and he let out his own roar of challenge.

Hey, when in Cimmeria, do as the Cimmerians do. I screamed too. It got lost in all the echoes bouncing around the tunnels.

Gard, running hard ten paces ahead of me, burst into a chamber. She gathered herself in a sudden leap, flipping neatly in the air, and plummeted from sight. The falling green light of the flare showed me that the tunnel opened into the top of a chamber the size of a small hotel atrium, and if Mouse hadn't stopped first and leaned back against me, I might have slid over the edge before I could stop. As it was, I got a really good look at a drop of at least thirty feet to a wet stone floor.

Gard landed on her feet, turned the momentum into a forward roll, and a shaggy blur the size of an industrial freezer whipped past her, slamming into the wall with a coughing roar and a shudder of impact.

The blonde woman bounced up, kicked off a stone wall, flipped over again, and came down on her feet, ax held high. She'd discarded the flare, leaving it in the center of the floor, and I got my first good look at the place, and at the things in it.

First of all, the chamber, cavern, whatever it was—it was huge. Thirty feet from ceiling to floor, at least thirty feet wide, and it stretched out into the darkness beyond the sharp light cast by the flare. Most of it was natural stone. Some of the surfaces showed signs of being crudely cut with hand-wielded tools. A ledge about two feet wide ran along the edge of the chamber in a C-shape, up near the top. I'd nearly tumbled off the ledge into the cavern. There were stairs cut into the wall below me—if you could call the twelve-inch projections crudely hacked out of the stone every couple of feet a stairway.

My glance swept over the cavern below. A huge pile of newspapers, old blankets, bloodstained clothes, and unidentifiable bits of fabric must have served as a nest or bed for the creature. It was three feet high in the middle, and a good ten or twelve feet across. A mound of bones, nearby, was very nearly as large. The old ivory gleamed in the eerie light of the flare, cleared entirely of meat, though the mound was infested with rats and vermin, all tiny moving forms and glittering red eyes.

A huge stone had been placed in the center of the floor. A metal beer keg sat on top of it, between the tied-down, spread-eagled legs of a rather attractive and very naked young woman. She'd been tied down with rough ropes, directly over a thick layer of old bloodstains congealed into an almost rubbery coating on the rock. Her eyes were wide, her face flushed with tears, and she was screaming.

Gard whipped her ax through a series of scything arcs in front of her, driving them at the big furry blur. I had no idea how she was covering the ground fast enough to keep up with the thing. They were both moving at Kung Fu Theater speed. One of Gard's swipes must have tagged it, because there was a sudden bellow of rage and it bounded into the shadows outside of the light of the flare.

She let out a howl of frustration. The head of her ax was smeared with black fluid, and as it ran across the steel, flickers of silver fire appeared in the shape of more strange runes. "Wizard!" she bellowed. "Give me light!"

I was already on it, holding my amulet high and behind my head, ramming more will through the device. The dim wizard light flared into incandescence, throwing strong light at least a hundred feet down the long gallery—and drawing a shriek of pain and surprise from the grendelkin.

I saw it for maybe two seconds, while it crouched with one arm thrown up to shield its eyes. The grendelkin was flabby over a quarter ton of muscle, and the nails on its fingers and toes were black, long, and dangerous-looking. It was big, nine or ten feet, and covered in hair. Not fur, like a bear or a dog, but *hair,* human hair, with pale skin easily seen beneath, so that the impression it gave was one of an exceptionally hirsute man, rather than that of a beast.

Definitely male. Terrifyingly so—I'd seen smaller fire extinguishers. And from the looks of things, Gard and I must have interrupted him in the middle of foreplay.

No wonder he was pissed.

Gard saw the grendelkin and charged forward. I saw my chance to pitch in. I lifted my staff and pointed it at the creature, gathered another surge of will, and snarled, *"Fuego!"*

My staff was an important tool, allowing me to focus and direct energy much more precisely and with more concentration than I could manage without it. It didn't work as well as my more specialized blasting rod for directing fire, but for this purpose it would do just fine. A column of golden flame as wide as a whiskey barrel leapt across the cavern to the grendelkin, smashing into its head and upper body. It was too dispersed to kill the grendelkin outright, but hopefully it would blind and distract it enough to let Gard get in the killing blow.

The grendelkin lowered his arm and I saw a quick flash of yellow eyes, a hideous face, and a mouthful of fangs. Those teeth spread into a smile, and I realized that I might as well have hit him with the stream of water from a garden hose, for all the effect the fire had on him. He moved, an abrupt whipping of its massive shoulders, and flung a stone at me.

Take it from me, the grendelkin's talents were wasted on the abduct-rape-devour industry.

He should have been playing professional ball.

By the time I realized the rock was on the way, it had already hit me. There was a popping sound from my left shoulder, and a wave of agony. Something flung me to the ground, driving the breath out of my lungs. My amulet fell from my suddenly unresponsive fingers, and the brilliant light died at once.

Dammit, I had assumed big and hostile meant dumb, and the grendelkin wasn't. It had deliberately waited for Gard to charge forward out of the light of the dropped flare before it threw.

"Wizard!" Gard bellowed.

I couldn't see anything. The brief moment of brilliant illumination had blinded my eyes to the dimmer light of the flare, and Gard couldn't be in much better shape. I got to my feet, trying not to scream at the pain in my shoulder, and staggered back to look down at the room.

The grendelkin bellowed again, and Gard screamed—this time in pain. There was the sound of a heavy blow and Gard, her hands empty, flew across the circle of green flare-light, a dim shadow. She struck the wall beneath me with an ugly, heavy sound.

It was all happening so *fast*. Hell's bells, but I was playing out of my league, here.

I turned to Mouse and snarled an instruction. My dog stared at me for a second, ears flattened to his skull, and didn't move.

"Go!" I screamed at him. "Go, go, go!"

Mouse spun and shot off back down the way we'd come.

Gard groaned on the floor beneath me, stirring weakly at the edge of the dim circle of light cast by the flare. I couldn't tell how badly she was hurt—but I knew that if I didn't move before the grendelkin finished her, she wasn't going to get any better. I could hear Elizabeth sobbing in despair.

"Get up, Harry," I growled at myself. "Get a move on."

I could barely move my left arm, so I gripped my staff in my right and began negotiating the precarious stone stairway.

A voice laughed, out in the darkness. It was a deep voice, masculine, mellow and smooth. When it spoke, it did so with precise, cultured pronunciation. "Geat bitch," the grendelkin murmured. "That's the most fun I've had in a century. Surt, but I wish there were a few more Choosers running about the world. You're a dying breed."

I could barely see the damned stairs in the flare's light. My foot slipped and I nearly fell.

"Who's the *seidrmadr*?" the grendelkin asked.

"Gesundheit," I said.

It appeared at the far side of the circle of light, and I stopped in my tracks. The grendelkin's yellow eyes gleamed with malice and hunger. It flexed its claw-tipped hands very slowly, baring its teeth in another smile. My mouth felt utterly dry and my legs were shaking. I'd seen it move. If it rushed me, things could get ugly.

Strike that. *When* it rushed me, things *were* going to get ugly.

"Is that a fire extinguisher in your pocket?" I asked, studying it intently. "Or are you just happy to see me?"

The grendelkin's smile spread wider. "Most definitely the latter. I'm going to have two mouths to feed, shortly. What did she promise you to fool you into coming with her?"

"You got it backwards. I permitted her to tag along with me," I said.

The grendelkin let out a low, lazily wicked laugh. It was eerie as hell, hearing such a refined voice come from a package like that. "Do you think you're a threat to me, little man?"

"You think I'm not?"

Idly, the grendelkin dragged the clawed fingers of one hand around on the stone floor beside him. Little sparks jumped up here and there. "I've been countering *seid* since before I left the Old World. Without that, you're nothing more than a monkey with a stick." He paused and added, "A rather weak and clumsy monkey at that."

"Big guy like you shouldn't have any trouble with little old me, then," I said. His eyes were strange. I'd never seen any quite like that. His face, though pretty ugly, was similar to others I'd seen. "I guess you have some history with Miss Gard, there."

"Family feuds are always the worst," the grendelkin said.

"Have to take your word for it," I said. "Just like I'm going to have to take these women. I'd rather do it peaceably than the hard way. Your call. Walk away, big guy. We'll both be happier."

The grendelkin looked at me, and then threw its head back in a rich, deeply amused laugh. "Not enough that I already have a broodmare and wounded little wildcat to play with, I also have a clown. It's practically a festival."

And with that, the grendelkin rushed me. A crushing fist the size of a volleyball flicked at my face. I was fast enough, barely, to slip the blow. I flung myself to the cavern floor, gasping as the shock of landing reached my shoulder. That sledgehammer of flesh and bone slammed into the wall with a brittle crunching sound. Chips of flying stone stung my cheek.

It scared the crap out of me, which was just as well. Terror makes a great fuel for some kinds of magic, and the get-the-hell-away-from-me blast of raw force I unleashed on the grendelkin would have flung a parked car to the other side of the street and into the building beyond.

The grendelkin hadn't been kidding about knowing counter-magic, though. All that naked force hit him and just sort of slid off of him, like water pouring around a stone. It only drove him back about two steps—which was room enough to let me drop to one knee and swing my staff again. It wasn't a bone-crushing blow, powered as it was by only one hand and from a fairly unbalanced position.

But I got him in the fire extinguisher.

The grendelkin let out a howl about two octaves higher than his original bellows had been, and I scooted around him, running for the altar stone where Elizabeth Braddock lay helpless—away from Gard. I wanted the grendelkin to focus all his attention on me.

He did.

"Behind you!" Elizabeth screamed, her eyes wide with terror.

I whirled and a sweep of the grendelkin's arm ripped the staff out of my hand. Something like a steel vise clamped around my neck, and my feet came up off the ground.

The grendelkin lifted my face to his level. His breath smelled of blood and rotten meat. His eyes were bright with their fury. I kicked at him, but he held me out of reach of anything vital, and my kicks plunked uselessly into his belly and ribs.

"I was going to make it quick for you," he snarled. "For amusing me. But I'm going to start with your arms."

If I didn't have him right where I wanted him, I'd have been less than sanguine about my chances of survival. I'd accomplished that much, at least. He had his back to the tunnel.

"Rip them off one at a time, little *seidrmadr*." He paused. "Which, when viewed from a literary perspective, has a certain amount of irony." He showed me more teeth. "I'll let you watch me eat your hands. Let you see what I do to these bitches before I'm done with you."

Boy, was he going to get it.

One of his hands grabbed my left arm, and the pain of my dislocated shoulder made my world go white. I fought through the agony, ripped Elizabeth Braddock's pointy-handled hairbrush from my duster's pocket, and drove it like an icepick into the grendelkin's forearm.

He roared and flung me into the nearest wall.

Which hurt. Lots.

I fell to the stone floor of the cavern in a heap. After that, my vision shrank to a tunnel and began to darken.

Which was just as well. Fewer distractions, that way. Now all I had to do was time it right.

A sound groaned down from the tunnel entrance above, an odd, ululating murmur, echoed into unintelligibility.

The furious grendelkin ripped the brush out of his arm and flung it away—but when he heard the sound, he turned his ugly kisser back toward the source.

I focused harder on the spell I had coming than upon anything I'd ever done. I had no circle to help me, lots of distractions, and absolutely no room to screw it up.

The strange sound resolved itself into a yowling chorus, like half a hundred band saws on helium, and Mouse burst out of the tunnel with a living thunderstorm of malks in hot pursuit.

My dog flung himself into the empty air, and malks bounded after him, determined not to let him escape. Mouse fell thirty feet, onto the huge pile of nesting material, landing with a yelp. The malks spilled after him, yowling in fury, dozens and dozens of malevolent eyes glittering in the light of the flare. Some jumped, some flowed seamlessly down the rough stairs, and others bounded forward, sank their claws into the stone of the far wall, and slid down it like a fireman down a pole.

I unleashed the spell.

"Useless vermin!" bellowed the grendelkin, its voice still pitched higher than before. He pointed at me, a battered-looking man in a long leather coat, and roared, "Kill the wizard or I'll eat every last one of you!"

The malks, now driven as much by fear as anger, immediately swarmed all over me. I gave them a pretty good time of it, but there were probably better than three dozen of them, and the leather coat couldn't cover everything.

Claws and fangs flashed.

Blood spattered.

The malks went insane with bloodlust.

I screamed, swinging wildly with both hands, killing a malk here or there, but unable to protect myself from all those claws and teeth. The grendelkin turned toward the helpless Elizabeth.

It was a real bitch, trying to undo the grendelkin's knotted ropes while still holding the illusion in place in my mind. Beneath the glamour that made him look like me, he fought furiously, clawing and swinging at the malks attacking him. It didn't help that Elizabeth was screaming again, thanks to the illusion of the grendelkin I was holding over myself, but hey. No plan is perfect.

"Mouse!" I cried.

A malk flew over my head, screaming, and splattered against a wall.

My dog bounded up just as I got the girl loose. I shoved her at him and said, "Get her out of here! Run! Go, go, go!"

Elizabeth didn't know what the hell was going on, but she understood that last part well enough. She fled, back toward the crude staircase. Mouse ran beside her, and when a malk flung itself at Elizabeth's naked back, my dog intercepted the little monster in the air, catching him as neatly as a Frisbee at the park. Mouse snarled and shook his jaws once. The malk's neck broke with an audible snap. My dog dropped it and fled on.

I grabbed my staff and ran to Gard. The malks hadn't noticed her yet. They were still busy mobbing the grendelkin—

Crap. My concentration had wavered. It looked like itself again, as did I.

I whirled and focused my will upon the giant pile of clean-picked bones. I extended my staff and snarled, "Counterspell this. *Forzare!*"

Hundreds of pounds of sharp white bone flung themselves at the grendelkin and the malks alike. I threw the bones hard, harder than the grendelkin had thrown his rock, and the bone shards ripped into them like the blast of an enormous shotgun.

Without waiting to see the results, I snatched up the still-burning flare and flung it into the pile of nesting fabric, bloody clothes, and old newspapers. The whole mound flared instantly into angry light and smothering smoke.

"Get up!" I screamed at Gard. One side of her face was bruised and swollen, and she had a visibly broken arm, one of the bones in her forearm protruding from the skin. With my help, she staggered up, dazed and choking on the smoke, which also blotted out the light. I got her onto the stairs, and even in our battered state we set some kind of speed record going up them.

The deafening chorus of bellowing grendelkin and howling malks faded a little as the smoke started choking them too. Air was moving in the tunnel, as the fire drew on it just as it might a chimney. I lit up my amulet again to show us the way out.

"Wait!" Gard gasped, fifty feet up the tunnel. "Wait!"

She fumbled at her jacket pocket, where she kept the little ivory box, but she couldn't reach it with her sound arm. I dug it out for her.

"Triangle, three lines over it," she said, leaning against a wall for support. "Get it out."

I poked through the little ivory Scrabble tiles until I found one that matched her description. "This one?" I demanded.

"Careful," she growled. "It's a Sunder rune." She took it from me, took a couple of steps back toward the grendelkin's cavern, murmured under her breath, and snapped the little tile. There was a flicker of deep red light, and the tunnel itself quivered and groaned.

"Run!"

We did.

Behind us, the tunnel collapsed in on itself with a roar, sealing the malks and the grendelkin away beneath us, trapping them in the smothering smoke.

We both stopped for a moment after that, as dust billowed up the tunnel and the sound of furious supernatural beings cut off as if someone had flipped a switch. The silence was deafening.

We both stood there, panting and wounded. Gard sank to the floor to rest.

"You were right," I said. "I guess we didn't need to worry about the malks on the way out."

Gard gave me a weary smile. "That was my favorite ax."

"Go back for it," I suggested. "I'll wait for you here."

She snorted.

Mouse came shambling up out of the tunnel above us. Elizabeth Braddock clung to his collar, and looked acutely embarrassed about her lack of clothing. "Wh-what?" she whispered. "What happened here? I d-don't understand."

"It's all right, Mrs. Braddock," I said. "You're safe. We're going to take you back to your husband."

She closed her eyes, shuddered, and started to cry. She sank down to put her arms around Mouse's furry ruff, and buried her face in his fur. She was shivering with the cold. I shucked out of my coat and draped it around her.

Gard eyed her, then her own broken arm, and let out a sigh. "I need a drink."

I spat some grit out of my mouth. "Ditto. Come on."

I offered her a hand up. She took it.

SEVERAL HOURS AND DOCTORS LATER, GARD AND I wound up back at the pub, where the beer festival was winding to a conclusion. We sat at a table with Mac. The Braddocks had stammered a gratuitous amount of thanks and rushed off together. Mac's keg had a blue ribbon taped to it. He'd drawn all of us a mug.

"Night of the Living Brews," I said. I had painkillers for my shoulder, but I was waiting until I was home and in bed to take one. As a result, I ached pretty much everywhere. "More like night of the living bruise."

Mac rose, drained his mug, and held it up in a salute to Gard and me. "Thanks."

"No problem," I said.

Gard smiled slightly and bowed her head to him. Mac departed.

Gard finished her own mug and examined the cast on her arm. "Close one."

"Little bit," I said. "Can I ask you something?"

She nodded.

"The grendelkin called you a Geat," I said.

"Yes, he did."

"I'm familiar with only one person referred to in that way," I said.

"There are a few more around," Gard said. "But everyone's heard of that one."

"You called the grendelkin a scion of Grendel," I said. "Am I to take it that you're a scion of the Geat?"

Gard smiled slightly. "My family and the grendelkin's have a long history."

"He called you a Chooser," I said.

She shrugged again, and kept her enigmatic smile.

"Gard isn't your real name," I said. "Is it?"

"Of course not," she replied.

I sipped some more of Mac's award-winning dark. "You're a valkyrie. A real one."

Her expression was unreadable.

"I thought valkyries mostly did pickups and deliveries," I said. "Choosing the best warriors from among the slain. Taking them off to Valhalla. Oh, and serving drinks there. Odin's virgin daughters, pouring mead for the warriors, partying until Ragnarok."

Gard threw back her head and laughed. "Virgin daughters." She rose, shaking her head, and glanced at her broken arm again. Then she leaned down and kissed me on the mouth. Her lips were a sweet, hungry little fire of sensation, and I felt the kiss all the way to my toes. Some places more than others, ahem.

She drew away slowly, her pale blue eyes shining. Then she winked at me and said, "Don't believe everything you read, Dresden." She turned to go, and then paused to glance over her shoulder. "Though, to be honest: sometimes he *does* like us to call him Daddy. I'm Sigrun."

I watched Sigrun go. Then I finished the last of the beer.

Mouse rose expectantly, his tail wagging, and we set off for home.

JIM BUTCHER enjoys fencing, martial arts, singing, bad science-fiction movies, and live-action gaming. He lives in Missouri with his wife, son, and a vicious guard dog. You may learn more at www.jim-butcher.com.

Roman Holiday, or SPQ-arrrrr

RACHEL CAINE

In My Big Fat Supernatural Wedding, *Cecilia Lockhart met her perfect match in an undead pirate captain. But even in calm seas, the course of true love never does run smooth. . . .*

BOSTON, SEPTEMBER

HONESTLY, IF SHE'D KNOWN THAT HER WEDDING WAS going to become the media event of the entire eastern seaboard, Cecilia would have gotten a better haircut. And a faster getaway limo, preferably one driven by a NASCAR star.

"Almost there," the limo driver said reassuringly as Cecilia clung to the arm of her groom and looked anxiously out the smoked windows at the flanking phalanx of news vans, reporters hanging out of car windows screaming questions, and bright popping strobes. "I can see the barricades."

The barriers were pulled aside, and the limo sailed sleekly through, coming to a flawless stop in a parking lot surrounded by marked police cars, all flashing their lights. No sirens, thankfully. Cecilia breathed a sigh of relief. She was pretty sure that the last black SUV to peel off pursuit had held Larry King *and* Oprah.

Cecilia looked at her groom, and hoped she didn't look as terrified as she felt. "That was—extreme," she said. Liam Lockhart—Captain Liam Lockhart—smiled.

"Lass, you've sailed with dead men, broken curses, and married a pirate," he said. "You might want to redefine how you measure an extreme."

He had a point. She studied him in the relative quiet of the limousine, and he looked back, perfectly calm. In the six months or so since they'd sailed the eighteenth-century pirate ship *Sweet Mourning*—Liam's ship—back into Boston Harbor and created a media firestorm, Liam had adapted to the modern world well in some ways, and not at all in others. He'd cut his hair, for example; it was a neat salt-and-pepper style, not exactly modern and not exactly antique, either. His wedding suit, however, was definitely a throwback—a fantastic black brocade coat and trousers made along the lines of what he'd been wearing when they met, only much cleaner and without the slashes, bullet holes, and various stains.

He was not conventionally handsome, maybe, but sharply intelligent, with black eyes deep and secret as the sea and a lovely kissable mouth. All in all, Liam looked utterly fantastic, and it gave Cecilia a goosebump-raising shiver of delight to see the sparkle of the gold ring on his left hand.

We're married. Not exactly a match made in heaven, a formerly cursed pirate and a slightly plain, too-round corporate wage slave who'd spent most of her not-quite-thirty years cultivating a fluorescent light tan in an office cubicle.

But when he looked at her, she felt like a goddess.

Liam lifted her hand to his lips and kissed it, mouth warm and gentle on her fingers. "In your own time, my love," he said. "No hurry."

"I'm ready," she lied with a smile, and he opened the door. He emerged first, then handed her out with the kind of flourish and elegance that she'd seen before only at Renaissance faires. On the other side of the press barricades, the cameras were eating it up. She was too terrified even to glance at the roaring crowd, but the pulse of strobes was so constant, it was like an extra sun.

Liam squeezed her hand, held her gaze, and winked. He bent close, put his lips to her ear, and said, "It'll be over soon. And then we'll have our leisure."

Cecilia fussed a little with her full silk skirts—a copy of a period wedding pattern from the eighteenth century, including a fiercely tied corset that had somehow managed to give her a dainty figure—and took his proffered arm to sweep past the rows of police officers standing at the barricades, heading for the wedding reception.

The *Sweet Mourning* loomed at the end of the dock, a massive ship with her sails currently lashed down, though Cecilia could see men swarming up into the rigging like spiders.

"That's odd," Liam said. "Should be an honor guard ready on the docks for our arrival." He pulled an elegant gold pocketwatch—his own—from his coat and checked it, frowning. "We're in good time, but not early."

With every step closer to the ship, Cecilia felt a tingle of foreboding building to an outright shiver. The crew was moving at a frantic pace on deck. Liam speeded up the pace, taking long strides in his polished black boots, and Cecilia had to hustle faster, with one hand holding her veil on her head. The guests wouldn't be far behind, although getting through security would delay them considerably, not to mention all the traffic.

The passenger ramp didn't lower for her, even when Liam shouted out a command. He cursed under his breath and gestured at the rope ladder hanging from the side of the massive ship.

"Climb?" she asked. "In this dress? Are you *kidding?*"

He wasn't. Her ascent wasn't nearly so graceful as his, and she was very relieved when he reached down to lift her the rest of the way and set her gently on the deck. The lift was performed one-handed. Liam was lean, but fearfully strong—cabled steel in those muscles.

Liam hadn't said anything about missing his ship, but she could see the change in him now, the brightness in eyes she hadn't even noticed had dulled, the subtle energy that ran through him. This was his home, not the apartment they'd gotten for him near the harbor. Liam Lockhart belonged here, on this deck—not on land, with her. Just for a second, she felt as though she was about to cry. *This is where he's happy.* It made her feel small, and second place.

Liam didn't notice. He'd been frowning and sweeping the decks with a captain's critical eye, and now he sent her a quick look of apology, and moved away from her to bellow, "Mr. Argyle, what the devil is going on here? *Argyle!*"

Cecilia realized belatedly that the supplies for the reception were piled in an untidy mess toward the bow—catering tables, tablecloths, punch bowls, silver cups, streamers, battery-powered party lights, speakers for the music. There were also people cowering there as well. Catering staff. The DJ. The wedding photographer.

As she stared in horror, a huge banner that read CONGRATULATIONS CAPTAIN AND MRS. LOCKHART fluttered from its place between the masts to the decks, was grabbed by two sailors, and flung onto the pile of reception debris.

Cecilia gasped as a pair of strange hands closed around her from behind. "Beg pardon, ma'am," said a rough voice. She struggled, but that was about as much good as fighting the tide; he simply put his arms around her, lifted her off the ground, and carried her off.

"Let go!" she screamed, and tried to twist to see Liam. She heard a clash of steel, and shouting. "Liam!"

"Quiet," her captor growled, and clapped a hand over her mouth as he hurried her down the darkened hallway, kicked open the door to the captain's cabin, and dumped her inside. "You've caused enough trouble already."

She fell to her hands and knees, twisted around, and glared back at him. He was a smallish man, compact and muscular, with wild dark hair and slightly mad eyes, arcane-looking tattoos crawling in a blue ring around his throat and down his chest.

In other words, scary.

"Stay here, witch," he ordered, and slammed the door on her. She tried the handle as soon as she heard his footsteps thump away, but of course, it was locked.

Perfect. Just *perfect*.

In the corner of the room, Cecilia spotted her blue suitcases—delivered ahead of time, thankfully—and charged for them. She skipped past the lovely going-away outfit and went for the blue jeans and comfortable white shirt at the bottom of the stack of clothing. She'd brought her own boots this time, and found a thick pirate-style belt in one of Liam's chests to finish out the ensemble.

Taking off the cute wedding lingerie would take too long. She left the white lacy underthings and topped it with more practical clothing, including the boots and belt, and began investigating the room for weapons. She'd found a dagger and was considering a cutlass when she heard the approach of a mob in full roar, noise that dumped a chill like cold water down her spine. It was coming down the hall.

The door rattled, then banged open, and Liam and Argyle charged inside. Mr. Argyle—a small, neat man with a Napoleonic haircut and Ben Franklin-style spectacles, primly dressed in a lobster-red eighteenth-century coat, white shirt, and black trousers, all sparkling new and clean—bobbed his head apologetically toward her as he shot the bolts on the door. "Ma'am," he said. "Felicitations on the happy day. Apologies for the general disaster."

Liam was ransacking the sea chests and coming up with weapons. A deadly looking double-edged knife. A six-shot revolver. A semiautomatic pistol, brand new. Liam caught the look she sent him, and shrugged half-apologetically. "Always be prepared."

"That's the Boy Scouts, not the pirates!" she said.

"Where do you think they got it from, lass?"

The roaring was loud now, right outside. Hammering started on the door. Argyle backed away from it toward them, his eyes cool and focused behind the spectacles as he held a pistol at the ready.

"Mr. Argyle," Liam said.

"Sir."

"What the sodding *devil* is going on?"

"Aye, well—"Argyle sent him a brief apologetic look. "I think the pink floral tablecloths were the last straw. But they've been muttering for months now, about how you've been bewitched again, about how devil-ridden this modern world is. I can't even convince most that the television box isn't some demonic spirit—"

A particularly loud *bang* on the door. Cecilia saw the wood shiver.

"Shortened version, Mr. Argyle, if you please," Liam said without a trace of alarm. Cecilia picked up another dagger from the pile Liam had amassed and jammed it firmly against her side, at an easy angle for a draw. "I don't think the door will hold for the epic tale."

Mr. Argyle nodded. "Mutiny, Captain. They're determined to take the ship out now, without delay."

"Well, it's not the first time that's happened," Liam said coolly. He ejected the magazine on the automatic he held, checked it, and slipped it back in with smooth efficiency.

"Respects, sir, it's the first time that we risk more than a temporary inconvenience," Argyle said. "Being mortal and all now." He sighed. "At least I convinced them to put the caterers and party staff safely on the docks. But they're taking the ship out, like it or not. I think the reception's off."

"There was no call for any of this. I'd have listened to them. I always listen."

Argyle looked briefly chagrined. "Aye. But—you must admit, sir, you've been a changed man, these last few months. And I've been no help to you. I admit, this modern world is a fair shiny place to my eyes; I failed to see how bad their morale was getting. My fault, Captain." He hesitated a moment, then said, "But perhaps it's a good thing, begging your pardon. They're pirates, black to the heart, the most of them. They don't belong out there, wolves among sheep. Better we keep them on the water where they can be watched."

"We can discuss it if we live," Liam said, and glanced at Cecilia, as if he'd suddenly remembered she was there. "My love, I'll need you out of the way. If the boys blame you for bewitching me, it's best not to give them your presence to glower at. Spark to powder."

"But—what are you going to do?"

Liam exchanged another look with his first mate, then turned toward the door. "Take back my command."

Cecilia nodded and withdrew to the farthest reaches, next to the stern window where the incoming glare would conceal her best. The cabin door shivered under a fusillade of banging.

"Here we go," Argyle muttered.

Liam reached the door, shot the bolt, and opened it, roaring, "Silence, the lot of you!" The impact was considerable. The crowd of men in the hall, fierce and brutal as they were, automatically stopped in the face of his rage, and there was a second of stillness. Liam stepped into it without a pause. "What the bloody hell are you playing at? Mutiny? Who stands for you? Come forward!"

There was a hesitation, and then one of the men stepped out. The same one who'd laid hands on Cecilia and hustled her into the cabin. "Josiah," Liam said, with a nod. "State your business."

"Captain," the man said. He had a low voice, a little rough, and he sounded firm but nervous. "The boys, we're in agreement. No more delays. This place, it's bewitched. We need clear sea air." Josiah's throat worked uncomfortably, and he sent a glance to a tall, thin, gawky man standing near him—a sharp, strong face, big eyes—who gave an encouraging nod. "You know it's true, sir. The men will go mad in this place. Best we put the witch over the side, like we done before, and—"

Liam, quick as a striking snake, put a cutlass at Josiah's throat, the point just tickling his Adam's apple. There was a collective intake of breath. Josiah didn't move.

"You're talking about my wife, Josiah Walker," Liam said softly. "Best think again, and well, before you continue."

Josiah clearly realized there was no good coming of that particular course, so he changed the conversational tack. "We'll not allow these mincing whoresons you call modern men to wander our ship and mock us, no matter what the excuse. We've had enough. Sir."

Liam lowered the sword and delivered a hard blow across Josiah's face, sending the man reeling into the arms of the other men in the doorway. "Have you," he almost hissed. "So have I. I wouldn't wish any of you on the modern world. You're a disgrace to the mothers who bore you."

Walker squared his shoulders and raised his chin, almost daring Liam to take another swing at it. "Been said before, sir. I'm sorry I called your woman a witch, but she brought us to this. And she has to go if we aim to live as we should. She's done her work—broke the curse—and that's done with her, aye?"

Walker's voice rose in a half question. He was nearly pleading, but his stare was still hard and direct, and Liam's was in no way softer.

"No," he said. It was almost a purr, deep in his throat. "And you put your hands on my woman under the penalty of a death you'd not wish on a rabid dog. Are we clear, Mr. Walker?"

Neither of them blinked. The other sailors murmured and jostled; Cecilia, heart pounding, palms sweating, faint of breath, could hear the tone of it rising, turning darker again. Liam had set them back on their heels for a while, but he was losing it quickly, and it was all because of her.

"Wait," Cecilia blurted, and stepped out of her shadows. To her surprise, they did; all of the mutineers, even Josiah Walker, paused in midmutter to shift their attention to her. "It's our honeymoon. You wouldn't kill me on the day of my wedding, would you?"

Walker frowned. Another man leaned in to say, "The wench has a point. That *would* be bad luck."

"Worse than having a woman on board?" Walker snorted. "*This* woman?"

Cecilia took a deep breath and plunged. "What if Captain Lockhart agrees to take the ship out for a period of—oh, I don't know, a month? Call it a honeymoon cruise. Then you put us back ashore, and go on about your business, if you still feel the same way. And we forget about the reception. I'll promise to keep out of your way." She gave them all a sudden grin. "Not that I expect you'll see either me or your captain much."

That woke a deep rumble of appreciative chuckling from the crew. Even Walker was forced into a slightly less vexed expression. "Well," he allowed, "that might do. Might do."

Liam deliberately relaxed, banishing his anger with an effort of sheer will. "Then as long as you all clear my cabin and let me get about the job of welcoming my new bride, you're all free to set sail, or to dive to Davy Jones for all I care."

A relieved sigh went through the men, and through Argyle as well. He'd been prepared to back Liam's play, of course, but Cecilia could see that defying the crew would have gone against his better judgment.

Liam turned toward Cecilia, just for a second, eyes burning into hers, and she forced a slight smile. He lifted her hands to his lips and kissed them. "Forgive me for leaving you," he said. "I'll be back as soon as I can."

And they all filed out, leaving her alone in the captain's cabin. After fidgeting for a while, Cecilia turned to the corner where Liam's hammock normally swayed. It was gone.

In its place was a luxurious feather bed, pristine and white, covered with fragrant red rose petals.

"Oh," she whispered, and tears stung her eyes. "Oh, Liam." It was a lovely thing.

She stretched out on it, feeling cold and lonely, listening to the thump of the crew's footsteps above her.

I should have brought a book, she thought.

Well, it was her honeymoon. Who'd have thought she'd need one?

SHE WOKE UP TO A RATTLE AT THE door, and it banged open to admit a man almost hidden beneath a massive silver tray, loaded down with an elaborate tea service. He staggered under the strain and expertly found his balance when the ship rocked and tilted.

When he lowered it, Cecilia was surprised to see it was Liam, and he was smiling.

"Good morning, love. We're well under way." Liam poured a cup of tea, added milk and sugar in the measures he already knew she liked, and handed over the delicate china. She sat on the edge of the bed and listened, nodding occasionally, as he told her details about where they were nautically in the world, what his plans were for the voyage, and all she could really understand of it was the light in his eyes, the lilt of pleasure in his voice. Although she loved seeing that in him, it also made her horribly uncertain. *I'm not good for him. This is what's good for him. If I take him away from this . . .* Maybe the crew was right. Maybe the best thing would have been to slip quietly away in Boston and let them go on without her.

Liam stopped talking and put his cup aside. She glanced down at her own and was surprised to find it empty; she'd sipped it without even noticing the taste, although she'd always enjoyed cream tea.

When she looked up, he was standing in front of her, and he

reached down to take the china from her fingers and place it care-fully back on the tray. "Biscuit?" he asked, with the blandest pos-sible tone. There were cookies on the tray. Oreos, her favorite. She nearly laughed out loud.

"No, thank you," she said. "Liam—"

He didn't waste time with another polite question, and before she could finish the sentence, he was next to her, capturing her lips with his. The kiss was a fierce, lovely thing, far different from the gentle one he'd given her at the wedding; this was a pirate's kiss, demanding surrender, and she felt her entire body give a joyous answer. When he let her up for breath, it was like rising lazily from a deep, skin-warm sea. She wanted to dive right back in.

Liam pulled back, and Cecilia shivered in response to the look on his face. She'd never had anybody stare at her in *quite* that way—and then a rush of heat flared up from her toes to melt her into a liquid, gorgeously decadent feeling of utter abandon. *Oh.*

Cecilia pushed him back onto the bed, then stood up and slowly unbuttoned her white shirt. It slipped off her shoulders and fluttered to the carpets, leaving only the fragile lace bra. The blue jeans were just as easy. Liam's breath left him in a rush.

"Permission to come aboard, sir," she said, and sat astride him. It was a long, damp, aching kiss, trembling with potential and need, and Liam's hands went around her to push her back, just a tiny bit.

"Lass," Liam murmured, "I'm not a gentleman. I wasn't born one, I wasn't made one, and the circumstances of my life haven't encouraged me to—"

She shut him up with a finger across his lips. "If I'd wanted a gentleman, I wouldn't have fallen in love with a pirate," she said. "Not even one with kind eyes."

He pulled back, frowning at her. "I do *not* have kind eyes."

"You do when you look at me." She took a deep breath. "If you're trying to warn me that you won't be a good, gentle lover, I think you're underestimating yourself," she said.

He captured her hands and held them tightly. Hers were stubby, small, and pale; his were large, square, darkened by sun, and heavily scarred. He didn't look up from his inspection of their differences as he said, "I'm saying that you are no doubt used to the refined ways of modern men who make a study of women, who understand how to—"

"Liam." She raised his chin with a finger under his chin. "If modern men have *ever* made a study of women, it's the first I've ever heard of it. If you think that I'm going to be comparing you to all my previous lovers, well, don't, because that's a list that includes two men, one of whom was a mistake, and one of whom was an *awful* mistake. And neither one of them gave a damn about how I felt during the process anyway."

Liam looked flummoxed. Appalled, even. "You mean, with all the magazines and writings and all of the visual—instruction—" He'd found the pay-per-view channels in his apartment. "—there is not a higher understanding of how to please—"

"Not a bit," she said.

He seemed completely relieved, and she had to stifle a laugh that she knew would be completely inappropriate. "So they weren't meant to be instructive."

"Did you *watch* the porn? Accuracy, not its strong suit."

He slid his palms up her arms, a warm glide of flesh. "Of course I watched it, my dear. I'm no Puritan."

"Prove it."

He slipped his hands under the thin lace bra, slowly, watching her face without blinking. He didn't restrain a smile when she let out a gasp, and it was one of his full, charming smiles, with a razor-thin edge of darkness—the kind that, she imagined, had spontaneously brought several women in his lifetime to shed their inhibitions.

Not a problem. She seemed to have left hers on shore, anyway.

"I've been thinking about this for hours," he said, and his voice was low, barely audible over the creak of timbers and rush of the sea. "There's a question I've been wanting to ask you, Cecilia. It's important."

"Yes?" Her voice came out almost calmly.

He put his lips very close to her ear. "Do you prefer the left side of the bed, or right?"

She laughed out loud, unable to stop herself. "Right side."

"Ahhh," he sighed regretfully. "That'd be a problem, then, lass, as *I* like the right side of the bed."

"Only one solution," she replied, straight-faced.

"Dice? A game of cards? Pistols at dawn?"

She kissed him, slowly and deeply. He groaned low in his throat, and pulled her closer.

"One of us has to be on top," she mumbled into his mouth. "I'll let you go first."

Under Liam's black trousers he wore, of all things, Joe Boxer briefs. With red lipstick prints. She stared. He shrugged. "Argyle advised me," he said, sounding faintly unsure. "All right?"

She smothered a laugh. "So long as they come off, I'm fine."

They did. Her lace top was also disposed of, though they took good time to enjoy the journey. It took a timeless, sunlit eternity for him to work his way from the relatively safe territory of her collarbones, nibbling down in slow, steady kisses, to her breasts. She couldn't keep herself from pulling in as much as her lungs could hold, arching toward him, desperate to have those clever, clever lips do more, go farther.

Oh, and they did. They definitely did. And it took a deliciously long time.

Liam paused for breath, looked up at her, and drew his fingertips in a slow, hot line down over her stomach, straight down. "Pace yourself, lass," he said, with a grin that took her breath away. "We've leagues to go yet." He hooked his fingers in the thin elastic band of the triangle of lace that pretended to be panties. "And plenty of territory left to explore. We've not even made landfall yet. . . ."

She heard a distant shout. Liam's smile vanished, and he turned his head, frowning. She hadn't made out any words, but evidently he had. He rolled off her, and roared, "God's *blood,* lads, we'd better be bloody *sinking!*"

She heard a kind of shrieking hiss, getting rapidly louder. He grabbed her and rolled her hard off the bed, thumping them both to the carpet between the bed and the cabin wall, an instant before something hit the stern of the ship so hard, it felt like a giant hand shaking the massive vessel. The mullioned window exploded in a shower of glass shards and lethal shrapnel.

By the time she blinked, Liam, stark naked, was already up on his feet, cursing with a bitter violence all the more alarming because he was doing it in a whisper. He shook broken glass from his trousers and stepped into them, not bothering with the fancy underwear, even while he asked, "All right?"

She nodded mutely, swallowed, and managed to say, "What's happening?" She could hear the alarm bells ringing on deck, running feet above her head, and felt the ship heel over hard enough to send her rolling against the wall. Evasive maneuvers.

"Bloody bad timing, at the very least," he said, and bent to give her a quick kiss. "Get dressed. If we're boarded, give a good account of yourself, you're the captain's wife now."

She gave him a shaky salute. "Aye aye, sir."

He eyed her with longing and great regret, touched his forehead in a casual salute, and dashed for the door.

Cecilia quickly dressed and armed herself with whatever was left over from his quick exit—a dagger, a spare cutlass, and a spare pistol. She checked. Fully loaded.

"I am *not* hiding in the corner," she said. That was a safe enough declaration; there was nobody to argue with her about it, at least not yet. She left the cabin and went down the narrow hall, blinking as she emerged into the bright shimmer of sunlight on deck.

The sails had been piled on, and the *Sweet Mourning* was cutting through the water at an incredible pace, flying like a bird. The rigging crew were on the masts and yardarms. Up on the quarterdeck, Liam was at the wheel, with Argyle leaning on the railing.

"She's got speed on us!" Argyle shouted. Cecilia ran to to the side to lean out for a look; behind them, far in the white wake, she saw another ship advancing on them. It was smaller, with a enormous single square mainsail, wider than it was tall, and a much smaller triangular sail at the prow. The design was thin and long, and somehow it put her in mind of a shark, the way it cut cleanly through the water. Argyle was right, it was frighteningly fast. Even though they had the advantage of more canvas, the other ship was rapidly gaining. "She's coming within range again! 'Ware cannon!"

Cecilia watched, wide-eyed, as a black dot traveled across the blue sky, grew in size, and ended its trajectory with a shattering crash amidships. It sent fragments spraying in every direction. Some of the shards had fallen near her feet, and she saw they were glazed pottery, not metal.

They were throwing *pots*?

And then a thick, greenish liquid that had splashed in a broad swath across the deck caught fire, an eerie flickering flame that took on a hellish intensity in less than a breath.

"Greek fire!" Argyle shouted from the quarterdeck. "No water! Smother it! *Move!*"

She got out of the way of a stampede of sailors carrying spare canvas, who began putting out the fire.

"Mrs. Lockhart!" Argyle bellowed. He no longer sounded friendly, or amused. "If you *must* expose yourself to every danger that presents, at least do so up here!"

She blinked, saw Liam and Argyle staring at her with identical expressions of disapproval.

"We'll discuss who wears the pants later," Liam said once she was on deck. "Argyle. Is it that damned madman Salvius?"

Argyle answered, and retrieved a spyglass from his pocket, studied the ship for a second, then passed the glass to his captain. "Aye. It's the *Aquila.*"

Liam flattened the spyglass with a snap and handed it back, no expression visible on his face at all. Someone from the crow's nest, far above, called out, " 'Ware ballista!" and Cecilia shaded her eyes to see something that looked like a massive, oversized spear arcing toward them. It hit toward the bow, ripping through wood like butter.

"That'll be a week in port," Argyle said with a sigh. "Hell and damnation."

"He's playing with us," Liam said, even as he spun the wheel, and the *Sweet Mourning* responded with another rapid change of course. "Any sign he's preparing to use his fire cannon?"

"Not as yet," Argyle said. "If he does, there's little enough we can do about it."

The other ship glided smoothly up to their port side, close

enough that Cecilia could see the elegant long lines of her form, and three banks of holes that were too small to be cannon ports—oar holes? There were men swarming the deck, most dressed in simple sun-faded tunics, but also a lot kitted out in armor.

One man stood alone toward the curved fishtail at the stern, muscular legs spread for stability. He was broad and sturdy, dressed in a splendid set of Roman-era armor, complete to shining helmet with a vivid crimson brush. The tunic underneath the armor was bloodred, and he glittered in the sun like some dangerously invincible god.

The Roman captain—what else could he be?—faced them as the two ships drew even with each other, and inclined his head. "Captain Lockhart," he said, in a voice loud enough to carry over a melee-filled battlefield, never mind a short span of water. "Well met on favoring seas."

"Better never met at all, you garlic-eating bastard," Liam shouted back. "What the devil are you playing at, Salvius?"

Salvius advanced to the rail of the ship, put both hands on it, and stared across at Liam. No, Cecilia realized with a shock, he was staring at her.

Liam realized it too. "What do you want, Roman?"

"Word travels," Salvius said. "I heard it from the Dutchman's own mouth that you'd broken free of your curse."

"So you came to gawp?" Liam said. "To put ballista holes in my deck for sport? To settle old grudges?"

Salvius unexpectedly grinned, showing a broad expanse of strong, if browning, teeth. "I like to see miracles for my own eyes. And now that I have—" He nodded sharply to another armored soldier, who shouted something to the men on the *Aquila's* deck.

" 'Ware arpax!" someone cried on the *Sweet Mourning,* and a massive bridge snapped up, as if spring-loaded, from the deck of the Roman ship, wide enough that two or three men could walk abreast on it. One end was fastened to the deck of that ship with some kind of hinges; the other had a lethal-looking bronze beaklike hook on the end, and it crashed down on the *Sweet Mourning*'s railing, splintering it, and dug deep into the wood of the deck, locking the two ships together.

And Roman sailors and soldiers began pouring across the bridge, roaring out a battle cry.

Cecilia pulled her pistol and cutlass. The pirates—*her* pirates—were already shouting and rallying to meet the invasion.

Captain Salvius hadn't moved from where he stood, still watching the three of them on the quarterdeck. His face was weathered, ageless, and very hard.

"As you said, Captain, your men are mortal now," he said. "Mine aren't. Stand them down, Liam. There's no need for deaths."

"I could send you to the bottom with a broadside. Short range. No misses."

"You could," Salvius said, and grinned. "For all the good it'd do you. By all means, waste the shot and powder, if you've an excess."

Liam made no reply for a few seconds, and then, "What terms?"

"Throw down arms and none of you will be harmed. I'll release you to sail off as clean as you please, once I have what I want."

Down on the decks, men were fighting, but Cecilia realized with a chill that they were also being hurt, maybe dying. She could see blood streaking the decks, and the Romans, despite being shot and stabbed, continued to press ahead with their attack. They would win. There was no other possibility.

Liam knew that too; she could see it in the stiff, angry set of his shoulders. He clasped his hands behind his back.

"And what is it you want, Salvius?"

Salvius shook his head. "After you throw down arms and give your surrender."

Argyle took hold of his captain's arm. "Don't," he said. "We can shake them. We've done it before."

"We've done it when we were invulnerable to shot and steel," Liam said. "We've done it when the *Mourning* had the devil's wind at her back and healed herself from the wounds she took in battle. We can't do it now."

They stared at each other, and then Liam shook off his first mate's hand. He took in a deep breath and said, "The ship is yours. You have my parole. Call off your sea wolves." And he put his cutlass and pistol down on the deck.

Salvius gestured to another uniformed Roman standing nearby, who gave some blasts on a shrill whistle; the attacking Roman sailors and soldiers backed off, giving the crew of the *Sweet Mourning* time to pull together in a defensive line and drag their wounded and dead out of the way.

"Throw down your arms, men," Liam shouted. "Do it now!"

Cutlasses, daggers, and pistols rained to the decking, some reluctantly. Cecilia realized she was still clutching hers, and forced herself to bend and lay them on the wood.

When she straightened, Argyle was still holding on to his, and Liam was facing him, sober and steady. "It's an order, damn you." Liam's voice unexpectedly softened. "*Duncan.* Put aside your weapons. I swear, I will not let him take you aboard that ship."

Argyle finally nodded, one sharp, convulsive nod, but his eyes were still wild and strange. He let his sword and pistol fall and assumed a stoic parade rest, as did Liam, as Captain Salvius moved through the crew of his own ship and crossed the temporary wooden bridge—the arpax?—and stepped onto the deck of the *Sweet Mourning*. He advanced toward the stern of the ship, sandaled feet thumping on the wood in confident strides, and his red cloak billowed behind him like a flag.

When the Roman stepped onto the quarterdeck, he smiled, and turned toward Cecilia.

"I am Aulus Salvius Lupus," he said. "I have the honor to be trierarch of the Roman vessel *Aquila*. And you would be . . . ?"

She licked her lips and tasted salt, either from sweat or sea spray. "Cecilia Lockhart. Wife of Captain Lockhart."

"Wife?" Salvius cut a look toward Lockhart. "Indeed. My congratulations. And how long since the happy day?"

"One," she sighed.

"Ah, that's good. Then he won't miss you much," Salvius said, and nodded to his second in command, who simply grabbed Cecilia, pinned her arms to her sides, and shoved her into the midst of a wedge of Romans, who closed ranks around her. "These are my terms, Liam. The witch goes with us, and I leave the rest of your crew untouched."

The color drained from Liam's face, leaving him as white and hard as bone. "Aulus," he said, low in his throat, "if you don't release her now, this will go badly. Very badly."

"I agree," Salvius said pleasantly. "Very badly indeed, for you. I'd rather not wash the decks with your blood, Liam, but one way or another, I'm having your witch."

Liam kept his calm, somehow. "Why?"

Salvius shrugged. "Profit. I expect the Dutchman will be along, soon enough, and Mad Peg, and all the rest, sniffing around for some hope of being freed of their eternal and well-deserved damnation. She's a valuable commodity." His voice hardened to ice and glass. "So don't stand in my way."

Liam looked at him as if he'd gone mad, or sprouted horns. "Commodity? What the devil do you mean?"

"She's a curse-breaking witch."

"She's not!"

"She broke yours, didn't she?"

"It was—" Liam controlled himself with difficulty. "It was an *accident,* you fool!"

Salvius shrugged. "Still." His smile widened, and grew chilling. "I'll try to keep her chaste and untouched until she's back in your loving arms. Unless of course she proves as difficult to control as your fine first mate, there. In which case I shall have to use persuasion."

Liam, without a sound, calmly bent, picked up his cutlass from the deck, and rammed it home in a gap of Salvius's armor with a savagery that took Cecilia's breath away.

Argyle grabbed Liam and dragged him back. Salvius looked down at the sword, driven to the hilt against his side, and pulled it out with a smooth, slow motion. Blood slicked its surface, but he showed no sign of pain. He tossed the cutlass to Liam, who caught it deftly out of the air and brought it immediately to guard. "Just for that, you can't have the witch back at all. I'll sell her to the Dutchman, or whoever else pays the best price for her services. Whatever those services may prove to be in the end is none of my affair."

Argyle had pinned Liam's arms behind him and was holding on with leverage and his full strength, whispering in the man's ear. Cecilia tried to struggle free, but the hands holding her were big, capable, and far too strong.

Aulus Salvius Lupus led the way back across the bridge of the arpax himself, and Cecilia found herself carried along like luggage. The massed smell of sweat, leather, and metal was almost overwhelming, and when she could catch a breath of sharp salt air, she was grateful.

She was dumped without ceremony by her guards so suddenly that, combined with the violent pitch-and-roll of the Roman ship, she fell face forward, catching herself at the last minute with her hands on sun-warm wood.

"Tie her to the mast," Salvius said. "Up arpax and rig for sail."

"Sir." The soldier closest to her saluted with his fist over his heart and repeated the order at top volume; two men grabbed her, lashed her tightly to the huge mast, and left her there as they went about their business. The *Aquila*'s boarding ramp creaked up, drawn by ropes and pulleys, and the ship pulled away from Liam's and heeled over, heading south with the wind. The speed was incredible—supernatural, as if the *Aquila* was driven by nuclear-powered engines. Something Liam had said came back to her: *the devil's wind.*

The *Sweet Mourning* fell behind quickly.

Facing Cecilia, about a dozen feet away, was a very curious thing: a large marble statue of a woman—a goddess, maybe—with curling upswept hair and a beautiful, empty face, her arms outstretched as if reaching for the sun. It was a beautiful piece of work, so lifelike, Cecilia could almost feel the whisper of the breeze that ruffled its draperies—elegantly rendered, almost lifelike . . .

. . . and then the stone eyes blinked.

It's the sun, Cecilia thought, and looked away. It wasn't. When she returned her attention to the statue, it was staring at her. Cecilia had been *sure* there were blank ovals in the face before, but now they were *eyes*. Blue eyes, the milky color of sea-blue chalcedony. Not quite . . . real.

The statue didn't speak, or move. It just . . . stared.

Cecilia became gradually aware of someone else nearby, an island of stillness in a sea of moving sailors. Captain Salvius. He stood, legs apart, feet braced, arms folded. Staring hard at the statue.

"What is this thing?" Cecilia blurted.

"Ah, you should be honored. Not every day you meet a genuine goddess," he said. "Her name is Larentina." He walked to the statue and caressed its cheek with one blunt fingertip. "Have you missed me, my love? Yes, of course you have. You see, I have to speak for Larentina because cruel Jupiter tore her tongue out for speaking ill of his romantic adventures." The statue closed her eyes, as if determined to shut him out. "Jupiter, now there's a god a man can respect, eh?"

"I don't understand. She's a *statue.*"

"Well, yes, now. Larentina came here to exact revenge over the sacking of her temples and raping of her virgin priestesses. Goddesses. So sensitive." Salvius tapped his grubby fingernails against her flawless white bosom. "Didn't turn out quite the way she expected, I dare say. Larentina's our luck. So long as we have her, death can't touch us. Even the gods have to let us do as we please." He faced Cecilia squarely; she thought she'd never seen a man with eyes like those, light gray and as empty as polar ice.

She drew in a steadying breath. "Are you sure you don't want me to break your curse?"

Salvius laughed. "Break all the other curses as you like, for all those sniveling fools like your precious Lockhart. Me and my men, we'll still be a power on Neptune's breast when the rest of you are gone whining to your graves. It's not a curse to us, woman. It's tactics."

He stalked away in a flutter of his bloodred cape, and Cecilia let out her breath in a slow, shaky sigh. She was facing toward the fishtail stern of the *Aquila;* over the curving coil of tail, she saw billowing sails. The *Sweet Mourning* was making her best speed to follow, but they were rapidly falling behind.

"Liam," she whispered. The world dissolved in sharp jagged colors as her eyes flooded with tears, and she bent her head and felt the pressure of panic weighing down on her.

No, she thought, and got hold of herself. *Liam wouldn't panic. Neither will I.*

As she shifted uncomfortably against the tight ropes, she felt her thick piratical metal belt buckle catch and hold against the hemp looped around her waist.

Was it even possible? . . .

Gritting her teeth, Cecilia began moving her hips back and forth, concealing it among the dips and lunges of the ship, and sawed at the rope.

This is going to hurt, some part of her complained. And she told it, *Shut up and shimmy.*

WHEN SHE FINALLY STOPPED, IT WAS BECAUSE SHE absolutely had to—her stomach and hip muscles simply refused to move another twitch. It felt like she'd been pounded in the stomach with a croquet mallet. She could see fraying in the rope where it had abraded against the belt buckle, but she couldn't tell from her angle whether it was enough. Probably not. *Should have gone to the gym more,* she thought dismally. A wave lashed over the side of the ship and splashed her arms, and the ropes. Not good. The wetter the ropes became, the tighter and stiffer they were when dry. Not that she really had any plan of what to do even if the ropes parted, barring diving over the side and swimming for Liam's ship. But being free had to have more options available than being tied.

Nobody paid the slightest attention to her. She'd become

aware of thirst some hours ago, and now it was getting to be a real problem. Her mouth felt like cotton, and even with the occasional splashed wave, she was simmering in the sun, which was only partly blocked by the sail billowing and booming overhead.

The sailors had water. She watched them dip it out of buckets set on deck, and stopped licking her salty lips when she realized she wasn't getting seawater, but blood.

The wind failed as night began to fall, turning the sky rich cobalt blue sprinkled with silver stars. Above her, the sails luffed and abruptly, the *Aquila* began to slow its knifelike progress through the water. Salvius frowned and looked up at the skies. Clear and cloudless. Even the waves felt unnaturally flat; the boat was hardly pitching at all now.

"Oars out!" someone roared from behind her. "Best speed!"

Cecilia heard the order echoed, over and over, growing fainter each time. Across from her, the statue's eyes had opened again, and for an instant, Cecilia could have sworn that the marble face took on a tinge of color. That the lips tried to move. But then it faded, and it was just a statue with eerily animated eyes, staring at her as if she was supposed to *do something.*

Which she couldn't, of course. Could she?

On the distant horizon, she thought she could still see the white flutter of sails. Liam wouldn't give up. She couldn't afford to, either. Cecilia tried moving against the rope again. It hurt a lot, but panic was a white-hot bubble inside her now, and she couldn't be helpless like this, she *couldn't.*

A strand of rope parted. She felt it go, and was barely able to restrain a sob of relief—but that was only one strand of the twist, and there were more to go.

I'm not going to make it, she thought, and felt tears trickle down her face. *I'm going to die.*

The statue's eyes opened and focused on her, and she heard it say, quite clearly, *Free me and live.*

"Uh—" Cecilia sniffled and tried to clear her throat. "I don't know how to do that."

You do, the voice whispered, faint and cold. *You will.*

The *Aquila* began to glide forward again, and she heard the rhythmic splash of oars driving it, along with the regular heartbeat of a drum.

"Captain Salvius!" Cecilia croaked. He turned toward her. "What's going on?"

Salvius stalked up to her, full speed, grabbed her by the chin and slammed her head back against the mast. "If you ever talk to me again without my permission, I'll have you screaming," he said flatly. "My bed's been cold for months."

She believed him, and it terrified her. She thought about Liam, about the rose-covered bed in his cabin, waiting for a night that might never come. About the gentle, fierce light of love in his eyes.

There was nothing at all in Salvius's eyes except calculation. She knew instinctively that if she showed him fear, weakness, it was all over.

So she smiled. "I can't imagine why," she said. "You're so charming and kind. The girls must be lining up to have a turn."

His teeth bared—strong, square teeth, surprisingly straight, considering that dental science hadn't exactly been advanced in his day. "When I tell you to hold your tongue, *hold it,* or you'll experience what our lovely Larentina did when Jupiter was displeased with her prattling."

From the bow of the ship, someone called out, "Sail, two points to starboard!"

Salvius didn't even look. "I expected him. That will be Ned

Low and the *Withered Rose,*" he said. "Well, this will either be
good business or bad, but either way, my lovely witch, you'll be in
someone's bed this evening. You'd better pray that Low makes his
usual pathetic show of force, then bids small, and that the bed
you're in is mine in the end. Low's hard on his wenches."

Whereas you're a great catch, Cecilia thought, but had sense
enough not to say. Quite. "*Another* cursed ship? Is there a *factory?*"

Salvius smiled, apparently amused by her defiance now. Almost indulgent. "Some of us are cursed by witches, some by gods,
some by their own ill luck. The only thing we have in common is
eternity. But the *Withered Rose* is in a class by herself. You'll see."

Salvius went to see to preparations. The *Aquila* struggled
against the flat sea, banks of oars propelling her sluggishly through
the water, but the fast-approaching vessel seemed to be running
under gale-force winds.

As the ship neared, Cecilia began to see details, and wished she
hadn't. It was built along similar lines to the *Sweet Mourning,* but
that was where the resemblance ended. Tattered rotting sails and
bodies, some skeletons, dangled gruesomely from the yardarms like
macabre wind chimes. The only sound it made, as it came frighteningly closer, was a hiss as it cut the water like a knife.

It suddenly slackened its pace as it pulled near the *Aquila.* A
wave of stench floated across the open water, thick and green and
fetid, and Cecilia struggled not to breathe. The *Mourning* had been
scary in the beginning, but this was—this was something beyond
that. Beyond just cursed.

This ship was *damned.*

There was something very creepy about the crew of the *Withered Rose* too. They seemed to be unnaturally still at their posts. Cecilia's eyes were drawn to a solitary man in the bow of the ship,

draped on the rotting figurehead's shoulder. He looked young—*very* young. Somehow, she'd been expecting someone of Liam's age, or Salvius's. But Ned Low—if that was him, and somehow she was sure it was—looked as if he'd barely seen his twentieth year. And he was very, very pretty.

"Young, isn't he?" Salvius asked, unexpectedly at her shoulder. "Old in all things vile, though. Some seek after evil, some are born prodigies. Edward Low was fathered by Pluto's cold member, and no doubt of it. You've been very unlucky if he's first to the table."

More goading. Cecilia tried to ignore it. She tensed as Salvius's hand touched her cheek, and felt the ropes creak. She tested them, but they didn't break.

"Well met on favoring seas," the young man on board the *Withered Rose* called. He had a rich, aristocratic English accent, reeking of insincerity. "How nice to see you again. Oh, do tell your poor slaves to leave off the oars. You're not going anywhere, you know that."

"My poor slaves need the exercise," Salvius said. "State your business, Captain Low, before I lose my temper."

Low laughed, and it was a gentle, evil sort of sound that had a lot in common with the reek of decomposition still drifting like fog from his ship. "My *business?* Captain, I am no crass merchant, I do not have *business*. I have—interests. And I heard you have something that could be of interest to me."

"I'd sell you my left nut for a decent price," Salvius said, and grinned with all his teeth.

"Tempting, dear man, but no, I already have a perfect set of my own which you, despite your best efforts, have yet to take from me. No, my interest is in a woman." Low's gaze fixed on Cecilia, and she deeply, deeply wished it hadn't. "That one would do nicely."

"Not for sale."

"But everything on the *Aquila* is for sale," Low pouted. "Don't be cruel, Salvius. It doesn't become you nearly so well as it does me."

"I said the witch is not for sale."

Low's eyebrows rose. "Witch, is she? Well, then. Even better. I've been shopping for one of those for a long time. They go bad so quickly, like unsalted meat."

Cecilia threw a frantic glance toward the stern. Far in the distance, she could see the dim outline of a ship. The *Sweet Mourning* was following, but it was too far away. Much too far.

Low laughed at something Salvius said in Latin. "Language, Captain," he chided. A plank was being put across from the *Withered Rose* to the *Aquila* by two silent, shadowy crewmen, and Low uncoiled himself from his catlike pose on the figurehead and glided to the railing. He leaped flat-footed up onto the narrow plank. It was unnatural, the way he balanced, and as he got closer Cecilia realized that there was a lot more unnatural about him. For one thing, he had a kind of black glow to him, a shadow clinging to him like a gray veil. For another, he moved like nothing human she'd ever seen, all boneless grace. Tigers moved like that.

And then she saw his face clearly, and her breath locked in her throat, because his eyes were clouded with white cataracts. The eyes of a corpse, in the face of an angel.

"Hmmm," Low said. He stalked around her, examining her far too closely for any comfort. "I suppose she might do. How much?"

"Ten thousand pieces of gold."

"Far too rich for my poor coffers."

"Then get off my ship," Salvius said pleasantly. "Maggotmeat."

"Your skills at salesmanship are second to none," Low drawled. "Is she virgin?"

"No idea. Want to check?"

They both looked at her thoughtfully. Cecilia's eyes widened. "I'm not!" she yelped. "I'm the wife of Captain Liam Lockhart, and I'm—"

Low took a sudden step toward her, and those pallid eyes glowed. He didn't say a word to her, but she couldn't breathe, couldn't speak for the dreadful weight of fear that crashed in on her.

"Well," Low said to Salvius, "I suppose I might be able to manage the price. Throw in a couple of slaves. I'm getting peckish."

"Need every hand I have."

"Oh, bollocks, Aulus, you can grab slaves anywhere, and I know you use them up regularly. A couple of juicy ones won't be missed." He flicked an elegant, pale, dismissive hand at the Roman.

"*One* slave."

"Agreed." Salvius snapped his fingers, and shouts passed along the length of the ship. Someone pulled up an iron grating, and after a short delay, a pallid, filthy specimen dressed in a tattered loincloth was pulled up and dragged to be presented to Captain Low.

"Perfect," Low said, and reached out to lay a hand on the slave's shoulder, a creepily friendly sort of gesture.

Salvius struck it away with the flat of his sword. "Take your pleasures on board your own ship, not mine," he barked. "You two, take him over to the *Rose.*"

He speared a couple of his soldiers with a stare, who then reluctantly took hold of the slave and marched him to the narrow plank. He tottered unevenly across to the other ship.

"Poor bastard," Salvius said without any real emotion. "Very well. That was a good-faith gift. I'll see my gold now, Captain."

Low's milky eyes went half-closed, and Cecilia thought she

saw a spasm of anger go through him, quickly gone. But he held up his hand in graceful surrender. "Very well," he said. "I'll go assemble the payment. But don't think to cheat me, my antique friend. You know what I do to those who don't hold their bargains."

Salvius nodded once, sharply. Low turned and glided across the deck, to the plank. He crossed without pause or misstep, perfectly balanced, and leapt lightly down on board the *Withered Rose*.

Salvius cursed under his breath. At least, Cecilia assumed it was profanity; it was Latin, and it sounded far too vicious to be anything else. He paced, back and forth, and the statue's blind blue eyes followed him with so much intensity that Cecilia could almost feel the hatred.

"What happens if he touches you?" she asked Salvius. He glanced over at her, and a corner of his hard, thin mouth curled.

"If you're wise, you'll try very hard never to find out," he said.

She heard the thud of boots on the plank between the two ships, and looked up to see that Captain Low was returning. Another man was with him, struggling under the weight of a heavy chest green and slimy with mold. They were both shrouded in shadows, and Cecilia couldn't get a clear look at the second man's face.

Low stepped onto the deck of the *Aquila* and took in a deep breath with evident satisfaction. "It's a tidy ship you run, I'll give you that, Salvius," he said, and waved at his sailor, who grunted and let the heavy wooden trunk thump to the deck. Cecilia felt the weighty impact through the soles of her feet. "As you asked. Now, I'll take my goods."

Salvius didn't move. He stared on at the other man, chin lowered, eyes fierce and wolflike in the dying sunlight. "Open it," he said. "I'll see the gold first."

Cecilia pulled in a breath and pressed against the ropes. She felt the one she'd been working on give . . . slightly.

Not enough.

Low's man opened the chest, and the Roman soldiers and sailors nearest to it to catch a glimpse let out an approving murmur as the thick glow of gold caught the sunset. "Stir it," Salvius said. "To be sure it's gold all through, and not your dinner leavings."

Low pulled his cutlass and stirred the gold, then reached down and pulled handfuls from the bottom, letting coins slip carelessly from his fingers on the way up. "Agreed?"

Salvius seemed to think about it for a long, uneasy moment, and then nodded. Two of his own soldiers grabbed the treasure dragged it out of the way, put it next to the statue, and stood at rigid guard.

Edward Low strolled slowly toward Cecilia. His dead eyes were the color of moonlight. He flicked his long fingers against the frayed part at her waist, smiling. "So nearly there, little witch," he said. "And so far away."

She turned her face away as he swung his cutlass, fast as a lightning strike; she felt it bite through the ropes and into the mast not more than a half inch from her arm. The bindings slacked, and she staggered as its support was removed.

She tripped over the mess of falling rope and almost pitched forward into Low's waiting arms. A hand pulled her aside at the last instant, and she caught a flash of steel, Roman red, and armor.

Salvius. "I said it before. Pleasure yourself on your own ship," he said flatly, and drew his sword as Low advanced on him. Low grabbed the sword in one hand as Salvius stabbed, and the entire blade turned first a sickly green, then brown . . . then just dissolved in the Roman's hand.

"Careful," Low said. "Someone might be hurt, Captain."

Salvius was pinned against the side of the ship. Low put those pale, destroying hands on either side of him on the rail of the ship, which turned a withered ancient gray, like old bone, and began to dissolve into wormy dust. He leaned forward, putting his face very close to the Roman captain's.

Salvius didn't blink, or flinch, but Cecilia saw it cost him a superhuman effort.

Low laughed, deep in his throat. "Don't toy with me," he said softly. "You wouldn't like how I play." He turned to Cecilia, moonstone eyes glowing. "Time's up, kitten," he said. "I'd take your arm like a gentleman, but the results would be—unpleasant, as you've seen." He nodded to the plank, and the creaking, rotten shape of the *Withered Rose* beyond. "On your own, or be carried by my man. Or rot here."

Salvius cleared his throat. "He means that last literally, girl. I've seen him reduce a man to maggots and bones in seconds. Don't test him."

"Conscience?" Low asked mockingly. "From a man who's fed children to the sharks rather than bear the price of their grain? Salvius. You have no higher ground on which to stand." He made a gesture, as if he intended to put his hand on Cecilia's shoulder; she instinctively flinched away, and he drove her relentlessly toward the plank.

And to her surprise, he *winked*.

She nearly fell, she was so shocked by it, and yelped when hands closed around her arms from behind and lifted her neatly up onto the boarding plank. Low's shadow-sailor who'd carried the chest—only his hands felt oddly familiar. Cecilia turned and peered at him, trying to see underneath the disguising smoke, and caught a glimpse of his dark, sparkling eyes.

"Shhhh," Liam warned her. "No time. We need a way to stop Salvius. Do you know of one?"

"Why ask me?" she whispered back fiercely. "I was a prisoner!"

"Aye, but an observant one. Resourceful. Well?"

"The statue," she said. "I think it's the statue—he said it kept death from taking him."

Captain Low, who'd been listening closely from where he stood just a foot away, still on the deck of the *Aquila,* nodded and moved back toward Captain Salvius. "One more thing, my lovely," he said, and lunged past Salvius to lay both his hands flat on the stone breasts of the marble statue. "Ahhhh, very nice. Fine piece of work."

The stone vibrated, cracked, and exploded into white dusty powder and chunks of stone, and left . . .

. . . a goddess. Tall, slender, with hair as red as the sunset glaring behind her, and milky blue eyes and marble-fair complexion. She was dressed in flowing, night-black draperies, and as Low stepped back from her she took in a deep breath, let it out, and fastened her merciless gaze on Captain Salvius. Chaos broke out— men screaming, wailing, some throwing themselves to the deck and begging for mercy.

Not Salvius, though. He stood and faced her as she came toward him.

Liam grabbed Cecilia and hustled her across the plank, yelling over his shoulder, "Ned! Damn you, don't dally!"

But Captain Low wasn't hurrying. He was watching the goddess Larentina as she reached out to tap her cool white fingers on Salvius's forehead.

He fell to his knees, swayed, and went down hard. Face down.

"Ned!" Liam yelled again. "She'll take you too!"

"Yes," he said calmly. "I'm considering it."

Larentina advanced on him. Low raised his eyebrows.

"Reconsidering, actually." Low backed away, leapt onto the plank, and ran lightly across it to drop onto the rotting, filthy deck of his ship next to where Cecilia stood with Liam's arms around her. Low pulled the plank away from the *Aquila* and let it splash into the water—it was already rotting from the touch of his hands. He leaned on the filthy railing and watched Larentina stalk the decks of the *Aquila,* relentless and beautiful, sending the crew to their long-delayed and no doubt well-earned deaths.

Larentina paused in her killing to look sharply across at them, and Cecilia felt a chill as if death were passing its shroud over her face.

But in its wake, she felt oddly restored. Her crippling thirst was gone. So were her aches, pains, sunburns, and when she licked her lips, she found them damp and supple.

"I think I'm in love," Ned Low sighed, and then shook his head. "Too clever by half, our friend Salvius. Not to mention careless. But I suppose he had to keep her close, or he'd have lost control."

The *Aquila* was sinking, rolling drunkenly in a sea that was suddenly churning with waves. And sharks. Cecilia turned away from the sight and buried her face in Liam's chest, and he wrapped her tightly in his arms.

She felt the wind snap the threadbare sails of the *Withered Rose* taut, and the gruesome ornamental skeletons dangling from the yardarms clinked their macabre music. Ned Low was watching her and Liam, not the wreck of the *Aquila.*

"I'll take you back to your ship," Low said. "As we agreed. Then we're squared, Lockhart. The next time I catch you in my grip, you'll rot like the rest. You and the witch." He hesitated, then said, "Unless she really can break curses, that is." It was half a question.

"No," Cecilia said. "I'm not a witch. Sorry."

"Ah," he said, and shrugged. His lovely young face smiled, but the dead man in his eyes didn't. "Pity."

Low made a languid gesture. Up on the deserted quarterdeck, the wheel turned, and the *Withered Rose* heeled over in a course change, making for the distant speck of sail that was the *Sweet Mourning.*

A fresh sea breeze blew over the deck, temporarily washing away the filthy stench, and tattering Liam's clinging shadows. Cecilia looked down at herself; she was wreathed in the stuff too, like a damp fog. She tried fanning it away, but it seemed to have a mind of its own. "Ignore it," Liam said. "It's when it disappears you have to worry. That's when Ned decides to make sport of you." He sounded grim, and his eyes were dark and haunted. He cupped his hands around her face. "Cecilia. I'm sorry it took so long. Ned's no easy mark and nobody's ally."

"Then why did he help you?"

Liam took in a deep breath. "I struck a bargain. It was the only way to get to you. Salvius's ship was too fast. Ned Low was the closest rescue I could find."

Oh no. "What did you promise?"

"Nothing I can't afford to lose."

Oh, Cecilia doubted that.

THE WITHERED ROSE GLIDED UP TO A BECALMED *Sweet Mourning* just as true darkness fell over the sea. The *Mourning* had lamps burning on board, giving the whole ship a party-barge atmosphere that left Cecilia with a sense of tremendous, knee-weakening relief.

She couldn't wait to be off this filthy, diseased scow.

Mr. Argyle was at the railing, holding a lantern, his narrow, clever face tense and anxious. "The *Aquila*?" he asked.

"Historical," Liam called back. "Coming aboard!"

Low sat at his ease and watched indifferently as Liam escorted Cecilia across the boarding plank and safely onto the deck of their own vessel. The crew closed around them protectively—amazing, considering a day ago they'd been willing to toss her over the side.

Maybe they just hated Edward Low that much.

She reached back for Liam, but he wasn't there. He was still standing on the boarding plank, looking at her, and while her dark shadows had blown free the moment she'd stepped on board the *Sweet Mourning,* his still writhed around him like toxic smoke.

"I'm sorry," he said, and his voice sounded choked and odd. "I'm so sorry, Cecilia. I love you."

And he turned and went back to the *Withered Rose.*

"No!" she screamed, and lunged for the boarding plank. Liam grabbed it from the far end and shoved; it was still fastened on the *Sweet Mourning,* so it banged loudly against the wooden hull as it fell. "Liam, *come back!*"

Argyle was holding her still. "Lass," he said somberly, "he can't. Ned Low's price. One had to stay, and he's made the choice. He wouldn't let anyone else do it for him. I tried. God's witness, I tried."

On board the other ship, Edward Low uncoiled himself from his perch and slipped down to walk to where Liam stood at the railing. He leaned casually against it, staring at Cecilia, and his moonstone eyes looked like twin moons reflecting the firelight.

"Do you believe in salvation?" he asked her.

She wasn't in the mood for his banter. "Let Liam go! *Please!*"

"All that binds him here is his honor," Low said. "But that's as strong as chain, for him. I ask you again, little witch, do you believe in salvation?"

"Yes!" She choked on the word, and a frantic sense of terror. "*Please.* I'd help you if I could. I really would."

He studied her gravely. "I believe you would," he said. "Although I'd never deserve it."

"I'm not your judge. *Please.*"

Low glanced sideways at Liam. "Your witch bargains hard," he said. "I'll hold you to your word, Lockhart. One year of service on the *Rose.*"

One year? Cecilia's heart turned to ice in her chest. She'd barely been able to stand an hour. What that would be like . . .

"I'll stand by my word."

"I know you will. You're a man of honor." Low put a mocking stress on the last word. "I never said when your service would commence, Captain."

Liam didn't move.

Edward Low rolled his eyes. "*Leave,* fool. I'm giving you parole. I'll decide when to collect my debt."

Liam's wrapping of shadow blew away, and Cecilia caught her breath and squeezed Argyle's hands in hers. Liam looked startled, and grim. "I suppose I should thank you."

"Don't," Low said soberly. "I expect to see full service from you. Just not today."

He made another of those eerie underwater gestures, and the fallen boarding plank rose up of its own accord and fastened back between the two ships. The ocean went as smooth and dark as painted glass.

Liam crossed over, dropped over on the deck of the *Sweet Mourning,* and Low reached out to put his hand on the plank stretched between them. It warped, molded, rotted, and fell away into dust and fragments into the waiting sea.

A devil's wind filled the sails of the *Withered Rose,* and the dark ship glided away into the night, silhouetted against the stars, and then gone without a sound. Low might have raised a hand in farewell, but it was just a shadowy impression, quickly vanished.

Liam let out a slow breath and closed his eyes. "You're an idiot," Cecilia said.

He nodded. "I know."

"I love you."

"And so you should," he said. "At great length."

THE CREW THREW A PARTY FOR THEM—IMPROMPTU feasts of cold smoked ham and canned pineapple and rum. Lots of rum. Their version of an apology for the ruined wedding reception. Cecilia had just enough food to sustain her, and enough rum to settle her nerves. Someone started up a hornpipe, and there was a spontaneous effort at a jig, which Cecilia gamely tried at the urging of the crew. When she stopped, breathless and glowing from effort, she saw Liam looking at her with dark intensity from the other side of the crowd.

"I think I'll retire for the evening," Cecilia said as she passed him. "Join me?"

Liam let a torturous second or two go by, then pushed away from the rail. "Aye," he said. "I suppose I might."

He was kissing her well before they reached the cabin—in the hallway, in fact, up against the wooden wall, perilously close to the tilting lantern. He kicked the cabin door open and pulled her inside, already unfastening her belt and leaving it in a pile on the floor as he walked her relentlessly back, toward the bed. Her shirt marked another step, and his joined it. Boots next. Trousers.

By the time they reached the bed itself, they were naked and warm and entirely consumed with tastes and touches and not at all with thought. Liam's hands slid around Cecilia's head, combing through her thick short hair, and he devoured her mouth in hungry, desperate kisses with all the feverish energy of lightning striking.

When he pulled back, Cecilia found herself shaking, panting, and very close to heaven. In the firelight, Liam's skin was the color of hot caramel, twice as sweet to the taste—burned darker on his forearms and hands and face, a true man of the sea.

"Maybe we ought to wait," Cecilia said. Lockhart's eyes widened.

"Wait?" he echoed, and she smiled wickedly.

"Something's bound to interrupt us."

Liam held up one finger, stepped back and turned to the door to bellow, "Mr. Argyle!"

The cabin door opened just a crack. "Aye, Captain?"

"You'll guarantee our privacy this time?"

"Oh, aye, sir. Totally guaranteed." And the door shut with a clank of metal.

"See?" Liam said. "Problem solved."

"Except that your first mate is listening *right outside the door,* Liam. I don't call that privacy."

Liam seemed honestly surprised. "Well, then, we'll have to be quiet, then, won't we?"

His kiss completely derailed her objections. The lovemaking was like a dream, waves hitting the shore, sleek and salty and irresistible. Cecilia floated in the currents, anchored only by his body, the sharp nip of his teeth on her neck, the electric-hot press of his hands.

In the end, there was nothing in the least quiet about it, but Cecilia quite forgot to worry about that.

"Ah, that's the way to mark the passing hours," Liam said drowsily, stroking her hair as they lay twined together in an untidy heap on the disordered bed. "One day down."

"Aye aye, Captain." She smiled against his chest. "And forever to go."

---

*RACHEL CAINE is the author of the popular Weather Warden series, the sixth installment of which (*Thin Air*) was released in August 2007. She also writes a young adult series, Morganville Vampires, with the third book,* Midnight Alley, *scheduled for an October 2007 release. In addition, Rachel has written paranormal romantic suspense for Silhouette, including* Devil's Bargain, Devil's Due, *and the recently released Athena Force novel* Line of Sight.

Visit her Web site: www.rachelcaine.com.

My Space: www.myspace.com/rachelcaine.

Her Mother's Daughter

P. N. ELROD

Gangsters, gats, and girls in Depression Era Chicago mean trouble, even for an undead shamus. Jack Fleming relates his latest case from The Vampire Files.

CHICAGO, FEBRUARY 1938

IT'S BEEN MY EXPERIENCE THAT A BLUSHING BRIDE usually waits until after the honeymoon's over before hiring a gumshoe to check up on her husband's whereabouts. When Dorothy Schubert, née Huffman, plowed into the office still in her wedding gown I figured she was out to break a record along with anything else in her path.

She was the angriest woman I'd ever seen—which is saying a lot.

I'd only stopped by to pick up the mail and hadn't bothered to turn on the light. She'd charged noisily up the outside stairs, shoving the door open so hard the glass rattled. Blindly she fumbled the switch, and the sudden brightness caught me behind the desk, envelopes in one hand, reaching under my coat for my .38 with the other. Chicago's a tough town; even a vampire needs an extra edge at times.

You heard right, but I'll get back to the Lugosi stuff later.

I eased off drawing my gun and put down the envelopes. The lady appeared to be unarmed, just remarkably upset. Her face was red, her brown eyes blazed, and she had very straight teeth, nearly all of them bared. I kept the desk between us.

"Is that you?" she demanded, jabbing a finger at the name painted on the door's pebbled glass panel. It read THE ESCOTT AGENCY.

I hesitated replying, wondering what my partner had gotten himself into, and then realized she'd not have asked the question had she ever met Escott. "No, but maybe I can help?"

"I need a detective," she said, tottering forward to grab the back of one of the wooden chairs in front of the desk. The charge up the stairs must have winded her.

"You look like you need a drink."

"That, too." She dropped onto the chair, her classy wedding dress making an expensive rustling sound. She was more arresting than pretty, with thick black hair, a hawk's nose, strong brows, and wide mouth. By turns she was the type who could turn ugly or traffic-stopping beautiful depending on her mood. A sculptor would have made much over her cheekbones, chin, and throat. I noticed the big vein there pulsing in time with her heartbeat, which was audible to my ears. She was calming down, though, the beat gradually slowing.

Her floor-dragging veil was half off, and she wore no coat over the gown. Last time I checked it was cold enough that even I felt the bite of Old Man Winter. The lady must have departed straight from the church in one spitfire of a hurry. Post-ceremony,

I noted, her rings were in place. One was a showy engagement sparkler, the other a more modest band with diamonds embedded in its gold surface. She had enough on one finger to buy the block, never mind the pricey trinkets hanging from her neck and wrists.

"You cold?" I asked. Her bare arms showed gooseflesh.

She considered, then nodded. The heat was down for the night; I took off my overcoat and draped it over her shoulders.

"You're nice. So polite," she said, pulling it close around her body like a blanket.

"Sometimes."

Escott kept a pint of Four Roses in the bottom left drawer— cheap stuff and strictly for clients in need of a knock-in-the-head bracer. I pulled it out and started toward the back room to get a glass, but the bride didn't wait. She had the cap off, bottle up-ended, and drained a quarter of it away in two shakes. It being her wedding day she had good reason to indulge, but still—impressive.

She slammed the bottle on the desk and whooped in a deep breath, her dark eyes watering. "Wow."

I'd given up drinking booze some while ago, but knew that Four Roses could peel varnish without much effort. "How may I help you, Miss—uh—Mrs.—?"

"Mrs. Jerome Kleinhaus Schubert as of an hour ago. I want you to find my husband."

"Uh."

Damn few things are a cause for flummoxing, but this peculiar situation had me nailed to the wall. Had Mrs. Schubert been a bad-tempered, gun-waving mug with one of the city's mobs I'd have known exactly what to do. Instead we traded stares for a long, much too-silent moment; then I remembered to fall back on procedure, and got out one of the agency's standard contracts, notepaper, and a fountain pen.

"Is that you?" She again pointed at the name.

"Mr. Escott's out of town. I'm his partner, Mr. Fleming. May I ask who referred you?"

She took a turn at assessing me. I was taller than average, leaner than some, and looked too young for my actual age of thirty-eight. Her gaze drifted upward. I removed my fedora and put it on the desk, and that summoned a glint of humor to her eyes. "Taxi driver. I told him I wanted a detective, and he took me straight here."

I peered between the blinds to the street below. A yellow cab was double-parked next to my Studebaker coupe. The driver waved up. I knew him slightly; he often hung out in front of my nightclub at closing, hoping to snag a late fare. It was no surprise that he knew about Escott's agency and that one or the other of us might be found there at odd hours. The club's doorman liked to chat when things were slow. They'd have plenty to gossip about with this development.

"Did you pay him?"

The bride glanced pointedly at her dress, which was unburdened by pockets, and she had no purse. "Put it on my bill. I'm good for it." She unpinned the trailing veil from her hair and began winding it loosely around one hand, apparently confident that her word alone was enough.

I hadn't said I'd accept the case, but decided this was one I couldn't miss. "No problem."

Excusing myself, I left to take care of her fare, trusting that she'd not run up an excessive amount in the brief time since her nuptials. I'm too much the optimist: the meter showed two-fifty. They must have come from across town. I gave the driver three bucks and asked if he knew what the hell was going on.

He was cheerful, shaking his head. "That dame shot out of

St. Mike's like one of them human cannonballs. Boy, was she mad. Never seen anything like it. She spotted me, was yelling for a PI, an' I thought of you."

"You were driving past?"

"Nah, waiting for the wedding to end. There's always someone needin' a ride after. Weddin's and funerals is always good for business, right?"

On that point I had to agree. I thanked him and trotted back to my client. The Escott Agency undertook the carrying out of unpleasant errands for those with enough cash and a need for discretion. Escott flatly refused divorce work. Finding a missing groom was a gray area, but odds favored an easy fix. He'd probably succumbed to cold feet and was hiding out with friends. Why wait until *after* the ceremony, though?

I asked Mrs. Schubert some basic questions, scribbling her answers in shorthand. Soon as I heard her maiden name a light went on.

"Are you related to—?"

"Yes, Louie Huffman. He's my father."

My interest in the case went up a few notches, along with a sudden urge to back out before things got more complicated. I knew Huffman slightly. He hung out at another club—the Nightcrawler—with half the mobsters in the city. He wasn't a big-time boss like my pal Gordy Weems, but one of the lesser chiefs.

Which still made him someone I didn't care to cross. My friendship with Gordy provided a certain amount of insurance against bad guys getting stupid with me, but it wasn't something I ever tested. Huffman oversaw debt collection, and he was very good at it. He had a reputation for being almost as handy with a baseball bat as Capone. You paid your debt or got shattered kneecaps or disappeared entirely. It was pretty simple.

That he had a daughter should not have surprised me. Many of the mugs were family men, they just kept their work well separated from their home life.

I wondered if the groom owed money to his new father-in-law. "What happened at the wedding?"

Dorothy Schubert melted a little at the memory. "It was beautiful. My favorite flowers—Daddy had them shipped up special from Florida—and the music and everyone was there and it was perfect. Jerome was so handsome; he looked just like Ralph Bellamy in that tuxedo."

An instinct within tipped me off that a flood was on the way. She made another whooping noise, but by then I'd ducked into the back room and returned with a box of tissues. I had it in front of her just as the dam burst. She tore out a handful and bawled into them.

"I—thought—he—*loved*—me!" she howled.

Crying dames are nothing to be afraid of, but for the next few minutes part of me wanted to run like hell; another said to put an arm around her and go, "There-there." A much more sensible part kept me seated until she'd recovered enough to continue.

"We'd come back down the aisle and went to the church's social hall for the reception. I was just *floating*."

"No pictures?"

"Did those yesterday. Maybe I shouldn't have let him see me in my dress before the ceremony—no, that's silly—*uh-uh-uhhhh* . . . " She soaked another wad of tissues and blew her nose. "I'm sorry."

"It's okay. The reception?"

"We had a line and a big cake and we cut the cake and it was *perfect*. Then Jerome wasn't there."

"What do you mean?"

"I looked away for just a moment talking to someone, and he was just *gone*."

"Men's room?"

"No—I sent the best man to check. Then they all started looking for him. No one saw him leave. Some thought it was a joke. Jerome's a kidder, but he knows when to stop and this didn't stop. I stood all alone while the ushers turned the church inside out. Then I couldn't take it anymore. How *dare* he humiliate me like that?"

"Your father have anything to say about it?"

"I didn't ask. This is my problem, not his."

She dabbed at her puffy eyes, which were rather raccoonlike from smeared makeup. In the pause I heard several sets of shoes clomping up the stairs. No knock, the door was thrown open yet again with violence. The glass panel thankfully held.

The man who trundled in was Big Louie Huffman. The tuxedo did little to mitigate his fundamental toughness. He was built like a balding fireplug with a solid trunk, thick arms, and seemed to use his raw muscle to suppress the force inside. His daughter had inherited his pronounced nose and downturned mouth. On her they looked good; on him they were intimidating. He looked ready to take the building apart.

Flanking him in the now much smaller office were two large goons also dressed for the wedding. Their tailor had failed to get the padding right, so you could almost tell the make and caliber of what they kept in their shoulder holsters. Each had a hand inside the coat, ready to pull out and blast away.

I held myself very, very still. "Uh—Mrs. Schubert—?"

"Don't call her that," Huffman rumbled.

"Oh, Daddy," she said, her voice creaking with the threat of more tears. "How did you—?"

"Followed your cab. Dot, what are you doing here?"

"I'm taking care of my problem myself." For this she squared her shoulders and raised her chin. "Just like you tell me."

He pushed out his lower lip, eyes going narrow as he thought that one over. "You're a grown woman, you know your mind, but we should keep this in the family."

She lowered her head and made a low noise deep in her throat. When my girlfriend made that kind of sound I knew to take cover.

Apparently so did Huffman. Even the goons backed up a step.

"I want," she said in a disturbingly level tone, "an impartial outsider to deal with this. I know you want to help, but I need to do this my way."

He thought that one over as well, then focused on me. Recognition clicked in his expression. "You're Jack Fleming—that creep from Gordy's club."

It beat being called a number of other, more colorful, descriptives. There was a lady present, after all. "Good evening, Mr. Huffman."

"Dot, we'll find another man for the job."

She rose and faced her father. With him and the others there for comparison I noticed just how tall she was, being eye-level with them. "I want *this* guy. He's got very nice manners."

"He's still a creep, sugar bun. I've heard stories."

By that point I was hoping she'd listen to her father so as to spare the office from damage, but young Dorothy planted herself, fists on her hips, feet apart, ready for a fight. My coat slipped from her shoulders. She looked just as scary as Huffman, yet somehow vulnerable.

I've got a sad and fatal weakness for dames in need. "May I suggest—"

All three men rounded on me. I could handle them more easily than Dorothy having another crying jag. "Mr. Huffman, if you would speak with Gordy he'll tell you I'm stand-up. Perhaps you've also had to deal with the burden that comes from having an undeserved reputation."

"He talks like a lawyer," muttered the older goon on the left. I took him to be Huffman's first lieutenant.

"Gordy'll give you the true blue," I said, less formally. Actually, I'd been trying to mimic my Shakespeare-raised partner. I must be getting better at it.

Huffman considered that. "I'm sure he will, young man. But just so we're clear, be aware that *my* reputation is very much deserved."

"Yes, sir." Yet another reason to be polite and not make any fast moves. I dialed the number for the Nightcrawler club's office, and one of the guys put me right through to Gordy.

That, if nothing else, got Huffman's attention. I said hello, told Gordy I had a guest with a few questions, then gave my chair up to Huffman. The goons watched, ready to shoot if I sneezed wrong. They didn't worry me. Not much. Cautiously, I picked up my overcoat, redraped it on the bride, then stood by the windows and made an effort to look harmless. Bullets won't kill me, but damn, they cost me blood, hurt like hell, and I liked this suit.

I could hear both sides of the phone conversation. Huffman identified himself.

"Problem?" Gordy asked.

"My kid wants to hire Jack Fleming for something. He said to call you."

"Your kid picked right. Hire him for what?"

"Find a missing person. It's a family matter."

"Fleming's okay."

"I don't like him," said Huffman.

"Get over it."

"He'll keep his yap quiet?"

"Like the grave." Gordy was in rare humor. He knew all about me.

Huffman cradled the receiver, stood, and gave me the benefit of a very effective glower. With a look like that he didn't need a baseball bat to make his point with slow-to-pay gamblers. He spotted the fedora and picked it up, checking the label inside. "You bought this at Del Morio's."

"Yes, sir."

He glared at the rest of my attire and the coat on his daughter. "All that, too?"

"Yes, sir." *What the hell?*

He gave a grudging nod. "All right, Dot. You can have him, but Becker and Cooley here go along, too."

She emitted another growling sound. So did the goons. No one looked pleased. She glared at Huffman; the goons glared at me. Maybe they'd heard stories, too.

"As chaperon," said her father. "For my peace of mind."

"Whatever makes everyone happy," I said.

She shot me a dark glance. "Okay, but just Cooley."

I got the impression that this father–daughter team did a lot of bargaining. Huffman agreed.

"And I'm in charge. What I say goes," she added.

Huffman nodded again. "Fair enough. Got that, Cooley?"

Cooley grunted. He was about the same age as Huffman, made from the same brand of tough. Becker had half as many years and looked frustrated at not getting picked for the job. He settled for giving me a threatening stare. Eager beavers annoy me.

"Now what?" asked my client.

I fished my car keys out. "Let's go to church."

STEP ON IT, WE HAVE TO HURRY," DOROTHY said as I pulled my coupe away from the curb. Cooley was a silent presence squashed between us, hard to ignore.

"Why?"

"Because the Pullman I reserved to get us to Niagara Falls leaves at midnight. I'll be on it with my husband or know the reason why."

"Could have mentioned that earlier. I can't guarantee we'll find him in time."

"If you don't, then I'll take my mother instead, I'm not wasting a perfectly good reservation. She likes Niagara. She went there with Daddy for her honeymoon. You married?"

"Not yet." I had hopes.

I'd proposed a number of times to my girlfriend, but she always turned me down. My being a vampire had nothing to do with it. With her singing and soon an acting career to look after, a boyfriend was okay, but not a husband. Apparently they take more work.

After one proposal too many she let me know the subject was closed, and if I opened it again she would get mad. Since she knows how to use a blackjack, most kinds of handguns, and even a crossbow, I decided there was no percentage in pressing things.

For the time being.

One of these nights she just might be in the right mood to say yes. When that happened I'd whisk her off to the nearest justice of the peace before she could change her mind.

"Your father gets his clothes at Del Morio's?" I asked.

"Uh-huh. He thinks very highly of Mr. Del Morio. If you buy there, then you're in."

"In what?"

"Daddy's good books. Mr. Del Morio doesn't sell to just any-one."

He hadn't sold to me, either, not knowingly. Not showing up in mirrors makes buying clothes awkward. Since my change I'd gotten into the habit of sneaking into the store after closing, helping myself, and writing up a sales receipt. I'd leave it and cash on the manager's desk with THANK YOU FROM LAMONT CRANSTON printed in block letters on the envelope.

I was a blood-drinking creature of the night, not a thief.

ST. MICHAEL'S CHURCH WAS IMPOSING YET APPROACHABLE, WITH a picturesque steepled clock tower and white stone trim against red-brown brick walls. I drove past the front and got a good look at the big statue of St. Mike himself in its alcove above the main door. Must have been a tough job to get him in place. If I wasn't so chicken about heights I'd be tempted to float myself up for a closer look at the art.

The surrounding streets were choked with cars, but Dorothy directed me toward the back where lights showed in some windows on the ground floor; the wedding reception was still going strong. A few must have left early; I found a space.

As I slipped into it, Huffman and his remaining goon parked at the curb by a door and went inside first. He said he'd give some excuse to everyone.

"I hope he doesn't tell them Jerome and I had a fight," she said. "We never fight. What are you doing?"

I'd gotten out and was checking all the cars within view. A LaSalle parked a dozen yards away had steam on the windows. "What does Jerome look like?"

"He's handsome, like Ralph Bellamy, and wearing a tuxedo."

I looked at Cooley.

"Black hair, twenty-five, medium build, dime-size brown birth-mark here." Cooley touched a finger to his jaw just under his right ear.

I crossed to the car with the steamed-over windows and yanked open the back door. The couple within screamed in unison, first shock, then outrage. Given my night vision the dim interior was no obstacle. The man did not look like Ralph Bellamy and lacked a birthmark—at least under his right ear. I tipped my hat, told them sorry, and slammed the door shut. The woman snarled, and there were loud clicks as someone belatedly locked things.

Dorothy emerged from the coupe, pulling my overcoat tight around her.

"Wasn't him," I reported.

"But Jerome would never—"

"Just covering the bases, Mrs. Schubert."

"I'm not used to hearing that. Call me Dorothy."

"What d'ya know, that's my favorite name tonight."

"And you're—"

"Jack." I started toward the church. "Inside."

"But they're all waiting to see me. I couldn't."

"Sure you can. You need to change clothes for the honey-moon."

"If there's going to be one."

"We've got a few hours." I offered my arm and took her in.

Good thing I don't have a problem about walking into churches or dealing with religious stuff, or I'd have to conduct my investigation in the parking lot. Cooley stalked behind. Like all good mobsters he had a poker face, but I thought the farce with the interrupted neckers had amused him.

People in fancy clothes were gathered in the hall, and a gaggle of bridesmaids rushed us, flinging questions. I winced at the noise in the small space and felt Dorothy flinch, her hand tightening on my arm.

"Pick one to help you change. I'll handle the rest," I murmured out the side of my mouth.

When the first wave subsided, she called the maid of honor over for help, and we were soon whisked off to some females-only area in the back. I was left in the hall outside the changing room with Cooley, half a dozen girls in matching blue satin gowns, stray wedding guests, and a lot of curiosity. No one knew who I was, but as I began asking questions they took me for a cop, and I was disinclined to correct them.

I got a lot of information about the wedding and the confusion following the groom's vanishing. It added up to what I'd already learned from Dorothy. By then the bride's mother, a formidable long-boned woman, sailed past, sparing me a single grim look but making no comment. When she went in to see her daughter, Cooley visibly relaxed.

"What?" I asked.

"Tough broad—uh—lady," he said.

"Oh, yeah?"

"Wouldn't want to be in Schubert's shoes if she gets hold of him. Nobody makes her kids cry."

I took the opportunity to get more background from him on the family. The Huffmans had produced four daughters, Dorothy being the eldest. If Big Louie planned to marry the other three off in similar high style he'd be giving his baseball bat a lot of wear to finance things. Maybe he'd arranged for Schubert to vanish, but it would have been cheaper to do that at the engagement stage.

"What's Schubert like?"

"Some college guy. He's okay. His people ain't hurtin'."

"What's their game? Jewelry?"

"Yeah."

I'd been kidding, thinking about the rocks Dorothy had worn. "You mean he's with Schubert Jewelers?" They were the biggest noise in five states for that kind of thing.

"Yeah, Siggy Schubert's only kid."

Good grief. "Has it occurred to anyone that he might have been kidnapped?"

From what I could read from Cooley's poker face, it had not.

"What'd you see tonight?" I asked.

"Usual stuff."

"How about unusual stuff?"

He shook his head. "I stuck with the boss. Didn't see nothin'. Dot started to get loud all of a sudden, yelling for Schubert, and next thing y'know she's running out the front. The boss took off after her, Becker 'n' me took off after him, then we followed her cab to your street."

"Not to the door?"

"Fast cabbie. He'd turned and was comin' back empty, so we knew he'd dropped her off."

"How did you—?"

"Car by the curb, light was on upstairs. Only one on the block."

Smart guy. "Anyone got a problem with Jerome?"

"The old man likes him, so's the ol—Mrs. Huffman."

"How 'bout the Schuberts? Any problem with them about Dorothy?"

"Not that I know."

"How do you feel about it?"

"Makes no diff to me. Boss's daughter does what she likes. Always has."

"You work for him long?"

"What're you getting' at?"

"The boss's daughter is one sweet pippin."

"I ain't blind, but she's not worth my kneecaps."

"Who thinks she is?"

He clammed up, lips going thin, gaze directed elsewhere. Not so long ago, before some bad things happened that ripped away the ability, I'd have hypnotized it out of him. That door was now shut forever. Any attempt to open it would probably kill me.

I could try beating it out of him, but there was a matter of mob etiquette. By having Gordy vouch for me, I was effectively his representative. One of Gordy's boys getting into a donnybrook with one of Huffman's boys—not good for business. I had to behave.

That aside, I now knew there was someone here who thought Dorothy was worth risking possibly lethal trouble. Chances were good they'd be on the Huffmans' side of the church aisle or Cooley would have given me a name. Better, he and his pal Becker would have quietly taken care of it themselves, and I'd never even have met Dorothy.

I knocked on the changing room door.

"Not yet!" Someone within yelled.

I'd seen undressed females before. The view never fails to fascinate. I opened the door two inches and called through. "Dorothy? You decent?"

"Let him in, it's all right," she said.

Her mother did the honors, reluctantly, not giving me much space to squeeze through. She'd provided Dorothy's somewhat hatchety face, but the grim look was all hers. Mama tigers were less protective. "She's not ready," she stated.

Dorothy was on a chair, using a shoehorn to lever her feet into some obviously new mules. She had on a graceful blue traveling dress, just the thing for a new bride to wear on her honeymoon trip. "I am now, Momma. Let him by."

"Just a few questions, ma'am," I said to Mrs. Huffman. My hat was already off or I'd have tipped it to her.

"You're the one," she said. Apparently her husband had had a word with her.

I didn't have a reply that would preclude getting my face slapped, so I smiled meekly and nodded.

The place looked like the backstage dressing rooms at my club, but much larger. A tornado had roared through, leaving behind all manner of clothing, makeup, and other feminine debris. My girlfriend had the same kind of clutter in her bedroom. God knew how they kept track of it all.

My coat was draped over a table on top of some long flat boxes. Not knowing where I'd end up or for how long, I pulled it back on again. It smelled of Dorothy's perfume. Nice stuff.

The maid of honor was busy folding the wedding dress into another long box. She was enough like Dorothy to be a sister. From the near-smirk on her face, she would be the bratty one of the brood. She glanced past me, looking puzzled for a blank second. That's when I saw a full-length dressing mirror in a corner. I angled out of range before she got a solid gander and realized I was missing from its reflection of that part of the room.

Finished with the shodding, Dorothy stood, smoothing her skirt down. Her makeup had been repaired. Her eyes were still puffy, but clean of black tear trails. Nose powdered and with a funny little blue hat atop her dark head, she seemed ready for anything. Don't ask me why, but a woman in a hat always looks able to take on any emergency. "What is it, Jack?"

Mrs. Huffman's face twitched. Her daughter being on a first-name basis with the hired help was none too pleasing to the lady.

I guided Dorothy out of immediate earshot of family, taking care not to trip over a set of matched suitcases. They were monogrammed, one each for the bride and groom: D.H.S. and J.K.S., respectively. I'd have to pass that detail on to my girl. She'd think it was cute.

"Why did you pick Cooley over Becker for chaperone duty?" I asked.

"Uh-um—I just did." Dorothy blinked more than was necessary.

"For a reason."

She hemmed a little more, her voice going so low that I had to lean close to hear. "Becker likes me. But he'd *never*—I mean if he—well—Daddy would *kill* him."

"Becker likes you. How'd he handle you being engaged and married, then? You must have noticed."

Her face reddened under the powder. "Actually, no, I didn't. I was so caught up planning the wedding and being with Jerome— you think Becker's done something?"

"I don't know. What do you think?" Distracted or not by her nuptials, she knew more than I did about the household, what was normal and what was not.

"Now that you mention . . . he was hanging close during the cutting of the cake. And I don't remember seeing him afterward— but then I was looking for Jerome. We need to get him, make him talk!"

"Hold your horses. If all Becker's doing is carrying a torch, there's nothing to that, he'll get over it. You make a big fuss and your father—"

"Would kill him, yes."

"You understand that's a literal thing, right?"

"I know my father. He's why I wanted to handle this myself. I was afraid he'd blow his top with Jerome."

"He'd do the same with Becker—who could be innocent."

"We still have to make him talk."

"That can be arranged. Any other unrequited loves?"

"Umm—don't think so."

Someone thumped hard on the door. Mrs. Huffman opened it a crack, then backed off to allow in another middle-aged woman. She had on diamonds. Not many, but the fires sparking from them looked obscenely expensive. I made a guess that she was the groom's mother. She'd also been crying, and wasn't done with it yet.

"Gerty?" said Mrs. Huffman, abruptly unbending. "What's wrong?"

"We found it on the table with the wedding gifts!" Gerty waved a scrap of brown paper in one shaking fist. "Sheila—it's terrible!"

Mrs. Huffman read it, her face clouding over. "Louie will kill him for this!"

"For what?" Dorothy grabbed the paper. "Oh, my God. Momma, you can't let Daddy know."

"Too late, he already does," wailed Gerty.

The maid of honor crowded in and had her turn to read and react. She dropped the scrap, scampered from the room, and about two seconds later screams of fury and dismay from the bridesmaids erupted in the hall. Another minute and whatever it was would make the *Tribune*'s bulldog edition.

Gerty was sheet white. "Sheila, you've got to stop Louie from doing anything. This has to be some kind of mistake. This isn't like Jerome—I raised him better than that."

I picked up the paper and read:

Dear Dot,
        I can't be your husband. Annul the wedding. I won't
bother you again.
        Jerome K. Schubert

There were things about the note that bothered me, but what jumped out the strongest was the scent of human blood on the paper.

THOUGH I DON'T BREATHE REGULARLY I TEND TO notice bloodsmell. It comes with my condition, no escape. That telltale whiff stopped me cold. Maybe Jerome had cut himself shaving . . . and maybe I'd take up sunbathing on Michigan Avenue.

Two edges of the crumpled sheet were uneven, torn from something larger. The writer could have lifted this from any waste-basket between here and the lake. No one puts a good-bye note in pencil on parcel wrap, though. Someone had been in a hurry and probably improvising.

I turned the sheet over. The back was marred with ordinary grime which served along with the dark paper to obscure the rusty traces of blood. It was not more than an hour old.

Dorothy looked like she'd taken a gut punch and jerked when I touched her arm. "Over here," I muttered, tugging.

There was no booze handy this time, so I made her sit and dropped on one knee before her, taking one of her cold hands. It was a parody of a proposal tableau, but no one was smiling.

"Dorothy." I said it sharply. "Come on, snap out of it. The note's fake."

She shook her head and blinked. "What?" How do you know?"

"You're going to tell me." I nodded at the monogrammed suitcases. "That's what you were taking to the train station?"

"Some of it. The trunks are already aboard."

"Right. Well, if Jerome had run off on his own don't you think he'd stop here on his way out to grab a packed bag?"

"Maybe—unless he went back to his parents' house."

"Let's figure he didn't. Look at the note. Is this his handwriting?"

"It's uneven . . . but yes."

I chose to take that as good news and had to hope he was still alive. "Next, what's he call you?"

"Darling . . . sweetheart . . . Dorry-kins . . ."

"Name? Dot or Dorothy?"

"Dorothy. Only my family calls me— Oh, no. You can't mean—"

"Not done yet. How about Becker and Cooley? They call you Dot, right?"

Her brown eyes started to kindle, and she made that dangerous back of the throat sound. "If they've laid a finger on my Jerome—"

"Atta girl. Now read it again. What's wrong with it?"

She did so. " 'Annul the wedding'? He wouldn't say that, he'd say 'marriage.' And he'd never sign his name with me. He always signs a *J* followed by a dash. Someone made him write this?"

"Looks it." She started to rise; I pulled her down. "But you've got to play like you believe it. Someone could be watching your reaction."

"But I have to—"

"That's my job. You know the layout of this church? The whole shebang?"

"Most of it."

"Make me a general sketch. I want to poke around and not have to ask directions."

"You think he's still here?"

"If only one person was in on it—maybe. Otherwise I'm just eliminating possibilities."

"But the ushers searched everywhere."

"Then they missed something." Like being able to pick up bloodsmell in the air. "Do the sketch and make like you believe the note. Ask for your father to come back here. If he's with you then he won't be hunting for Jerome."

DOROTHY SLIPPED ME HER ROUGH MAP JUST AS Louie Huffman arrived. He looked like a bear with a headache, but didn't let that roll along to his daughter. I'd suggested she let her parents know the note was a fake, and that they not share the information with anyone. The three of them went off in a corner, heads together, expressions grim. If it turned out that Jerome had disappeared himself after all, then it was his own hard luck if the Huffmans ever caught up with him.

Missing from the picture were Cooley and Becker. A different set of armed goons in imperfectly fitting tuxedos stood guard at a respectful distance. I asked after the missing lieutenants. Cooley was down the hall; no one knew where Becker was.

I was just guessing about a possibly lovesick Becker being the perpetrator. That would make things simpler, but any of the mob muscle working for Huffman could be behind it. This shenanigan might not be about removing a rival for Dorothy, but a diversion. For all I knew Siggy Schubert could have been slipped a ransom note on the side. He was damned rich.

No point questioning him just yet. I had to let this play out as expected and keep my eyes open.

Since Jerome had vanished from the reception hall, I went there first.

A couple questions got me the location of where he'd last been with the bride: at a table shaking hands and helping serve out wedding cake. The table was in front of double doors leading to a kitchen where a number of ladies were washing up and in deep discussion about current events. There was a collective pause when I walked in. I smiled and gave a "don't mind me" wave, checking for other doors. One led to the outside, another to a different hall. Either worked well for a fast exit.

It wouldn't take much for someone to sidle next to Jerome, jam a gun muzzle into his ribs, and tell him to come along quietly. Done right and it would seem as though he'd truly vanished. Take him into the kitchen, then where—outside to a car trunk or stash him in a quiet spot in the church to write a note to the bride?

"Excuse me—were any of you ladies here when the groom went missing?"

That netted me half a dozen replies at once. I finally got that they'd been away to see the cake-cutting and get a closer look at the wedding dress. Only one had remained in the kitchen, and she'd not noticed anybody ducking outside.

I thanked them and tried the hall. Dorothy's map got vague at this point. St. Mike's was pretty huge.

The lights were out, indicating the area was closed for the night, but there was enough glow from the windows to allow me to navigate. More doors lined the wall opposite, and I tried a few. Classrooms and meeting rooms. I made fast work of them, listening for heartbeats, sniffing for blood.

A broom closet stinking of floor polish, old rags, and dust came up trumps. On the floor was a cravat; its dark blue matched the color of the bridesmaids' dresses.

Bloodsmell. All over it.

A broad stain on the material made my corner teeth itch.

Still damp. If Jerome had bled that much . . . damn.

I backed out and checked the polished floor for blood spots. None visible, but two parallel drag marks such as might be made by shoe heels led farther into the building. I'm no trail scout, but they were as good as a neon arrow.

They ended at a stairway going down into profound blackness and silence. I looked for a light switch, but the walls were clean.

Dammit.

My eyes could make use of the least little shard of light—if it was present. An interior chamber like this put me back on a level with normal humans. Maybe this check had discouraged the ushers on their initial search for Jerome. Couldn't blame them; it sure as hell had me hesitating.

It's wholly irrational and no one knows of it because it is a source of great personal embarrassment to me, but I hate the dark. Forget an ordinary dim room, I'm talking about the kind of utter absence of light that makes you think you've gone blind. That's enough to freeze me. I always have to fight off a stab of panic.

Crazy enough for a grown man, but a vampire?

I've got reasons. Bad things have happened to me, and though much took place in well-lighted spots, enough occurred in pitch blackness to leave permanent scars.

Wincing, I pushed forward. I couldn't let it keep me from doing my job. If my partner had been along I'd have bulldozed ahead, bolstered by his moral support and dry humor. On my own I had time to imagine and remember past terrors.

I made it to the first landing before my nerve gave out and I stumbled back again, getting away from whatever creepy things lurked unseen below.

Stupid, stupid, STUPID.

I couldn't kid myself out of it, either. It hadn't been so very long ago that I'd been trapped and helpless in another black cellar. The memory was only too ready to surface. I closed my hands on a banister rail to keep them from shaking.

Schubert didn't have time for this. Chances were good that he was down there in need of help. I took a deep cleansing breath to clear my head . . . and picked up a faint trace of blood-smell.

Damn. I had to force myself no matter what, but internal terrors aside, it was truly dangerous to go blundering around in unknown territory. I needed a flashlight or—

Oh. Big Catholic church. If anyone had candles by the gross . . .

A minute later, sheepish and annoyed, I took the stairs with considerably more confidence. I found candles and a box of matches in the broom closet. They made me sane again.

I see more by a single candle flame than other people can get from a lightbulb's glow, but a flame jiggles. Shadows dancing and leaping in the corners spook me the same as anyone else; I took it slow and listened.

The only noise was above and behind me. Someone came striding up the hall at a good clip, closing on the stairs. I didn't want to be caught, so I vanished.

Handy talent. Now *I* was one of the creepy things lurking unseen.

Pressing my amorphous presence against a wall, I floated gently downward until coming to a turn, then held myself out of the way in the corner. My hearing was muffled in this state; all I could tell about the newcomer was that he seemed to be alone. I waited until he was well past before going solid again.

Returned to reality as well, the candle burned cheerfully bright. Huh. I'd known that might be a possibility, but it's still interesting to see firsthand.

I eased down a little farther, then halted again and vanished as a *second* person followed the other guy. He had his shoes off, moving along swift and quiet.

The temptation to reappear behind him and lay a hand on his shoulder like Death's harbinger was very strong, but I resisted. When this one was well ahead I took form again and listened, but apparently he was the caboose of the train.

They must have had flashlights. Past the glow of my one flame I picked up the brighter radiance of modern invention playing against the walls of the bottom landing.

It faded, though. I hustled to catch up.

The basement was enormous and used for storage, *lots* of storage. All kinds of stuff, ecclesiastical and other, more worldly items, filled the place to the ceiling. Tables, stacks of chairs, candle stands of every shape and size, sporting equipment, folding beds, and a thousand dusty crates kept me from seeing very far into a maze of junk.

Deep into the jumble someone had left on a light. I moved toward it. My candle was a liability. I pinched it out.

Just a fraction too late I caught a surge of movement on my left.

Something cracked against my shins and down I dropped. In the background against that burst of pain I heard a woman gasp and let fly with a short scream. Almost at the same instant something far worse slammed into the back of my skull. I kept on dropping, but was unaware of hitting bottom.

It was cold there, though. Really cold.

IF I GET HURT BADLY ENOUGH VANISHING IS an involuntary thing. My body simply takes over and gets me away from whatever grief has inflicted itself—unless the injury involves wood. I don't know why, and I sure as hell try to avoid it, but wood hates me. It shorts out my disappearing act, leaving behind what others might mistake for a dead body. I go completely inert, no breathing or heartbeat, dilated and fixed pupils, the works.

Considering my circumstances as awareness trickled back, being dead was a pleasant alternative.

I lay on my back, limbs sprawled, and an unbearable pressure between my ears had the world spinning. Eyes open or shut, it made no difference. Muscles twitching, I wanted to vanish and thus heal, but wouldn't be able to until the shock wore off.

That would take a while. My head would have to be smashed flat by a steamroller to feel better. I took care to keep still and not groan.

When raising my eyelids seemed like something that could be done without too much agony, I gave it a try.

Not good. Pitch black all around, but the head pain was distracting and staved off the usual stutter of panic. When I'd recovered enough that the darkness bothered me I snarled at the monsters hiding there. In my present mood I'd strangle anything within reach . . . when I could move again. Getting what should have been a fatal bash to the brain had tossed my nebulous fears into the next county.

After a few minutes I figured out someone had thrown a tarp over me. That's what you do with the dead, cover 'em up because it could be catching. Entirely true: soon as I was able, I would kill someone for this.

Before long I thought sitting up wouldn't be too bad, and it wasn't—it was horrendous. I pushed off the tarp and let my body get used to being almost vertical. Whatever light had been on was gone now.

Sluggish memory reminded me I should still have matches

and candles in my pockets. I made my unsteady fingers work and
fired up a match.

That was bright. Ow.

I lit a candle and checked around. Someone had dragged me
off the main path, stashing me by a battered old table. Record
books and clipboards suggested that it served as a work desk for
some fearless soul. A bare bulb with a frayed string pull dangled
temptingly overhead.

Getting to my feet was hard, but once there it wasn't unbearable so long as I didn't move my head much. I yanked the light on,
bathing the place in twenty-five watts of electric glory.

No one came charging from the remaining shadows. I was
happy.

Having been through this before I knew better than to touch
the sore spot on my head. Nothing good ever came of that.
Bloodsmell hung in the still air, but wasn't mine. It was some lin-
gering trace of the trail I'd followed, meaning the damage hadn't
broken my skin, probably due to—

Where the hell was my hat?

I squinted around in the too-bright light. No hat. That made
me mad. I liked that fedora.

No, I wasn't thinking straight, but after the whack I'd gotten I
was doing pretty damned good.

Staggering down the maze, I found my now rumpled topper
on a crate along with my first candle. Its wax was still soft, not
more than five minutes had passed since the attack. Damn, I hurt
worse than a lousy five minutes' worth of unconsciousness. Someone had blended the items into the general junk. Add a little dust
and they'd stay lost in the background for years.

Was that the plan for the missing Jerome Schubert? I looked
at the mountains of tarp-shrouded boxes with fresh unease, and

listened hard, but no sound of a heartbeat came from any of them. Good if he was alive, really bad if he was not.

Off to the side on the bare cement floor lay a woman's shoes. They might have been my client's new mules, but female footwear all looks the same to me. I thought I'd recognized her tone in that gasp and brief scream. Perhaps she'd followed me. When I got clobbered, she sensibly ran. If she was anywhere near I'd have heard her.

Farther into the basement, then, where there was at least one bad guy who'd already decked me. No chance that he would get a second try.

I was still armed, my .38 Detective Special snug in its shoulder rig, but if Dorothy was down here I was reluctant to start slinging lead, however much someone deserved it. This place was full of alternative weapons, though, and in two seconds I had the reassuring weight of a genuine Louisville Slugger in one hand. For all I knew it could have been the same hunk of wood applied so effectively on my shins and skull.

Which still hurt. I limped along until the faint *lub-dub* of a heartbeat teased at my eardrums.

Not far ahead.

Loose-limbed and dazed, Cooley lay in the glare cast by another hanging bulb that had been left on. As I came within his field of view his eyelids flickered with awareness but no real conviction. He looked the way I felt, which was damned awful. Someone had lambasted him good, which was tough luck for the guy. At the same time I wondered what he was doing here. His heartbeat told me he wasn't a member of my particular union, so he couldn't have been following the scent of blood.

I set the bat and candle to one side, patted down his pockets, and found a flask. Plenty of people had gotten into the habit of carrying one during Prohibition. Back during my non-blood-drinking days I'd done the same. His was silver-plated with a cap that doubled as a shot glass. Nice. I dribbled half a finger's worth of hooch in and held it to his lips, careful not to move his head. He wouldn't thank me for that.

The smell of the stuff was about as appealing as gasoline, but I still felt an urge to take a sip as well. Fresh blood was my only poison now, but I could wait.

Cooley choked down his booze and grimaced.

"Who's the bad guy?" I asked. "Becker?"

He growled.

"Where is he?"

Another growl, accompanied by his right hand flapping once against the floor. I took that to mean Becker was not too far ahead.

"Is Dorothy with him?"

"Donno," he managed to say with some effort.

I gave him another shot of firewater, pulled a tarp from something, and covered him to the chin. Maybe I don't feel it much anymore, but it had to be cold down here. His eyes flickered again, puzzlement crossed with I wasn't sure what. Some of these tough guys don't know how to react to common decency.

Snagging up the bat and snuffing the candle, I moved on, trying to be quiet by going on the balls of my feet. In my own ears I sounded like a stampede. At least someone was leaving the lights on ahead.

Before long I picked up the faintest mutter of voices. The speakers were around a corner made of thick support pillars and shelving. Some of the stuff must have been down here since before the Spanish-American War.

A man and woman were arguing, the tones intense.

I peered around a final obstacle.

Becker was faced away from me, arms down stiff at his sides, hands clenched, a baseball bat in one fist. Sometimes I hate being right.

Dorothy, flatfooted without her shoes, was backed into a dead end, this part of the maze stopped by a brick wall. For all that, she looked defiant and sounded dangerously angry. "Tell me where he is."

"You need to get out of here," said Becker. It had the tired cadence of repetition.

"Not without my husband."

"You go back upstairs and don't say nothin' to—"

In the time it took them to make that exchange I'd slipped behind Cooley and with remarkable restraint lightly swatted the back of his head with the slugger, using just enough force to rattle him. He dropped, stunned to immobility, but not unconscious. I kicked his own bat away and put my foot on his throat.

Dorothy stared at me, mouth wide open, big brown eyes popping.

I grinned back. Though my corner teeth weren't out it still seemed to scare her. "You okay?"

"I thought he'd killed you! When you fell and didn't move and—"

"Not even close. Where's Jerome?"

That jarred her from further questions about my miraculous recovery. "I don't know." She looked down at Becker, eyes going hard. "Yet." She picked up his bat and hefted it.

"Let's just get out of here, find your father, and . . ."

She shook her head. "My problem, and I will take care of it."

I heard the scrape and scuff as someone approached. Cooley rounded the corner, wobbly, but with his gun in hand. He took in the little scene, scowled at Becker, then holstered the gat.

"Cooley," she snapped, "where's Jerome?"

He started to shake his head, then stopped, one hand half-raised to touch the sore spot. He must have known better too, and turned it into a shrugging gesture. "Donno. I thought he might and followed him down here." He pointed at me.

"Why would I know?" I asked, surprised.

"I hear stuff. You get results an' no one can figure out how. You seemed to be on top of things."

Only partially, after I'd picked up on the scent of blood. Clearly he'd missed my ignominious retreat up the stairs away from the big bad dark below. The rest had been luck. The sour kind. My head . . .

"You followed him, and I followed you," said Dorothy. "And Becker was here already. Jerome must be here too, right?" She looked to me for concurrence.

I stalled, using the moment to sniff the stale air for blood—nothing—and listen for a fourth heartbeat in the immediate area. The three that were present would mask its sound. "We'll have to search."

"This place is too big, and I'm in a hurry. Slap it out of Becker."

"What?"

"You heard me."

I'd have thought she'd seen one too many Cagney movies but for the fact she was her father's daughter. "Uh . . . well . . ."

"You're not going sissy on me, are you?"

Cooley stepped in to rescue me. "He can't, Dot."

"Why not? I hired him."

"He's friends with Northside Gordy. Your pop works for him, but in a sideways kind of direction. If you have Fleming beating up one of your pop's guys, that could make for trouble. Big Louie would have to retaliate on this guy, and then Gordy would have to retaliate on Louie."

She steamed and stewed, but offered no counterargument, just a single contempt-laden comment. *"Politics."*

"Yeah," I said. "Sorry."

"All right. Will it start a gang war if you two just tied Becker up for me?"

We consulted with a wordless exchange of looks. "We can do that," I said.

"Yeah, we can do that," Cooley echoed.

He was pretty gray in the gills. I was a little better recovered and did the honors after finding a coil of rope.

Dorothy was specific about how she wanted Becker immobilized. Being in no condition to object, he was soon wrapped tight in a hemp cocoon. While I was busy Dorothy found a stack of folded tarps and dragged them down, filling the air with dust. She and Cooley sneezed, but I was immune so long as I didn't breathe.

Becker revived enough from my gentle tap to sneeze too.

Dorothy paused, throwing him a Medusa's stare, and he did go still. "Where's Jerome?"

"He's not right for you, Dot."

"And you are?"

"I'm a better man than him."

"I can almost see why you'd think that. But brass tacks—*I* get the final say, and that's what matters. I love him, not you. Now *where* is he?"

"Cooley, you tell her that I—"

"Leave me out of it!" Cooley snarled. "I told you to stay clear of her. You're an idiot, ask anyone." He sank to the floor, his back to some junk, and took a swig from his flask. He seemed content to watch but not interfere. That was a reasonable course to me. I remained standing, using my bat for a cane to keep me steady.

Dorothy leaned in close. "Becker. Look at me. Tell me where Jerome is, and we'll keep this between ourselves. Even Daddy won't know."

"I don't care if the boss finds out!"

If that was her trump card, she didn't seem disappointed by his reaction. "You should."

"He can do what he likes, I'm saving you from—"

She picked up his baseball bat and gave it an experimental swing.

Becker went white, but kept the stubborn face. "You wouldn't."

"If Daddy was here, probably not. He'd do it himself, and probably kill you before you talked. But this is your lucky night. I'm here instead."

"Aw, Dot," said Cooley, "you don't wanna do that."

"Yes, I do."

"You could really hurt him."

"Exactly." Her gaze never left Becker.

"I mean you could kill him. Accidental-like."

"If I kill him it will be entirely on purpose. But that won't happen. He'll *wish* he was dead, though."

She dropped the bat and began throwing folded tarps across Becker's tied-up body. He tried to roll around to get out from under, but their combined weight got to be too much. In a very short time he was nearly gone from view except for his head. Must have been hot, I thought, watching his face go red from either heat or rising fury.

"Dot . . . ," he said. "You need to—"

"Where's Jerome?" she asked, picking up the bat and tapping the fat end against the cement floor.

When he didn't reply, she raised it high and brought it down hard across his tarp-insulated midsection.

Cooley yelled something, but it was drowned out by Becker's much louder, outraged bellow. Despite the thick layers of canvas he'd obviously felt the force of it. Never underestimate the determination of a woman being deprived of her honeymoon.

Dorothy took a few more swings, full power, then paused to sneeze. Each time she connected, more dust got thrown up. I offered her my handkerchief. She gave me a sweet, heart-melting look of gratitude and noisily blew her nose. "You're *so* polite," she said.

I didn't know what to say to that and stepped out of range as she wound up for another inning.

"Dorothy!"

We all froze—except for Becker, of course—as Mrs. Huffman stepped into the improvised arena. With her was Mrs. Schubert. Both ladies were wide of eye.

"What *are* you doing?" demanded the mother of the bride.

Dorothy lifted her chin, resting the bat on her shoulder. "*He* knows where Jerome is. I'm persuading him to cooperate." She gave a brief meant-to-be-reassuring nod at her shocked mother-in-law.

"Oh, Sylvia," said Mrs. Schubert.

"You're right, Gerty." Mrs. Huffman stepped forward. "This isn't the way to do it." She pulled a four-inch-thick layer of tarp from Becker and glanced at her daughter. "Too much padding, dear. He won't feel anything with that much in the way. Try it now."

"Sylvia! We're in church!" Mrs. Schubert pointed out.

"Just the basement. It doesn't count. If this was the sanctuary it would be completely different."

"Well, if you're sure . . ."

She put an arm around other woman's shoulder and gave a re-assuring squeeze. "Your Jerome is family now. We look after our own." Mrs. Huffman offered suggestions on where best to strike to get a faster result.

Dorothy slammed the bat down, clearly in a take-no-prisoners mood.

Cooley and I winced.

Becker howled. I didn't think he could get louder at it, but he managed. At one point he tried to babble to Mrs. Huffman that he was in love with Dorothy, but it cut no ice with her.

"Sweetheart," she addressed her daughter, who'd paused again. "Make him fall *out* of love with you."

Dorothy made that ominous back-of-the-throat sound and obliged, having gained her second wind.

Mrs. Huffman glanced at Cooley. "You will see to it that this fellow leaves town?"

"Yes, ma'am," he humbly replied.

"If there's anything left of him," I added.

I got a hard, haughty look from the lady. "Young man, he won't even show a bruise."

That set me wondering if she was the source of Big Louie Huffman's reputation for swift persuasion. Maybe behind every successful man stands a woman—holding a baseball bat.

Wham, thump, wham. I winced again, sympathetic, but not about to get in the middle of the proceedings.

It seemed to take longer, but a couple minutes later Becker cracked. His color had gone from white fear to red anger and finally bilious green as he blurted out where he'd hidden Jerome. Now I stepped in quick, threw off the tarps, and rolled him on his side. The pounding had a predictable effect on his digestive tract, and I didn't think it a good thing for him to choke to death in front of the ladies. They withdrew from the immediate area, hands over their noses, and went after Dorothy as she darted off to find her husband.

Moving more slowly, I followed the women back to the old table where I'd been dragged. There was a door in the shadows I'd not noticed earlier, distracted as I was by the skull-busting. Dorothy was trying to pry it open with a crowbar.

"Jack! I'm not strong enough—could you—?"

No problem. I didn't need the crowbar, but used it anyway. No point in impressing them by ripping the doorknob from the thick panel; I might have to pay for it. A minimum amount of el-bow grease popped the door wide. Dorothy rushed in, crying Jerome's name, kneeling and covering him with kisses.

He was tied, gagged, and groggy, with blood down the front of his once-pristine white shirt—from a punch in the nose, it turned out.

And dammit, he *did* look like Ralph Bellamy.

Once free and able to catch his breath Schubert filled in the blanks while the women fussed over him.

At the cake-cutting Becker had threatened to ventilate him un-less he came along quietly at gunpoint. Schubert was too surprised even to think to fight until they were in the hall broom closet. Becker had been itching to punch him for weeks. One smack in the kisser did the trick. That satisfaction taken, he'd forced Schubert to write the good-bye note, which he'd done with one hand holding the pencil, the other pressing the blue cravat to his bloody nose. For all that, he'd tried to put in a few clues that would make the note read wrong. Smart guy.

Then Becker coshed him solid and dragged the unconscious groom down to the basement. With Schubert safely stowed, Becker was free to resume goon duties for his boss until such time as he could return and permanently remove his rival. The bride's violent reaction and bringing in outside help must have been a shock.

Dorothy enthusiastically gave credit where it was due, and Schubert shook my hand. I don't think one word in ten was getting through to him, but he was willing to agree with his wife. If he continued doing that I figured they'd have a long and happy partnership.

As it seemed only right, I asked and was allowed to kiss the bride. My chaste peck on the cheek made her blush. Then the mothers stepped in and insisted everyone go back upstairs. They'd already decided to tell their guests the whole thing was an elaborate wedding prank that had gotten out of hand.

Soon as they were far enough away, I vanished, cutting myself off from the head and shin pain. That was almost as good as kissing Dorothy. As I floated in the gray nothingness I wished them a happy celebration in their Niagara-bound Pullman.

Then I wondered what my girlfriend was up to; plenty of time to call on her, see if she might be in the mood for some amiable canoodling. How many other couples who had attended the wedding would have similar thoughts in line with the bride and groom's wedding night?

When I went solid again the headache was gone along with the bruises. I was tired from the healing, but straight-from-the-vein refreshment at the Stockyards or even a pint of red from a butcher shop would take care of that.

I still had some cleanup work to do, though, not unlike those ladies in the kitchen, but with more heavy lifting involved.

Cooley was where I'd left him, taking it easy on the floor while scowling at the miserable rope-swathed bundle before him. When I returned, he tiredly levered himself upright, pulled out a knife, and cut Becker free. "We need to get him outta here before Big Louie steps in."

He took it for granted that I'd help him. Well, why not?

"The kid's okay," Cooley went on, "but an idiot for skirts."

"Aren't we all?"

"Yeah, but use a little judgment on which skirt you fall for."

"Like Mrs. Huffman?"

That shot got me a sharp look, and for an instant before covering it up he looked like a raw and vulnerable kid himself. Maybe some twenty years ago Mrs. Huffman had used similar means to make him fall out of love with her.

"Oh, yeah," he said slowly. "I hear stories about you. You don't go spreadin' that one, punk."

I raised both hands in a "not me" gesture. "It stays right here, pal. Like the lady said, we're in a church."

He grunted and, with more care than I'd have given him credit for, helped get the luckless Becker to his unsteady feet.

P. N. ELROD has sold more than twenty novels, at least as many short stories, and edited several collections, including My Big, Fat Supernatural Wedding. *She's best known for her* Vampire Files *series, featuring Jack Fleming, and would write books more quickly but for being hampered by an incurable chocolate addiction.*

Information on her toothy titles may be found at www.vampwriter.com.

Newlydeads

A Tale of Black London

Caitlin Kittredge

This story takes place in the world of the Black, place of fae, demons, and magic-users that hides in the nooks and crannies of the real. As far as human denizens go, Pete Caldecott and her friend Jack Winter are by far the most notorious. . . .

BLACKPOOL APPEARED OUT OF THE FOG, A THOUSAND neon eyes winking from a hunched and gleaming body.

Pete Caldecott stood in the swirling salt-scented mist and glowered at the edifice of the Paradise Palace Casino & Resort. The pink neon letters blinked lethargically, a beacon to middle-aged couples, poor young families, and gamblers on their last shilling. Not so common were detective inspectors, like herself, and sneaky gits like her companion.

Pete turned her head to glare at Jack Winter, the titular companion. "This is *not* my idea of a bloody holiday."

Jack shrugged, producing a Parliament from the thin air between his fingers. "You said you needed a change. This is a change. Chin up, lip stiff or some rot. Besides, you love the seaside." He clicked his fingernails together and an ember flared on the Parliament's tip.

Pete ignored him. Jack used magic on her only when he was trying to weasel out of an apology. "Get the bags, then," she said. "Can't wait to relax in the confines of a double-twin between the lift and the ice machine."

Jack grabbed up their suitcases from the back of Pete's Mini and jogged after her. "Oi! Come back here!"

Pete quickened her pace in retaliatory spite. The carpark was silent and empty except for the Mini's red beetle-backed shape, pavement slick and slimy in the descending twilight. The mist gathered behind her, obscuring Jack's bowed platinum head for a moment, and a wind brought the scent of rotting sea things. No bird cries carried from the Irish Sea and no drunken holiday chatter, which there should surely be in Blackpool of all places, reached her ears.

Just for a moment, she could be anywhere, trapped in fog ancient as the marshes around the city, lost to the Black like the women of fireside stories.

A doorman in a crumpled pink coat slumbered at the lobby doors when Pete reached them. Moisture dripped from the brim of his cap. The doors were frosted glass, etched with the image of kissing swans.

Jack caught up to her, wheezing equal parts wet air and smoke, his jackboots raising a clatter. The doorman did not stir.

"You going to be in a mood for the entire weekend?" Jack demanded, dragging deeply on the end of his Parliament before flicking it into a puddle. It hissed and sparked out with a little question mark of smoke.

"Very probably," said Pete. Jack got *his* smile, the curled ends pushing at the early lines in his face and the little spark of imp-light in his eyes. Pete always thought of it as the devil-smile.

"I promise you—no, I *wager* you, Pete Caldecott, that before this holiday is over you'll admit that you've had a bit of fun."

Pete opened the lobby door. "Never happen. Ten quid?"

Jack hefted the suitcases. "I'm a confident bloke. Make it twenty."

The swans whooshed shut behind them, kissing once more. The Paradise Palace's lobby was done in bloodred carpet and pink satin chairs, walls the color of a poisoned tide washing sand.

Pete said, "I'm surprised you have that much to bet, after the horrendous expense of dragging me to a family casino resort done entirely in swans." The motif repeated through the lobby, the only relief a gilt-edged oil painting over a fake fireplace that depicted a marsh scene, a deep swirl of blacks and fleshy greens.

"They're having a special," said Jack smugly, shoving Pete's suitcase back into her arms. "St. Gummarus's Feast rates for all of the week. Get ready to pay out on Monday, Miss I'm-So-Sure."

Jack Winter had many vices, not the least of which was usually being right. Pete pointed at the black marble reception rather than admit she was out of retorts. "Go check us in. I'm tired and I'd like to go claim my glorified broom closet so I can lie down."

"You wait, Caldecott," Jack assured her, strutting over to the reception. The clerk eyed his black denim, jackboots, and nicotine-tinged Dead Kennedys shirt with something approaching stark horror. "You wait. You'll have the time of your life. Mark my words."

JACK GRINNED SILENTLY THE ENTIRE TIME THEY WAITED for the lift, and practically cackled when he reached across Pete and punched the button for the top floor of the hotel.

"All right, *what?*" she finally demanded. Jack burst out into laughter, which quickly turned to a cough.

"Bollocks, is it sodding damp enough in this place? My insides are growing mold."

"*You* chose it, *you* don't get to complain," Pete said, punctuating her speech with her best I'm-going-to-fetch-you-a-bloody-smack glare. "What's so bloody amusing?"

Jack rummaged about the inside pocket of his tatty black longcoat and pulled out two plastic cards emblazoned with—what else—the kissing swans. The cards were gilt-edged, like some sort of psychotically romanticized Golden Ticket. "Here, you look at this," Jack said, still barely containing his mirth, "and you try telling me that this won't be the best bloody holiday in the history of Britain."

The plastic card read *Honeymoon Getaway—Suite Access Key* in flamboyant red script.

Pete felt as if the lift had abruptly reversed direction. "Jack, what did you do?"

"I told that sad bloke at the counter we were married," said Jack, eyes alight. "And it being our honeymoon, and us having so little money with the baby on the way, it might be nice if he offered us a sort of upgrade. . . ."

Pete dropped her suitcase and moved for Jack's throat. Height advantage he may have, but she was a trained inspector with the Metropolitan Police. She'd faced down demons and rampaging ghosts, and more important, she was *angry.*

"Oi!" Jack shouted, her blow glancing off his shoulder as he ducked. "Settle down! The honeymooner's suite gets free room service! And a whirlpool bath. You bloody women love that sort of thing."

"Jack," said Pete, pitching her tone to cut steel. "We are not married. We are not sleeping together. Right at this moment in time, I don't even *like* you."

"It was just a lie, Pete," he sighed, leaning back against the satin-draped wall of the lift. "Lies don't draw blood. And besides, we got free liquor and a big fancy hotel suite out of it."

"You did," Pete hissed, jabbing him in the chest. "*You* did all of this. Dragged me along off the bloody cliff, as usual."

The lift doors rolled back with a soft chime. Jack threw up his hands. "I give up," he snapped. "I thought if I took you away like you wanted, maybe you'd stop being so bloody serious, but I was wrong."

Pete bit the inside of her lower lip and looked at her shoes. Jack didn't complete the thought, didn't say *took you away from what happened in London*. But then, he needn't. Pete dreamed it, every night, cinematically and vividly and with the same gut-ripping terror of the real event. As a Weir, she dreamed colors, smells, letters and sounds, and always had. Once upon a time, she'd dreamed about the day when they were young that Jack had nearly died the first time.

Now, it was all ghosts and blood.

The lift started to close and Pete slipped out, following Jack down the muffled hallway of bleeding floor and medium rare walls. "I'm sorry," she said when he could hear her. He was trying to jam the keycard into the reader slot to the side of their suite's double doors.

"Yeah, well, me too," Jack muttered. "Let's just get through the weekend and forget this whole event, right? Chalk another win on the board for me and my brilliant bloody ideas."

Pete looked at the doors of the suite. They were black, carved with a swirling symbol that evoked the painting in the lobby, artful strands curling around the central point. Circles were supposed ff .

to be safe, for mages. Jack never went anywhere without odd ends of chalk in his pockets. "It could be worse," she said finally.

Jack ripped the card out of the reader. "Bollocks!"

Pete took it from him. "Just let me." He backed up, glaring.

"There better be a sodding lake of free booze in there. I need a bloody drink."

INSIDE, ALL WAS BLACKNESS. PETE CLICKED THE SWITCH next to the door, with no response. "That's odd."

Blue shine blazed behind her, illuminating overstuffed and gilded furniture and a bed the size of a football pitch on an elevated dais at the far side of the room. Jack shuffled past her, the witchlight flickering in the curve of his palm, and turned on a floor lamp. "Bad wiring. Not surprised. This whole city is sinking back into the fucking marshes."

He fished in his jacket pocket and found chalk, and drew a sloppy warding hex on the inside of the door.

"Jack, no," Pete protested. He jabbed the stubby end of the chalk at her.

"When some bloody beastie from beyond the beyond is on the other side, you'll thank me." He dropped his bag, his coat, and his boots in a heap in the center of the hearts-chamber carpet, emptied the gold-painted bar of its supply of tiny whiskey bottles, and went into the bathroom. The door slammed in Pete's face.

"Oh, of course," she muttered. "Because *I* don't need a shower after four bloody hours of M-55 Saturday traffic. Tosser."

At least he hadn't claimed the bed. Pete smiled grimly and laid her suitcase on the satin duvet, the color of bone mellowed by centuries. Except for this white, the whole suite repeated the rest of the hotel. The colors and slippery fabrics gave Pete the uncomfortable feeling of being *inside* something huge and crimson and beating.

She shivered the feeling away, and opened her case. The file inside, on top of her weekend's worth of holiday clothing, was accusing as a murdered man's open eyes.

Pete knew that nothing would have changed since the last time she'd read the file's contents, but she opened it anyway and scanned the first line.

Detective Chief Inspector Geoffrey Newell
SO5, Metropolitan Police Service, London
Dear Sir,
    I regretfully tender my resignation from the position of Detective Inspector . . .

It went on, with the required platitudes. *Invaluable experience. Due to recent events . . . Do not feel able to discharge my duties . . .*

The memo didn't give her room for much more than that, just the entrails of a promising career that, thanks to Jack, she was considering chucking. And on cue, Jack had turned into an absolute wanker.

"Should have told him," Pete castigated herself out loud, pulling a jersey and sleep pants out of the case. She shoved the file to the very bottom, crumpling the edges. Jack would tell her she was bloody stupid—bloody *fucking* stupid, if he were actually talking. That it wasn't his fault. She hadn't *had* to go looking for him four months ago, and her slippage into the Black, her awakened but not controlled Weir talents and her entrée into magic was entirely her own doing.

Jack would tell her all of that and then turn around, with his self-satisfied smile, and leave all over again. Jack was good at leaving—twelve years long the last time he and Pete had parted. If she admitted she needed his help now, he'd be off again. Jack Winter was not a fan of commitment, to anything except his own skin.

How do I ignore it? How did she go on chasing shoplifters and prosecuting hooligans who got pissed and went Paki-bashing once she'd looked on the face of ghosts hungry for a living heart's essence and seen what crawled away into the shadowy places of London when the light hit its scaly hide?

Jack yelped, from the bathroom, "Bloody buggering fuck!"

Pete's skin leapt as she jerked back into herself, and she cleared the dais and the distance to the door in two steps. If there was one thing her time with Jack had taught hard and surely, it was that screams of terror were never to be ignored.

She hit the door with her shoulder, popping the gilt latch off its hinges, and nearly skidded into Jack. He had his shirt off, half-empty mini-bottle in one hand and an expression traveling the road from shock to revulsion on his face.

"What is it?" Pete demanded, expecting to see a shade, those angry howling scraps of a human soul stranded after death, or something worse, like the slime-mold demons Jack claimed lived under London Bridge.

Jack tossed down the rest of the whiskey and set the bottle with its empty brothers on the vanity. "Look," he said, pointing into the basin of the whirlpool tub. Pete stepped around him and peered in, then clapped a hand over her nose to shield against the smell of rotted seaweed and sundered guts that rolled out to meet her.

"Bloody hell." A dead thing lay in the basin, and Pete thought *thing* because that's exactly what it was—it could have been a gull, or some other waterfowl at some point, but instead of legs it had sadly curling feelers, rubbery and yellow, and a beak that hooked like the letter *C,* black and scarred. Its eyes bulged out and its neck had been twisted around. The thing's greenish blood, a color like absinthe mixed with motor oil, smeared the pale porcelain.

Pete stared for a long two heartbeats. The ripples in her head, the pulse of the magic wound through everything, gave an unpleasant twinge, as if just for a second she'd brushed her hand against something still and slimy. The dead thing's bulging eyes took on a shine, and Pete turned away.

"Just a thought," she said to Jack, as she got an armful of pink towels from the rack and threw them over the corpse, "but perhaps we shouldn't indulge in a sea swim anywhere in the greater Blackpool vicinity."

"Most bloody disgusting thing I've ever seen," Jack muttered. His shoulders twitched and he started on a fourth bottle of whiskey, emptying it in a swallow. Jack was heavily tattooed and at the moment the ink and his old track-mark scars stood stark against his skin. He looked like his body was engaging him in debate about whether to vomit.

"Who could have done it, is the question," Pete murmured. "If it's someone in the hotel, they've got a bloody twisted sense of humor." She gathered the towels into a bundle and lifted the dead creature out of the bath, sadness pricking her. "Poor thing."

"Poor thing?" Jack demanded. "No, not poor thing—what about poor *me?* My nerves are utterly shot! I'm from the city—we don't find dead wildlife in the loo very often!"

"*Yes,* poor thing," Pete said sharply. "It was ugly and smelly, but it was defective too—defenseless. It couldn't run or fly from whatever human wrapped hands around its neck. If I meet the tosser, I'll kick him in the sodding bollocks."

"Just get it out of here," said Jack. "And ask room service if they can bring about ten liters of bleach for the bath."

Pete found a spare garbage bag in the outer suite and slid it around the mass of towels. Jack would just have to pay for them. A few oily gray-green feathers slid loose and stained the carpet at her feet, and Pete felt that lap of discomfort again, the faintest pinprick of the disturbance against the smooth surface of the Black. An experienced Weir, a shaper of magic, would probably know what it meant, but all Pete knew was that it made her head hurt like she'd just woken up hungover.

She shoved the feathers into a desk drawer so she wouldn't have to look at them, and put the corpse outside the suite's front doors, locking them firmly behind it.

I'M HUNGRY," JACK ANNOUNCED WHEN HE CAME OUT of the bath. A towel sat low on his skinny hips, and he padded about on bare feet.

Pete threw his jeans at him from the bed, where she'd ensconced herself under the satin sheets with a novel. "Put some bloody clothes on."

"Easy, luv—we are married, after all." Jack grinned at her and fished a cigarette out of the pocket of his pants before tossing them aside in favor of a pair of slim suit trousers.

"I'm going to bloody murder you, Jack Winter," Pete muttered. It was a threat she delivered often, and usually hollow, but she was in no mood. "I mean it. Don't sleep tonight."

"Well, there'll be no sleeping when I'm dead of bloody starvation," Jack said, exhaling smoke through his nose. He pulled on the trousers and shucked the towel. "There's a restaurant downstairs. Romantic dinner for two included in the package. What do you say?"

"I say that I'm comfortable where I am," said Pete. "You and your prodigious talent for ticking me off are welcome to the restaurant."

Jack sighed, dumping the candy out of a china dish on the wardrobe and putting out his Parliament in it. He came over to the bed and sat next to Pete. She scooted away, but he trapped her wrist with wire-strung fingers. "Pete. I know you're unhappy and bloody angry at me, but it's just dinner. Come eat and raise up your blood sugar and I wager you'll be a deal less cranky."

"More wagers?" Pete arched her eyebrow. "We're up to forty quid. You can't play in these leagues, Jack." She *was* hungry, and Jack's sincere blue gaze was very hard to ignore. His eyes were changeable, like a sky, glacial and bright when he was intent, the burning base of a candle flame when he was angry. Mage's eyes, flaring and settling depending on mood and magic.

"I'll match it if you can." Jack grinned. Inwardly, Pete felt the lump of resentment toward Jack's arrogant, bugger-all decision about this stupid holiday like a malignancy. Whatever else he'd done, Jack *was* trying.

Pete sighed. She didn't want to look at him. Jack pleading or discomfited was out of order. She settled her stare on the twin Eyes of Horus tattooed on his collarbones, touching one to change the subject. "The ink's holding up?"

Jack lifted a shoulder. "Better than nothing." The black Eye tingled under Pete's fingers. The light Eye looked toward the world of the living. The dark saw the land of the dead. Both served to take the edge from Jack's psychic sight, so it couldn't catch him unaware.

"Are you close to edge? Going to have an episode?" Pete asked anxiously. Jack shook his head.

"Hotels are good for that. So much humanity, so much fear and strain and pleasure too—like listening to a radio tuned just out of frequency. Peaceful, really. Sort of a white noise."

Pete's heart beat normally again. Jack wasn't going to disappear into the well of his sight, when it bounced back from his mage sensitivities amplified to the point where he sometimes couldn't tell the murdered, gibbering ghosts from flesh. He wasn't going to control it with a needle as he had before. *The ink holds,* she told herself firmly, and nearly believed it.

"I guess I *am* a bit peckish," she conceded, on the heels of her relief. Jack gave a bounce on the mattress next to her.

"Bloody right! Get dressed." He dropped a kiss on Pete's cheek, featherlight and dry, and then jumped up and went to root in his case. "What d'you think will give those stick-up-the-arse hotel staffers a bigger coronary?" He held up two jerseys, one featuring Iggy Pop flipping the bird and one a River City Rebels bit that proclaimed CORRUPT THE KING WHILE YOU FUCK THE QUEEN!

"Rebels," said Pete. She slid off the bed and got a black sweater and jeans to change into. Another hard and fast rule of life in the Black—never clothe yourself in anything you weren't able to run in, or willing to sacrifice to burns, blood, or demonic spittle.

THE RESTAURANT, MI AMOR, WAS DECIDEDLY NOT A denim-and-sweater sort of place and caused a fidgety response in Pete akin to stepping into a dowager aunt's parlor.

White and pink linen billowed over the tables, and a terrace looked out on the sea. The entire arrangement was lit only by candles, and red-jacketed waiters moved among the bowed heads of diners like phantoms. Torches on the terrace flared valiantly against the fog and the wind that had sprung up. Pete smelled the tang of the bog through the doors, open even though it was late autumn. She shivered involuntarily. The closer she got to the sea, the louder the magic hissed, like standing too close to an amplifier.

"Winter, Suite 103," Jack told the maître d'. The maître d', shaven-headed and wearing a tuxedo that fit like he'd hastily buttoned it over his footie jersey, ran a stubby finger down the list.

"Ah," he said, grinning and displaying the sort of teeth that gave England a bad name, "The honeymooners."

"Bloody right." Jack grinned back, throwing an arm around Pete. His hand wandered south toward her chest and she twisted his index finger, hard. Jack hissed but managed to keep smiling.

"Right this way," said the maître d'. He shuffled through the candlelit cavern, flames and linens rippling in the wind off the sea.

"Reminds me of a bloody tomb," Pete muttered. "All shrouds and saint's candles."

"Anyone ever tell you you've got one bloody morbid set of sensibilities?" Jack muttered back. Pete shrugged out from under his arm and wrapped hers around herself. The mist swirled beyond the French doors and obscured whatever was beyond the torchlight. Somewhere far away in the night, waves hit the rocks with a hushed, wind-driven desperation.

"Here we are," the maître d' said, pulling out Pete's chair. She sank down, still shivering. Jack took her hand, a pretense of a romantic gesture, but in reality he squeezed her fingers and mouthed, "All right?"

"Donovan will be your waiter," said the maître d', and withdrew with another rotted-out smile.

"I'm fine," Pete said, low toned. "Just cold."

"I feel it too," Jack assured her. "It's wild out there. The hunting moon is whipping everything into frenzy. Just eat something and have a drink and a laugh. It'll settle once midnight passes."

Pete nodded to placate Jack, sipping her water. It wasn't just the impending moonrise, pushing against her skin as the ambient magic of the world gathered and sparked wild hunts and bonfire dancing. It was the slithering sensation, the closed-in mist that penetrated everything in Blackpool, closed off the famous neon lights and Spire, and wrapped the hotel in silence. She felt like something was stirring, just behind her eyes, ancient and terrible. Was *this* what she looked forward to if she left the Metropolitan Police and went with Jack to learn what he had to teach about magic? This horrible *birthing,* that struggled to surface?

"Drinks?"

Pete gasped and stared up—and *up*—into the face of possibly the most grotesque man she'd ever seen. The waiter had a brow that jutted like a Cornish cliff, ginger eyebrows parading across the bone ridge. Birdlike black eyes burned from sunken sockets and his jaw was knotty and misshapen, like he'd taken a bad hit during a rugby match. A scar ran from the left side of his mouth, disappearing in a serrated line down his neck. "Drinks?" he said again.

Jack shook his head once and put on his congenial, one-of-the-blokes face. Jack was good at instant masks of true feeling. "Whiskey here, mate. Straight with no nonsense, if you please."

The waiter, who had shoulders that a yeoman could have yoked a wagon to under his starched red shirt, grunted and wrote on a pad. His name tag read DONOVAN in the same overwrought, near-unreadable print repeated throughout the resort.

"And you, miss?" Donovan had a Geordie accent, and it came out more like "Anyewmess?"

"Red . . ." Pete swallowed, tracing the terrible scar down his neck and into his collar with her eyes. How had he *survived* such a slash? Maybe because he was built like a mountain troll . . . "Red wine," she managed.

"It were a gaff," Donovan said. He touched the scar with hands that could have turned Pete's head into a cracked egg. "Used to work the fishin' boats out on the North Sea. Me mate turned and caught me with the gaff one day, in the fog. Didn't see me comin'. I were real quiet-like, back then. Made no more noise than smoke." He grinned, although his bulging jaw made the expression sag on one side.

Pete, and Jack, who was making a valiant effort not to burst into laughter, if his snorts were any indication, were saved from a reply by a keening, gull-like shriek from the front of the restaurant. There was a commotion of linen and dropped silver, and a woman stumbled through the tables and launched herself at Donovan. "You stole my husband!"

Donovan batted the slim, sandy-haired girl away with the brutal grace of a big bloke who fights dirty. The woman rocked backward into an empty table, shattering wine goblets. "Bastard!" she screamed and grabbed Donovan again, beating at the waiter's oak-barrel chest with bloodied fists. The chatter of the restaurant stilled and even the couple snogging at the next table stopped for a moment to watch.

Donovan grabbed the woman by her torn sweater, soaked in mud and bog water like the rest of her, and held her at arm's length. "Gerroff, you!"

"You stole him!" the woman sobbed. "You sons of bitches stole my Sheldon. . . ."

"Here," said Pete, standing up and inserting herself between Donovan and the woman. "What's happening?"

"She's mad as a hatter, is what's happening," Donovan growled. "Was ejected from hotel grounds just this morning for causing a fuss."

"They crawled up," moaned the woman. "Across the tow-path. They wrapped him in rot . . . oh God . . . they were *writhing . . .*" Her eyes were bloodshot and unfocused and sweat stood in a line of beads across her cheeks. Pete sniffed. No alcohol on the woman's breath, and Pete felt the instinctive flinch that occurs when in the presence of someone quite mad.

"What's your name?" Pete asked her quietly. "Do you know it? Do you know where you live?"

"Henrietta," the woman shuddered. "Henrietta Phillips. From London."

"Oi," said Donovan. "Who're you to be askin' all these questions?"

"Pete Caldecott," said Pete. "Detective Inspector. Also of London."

"Here, now," said Donovan. "No police needed. This bird's just had a falling out with 'er medications."

"I *saw* it," Henrietta hissed, and there was terror in her creaking tones, the kind brought on by witnessing something a human was never meant to endure. A touch of cold prickled the back of Pete's neck. She listened when Henrietta said, "I saw it, coming out of the mud and the salt . . . I heard it speaking . . . and the smell—oh God, the *smell* . . . death and rotted fish and Shel let out this scream—"

Donovan pulled Henrietta close and slapped her cheek, leaving a handprint. "Shut yer gob! Gerry!" he yelled to the maître d'. "Call up security!"

"Oi!" Pete shouted in turn. She shoved Donovan back from Henrietta, laying a hand flat on his chest and holding him away. "I think you've done quite enough to help the situation."

"Touch me again and I'll lay a smack on you that'll have teeth out of yer head," Donovan growled.

In less time than it took to blow out a candle, Jack was on his feet. "Lay one hand on her, and you'll be fit for a closed coffin," he said. Jack didn't snarl, or posture, he just stood at Pete's shoulder, over her left side. The hairs on her neck crackled from the power gathering around him, dark blood–fueled magic that clung to Jack when he was angry.

Donovan's eyes flared; then he dropped his chin and backed up a step. Jack smiled in a manner that managed to be genial and terrifying at the same time, all Big Bad Wolf teeth and menace. "Glad we understand one another, mate." He produced a cigarette and lit it off the hurricane candle on the table. No magic in front of the mundanes.

"Sheldon . . . ," Henrietta moaned. "My Shel . . . we were just on our honeymoon, no time at all . . . he's gone into the mud now. . . ."

"Is anyone *not* on their honeymoon in this place?" Pete muttered. Gerry the maître d' and two sufficiently burly members of the hotel staff, clad in satin vests and breeches, rushed up.

"I think maybe this does merit the local constabulary being called . . . ," Pete started, but Gerry pointed a furious finger at her, palm raised. A small tri-pointed tattoo flared from his palm.

"Set down and eat your supper, miss. We are handling the matter and it is none of your concern!"

Pete was set to inform the maître d' that it was more her business than his when Jack yanked her back into her seat. "Don't," he said. "Just sit and eat, like the man said."

"The smell . . . ," Henrietta moaned as they dragged her out, heels wrinkling the carpet. "Brackish oil . . . the police laughed, and you can as well, but you'll see, you'll all see it soon enough. . . ." Her sobs and screams faded as the arched doors of the restaurant whispered shut. After a moment, the canned music resumed and diners around Pete and Jack ducked their heads back to their plates.

"We better get a complimentary lunch or something for all of this ruckus," Jack said. "Puts off my digestion."

Pete tore a roll into tiny crumbs and watched the breathing dark mist beyond the terrace doors. "Jack, something's going on," she said, finally giving in to the whispers and the pressure on her mind.

"No bloody kidding," he muttered. "That shambling Gerry's been branded with the Tridach mark."

"The what?" Pete always felt as if she were sitting her A-levels while still in first form when Jack talked about the arcane.

"It means he worships the devil," said a burbling female voice from over Jack's shoulder. American, it burred on the skin like a fingertip's touch.

Pete canted her head to the left and caught a shadowed mixture of red lips and curling chestnut hair, lit by eyes the color of rain-washed evergreens, shot with gold. The woman, poured into a black satin dress, sat on the lap of a bloke who was trying hard to be Joe Strummer, and not managing it.

Jack turned in his seat, face lighting when he met the woman's eyes. "You know something about demons."

"I have an affinity for the darkness," said the woman. "And what lives in it."

Pete rolled her eyes. Jack seemed to have no such compunctions. "Do you, now." He let the easy, familiar smile he'd perfected in his days as a front man for the Poor Dead Bastards bloom into being. "Then you know the Tridach mark doesn't really mean he's a devil worshipper. It represents the Triumverate, the ruling body of Hell, and all the associations of being a faithful servant. According to demonic law, he was placed on earth to serve some special purpose. The Triumverate doesn't mark mortals very often."

The woman's lips parted and she looked positively aroused. "You know something about darkness yourself. Delicious." She extended a hand, red plastic talons crowning it in a wet gleam. "I'm Charlotte, and this is my husband, Roy. From Cincinnati."

"Yo," said Roy.

"We're on our honeymoon," Charlotte continued. "Exploring the mysteries of the Old World."

"Of course you are," Pete murmured, fighting the urge to shove the remaining dinner roll into Charlotte's mouth to shut it. "Very image of the virgin bride, you."

"Our fair isle has a lot of secrets to be found." Jack took Charlotte's hand, turning it over instead of shaking it, stroking his thumb over the palm. "May I?"

Charlotte's husband grunted, but her pupils expanded with delight. "You do divination?"

"Luv, I do many things," said Jack. He held Charlotte's hand close to his face and traced each line with the side of his thumb in turn. "A *long* love line," he intoned. "Life-line . . . is . . ."

Jack's shoulders stiffened, like he'd just choked on a sip of water, and his eyes suddenly went nearly white, color leaching. He let out a low moan as his sight gripped him.

"Bollocks," said Pete. She grabbed Charlotte's wrist and Jack's, and yanked them apart, fighting against the iron hold Jack had on the American's hand. Released, Jack slumped over, the pulse in his neck beating like a trapped bird.

Charlotte blinked at Pete. "Christ. He gonna be okay?"

"Fine," Pete snapped. "Just bloody fine, once he learns not to be so *bloody stupid and careless!*" The last was directed at Jack, but he was staring into the middle distance, color slowly drifting back into his face. He blinked, and his eyes were glacial blue again. Pete unclenched her fists, breathing deep to tell the shrieking part of her mind that it was past, the episode was averted, Jack was fine. It didn't work terribly well. They needed to get out of the restaurant.

"It was lovely meeting you," she told Charlotte. The woman

acknowledged her insincere smile with a startled doe-in-the-headlights expression. Pete didn't bother trying to explain Jack's reaction away. *Sorry, Charlotte, but my friend here sees dead people with regularity and sometimes it makes him a bit odd.* . . . Henrietta wouldn't be the only crazy person thrown out of the hotel tonight.

Pete took Jack's arm and he obediently followed her up, leaning against her shoulder like he'd had half a dozen pints. "Charlotte wanted to shag me," he muttered as he stumbled to the lift with Pete. "I give them six months . . . tops. 'Sides, she's going to die soon, and who would want to shag a corpse? . . ."

Pete punched the button for the lift with her free hand and settled Jack against her shoulder. Seeing death for a person still living was the worst of the sight. The crushing inevitability of it could send Jack out of commission for days.

"And you wonder why I don't want to get married."

JACK SLEPT, AFTER DEMOLISHING THE LAST OF THE minibar's whiskey, lying lengthwise across the bed. Using his sight was like popping a handful of Valium, or so he'd told Pete. He could sleep forever, completely blank and dreamless.

Pete grumbled him out of his shoes and socks and left him sprawled. She turned out the lights and curled on the sofa under a pink throw. If it were just her, she'd be on the motorway back to London. The hotel was wrong, like being trapped inside the skeleton of a giant desiccated beast. Lines of black power crossed under their feet, and Jack seemed oblivious.

Or maybe he was just used to it. *And you would be as well, you poor excuse for a Weir, if you'd learn to block out feed from every stray spurt of magic floating on the wind.* She couldn't very well shake Jack awake and say, "We have to go home. The hotel gives me the creeping spooks for reasons I can't fully explain." Jack would laugh himself weak, and then tell her she was being bloody stupid. "Besides, I'm a sodding inspector," she muttered, "and I'm afraid of harmless hotel ghosts." "Harmless" here being a subjective term, of course. She groaned at her own pitiful state and pulled the throw up to her chin.

Since the incident in London, sleep was a reluctant and elusive partner, but Pete nevertheless felt her lashes flutter down against her cheeks. The sofa was soft and the throw was warming her and the *hush-hush* of the sea coaxed her to sleep, just sleep. . . .

No nightmare forced Pete to wake or perish, just a repetitive, steady *boom boom boom,* like the beating of a great three-chambered heart.

Jack stirred and turned over on the bed, a shaft of weak fog-filtered sunlight turning his platinum hair white. The beating came again, *boom boom boom.* "Room service," a guttural voice spoke.

"Bollocks," Pete muttered. She was awake, and her neck and spine were on fire from sleeping crumpled against the sofa like a scarecrow. "Coming!" she shouted, tripping over her own shoes on the way.

Donovan the waiter stood outside the suite door, holding a covered silver tray. "Morning, miss." His slippery grin gave Pete an involuntary twitch between her shoulder blades.

"We didn't order room service," she said, keeping her frame fully blocking the doorway.

"Course you didn't," said Donovan. "Morning-After Brunch. Compliments of the management." He craned and caught sight of Jack. "Wore the wee lad out, did you?"

Pete snatched the tray. "Give *the management* my thanks." She shut the door in Donovan's face. "Tosser."

"Whossat?" Jack muttered, an arm over his eyes to block out the sun. "I smell sausages."

Pete set the tray down and regarded it. Silly, of course. Nothing but breakfast under the cover, but at the same time, she felt a spurt of pure animal fear when she thought about what *could* be under the innocuous nickel-plate lid. . . .

Jack came up and snatched the top off, missing Pete's sharp intake of breath. "Toast is soggy," he muttered, tossing it into the bin. He shoveled eggs and sausage onto a plate and flopped down on the sofa, flicking on the telly. Pete ignored the food and opened the French door onto the balcony. Salted moisture kissed her hair and face. She could see a little ways down the beach in daylight, a lone figure weaving along the sand just in the mist, a lanky black-clad shadow.

Something about the cant of the figure wasn't right, he moved like a drunk or someone who'd been dealt a blow. "Jack," she called. He didn't stir himself. "Jack!" Pete shouted to make herself heard over the popcorn guns of a black and white Western film.

"What!" he bellowed irritably. "Can't a bloke eat breakfast in peace?"

The figure emerged into the slice of vision granted by the sun, and Pete saw Roy the American staggering along the beach. Blood ran down his face, tributaries and deltas along the stark lines of his mouth and neck, and he held his hands in front of his body. His fingers and palms were crimson too. As Pete watched, rooted like an ancient oak, Roy shuddered and then fell over, curling into the fetal position and growing still.

"Bloody hell," Pete muttered, whirling and making a dash for the front door of the suite. Jack watched her go.

"What's the matter, then?"

"That American bloke from last night," she panted, jerking on her shoes. "I think someone's killed him."

ROY'S BODY LAY IN THE SAND LIKE A broken marionette, blood patching the earth a darker brown. Pete skidded down the half-rotted wooden steps the hotel provided as access, and felt the wet sand suck at her feet as she dashed for Roy. Jack appeared behind her, like he sometimes did, panting like he'd just run a hundred meters.

"Call an ambulance!" Pete yelled over her shoulder. The ever-present fog dampened her shout, thinned it so that it remained trapped beside her. The hotel and the rest of the beach disappeared as the wind picked up and it was just herself and Roy's mangled form.

Jack appeared, hair like a spiked sun. "Pete. Don't touch him!"

Pete skidded to a stop, going to her knees next to the body. Seawater soaked through her trousers. The tide was coming in, and a crab with an extra claw protruding from its back scuttled through the mushy pool Roy's blood made. Jack dropped beside her and pulled back her wrist just before she felt for Roy's pulse. "Look."

An iron shackle was locked around Roy's neck, dug deep and sharp enough into the skin to form a necklace of blood droplets. The shackle was like nothing Pete had ever seen, metal holding a shine, forged with curling, roiling designs that caused the point between her eyes to ache. The broken end of an equally foreign chain link dangled from the collar.

"Bloody hell," said Pete, because anything else would have been insufficient. Jack wrapped the end of his t-shirt around his hand and flipped Roy's body over onto its back. What Pete had taken for cuts on his cheeks were more like *burns,* like something thin and coated in acid had taken Roy's face in its hands. But not hands. Diamond-shaped markings bubbled where the . . . where whatever it was had touched him. "He's been kissed by the Black, luv," said Jack, brushing his hand off. "Touch might transfer it. Just looking out for you."

Pete swallowed as she met Roy's open eyes. The magic was so thick around him, it choked the air out of her, and she let Jack pull her away. "All right?"

Laughing, Pete shook her head. "How would I bloody be all right? He was alive not twelve hours ago. Him and his silly bint of a wife." Her gut twisted, nothing to do with the dark energy around them. "Oh, God. Where's the wife?"

Jack conjured a Parliament and lit it, drawing deep before he said, "That thing you feel, like congealed grease on skin, is sacrificial blood magic. Old Roy's soul is half out of his body, waiting to be called as power in someone's ritual. Poor sod."

Pete looked down at Roy again, thought of dark wet things and mist-hidden shadows. "Who would do something like this?"

"A sorcerer," said Jack, flicking his cigarette away. The wind brought it back and spread embers across the sand. "A practitioner of black arts attempting to call something from the otherworld. Unusual that they'd just take two, even if this bloke did manage to get away. Usually sacrifices are threes, or sevens. Darkness loves the prime numbers, you know."

"Henrietta," said Pete, the woman's shattered eyes and disconnected ramblings jumping back to forefront. "That crazy bird from the restaurant last night. She said that something had stolen her husband."

Jack rubbed his chin, making a sandpaper sound against his morning shadow. "Three bodies needed, then, and they used old Roy's soul as kindling for the fire." He paced around the body, muttering. "Not phases of the moon. Not a demon. Might be amateurs. Chanting naked, bathing in blood. Some stupid shite like that."

"This is not an amateur anything," said Pete, pointing at Roy. "We have to call the police. Then we have to find Charlotte."

"What are you on about? What sodding *we*?" Jack asked. " 'M staying right here, in me honeymoon suite. Let the coppers sort it out. Always fun to watch you lot try and figure out creatures of the Black."

Pete seized Jack by his upper arm and jerked him to her. "Take my mobile. Call the police. I'm going to try and find Charlotte before something in this freaky place eats her insides." She pressed her mobile into Jack's palm. "Hurry."

"Can't, luv," said Jack. Pete turned on him, ready to scream, and he held up her mobile. NO SVC blinked in the center of the screen.

"Bollocks." Pete kicked a lump of sand, pacing away from Roy's body. She couldn't stand to feel the displaced magic any longer—it hurt, like a boil under the skin.

Roy's footprints came out of the fog, and just behind and to the left of him, twin webbed tracks moved, taking one step for Roy's four. They were like gull's feet, but human-sized and with far too many toes. A thin miasma of slime coated each track, sending the smell of overripe mud to Pete's nose. "Jack." She pointed numbly when he came to her side. "It followed him. All the way back. And then it just vanishes."

"Watched him die," said Jack. "Made sure he couldn't babble like that Henrietta bird."

"A demon?" Pete wrapped her arms around her torso, suddenly chilled beyond measure.

"No," said Jack. "No, a demon free in the world would be

wearing human skin. This is . . ." He sighed and brushed the
dampness from his hair, leaving it wild like a Celt's. "Bugger all,
Pete. I don't know what this is." For Jack to admit ignorance made
the situation bad, bad in the way that had ended in blood once before. Pete bit her lower lip hard to blot out memories of London
that had no place.

"Knew this place was wrong," she muttered, retracing Roy's
footstep. Knew that something sinister was lurking under the
tacky cheerfulness of the Paradise Palace. *Knew it,* and doubted,
and kept her mouth shut. Now Roy had been killed by it.

"Oi, where're you going?" Jack shouted when she started to
walk away. Pete stopped, not looking back.

"I'm following it," she said. "Coming?"

PETE WALKED, UNTIL SHE WAS SURE THE WIND and wet had sunken
into her bones and she would become soft and gibbous, a water-
logged shade who would never be warm again. Roy's footprints
led down the beach, past casinos blinking their promise of FREE
BINGO WEEKLY out to sea, past a boarded-up boat rental shack and
finally into the wild, scrubby little trees and the phantom bones of
driftwood clustered where the tide had left them.

The tracks took a turn inland, and Pete and Jack crested a
hillock and descended into the bogs. The sound of the sea was muffled by winter-blackened dead trees and the salt air became clammy
and sour. Roy's reversed tracks deepened, running for his life.

Pete slipped in the mud, but Jack, in his workman's boots,
tromped along merrily champing on a cigarette like he was taking
a turn through Regent's Park.

"Bloody kill you," Pete muttered.

"Here," said Jack from ahead of her, gesturing with the lit end
of his Parliament.

Pete examined the spot where the web-foot tracks dragged themselves out of the peat muck and began to follow Roy's shaky strides. His ended a few meters farther on, seemingly in the flat marsh water that reflected Pete's frown back at her.

"This *can't* be where he came from."

"Maybe he swam," Jack shrugged. He did a slow circle, looking out over the brackish-colored marshland visible through the fog, and then flicked his cigarette butt into the water.

"That's a cartload of bollocks," Pete told him. She crouched and dipped her fingers into the marsh, recoiling as sinuous underwater plants grasped at her skin. "The water's no more than a couple of degrees. And he wasn't wet on the beach."

Jack sighed. "Pete, it's bloody strange, yeah, but what do you want *me* to do about it, grab a ruddy iron hook and drag the bottom? I'm on holiday!"

"That Charlotte girl could still be alive!" Pete cried. "Can't you call up an imp and offer it Roy's blood or something to reveal her true location?"

"Doesn't work that way and you know it," said Jack. "Magic isn't tricks and forcing it to do what *you* want. It's the fabric of the Black and it has its limitations."

"And by limitations, you're meaning that you're a lazy git," Pete snapped. "This place is *doing* something to the people in the hotel. You *know* it is." A bird screamed from somewhere invisible. She shuddered. Her skull felt like it was splitting apart from the inside the longer they stayed out here in the fog and if she stared at the water, she swore that glimmering ebony tendrils *moved* underneath the tiny ripples stirred by the wind. "I can feel it," Pete muttered. "I'm *not* imagining things and neither was Henrietta."

"There might be something evil here," said Jack, in what for him was a gentle tone. He clasped her on the shoulder, fingers knobby as a skeleton. "It's not ours to rush in with flaming swords, Pete. Charlotte's gone, probably dead. 'S what I saw for her last night, anyway. I don't know about you, but I'm wet and tired. Let's go back to the hotel, sleep, and go back to London, right?" He rubbed both hands up and down Pete's arms when she shivered. "Charlotte will either turn up or she won't. Dead, or not. It's not in your hands, luv."

"And when we get back to London," Pete said quietly. "Everything will be safe and nice and normal? Is *that* what you think, Jack? You think a cheap hotel suite and lies to get a free dinner made me forget you nearly being killed, or being left alone with that sorcerer's spirit to fight off?" She shook her head, venom coursing in her veins. For just a moment, the air was breathy with corpse-dust and the glowing eyes of the spirit Jack had released shone down on her with the light of damnation.

"You're pathetic," Pete spat at Jack. "You fob off problems and expect the world to flow around you and everyone to forget what a bastard you really are. Well I *won't* forget, Jack, so you and your holiday can go bugger yourselves."

His face clamped shut over the flicker of pain Pete saw, and his lip curled. "You aim for the killing cut, luv. Well done." He pushed past her and walked back down the path. After a moment more staring into the fog, trying not to sob from sheer frustration, Pete followed him because there was nothing else she could do.

THE SKY WAS THE GRAY OF A DEAD WOMAN'S hair when they finally reached the hotel. The light was moving on toward evening, if there was such a thing in this endlessly fogbound place. Jack made a beeline for the hotel bar and Pete stormed over to the lift and punched the button to take her back to the room.

"You've left mud on the carpet, Miss," Gerry the maître d' sneered, creeping up at her elbow. Pete hit the button again.

"Ask me if I bloody care. Isn't it your job to clean these things?"

"You're fighting with the other half, then?" Gerry said, his smile growing wider. Pete glared at him as the lift dinged open.

"Poke your shiny head into someone else's business."

"That's a yes, then," said Gerry as the door rolled closed. Just for a second, her Weir gift flared and Gerry had pointed teeth and a frog's webbed hands. He laughed, flicking a forked tongue.

Pete leaned her head back against the satin wall and the tears did come, unstoppable against the tide of the Black. The city and the bog and the hotel were dark places, evil, and she just wanted to get away . . . Pete clutched at her head as a flood of whispers engulfed her, sliding into a crouch against the pain and the unbearable pressure of magic. "Stop it," she begged. "Stop it, stop it. . . . I see. *I understand.*"

Hissing, the whispers faded away, slowly, and she realized that the lift doors were standing open on the top floor. Everything was normal—cheesy gilt wallpaper, kissing-swan mirrors and the plastic carved paneling on the suite's door.

The thought that she might be going mad crossed Pete's mind.

She slammed the door to the suite behind her and locked the chain bolt, not that it would stop Jack, when and if he came upstairs. If he'd lived a hundred years ago, he could have easily plied a trade as a sneak-thief in the alleys of London.

Pete threw off her shoes and collapsed on the bed, sundown darkening the room to velvety gray-black. Jack came in after a time, stumbled in the dark, smelled of whiskey and too many Parliaments, and then Pete slept, fitfully and with dreams of dark things rolling beneath marsh water.

PETE WOKE WITH A GASP AND THE SOFTLY glowing face of the bedside clock staring at her. Twelve midnight. She breathed deeply and put a hand over her heart, which was thumping the way it did when she had the nightmare that Jack had died, and she'd been too late to save him. The sorcerer spirit touched him and stole his magic. And then Pete killed the ghost wearing Jack's face.

Jack let out a soft drunken snore from the sofa and Pete relaxed, using the still rush of waves and the cool touch of the utterly black night to calm herself.

In the darkness by the wardrobe, something slithered.

Pete bolted upright, out of the satin sheets and over the edge of the bed, scrabbling away from the sound toward the balcony. "Jack!" she hissed.

The sounds were all around her, not half-imagined offshoots of ambient magic but real, wet squelching of misshapen limbs over the carpet and gibbering moans. For a dreadful instant, the fog parted and moonshine struck the room. Pete saw hundreds of wet black-green bodies gleaming, while triple rows of eyes lolled in protuberant exoskeletons and bone teeth with razor points dribbled ichor from misshapen mouths.

In her lifetime, Pete had faced too many of her fears without flinching, because it was what was required. Gang members with guns. Jack, alive and dead. The bottomless cold power of the Black that burned you from inside your skull when your magic took hold.

The nearest marsh-creature's tentacle wrapped around Pete's ankle with a cold so icy, it burned, and Pete decided *Bugger all that for a lark*. She screamed to wake the dead. *"JACK!"*

For a horrible second nothing happened, and then witchfire flamed to life in the vicinity of the sofa and Jack's tousled platinum hair and face coalesced, hollow-eyed in the blue light. "Bloody hell, can't a bloke get a decent night's—?" He saw the things, then, although they hissed and drew back from the witchfire into the dark.

Pete grabbed the digit around her ankle and pulled, but it only contracted harder, squashy and palpable like a muscle with no bones inside. "Do something! Get rid of these fucking things!" she screamed at Jack. More feelers attached to her wrists, her legs, snaking up from the floor to bind her, or worse.

Jack stomped on the creatures underfoot. The witchfire in his palm matched by twin flames in his eyes. "*Saighid!*" he bellowed. The chalk warding on the door flared to life like a flashbulb, and then just as quickly threw violent blue sparks and went out.

"Well, bugger me sideways with a barbell," Jack mused. "That should have worked."

Pete snatched the cut-glass candy dish Jack used as an ashtray off the wardrobe and began beating away the beasts, some of which looked like many-legged octopods, some just gaping mouths with three or four eyes supported by flimsy nets of tissue. She was nearly free when a pair of crushingly strong arms wrapped around her torso and lifted her off the ground.

"It didn't work, Mr. Winter," said Gerry the maître d', now attired in a black sweater and slacks, a watchcap covering the sheen of his bald head. He appeared from out of the loo, the long kitchen knife in his hand catching light like the tooth of a great wolf. "Innocent blood spilled is piss-poor for warding hexes. Degrades their magic right down to nothing."

Jack gaped at him, looking more outraged that his hex had failed than at the fact his hotel room was full of bog-spawned horrors. "Innocent blood?" he managed. "What sodding blood? I cut meself shaving, but in case it escaped your attention, I'm far from innocent as Leicestershire is from Los Angeles."

"The creature," Pete managed, although the person holding her was doing it tightly enough to crack ribs. "The dead thing, in the bath. Innocent blood."

"Oh, you have *got* to be jerking me!" Jack shouted. "The bloody hell is wrong with you freaks? Drink too much swamp water on the job?"

A small five-legged octopod with a sucker mouth crawled up Pete's leg, and she kicked it away. It gave a high squeak as it bounced off the opposite wall. The man holding her grabbed her hair with one hand and jerked her neck back almost to breaking. "I'll thank ye to leave my creatures alone, miss."

"Donovan?" Pete rasped.

He grinned. "The same."

"Let go of her," Jack said, his eyes narrowing to fiery slits. "You've made me ask you twice now, and I'm all out of patience for it."

"You're coming along quietly," said Gerry. "Or my servant is going to snap your wife's neck. We'd hate for an accident to occur on hotel grounds, but some things are simply unavoidable."

"It's all right, Jack," said Pete. An involuntary tear worked out of her eye when Donovan twisted her neck. "Just go with him."

Jack looked from her to Gerry, then slowly lowered his hands. The witchfire flickered out of existence. "You've got me," he muttered quietly. "I'll do anything you sodding want. Just don't hurt her."

Pete slumped. Jack wasn't supposed to surrender—he was supposed to bloody get away and help her escape when the opportunity presented. Noble gestures were so contrary that she almost started crying again.

"Unfortunately," said Gerry with a wide smile. "I'm not sure I can fulfill that promise, Mr. Winter. You and the missus make a pair, you see." He jerked his head at Donovan. "Get her to the boat."

DONOVAN AND GERRY TOOK THEM THROUGH A BASEMENT service door that backed onto a canal filled with garbage and brown sludge that looked more like intestinal distress than water. A pole launch bumped gently against a pier made of old plastic drums sealed with tar.

Pete fell on her knees in the aft of the launch when Donovan shoved her. "Not so chatty now, are ye?"

"I'll set a badger on your bollocks," Pete muttered. Donovan kicked her and she felt something give, low down near her stomach. She bit the insides of her cheeks. She wouldn't get Donovan off by yelling.

"Knock that off," Gerry commanded as he wrestled Jack into the launch. "You remember what happened last time you bruised the sacrifices, surely."

Donovan grunted, and Jack raised his eyebrows. "So you two are the silly gits playing doctor with creatures of the Black. Have to say I'm a bit let down."

"Shut up," Gerry said. "This is older and larger than you, mage, and I don't expect you to understand." He pushed Jack down next to Pete, and cast off the line. Donovan poled the skiff into the channel and they drifted toward the sea.

"You all right?" Jack muttered without moving his mouth too much. Pete sucked in a breath. A dull shiv of pain slid between her broken bones.

"Hurt, but I can run for it if I need to."

"Quiet, you two," Donovan warned.

"Go bugger yourself," said Jack loudly. "If you hurt us, you'll be stuck sacrificing that bloody overcooked roast you served me last night." To Pete, he murmured, "Sorry."

Pete blinked. Never mind creatures in the suite and the thick dark magic that lived in the air around Blackpool—Jack apologizing was truly a phenomenon. "You are?"

"Should have listened to you," he said. "This *is* a dodgy place."

"Yeah, and the time for guilt has cruised past like a missed bus," Pete said. "So what are we going to do?"

The launch drifted through connected channels and the salt tang told Pete they were near the bog, moonlit mist curling away from the prow. Were it not for the pain in her ribs and the thrumming of darkness in the waters, they could have been on the hidden path to Avalon.

"We wait, for now," said Jack. "Until we get where we're going. I want to see what these sods are on about."

"That's a terrible plan," Pete hissed. "We need to swim for it. Where we're going to is an untimely death!"

"No . . ." said Jack slowly, his head swiveling as the skiff began to slow. Pete struggled up and followed his eyes. Jack tilted his head. "That's where we're going."

Something massive and hunched rose out of the water, taller than the windbroken trees along the shore. It was stone and moss, slimy and shining as if it had just woken from under the mud. Columns held a crooked roofpiece made of insectoid carapaces and steps covered in algae led to the round opening, jagged pieces of broken stone lining it like rotted teeth.

The skiff bumped against the bottom stones and Donovan hauled her up, nearly dislocating her arm.

"Any tricks from ye," he told Jack, "and she breaks like a matchstick."

"I'll enjoy feeding you your still-beating heart, you bastard," Jack said pleasantly as Gerry pushed him out of the boat.

"Hear that, Donnie-boy?" Gerry said. "That's a sentiment born of true love." They laughed as Pete and Jack were herded up the steps to the temple door.

It *was* a temple. That was the best way Pete could describe it. The stones were massive and hand cut, carved with curling tentacles and lidless eyes and the great humped backs of creatures rolling through deep waves. Gaseous fumes tinged the air of the single open chamber yellow. The temple wasn't Roman and it wasn't Celtic or Saxon—the place was slightly out of focus, as if built by something with an idea of human shapes but no practice.

Moss and algae covered almost every surface and Pete slipped, going down hard. Donovan dragged her the rest of the way by her scruff, locking her next to Jack into the neck cuff and a pair of iron shackles, chains bolted to a collapsing column.

Jack winced. "Iron's cold," he said by way of explanation.

"You better have a *bloody* good plan," Pete whispered. Witchlight flamed up in alcoves along the walls, and Pete saw the chamber was larger than it appeared, stretching to a massive fallen-in piece of the floor leaking bubbling marsh water. Tiny waves sloshed at her bare feet.

"Trust me, I'll be thinking of one right quickly," said Jack. "Interesting place, though. Appears to be some kind of death cult, chaos worshippers."

"Two pathetic sods without girlfriends," Pete muttered. "Not much of a cult."

Gerry hit a bronze gong mounted near the edge of the water pit, and with a low moan and a shuffling of feet a row of robed figures shuffled in. Their tattered black garments bore the tridach mark. Pete recognized the doorman from the hotel, and a friendly clerk at the petrol station where she and Jack had stopped on their way into the city.

"Bugger all. Look at them."

"Patience," Jack sighed. "I'm sure they'll eventually free us for the sacrifice, and then you can kick them, and I'll send up a little smoke, and we'll be off in the bloody boat."

"That's about as well-planned as this holiday was," Pete snapped.

"Listen!" Jack shouted. A few of the cultists glanced at them. "You didn't have to come along, but I was trying to do something for you because I felt bloody guilty about what happened in London and now that we've managed to end up like this, I just feel bloody stupid, neither of which is improving my mood, and on top of it all I feel a hangover coming on, so you can just *bugger the bloody hell off, Petunia!*"

Pete blinked, fury for just a moment overriding her fear. Then she hissed, "You are a selfish, self-absorbed git, Jack, and if you'd bothered to check on me after you almost *died* and I had to kill a ghost that sucks out people's souls—and do you know how hard it is to kill a ghost, Jack? Sodding hard!—if you'd just thought for one *second* about doing what I *needed* instead of what was *easy,* we wouldn't be in this mess!"

"Silence!" Gerry bellowed. He had donned his own robe, as had Donovan. "That's better," he said when Pete just glared at Jack in mute rage. He turned to the assembled cultists and raised his arms. "Brethren, we have joined thrice on this, the feast cycle of St. Gummarus the hunter, to bring prey and offerings to our lord, the immovable and towering Lord of Rage, Mnarhoteph."

"Mnarhoteph, fear his Name," the cultists chorused unevenly.

Pete met Jack's eyes, and even though she wanted to loose her chains and wrap them around his skinny tattooed neck, she felt a bubble of laughter when she saw he was trying to bite back a grin.

"Every cycle of the seasons we feed the unending and bottomless anger of Mnarhoteph, and when his hunger has been satiated, he grants us the power of his hatred."

"Mnarhoteph, praise his Fury," the cultists droned.

Gerry hit the gong again, three times, and it reverberated inside Pete's skull like a rusted dull blade scraping bone. "Mnarhoteph, the moon is high! Arise!"

The waters in the pit began to boil and heave and then in a vast sigh of fetid air and a groaning of chains, a massive body filled the pit, reaching for the temple roof. Mnarhoteph had row upon row of eyes, tentacles the size of tree trunks, suckers and feelers rimmed with teeth all studding a gleaming black hide. Pete felt his magic hit her, felt as if her sanity and her skull had split by gazing upon Mnarhoteph's silently shrieking edifice. "He's the source . . . the source of what I feel here . . ." And she lost the ability to speak, mesmerized by the awful beauty of the creature.

Jack went paler than usual, making him look dead. "Bollocks. I thought these gits were just *playing* at chaos worship." He began to jerk his chains frantically. "Pete, we need . . ." His eyes roamed over the witchfires in the alcoves and the poisonous yellow air, over Mnarhoteph and the great salt-bitten chains studded to his skin with harpoon spikes that held him in the pit. "We need a spark," said Jack finally.

"Thrice we have brought you sacrifices to fuel your towering hatred!" Gerry cried. "A female, a male, and now both aspects of the human filth lie before you in offering. Feed, master, and be strong!"

"A spark," Pete repeated, clinging to Jack's voice as her

breadcrumb trail of sanity. Her words were lost as Mnarhoteph opened its maw and roared, a sound of pain that shook the temple to the stone bones.

Pete sobbed as Mnarhoteph's cry went through her and wrapped around her heart, filling her with agony heavy as iron.

"Pete," Jack muttered urgently as Mnarhoteph's tentacles snaked across the floor, bleeding black ichor from the piercing iron bonds. "Pete, make a spark. Small, large, in-between, just hurry!"

Her mind still raged with Mnarhoteph's cry—trapped, alone and in pain—but Pete gathered herself, just as she had when the sorcerer's ghost took Jack's face, and banged her wrist against the stone column she was shackled against. The wet stone elicited nothing but pain in her hand.

Jack's eyes went milky and rolled back in his head, and he murmured wordlessly as Mnarhoteph moved inexorably out of the pit. His chains shrieked against the rock.

Pete made a fist and banged the shackle against stone again, and again. Purple bruising and crimson blood sprouted around the edges of the band, but she kept hitting stone, chipping off centuries of muck until, sure her hand was pulp, she hit dry rock.

A bright orange spark flew off the iron and Jack's eyes snapped back, twin flames replacing the color. *"Aithinne,"* he breathed. A wind sucked the air from Pete's lungs and then with Jack's magic fire—real, crimson fire—sprouted from her spark and the gaseous air all around them began to burn. The initial explosion cracked the pillar Pete was chained to and drove Mnarhoteph's rubbery tentacles back.

Tracers of fire floated through the air, catching cultists as they attempted to run and roiling a bluish smoke from the burning algae. Donovan, robe and hands aflame, slid in the burning muck and cracked his head against broken rock, falling still.

Pete slipped her shackle with her blood-slicked hand and went to Jack. He was bleeding from a cut in his forehead and lying still, but breathing.

Pete turned to watch the fleeing cultists as the fumes burned away, leaving the air damp and salty as it had always been. "I guess that was a plan, all right. A bloody *stupid* plan, but a plan nonetheless."

From the pit, Mnarhoteph groaned. In a voice bottomless and liquid as the sea, he said, "Please."

Pete's heart thudded as she walked ankle-deep into the water pit and stood, close enough to touch Mnarhoteph's hide. "What did you say?"

"Please . . ." he grumbled. "Hurt . . ."

Jack stirred and pulled himself up, freeing himself now that his shackles were loosed. "What the bloody hell are you doing, Pete? Get away from that thing!"

"It's hurt," Pete said. Jack's sight let him perceive the dead, but Weirs were the conduits for the old gods, shapers of magic who spoke to all of the Black. Jack couldn't hear the creature's pain.

Pete placed a hand on Mnarhoteph and this close, the dark churning of magic was loneliness, not evil. "What do you want?" she whispered.

He pulled against the massive chains and harpoons that held him. "Home . . ."

Pete looked at the carvings along the temple walls, the deep waves and open seas—not a shallow and polluted bog on the edge of civilization.

Jack came to her side. "Guess he's not such a nasty chaos beastie, after all. Some ancestor of those blithering idiots in the robes must've summoned and trapped him here."

"How long, do you think?" said Pete. Jack shrugged.

"Centuries, at least."

To be trapped and forced to feed power into these small, grasping people . . . Pete met Jack's eyes. "Could you—?"

He sighed and she felt the crackling of air as his magic took hold. So different from the bottomless darkness of Mnarhoteph's power, but just as strong. The chains fell away from their bolts in the stone, and Mnarhoteph shuddered, the harpoon spikes falling away from scarred and rendered flesh.

"Go," said Pete, stepping back. "We don't mean you any more harm."

Mnarhoteph's nearest row of eyes focused on her, and he trumpeted. "Home."

Pete and Jack followed in the shining trail Mnarhoteph's body left as he slithered down the temple steps and splashed into the water. The light was the gray of a nearing sun, and the mist had disappeared so that Pete could watch him swim, all the way to the sea.

AFTER PETE HAD CALLED THE BLACKPOOL POLICE FROM a cultist's unmelted mobile, she sat next to Jack on the steps of the temple. He produced a lit Parliament. "Fag?"

"I'd murder one."

Jack handed it to her, and then exhaled before he said, "You really meant what you said before the bloody creature from the black lagoon showed up, didn't you."

Pete bit her lip. Jack's eyes weren't fiery or glacial or masked. They were just hurt. "Bits of it, yes," she said finally.

Jack started to say, "I guess that means . . ." but he was knocked into the water by a flying, charred shape in a black robe.

"Infidels . . . usurpers!" Gerry groaned. Burns covered one side of his face and head, and his eye was a leaking pit. His lips were twisted and swollen, most of the tender flesh gone. "Down into the black pit with you!" he growled, grabbing Jack by the neck and pushing his face into the bog. Jack clawed at Gerry's burnt hands, raking away long strips of flesh, and came up sputtering.

"Leggo, you git!"

"Die!" Gerry howled, hitting Jack with his good hand. Jack spat blood and swamp water.

"If I'm allowed last words, I'd say look behind you."

Pete slammed a mossy chunk of rock into Gerry's bald, roasted skull. The cultist folded like a puppet with his strings cut. She grabbed Jack's hand and pulled him out of the water. He collapsed next to her, shivering.

"I win."

Pete blinked. "Pardon me?"

"I win," said Jack with a wide grin. "Did I not tell you you'd have a bit of fun?"

Pete looked at him, looked at Gerry's still form, and contemplated telling Jack he was incurably deranged. Then she started to laugh. "Smacking that arsehole was the most fun I've had in months."

"Forty quid," Jack reminded her.

"I'll write you a check when we get out of this bloody swamp," she promised.

"Am I right you'll be finding your own flat, then, when we get home?" Jack said. He went on before she could answer. "Pete, for what it's worth, those bits you meant—I *am* a bastard and a selfish git, but I kept alive this long because of it. I'm sorry I can't undergo a miraculous transformation for you, luv. Truly I am."

Pete reached and took Jack's hand. He started, then squeezed her fingers and didn't loosen his grip. "I'm quitting," Pete said.

"The Metropolitan Police. I can't do that and be this." She gestured at the bog and the temple.

Jack's forehead crinkled. "But you love your job."

"I did," said Pete. "But you taught me that you're part of the Black first and a member of society second. And . . ." She almost swallowed down the words, jumped up and ran far away as she could, "I'd like you to teach me more."

Jack looked down on her, for a long time, smoke trailing out of one nostril. "You're bloody mad, Caldecott. You honestly think I'm any kind of qualified to take an apprentice? Bloody buggering fuck, you've *seen* what happens when things go bad with me. You'd sign on willingly for that?"

Pete nodded once, and was telling the truth.

"I'll be hard," Jack warned. "I won't let you be because you're my friend or because I care for you. It won't be any sort of pleasant and if you work with me there's a good chance you'll be buried in an early grave. So quit being so bloody stupid, go back to the Yard, and forget it, Pete, because if you take me as a teacher, I'll make bloody sure you regret it." He glared at her, but there was an expression in his eyes that was entirely new to Pete. She'd call it hope, if it were anyone but Jack.

"You're right, Jack Winter," she said. "You are a git."

"I told you," Jack started, but Pete leaned up and over and kissed him firmly, until he stopped trying to talk.

"I knew what I was getting into the first moment we met," she said. "And I don't want a transformation. I knew what I got the day I met you and you don't frighten me. Never did and never bloody will."

He grinned at her, but his eyes were calm cold glaciers in a choppy sea. "We'll see, luv."

Pete put her head on Jack's shoulder and they sat on the steps of the old temple in the bog, waiting to be rescued and watching the neon spires of Blackpool fade into daylight, skeletons of a nightshade world that crumbled away under the sun.

CAITLIN KITTREDGE is the author of the Nocturne City series, featuring were-wolf detective Luna Wilder, and is currently hard at work on the first full-length volume of Pete and Jack's adventures in Black London. By day, her mild-mannered alter ego works as a video game designer. Hobbies include listening to old-school punk rock, collecting comic books, and mocking bad films. She enjoys a nice cup of tea. Find her online at www.caitlinkittredge.com.

Where the Heart Lives

Marjorie M. Liu

The Dirk & Steele series is set in contemporary times, but in a world where magic rubs elbows with science, where men and women with more-than-human powers secretly risk their lives to help others.

This story, however, takes place long before the events of the series, and is a glimpse into the lives of those who influenced the creation of the Dirk & Steele detective agency.

WHEN MISS LINDSAY FINALLY DEPARTED FOR THE WORLD beyond the wood, it meant that Lucy and Barnabus were the only people left to care for her house and land, as well as the fine cemetery she had kept for nearly twenty years outside the little town of Cuzco, Indiana. It was an important job, not just for Lucy and Barnabus, but for others, as well, who for years after would come and go, for rest or sanctuary. Bodies needed homes, after all—whether dead or living.

Lucy was only seventeen, and had come to the cemetery in the spring, not one month before Miss Lindsay went away. The girl's father was a cutter at the limestone quarry. Her brothers drove the team that hauled the stones to the masons. The men had no use for a sister, or any reminder of the fairer sex; their mother had run away that previous summer with a gypsy fortune-teller, though Lucy's father insisted his absent wife was off visiting relatives and would return. Eventually.

When word reached the old cutter that a woman named Miss Lindsay needed a girl to tend house, he made his daughter pack a bag with lunch, her comb, and one good dress from her mother's closet—then set her on the first wagon heading toward Cuzco. No good-byes, no messages sent ahead. Just chancing on fate that the woman would want his daughter.

Lucy remembered that wagon ride. Mr. Wiseman, the driver, had been hauling turnips that day, the bulbous roots covered beneath a burlap sheet to keep off the light drizzle: a cool morning, with a sweet breeze. No one on the road except them, and later, one other: an old man who stood at the side of the dirt track outside Cuzco, dressed in threadbare brown clothes, with a thin coat and his white hair slicked down from the rain. Pale eyes. Lost eyes, staring at the green budding hills like the woods were where his heart lived.

In his right hand, he held a round silver mirror. A discordant sight, flashing and bright; Lucy thought she heard voices in her head when she saw the reflecting glass: whispers like birdsong, teasing and sweet.

Mr. Wiseman did not wave at the man, but Lucy did, out of politeness and concern. She received no response; as though she were some invisible spirit, or the breeze.

"Is he sick?" Lucy whispered to Mr. Wiseman.

"Sick and married," said the spindly man, in a voice so loud, she winced. He tugged his hat a bit farther over his eyes. "Married, with no idea how to let go of the dead."

"His wife is gone?" Lucy thought of her mother.

"Gone, dead. That was Henry Lindsay you saw. Man's been like that for almost twenty years. Might as well be dead himself."

Which answered almost nothing, in Lucy's mind. "What happened to her?"

A sly smile touched Mr. Wiseman's mouth, and he glanced sideways. "Don't know, quite. But she up and died on their wedding night. I heard he hardly had a chance to touch her."

"That's *awful*," Lucy said, not much caring for the look in Mr. Wiseman's eye, as though there was something funny about the idea. She did not like, either, the other way he suddenly seemed to look at her; as though she could be another fine story, for him.

She edged sideways on the wagon seat. Mr. Wiseman looked away. "People die, Miss Lucy. But it's a shame it happened so fast. I even heard said they were going to run away, all fancy. A honeymoon, like they do out East in the cities."

Lucy said nothing. She did not know much about such things. In her experience, there was little to celebrate about being husband and wife. Just hard times, and loss, and anger. A little bit of laughter, if you were lucky. But not often.

She twisted around, looking back. Henry still stood at the bend in the road, his feet lost in deep grass, soaked and pale and staring at the woods, those smoky green hills rising and falling like the back of some long fat snake. Her heart ached for him, just a little, though she did not know why. His loss was a contagious thing.

Honeymoon, she thought, tasting the word and finding it pretty, even though she did not fully appreciate its meaning. And then another word entered her mind, familiar, and she murmured, "Lindsay."

Lindsay. The same name as the woman she was going to see. Lucy looked inquiringly at Mr. Wiseman.

"His sister," he replied shortly, and smiled. "His very pretty sister, even if she's getting on in years." He stopped the wagon and pointed at a narrow dirt path that curled into the woods. "There. Follow that to her house."

Lucy hesitated. "Are you certain?"

"There isn't a man, woman, or child in this area who doesn't know where Miss Lindsay lives." He reached behind him, and pulled out a bulging cloth sack. "Here, give this to her. Say it was from Wilbur."

Lucy clutched the sack to her stomach. It felt like turnips. She slid off the wagon, feeling lost, but before she could say anything, Mr. Wiseman gave her that same sly smile and said, "Stay on the path, Miss Lucy. Watch for ghosts."

"Ghosts," she echoed, alarmed, but he shook the reins, tipped his hat, and his wagon rattled into motion. No good-byes. Lucy watched him go, almost ready to shout his name, to ask that he wait for her. She stayed silent, though, and looked back the way they had come. Home, to her father and brothers.

Then she turned and stared down the narrow track leading into the woods. It was afternoon, but with the clouds and misting drizzle it could have been twilight before her, a forest of night. Birdsong rattled; again, Lucy thought she heard whispers. Voices airy as the wind.

Ghosts. Or nothing. Just her imagination. Lucy swallowed hard, and walked into shadow, the wet gloom: dense and thick and wild.

She thought of her mother as she walked. Wondered if she had been this frightened of leaving home, or if it had been too much a relief to unburden herself of husband and children. Then Lucy thought of the old man, Henry Lindsay, and his lost eyes and lost wife and lost wedding night, and wondered if it was the same, except worse—worse because her mother had chosen to go, worse because her father did not have eyes like that man, or that sorrow. Just anger. So much bitter anger.

The path curled. Lucy walked fast, stepping light over rocks and ivy. In the undergrowth, she heard movement: a blue bird broke loose from the canopy, streaking toward the narrow trail of gray sky; to see it felt like she was watching some desperate escape, as though the leaves on either side of the track were walls, strong as stone and insurmountable. She half expected a hand to reach from the trees and snatch the bird back.

A chill settled between her shoulders. Lucy heard a whisper, wordless but human. A hush, heart-stopping. She paused in mid-step and turned. There was no one behind her.

Lucy heard it again, and terror squeezed her gut like a cut lemon. Ghostly, yes; a voice like the wind, high and cool. She caught movement out the corner of her eye—cried out, turning—and saw a face peering from the shadows of the underbrush.

A woman. A woman in the wood, pale and fair, with eyes as blue as cornflowers. Lucy stared, trying to make sense of it—unable to speak or move as she met that terrible gaze, which was lost and so utterly lonely, Lucy felt her heart squeeze again, but softer, with a pang.

"Help me," whispered the woman. "Please, help me."

Lucy tried to speak, and choked. Around her, other voices seemed to seep free of the wood; whispers and hoarse cries and birds screaming into the cool wet air, a rising wind that blasted Lucy with a bone-chill to her heart, swelling like her insides were growing on the hum of the wood, engorged on sound.

She heard a shout—a man—but she could not turn to see. Her body felt far away, lost, and the woman cried, *"She's coming."*

Something broke inside Lucy: she could move again. She tried to run—heard another shout, desperate, and turned in time to see a brown flailing blur, a streak of silver, a shock of white hair.

Arms caught Lucy from behind. She cried out as she was lifted into the air, screaming as the sky and trees spun into a blur, so sickening, she closed her eyes. She heard the woman sobbing, a man crying a name—*Mary, Mary*—and then nothing except a heartbeat beneath her ear, sure and steady as a hammer falling.

Her heart hurt. Lucy opened her eyes and found the world changed.

She was no longer caught on the path in the woods. A meadow surrounded her, small and green and lush with grass and wild daisies, scattered with heavy oaks; somewhere near a creek burbled and goats bleated. Lucy saw a small white house behind a grove of lilac trees, and beyond, again, the rising forest; only gentler, without the dense shadows that seemed to live and breathe. No women lost in the leaves.

There were arms around her body, and movement on her left. Lucy struggled, managing to pull away until she could dance backward, staring.

Two men stood before her, one young, the other older. The elder man was Henry Lindsay. Lucy remembered his face. Up close, however, he did not look quite so aged. His body was straight and hard and lean; he had few wrinkles and his eyes were bright, startling, the color of gold. His white hair was the only symptom of age, but that seemed a trivial thing compared with the fire in his gaze, which was so alive, she thought she must have imagined the man who had stood at the side of the road, with a face as slack and dead as a corpse.

The young man with him had quieter eyes, but just as bold. He wore a soft blue cotton shirt that had been patched with bits and pieces of rags, the stitches neat, made with thick red thread, a complement to his color: blue eyes, skin brown from the sun, hair dark and wild like a scarecrow. He glanced at Henry, just before the older man lurched toward Lucy: a half step, the edge of a full run, stopping as though pulled back by strings. His hands clenched into fists. Lucy noted the silver mirror jutting from his coat pocket.

"She spoke to you," said Henry, his voice deceptively controlled: quiet, easy—frightening, because Lucy could tell it was a lie. She said nothing, uncertain how to answer him, and in her head she could see the woman in the wood, her pale face and lost eyes: a mirror to how this man had looked while standing on the road.

Henry said it again, louder: "She spoke. Tell me what she said."

Lucy stared, bewildered, and he rocked toward her with a low cry, hand outstretched. She staggered back, holding up her arms, but the young man stepped between them and caught Henry before he could get close, holding him back with his size and easy strength. Lucy readied herself to run.

"Stop this," said a new voice. *"Henry."*

Lucy turned. She had to steady herself—all of this was too much—but she dug her nails into her palm and gazed at the newcomer: a woman who stood a stone's throw distant, her mature face a reflection of Henry Lindsay, who quieted and stilled until the young man let him go.

Black hair, threaded with white; golden eyes and an unlined face; a small narrow body dressed in a simple dark red dress, finely mended. The woman stood barefoot in the grass, hair loose and wild; proud, confident, utterly at ease. Lucy felt drab as a titmouse compared to her. In the trees, crows shrieked, raucous and loud.

"Miss Lindsay," she whispered, following her intuition. "Ma'am."

The woman tilted her head. "I don't know you."

"My father heard you were looking for a girl," she replied hoarsely.

Henry swayed. Lucy forced herself to stay strong, to look him in the eye as her father had always said to do, that eyes were important when dealing with strangers, especially men.

He said, "She spoke to Mary. She spoke to Mary in the woods."

"Did she now?" said Miss Lindsay slowly, her gaze sharpening. She moved close, hips swaying gracefully. "Did you speak to someone in the woods, child?"

"No," Lucy said softly. "But the woman . . . the woman in the trees spoke to me. And I heard . . ."

She stopped. Miss Lindsay stood near, her golden gaze like fire: hot, burning. She reached 'out and touched Lucy's forehead with one finger, just between the eyes, and whispered, "What did you hear?"

"Voices," Lucy replied, compelled by those eyes, that searing touch. "Many voices."

"Mary," said Henry, in a broken voice. "Tell me what she said."

Lucy looked at him, and finally could see again the man from the road, lost and dull. She was sorry about that, and said, gently, "The woman asked me to help her. And then . . . then she said . . . someone was coming."

She's coming, echoed that urgent voice, inside her head. Lucy felt a chill race through her body. Miss Lindsay flinched, and moved away. She turned her head, until her hair shifted and Lucy could not see her eyes.

"You'll do," said the woman softly. "Yes, if you like, I'll hire you."

"If she wants to stay," said Henry, also turning away, his voice rough, his shoulders bowed. His hand was in his coat pocket, clutching the mirror. A wedding ring glinted on his finger.

Lucy stared at them all, helpless, unsure what to do. Her gaze finally fell on the one person who had said nothing at all—the young man, who was calm and steady, and who watched her with that same straightforward regard. Lucy imagined a clear pure tone when she looked at him, and it was an unexpected comfort.

"I'll stay," she found herself saying—two words that could have been a leap off a cliff for the falling sensation she felt on uttering them. It was dangerous, something was not right; there were ghosts in the woods and spirits unseen, and here, here, these people knew of such things. And she was joining them, would cook and clean for them.

But it was better than going home.

Lucy imagined a whisper on the wind. Miss Lindsay briefly closed her eyes, then held out her hand and gave the girl a long piercing look.

"Come," she said, in a voice gentler than her eyes. "I'll show you the house."

And that was that.

NOTHING HAPPENED THAT FIRST WEEK, EXCEPT FOR THE fact that afterward, Lucy's life felt irrevocably changed. The sensation crept on her slowly, nudged along by little things that she had never had a chance to experience: reading as a leisure activity, for starters (Miss Lindsay insisted on it, in the evenings); or being treated as a thinking person, something more than a girl or daughter or sister or future wife. Something beyond drudge. An equal, perhaps.

It was a fine house, much larger than anything Lucy was accustomed to, with a second floor and an actual parlor and fireplace just for sitting and warming the feet. There were books shelved against the walls, more than she had ever seen—a library of them, all around—as well as journals and odd paintings, and stacks of newspapers bound with string. Most of those were crumbling and yellow; Lucy was careful as she cleaned around them, gazing as she did upon faded images of President Lincoln, as well as cramped headlines about the War, some fifty years past.

Lucy had her own room with a lock on the door, just off the kitchen. Miss Lindsay slept upstairs, as did her brother, Henry. The young man, Barnabus, kept his bed and belongings in the work shed off the garden. He was like her—there for odd jobs—although unlike her, he was treated more like family, though Miss Lindsay explained that he was not. Or rather, not by blood.

"A child of the forest," the woman called him, that first night. "Found in the woods as a boy, living wild as the coyotes and foxes. Folks brought him here. It was that or the circus, with those men. So I raised him. Taught him. Oh, he's a good one, that Barnabus. Talk to him as you like—he's as smart as you and I—but don't expect a word from his mouth. He can't speak. Not like us. The forest stole his voice."

Given what Lucy had experienced, she thought that might be the literal—if not fantastical—truth. And it disturbed her greatly. She did not know what to make of it. The forest was dangerous— she knew that in her heart—and while it went unspoken that she should not walk near the tree line, ever, the others did so all the time.

No one ever explained the threat that she felt so keenly. She tried asking, but Miss Lindsay always managed to change the subject—so smoothly, Lucy hardly realized what she was doing until it was too late and she was off scrubbing a floor or cooking or weeding, and thinking hard about why she was here, and how

Miss Lindsay had managed, yet again, to deflect a question about a situation that Lucy found dangerous and frightening and undeniably odd.

She dreamed of the woman at night, the woman in the wood, and listened to her pleas for help beneath a wail of wind and whispers, endless and cold and pained. Sometimes she sensed another voice beneath the other—*Mary, Mary,* she would hear Henry cry—and something else, bells and the pound of hooves, and music playing high and wild like a storm of thunder and fiddle strikes.

And sometimes in her dream she would open her eyes and Miss Lindsay would be sitting by her bed, with that cool hand pressed against her forehead and her golden eyes shining with unearthly light. And in those moments of fantasy Lucy would think of her mother, and stop feeling afraid, and slip into softer, gentler, dreams: buttercups and horses, and afternoons by the river with her feet in the sun-riddled water. Sometimes Barnabus was there, holding her hand. She liked that, though it scared her too. In a different way.

There were several surprises that first week, the biggest one being that Miss Lindsay had a cemetery on her land, only a short walk away along a narrow wagon track. Her family was buried there, but mostly other folk—from town, the surrounding areas—anyone who did not have the money to be planted in one of the church plots near the bigger towns. Miss Lindsay called it a service to the public, and several times Lucy saw strangers exit the trail through the forest bearing gifts of cloth and food. Payment served.

Folks never lingered, though. They visited the graveyard, then left quick, hardly looking around, as though afraid of what they would see. Lucy wondered how they managed to make it through the forest unmolested, and said as much to Henry, whom she found one afternoon in a rare moment of responsiveness—sitting in the sun, reading a book by someone with a long, rather familiar, name. Shakes Spear, or something of the kind. She settled down beside him with a pile of mending in her lap. Barnabus was nearby, chopping wood. His shirt was off, draped over a low tree branch.

"The forest has a mind of its own," Henry replied, after some deep thought. He gazed at the tree line, and his eyes began to glaze over, lost. Lucy pricked him—accidentally, of course—with her needle. He flinched, frowning, but his expression cleared.

"You were saying?" Lucy prodded.

"A mind, a spirit. This the forest primeval," murmured Henry, "darkened by shadows of earth." He looked at her. "Longfellow. Do you know him?"

"We never met," she said, and then blushed when she realized that was not at all what he meant. Henry smiled kindly, though, idly tapping the book in his hands. Lucy, in part to hide her embarrassment—but mostly because she was suddenly quite motivated to educate herself—pointed and said, "What are you reading?"

"The Bard," Henry replied, handing her the book. "Specifically, *Romeo and Juliet*. A great and tragic love story."

Lucy made a small sound, savoring the smooth feel of the slender red volume in her hands. "Seems like tragic is the only kind of love there is."

Henry tilted his head. "Broken heart?"

She frowned. "Oh, no. Not me, sir. Never been in love. Just . . . I've seen things, that's all."

"And I suppose you've heard of *me*," he said with a hint of darkness in his voice. Lucy felt a moment of panic, but then she looked at him and found his eyes thoughtful, distant—but not lost. Nor angry.

"I heard something from someone," Lucy said slowly. "First time I saw you on the road, coming here."

"You saw me?" Henry looked surprised. "Ah. Well."

"You were . . . distracted," Lucy told him, not wanting him to feel bad. "Staring at the forest."

A rueful smile touched his mouth. "That happens."

Lucy hesitated. "Because of the woman? Mary?"

She knew it was a mistake the moment that name left her mouth. Too much said, too fast. Henry's expression crumpled, then hardened; shadows gathered beneath his eyes, which seemed to change color, glittering like amber caught in sunlight. Lucy had to look away, and found Barnabus watching them with a frown. He put down his ax and began walking toward them.

"I'm sorry," Lucy said to Henry. "Please, I'm—"

He cut her off, leaning close. "You saw her. In the forest. What did she look like?"

Barnabus reached them. He sat beside Lucy, the corner of his knee brushing her thigh. He was big and warm and safe, and she was glad for his presence.

"She was beautiful," Lucy said simply, and then, softer: "She was your wife."

"My wife," echoed Henry, staring at his hands. "She is still my wife."

Lucy stared. "I thought . . . I thought your wife was dead. What I saw . . . just a ghost." The ghost of a woman lost in the forest; the walking, speaking, dead; an illusion of life. Nothing else made sense. Even the forest, a forest that had almost captured her—a terrible dream full of ghosts, spirits.

Barnabus went still. Henry exhaled very slowly. Lucy felt a whisper of air against her neck, a chill that went down her spine. Miss Lindsay was behind her. She could feel the woman, even though she could not see or hear her. Lucy always knew when she was close.

Miss Lindsay said, "Perhaps you'd like to walk with me," and Lucy rose on unsteady legs, and joined the woman as she turned and strode away toward the cemetery.

"I'm sorry," Lucy said.

Miss Lindsay raised a fine dark brow. "Curiosity is no crime. And you have a right to know."

"No." She shook her head. "I'm just the house girl. You didn't hire me for—"

"Stop." Miss Lindsay quit walking and gave her a hard look. "Close your eyes."

Her demand was unexpected, odd. Lucy almost refused, but after a moment, Miss Lindsay's gaze softened and she said, "Come, I will not hurt you. Just do as I say. Close your eyes."

So Lucy closed them, and waited. Miss Lindsay gave her no more instructions, which was curious enough in itself, though the girl did not break the silence between them. The darkness inside her mind was suddenly fraught with color, images dancing; not memories, but something new, unexpected. Like a daydream, only as real as the grass beneath her feet.

She saw a thunderstorm, night; felt herself standing in a doorway, staring at the rain. A warm hand touched her waist.

And then that touch disappeared and she stood in the forest, within the twilight of the trees, and the woman was once again in front of her—*Mary*—hands outstretched, weeping.

Gone, again, gone. Other visions flashed—feathers and crows, golden glowing eyes—but it was too quick and odd to make sense. Except for one: Henry, younger, standing beneath a bough of flowers, holding hands with the woman from the wood. Mary. Smiling. Staring into his eyes like he was where her heart lived.

Then, later: Henry and Mary, riding away in a buggy. Henry and Mary, kissing. Henry and Mary, in the dark, his hands shaking against the clasps of her wedding gown, the white of the cloth glowing beneath the dappled moon. On a blanket, in the forest.

Lucy saw a shadow behind them, something separate and unnatural, creeping across the forest floor. She tried to shout a warning, but her throat swelled, breath rattling, and all she could do was watch in horror as that slither of night spread like a poison through the moonlight, closer and closer—until it nudged Mary's foot.

And swallowed the rest of her. One moment in Henry's arms—in the next, gone. Gone, screaming. Henry, screaming.

Lucy, screaming. Snapping back into the world. Curled on her side in the thick grass. Arms around her. A large tanned hand clutching her own and Miss Lindsay crouched close, fingers pressed against Lucy's forehead.

"You're safe," said the woman, but that was not it at all. Henry and Mary were not safe. Henry and Mary had been torn apart and Lucy could not bear to think about it. Not for them, not for herself—not when she suddenly could remember so clearly the night her own mother had disappeared, swallowed up by the world. Her choice to go—but with the same pain left behind.

"Ah," breathed Miss Lindsay, and her fingers slid sideways to caress Lucy's cheek. "Poor child."

Lucy took a deep breath and struggled to sit up. The world spun. The arms around her tightened—*Barnabus*—and she closed her eyes, slipping back into darkness.

SHE WOKE IN HER BED. A CANDLE BURNED. Outside, strong winds rattled the house; rain pattered against the roof and window. Miss Lindsay sat in a chair. Her hands were folded in her lap and she wore a man's robe that smelled of cigar smoke.

Lucy tried to speak, found her voice hoarse, hardly her own. "What happened?"

A sad smile edged Miss Lindsay's mouth. "Impatience. I pushed you too fast."

The girl hesitated. "Was it real, then? What I saw?"

Only after she spoke did she realize the foolishness of that statement; Miss Lindsay could not possibly know what she had seen. But the older woman denied nothing, nor did she look at Lucy as though her mind was lost.

"Real enough," she replied softly, and then, even quieter: "Did you understand what you saw?"

"Some of it. Except at the end . . . what took Mary . . ." Her voice dropped to a whisper as a chill swept deep. "That was not human."

"So little is," murmured Miss Lindsay, but before Lucy could ask what that meant, she said, "The woman you saw in the forest the day you came here is my brother's wife, Mary. She did not die, as other have said, but was stolen away. Captured, with the woods as her cage. She cannot leave, and my brother . . . my brother cannot enter. He cannot see her. He cannot speak to her. But he knows she is there and so he stays and watches, for just one glimpse." Miss Lindsay looked at her hands. "He loves her so."

Lucy curled deeper under the covers, staring. "I don't understand how any of this could happen. It's not . . . normal."

"Normal." Bitterness touched Miss Lindsay's smile. "Some would say the same of the moon and stars, or the wind, or a flight of birds, but all those things are natural and real. We accept them as such, without question." She leaned close, candlelight warming her golden gaze. "You should know, Lucy, that I hired you on false pretenses. Not merely to cook and clean and stay silent in your room. You live here, my dear, because you are the first person in twenty years to see my brother's wife. And *that,* if one wished to speak of such things, is *not* normal."

Lucy shook her head against the pillow. "The driver, Mr. Wiseman, told me about ghosts. That's all I thought she was."

"Ghosts." Miss Lindsay's fingers flexed. "To tease a child about ghosts is simple because of the cemetery I control. Because of the dead that people bring. Not because of Mary. Those in town think she's buried here. And she is, in a way. But the woman you saw is flesh and blood."

"How?" Lucy breathed, thinking of Mary—Mary in the forest, so lost—Mary in the forest twenty years past, so in love. "Why?"

Miss Lindsay closed her eyes. "Tomorrow. Tomorrow, I will tell you that story."

"No," Lucy protested, but the older woman stood.

"Tomorrow," she said again, and blew out the candle. Lucy reached out and caught her hand. Miss Lindsay gently disengaged herself, swept her fingers over the girl's brow, and walked from the room. She closed the door behind her.

Lucy lay in the darkness for a long time, listening to the old house, the rumbling storm. It occurred to her, briefly, that she could leave this place and go back to her father and brothers, but the idea made her heart hurt and she realized with some surprise that this place, despite its mystery, felt like home. A better home than what she had left behind. What she had been forced from by her father.

Mother was forced to leave, in a different way, whispered a tiny voice inside her mind, but that was too much, and Lucy pushed back her blankets to rise from bed. She still wore her clothes from that afternoon, but did not bother with her shoes.

The house was quiet. Lucy walked silently through the

kitchen. She wanted water, but as she reached for the pump above the sink she noticed a warm glow against the wall in the parlor, and heard the sound of pages turning. She peered into the room.

Henry and Barnabus sat before the small fire, reading. Her heart jumped a little at finding them; she was not quite certain she was ready to face the older man, not after what she had seen inside her head. And Barnabus . . .

The young man looked up from his book. He had not been long from the rain; his hair was damp, as was his shirt, which strained against his shoulders. She tried to imagine him as a child, wild in the forest—still wild, maybe—and it was easy, as simple as looking into his eyes. She felt shy, looking at him. He was so handsome, breathtakingly so.

Barnabus stood and gestured for her to take his seat. When she did not move, he held out his hand to her, and she let him take it and guide her. His skin was warm. His touch, gentle. Her heart beat a little faster.

Henry closed his book. "Are you better?"

"Yes," she said, hardly able to look at him. But she did, and though she found terrible sadness in his eyes, there was also compassion. Barnabus very quietly settled himself on the floor beside her chair, the edge of his hand brushing her foot.

Lucy fidgeted, staring at the fire. Henry said, "You want to ask me something."

She hesitated. Henry frowned, laying his book on the floor. "I'm sorry for earlier. I scared you this afternoon. I didn't mean to."

Barnabus sighed. Lucy glanced down at him. "I'm sorry too."

"So? Ask me what you want." He smiled gently. "I am here, Lucy."

You are with your wife, she thought, and summoned up her courage. "Please . . . why was Mary taken?"

Henry paled. Barnabus's hand shifted against her foot. A warning, perhaps. Lucy ignored him, refusing to take her gaze from the older man's face. She watched his struggle—battled one of her own, resisting the urge to take back her question—and thought instead of Mary. Mary in her wedding gown. Mary in the forest, begging for help.

Lucy thought of Miss Lindsay too. She was defying the woman; she doubted that would end well. But she needed to know.

Henry looked at the fire; for a moment his eyes seemed to glow. "Mary did nothing. It was me. I was . . . foolish. I had a temper, and there was a woman who had too much interest in me. I rejected her, badly. And because she could not hurt me. . . ."

He stopped. Lucy forced herself to breathe. "Does this woman live in the forest?"

Henry closed his eyes; a bitter smile touched his mouth. "She *is* the forest. She is a witch and its queen."

"A witch," Lucy murmured, thinking of fairy tales and crones, women in black hats with cats in their laps, cooking children for supper. "How do you stop a witch?"

"You don't," Henry said heavily, and picked up his book, tapping his fingers along its spine. "None of us are powerful enough."

"She couldn't hurt *you,*" Lucy pointed out, and Barnabus once again touched her foot—yet another warning.

Henry's jaw tightened; his eyes were quite bright. "Do you have any more questions?"

"Just one," Lucy said softly, thinking of her mother. "What is it like to be married?"

Barnabus went very still. Henry glanced at him and said, "It is a sacred art. A union of souls. To be together is the grandest adventure."

Lucy shook her head, trying to picture Henry and Mary as her father and mother, to imagine what that would be like, to have parents who loved. It was difficult to do, and disheartening. "It seems like a lot of work."

Henry studied her. "And?"

"And, nothing," she said, but hesitated, still chewing on her memories. "I heard a word once, talking about such things. *Honeymoon,* someone called it. I liked the word, but I still don't know what it means."

"It doesn't mean much by itself," Henry replied slowly, with a distant look in his eyes. "It's a symbol, I suppose. You're married, so the both of you run away where no one knows you, no one can find you, and you make a world that is just your own. For a short time, your own." He smiled gently. "A month, the span of the moon. Sweet as honey. And if you're lucky, perhaps you turn that honeyed moon into something longer, a lifetime."

"But I still don't see how it makes a difference," Lucy said, feeling stubborn. "If you're married, you're together anyhow. Happy or not. You don't need to be all . . . sticky about it."

Barnabus shifted slightly, but not before she saw his small smile. Heat flooded her face; she felt deeply embarrassed to have said so much in front of him. She had forgotten herself—was far too comfortable in his presence—far too at ease with all these people, who were supposed to be her employers. Not her family.

As if you were ever made so welcome by your own flesh and blood.

Lucy stood. Barnabus caught her ankle in a loose grip. The contact seared her skin.

"The heart loves," Henry said softly, so gentle, it made her chest ache. "Listen to your heart, Lucy. Don't be afraid of it."

"I'm not," she whispered, feeling captured, trapped; Barnabus's hand felt too good. She nudged her foot and he released her.

"Good night," she said, not looking at either man, and fled the parlor for the kitchen. She almost went straight to her room, but she needed air and flung open the kitchen door that led into the garden. Wind blasted her, as did rain. She worried about others feeling the draft and began to close the door behind her. It caught on something, Barnabus.

Thunder blasted. Barnabus touched her waist, drawing her back until heat raced down her spine, and her shoulders rubbed against his hard chest. His hand closed over hers and they held the door together, blasted by white lightning and tremors of sound.

Barnabus shut the door when the rain began coming in. Cut off from the storm, the air inside the house felt closed, uncomfortably warm. No lightning, no candle, no way to see except by touch and memory.

Barnabus still held her hand. He guided her across the kitchen until she touched the door of her room, and there he eased away. Lucy listened to his soft retreat, the creak of the floorboards, the rustle and whisper of his clothing, the faint hiss of the wind as he left the house for his bed in the work shed. Her hand tingled with the memory of his fingers. Her waist still felt the pressure of his palm.

Lucy lay down on her bed and closed her eyes. She dreamed of a world that was her own, and a sweet moon made of honey in the sky.

LUCY ROSE EARLY THE NEXT MORNING. BARNABUS WAS already awake; she could see him in the distance, in the cemetery, digging a grave. Lucy vaguely recalled Miss Lindsay mentioning a death in town. She watched him work for a moment, and then went about her business, feeding the chickens and milking the goats. Crows gathered along the eaves of the house, watching her.

They made a ruckus only once, and Lucy looked up at the sky just long enough to see a streak of golden light in the shape of a bird fall behind the work shed. She did not know what to make of it—again her imagination, perhaps—until she heard a rustle of clothing and Miss Lindsay walked out from behind the small structure, buttoning the top of her dress.

She did not appear surprised to see Lucy, but merely said, "Good morning," and walked into the house. The girl stared after her, perplexed. So much was odd about this place. Or perhaps Lucy was just odd herself. That did not bother her, she knew, as much as it should. As much as it would have, not so long ago.

The funeral took place that afternoon. Few people came, but one of them was Mr. Wiseman, hauling a coffin in the back of his wagon. Lucy did not feel any great pleasure in seeing him. He was a very real reminder of the world beyond the wood—a world that felt like a distant place—and the sight of his face made her stomach twist with dread.

"I see the ghosts didn't get you," he said loudly, with that same sly smile.

"Ghosts are for children," said Miss Lindsay, coming up behind his wagon. She stood beside Lucy, and rested her hand on the girl's shoulder. "Don't you have something better to do with your time, Wilbur, than tease young girls?"

Mr. Wiseman tipped his hat. "Helena, you're still as handsome a woman as I've ever met. I don't suppose your brother would consent to me courting you?"

"I believe my brother would have very little say in the matter," replied Miss Lindsay dryly, "nor would your wife be all that pleased with the arrangement."

His smile was all teeth. He tore his gaze from Miss Lindsay and looked at Lucy. "Got a message for you, girl. Your father's come down with some kind of sickness. He wants you to come home straightaway to care for him."

Lucy stared. "He was fine when I left."

"But he's not now. You're to ride with me after I'm done here."

"No," she said without thinking.

Mr. Wiseman's smile slipped. "Maybe you didn't hear me."

"I heard you." Lucy drew in a shaky breath, swept away by such hard emotions that she almost quivered with tension. "No, I won't go."

"He's your father."

Desperation rode over guilt. "I'm doing a job. He wouldn't give up his place at the quarry for me. I know that. He told me often enough."

Mr. Wiseman's jaw flexed. "You'll do as you're told, girl."

Miss Lindsay's hand tightened on Lucy's shoulder. "Wilbur. You and I will discuss this later."

"No time for that," he snapped, eyes narrowed. "You been twisting this girl's mind, making her turn from her family?"

"I like working here," Lucy told him, voice rising. "And my brothers are still at home. They don't need me. They didn't even *want* me."

"Go on, now," Miss Lindsay said to Mr. Wiseman, drawing Lucy away. "There are people waiting on that body."

He looked ready to argue, but it was true—there were mourners dressed all in black standing at the little cast-iron gate in front of the cemetery, and they were watching Mr. Wiseman with a question in their eyes. The old man grunted, giving Lucy a baleful glare.

"You be packed by the time I get back," he told her. "Or else I'll take you as you are."

Lucy flinched. She saw Barnabus running toward them, and

caught Mr. Wiseman also staring at the young man. Something passed through his gaze, and he slammed the reins against his horses, jolting them into motion.

"Coward," Miss Lindsay murmured, but Lucy hardly heard her. All she could do was stare at Barnabus as he moved close. He looked dangerous, furious—like he was ready to fight, something she had never imagined of him. He touched the small of her back, his mouth set in a grim line that only grew deeper, darker, as he gazed past her at the old man's retreating wagon.

And then he looked at her, and in his eyes, a question. Uncertainty.

"If I go, I won't be back," Lucy said, speaking to them both, but looking at Barnabus. "I know it."

Knew it like truth. Just as with those visions of the day previous, she could feel inside her head the future tumbling away into a dark cold place, and if she went with Mr. Wiseman, that would be her fate. Something lonely and awful. Like having her wings cut after a taste of flying.

Miss Lindsay's eyes flashed golden, and this time Lucy was certain it was not her imagination. "You want to stay here? You're sure of it?"

Lucy nodded, struggling with her fear. She knew it was terrible—*she* was terrible—and her father, her father would think *she was just like her mother*—but she did not care. She had to stay. Something would break inside her if she left this tiny world within the forest—this dangerous forest—this little place with these strange and wonderful people who made her feel safe and welcome. If her mother had felt this way, all those years ago, then Lucy could forgive her. She understood now, what could drive a woman to abandon all. She understood, and if it was selfish, then so be it. She would be selfish, and happy.

"Barnabus," said Miss Lindsay crisply, "take Lucy to the pond at the bottom of the hill. I'll handle Wilbur. When he's gone, I'll come fetch you both."

"I'm sorry," Lucy said, suddenly regretting the trouble she was causing the woman. "If *you* don't want me—"

"No." Miss Lindsay brushed her fingers across the girl's forehead. "You are no trouble to me or this family. This is your home."

And with that, she turned and strode away toward the cemetery, where Mr. Wiseman was helping the mourners unload the coffin. Barnabus tugged on Lucy's hand. It took her a moment to follow; she kept hearing those words, seeing those golden eyes, and felt inside her a flush that could have been what Henry spoke of, that sense of running away. The grand adventure. Making a new world from the old. She was not married, but it felt the same: a union, in its own way.

She and Barnabus crossed the meadow, chased by crows. They climbed a gentle slope through scattered oaks, and at the crest of the hill gazed down upon a body of still water, blue from the sky and filled with lily pads and brown ducks. The forest nudged the northern edge of the pond, but the sun chased back the shadows and the grass was tall and green.

There was a rough dock jutting from the green shore. Barnabus and Lucy sat at the end of it, careful of splinters, and dangled their feet in the water. After a short time, he reached over and held her hand.

She liked that, and felt a stab of fear that she might have to give it up. But then she remembered Miss Lindsay's calm strength and said, "They're good people, aren't they? Henry and Miss Lindsay. But they're not . . . like other folk. Regular, I mean." She had been about to say *normal,* but recalled Miss Lindsay's feelings about that word.

Barnabus nodded, squeezing her hand. He did not appear at all perturbed by her question or the implication, but rather, seemed comfortable with the truth: that Henry and Miss Lindsay *were* different, inexplicably so, and that it was natural. Like the wind or the moon. She liked that too.

"How long have you lived here?" Lucy asked him, jumping slightly as fish nibbled on her toes.

He spread out his fingers. Five, then two. Seven years.

"And before that? Did you really live in the forest?"

Barnabus shrugged, gazing past her at the dense tree line. His mouth moved, but not a sound emerged except the whistle of his breath. He looked, for a moment, frustrated—and Lucy wondered what it would be like to have no voice, to have a lifetime bottled up inside her without words or sound. She reached out, unthinking, and touched his lips with her fingers. She only meant to tell him it was all right, that he did not need to explain, but his face was so close and his eyes were so deep and blue, that she found herself leaning, leaning, until she felt the heat of his breath and her fingers slipped away, only to be replaced by her mouth.

Lucy had never kissed a boy before. His taste was sweet and hot—toe-curling, a delight. It frightened her, but not enough to give it up.

It did not last. Lucy heard a weeping cry, and broke away, staring at the woods. She heard it again, a voice calling out, and it took her only a moment to find that pale feminine face, luminous in the rich green shadows of the forest. Lucy leapt to her feet and ran. She felt Barnabus behind her, but she did not look back, afraid if she did the woman would disappear.

Mary. She heard a crow shrieking above her head—an animal caw that suddenly sounded very human—but she ignored that, as well.

She reached the edge of the forest just as Barnabus caught up with her. She thought she heard Henry shouting, but Mary was there—right in front of her—and the woman whispered, "Please, help me."

Lucy sucked her in breath—fighting for courage—and jammed her hands through the underbrush toward Mary. Barnabus grabbed her waist—another set of hands joined his, as well—but it was too late. Something took hold of her wrists, yanking hard— and the face in front of her changed. It stopped being Mary, and became instead a shadow, a gasp of night, like that slithering tendril of nothingness she had witnessed in her vision.

Raw terror bucked through her body. She tried to pull back, fighting with all her strength. Whispers rose from the trees—all those voices she had almost forgotten, soaring into her head like a scream.

Lucy was pulled into the forest.

THE FIRST THING SHE NOTICED, WHEN SHE COULD see again, was that the world around her seemed quite ordinary. She was in the forest, yes, but she had been inside forests before, and this was no different. The shadows were long and the canopy thick, and the twilight that filled the air was neither gloomy nor particularly menacing. It was simply dense—with vines of wild rose and new spurting growths of seedlings; poison ivy, ferns, tiny bowing cedars and those massive trunks of oak that spread fat like squatting giants all around her. She smelled the earth, something else—like rain— and the air was still and warm and humid.

Lucy turned in one slow circle, trying to find the edge of the forest. She was close, she knew she should see Barnabus or Henry—at least hear their voices—but even the birds did not sing, and all she could see was leaf and branch and shadow.

"Hello?" she called out, thinking of that creature which had pulled her inside the wood. Fear clutched her throat, pounding against her heart, but she steadied herself, fought herself, and regained control. She thought of Mary too. Trapped here for twenty years. She wondered if the same would happen to her.

She heard something, and turned in time to see an immense pale figure part the gloom. A white stag. Tall and broad, with a deep chest and a long neck that glittered as though sprinkled with dew. Its hooves had been polished to the sheen of pearls, and its eyes glowed with a wild raging light. Tiny bells hung from its silver antlers, and the sounds they made were those same whispered voices Lucy had heard in her head—now louder, cries and sorrow ringing with every delicate knell.

A woman sat upon the stag. She was divine: pale and slender, sparkling as though spun with stars and diamonds, her hair so long, it almost swept the ground. A Snow Queen, with a manner that begged a bow. White furs and silks crisscrossed her high breasts, which were quite nearly exposed, though covered with faint lines of pale rose, curling like poems and wings upon the skin below her throat.

She held herself with such lightness, Lucy imagined she might float to fall, and as the stag stepped near, Lucy saw that the woman was perched on a fine dainty saddle shaped like a frog.

"Witch" was not the right word for this woman, Lucy thought. A witch was human. And this . . . creature . . . most definitely was not.

"You are trespassing on the land of the *Sidhe,*" said the woman, her voice strong, ringing. "What say you?"

"I say no," replied Lucy awkwardly, fighting for courage. "You brought me here. So I was invited."

A faint smile touched the woman's mouth. "You thought you

were saving a heart that belongs to me. So you are a thief. Much worse, I think."

Lucy steeled herself. "You're talking about Mary. Mary doesn't belong to you."

The stag shook its head and the bells wept. Lucy thought she heard Mary's voice within those tones. She closed her eyes for just a moment, searching, listening hard, but when she looked again at the woman, she was gone from the stag.

A cold hand caressed the back of Lucy's neck, and she flinched, whirling. The woman stood before her, impossibly tall. Her eyes were as green as a spring leaf in morning sun: crisp, sharp, ageless. She peered at Lucy like she was a snowy owl, and the girl a mouse, and there was a hunger there that was implacable and terrifying.

"All that enter the forest belong to me," said the woman softly. "And now you, as well."

"No," Lucy said. "I want to go home."

"Home." The woman smiled. "This is home."

"There are people waiting for me. For Mary, too."

"Mary," she said quietly. "Mary betrayed my trust. She tried to fetch help. You. Quite shocking that you were able to see and hear her. I find that fascinating."

Lucy did not. "Let us go. Please."

"For what reason?" The witch smiled, tilting her head. "Shall I tell you a riddle and have you guess the answer? Or perhaps have you perform three impossible tasks, each more harrowing than the other. Oh, better still, tell me stories to keep me amused. Be my fool, my jester of the wood, and *perhaps* in a year or twenty I will release you."

Lucy doubted that. So she said nothing, instead waiting, watching, refusing to let herself feel a moment lost. The woman's smiled faltered, just slightly, and that momentary weakness humanized her presence in ways that made her seem less regal than ridiculous—as though her shocking appearance was nothing but an attempt to impress, awe and intimidate.

Lucy suddenly felt stronger. "I won't beg you. I won't be a fool."

"You already are," said the woman darkly. "You are nothing."

"No more than you," Lucy replied recklessly, following her intuition. Perhaps too well: a cold hand grabbed her chin with crushing strength, yanking up until she stood on her toes, forced to look the woman in the eyes.

"You love," she whispered harshly. "I can smell it on you. Should we test that love? Do you truly think the one your heart cares for would wait? That handsome young man who used to be mine?"

"Barnabus," Lucy said, hoarse.

"*Barnabus,*" she hissed. "I raised him long before that old crow sank her claws into his heart. He was *mine*. My *son,* in every way but one. But *that* one . . . he remembered."

"He did not love you." Lucy could feel it, see it: a little boy with blue eyes running naked and wild, engaging with the woman, but never with emotion. Never with affection, or a smile.

The woman glanced away, and then, softly, almost to herself: "He would never call me mother. He refused. And so I punished him."

"You took his voice."

"I could not have him calling another by the name he refused me."

"So if someone refuses you, you hurt them? What good does that do?"

The woman gave her a sharp look. "Respect must be shown. And I am a queen."

"You are a queen who is alone," Lucy said, and the woman released her so quickly, she staggered, rubbing her aching chin. The woman—the queen, the *Sidhe,* whatever that might be—watched her with cool steady eyes, a gaze she now knew Barnabus copied well. Lucy met those ageless eyes, letting her thoughts roam, picking up as she did tendrils of thought and vision: the woman in her finery, wandering the endless expanse of forest, alone. So very alone.

"You wanted Henry to love you as a man loves a woman," Lucy whispered. "You wanted Barnabus to love you as a mother. And there have been others, haven't there? People who caught your eye. You brought them here, and then you hurt them because you couldn't understand why they didn't return what you feel."

"Love," whispered the woman. "It is a myth that belongs only to humans, and those who pretend to be like them. It cannot last."

"I used to think that," Lucy told her. "Until I met Henry, and I saw how he loves."

"Henry will give up on his wife."

"Henry will love her forever."

The woman smiled coldly. "Forever does not exist for mortal love."

"It doesn't exist for immortals, either," Lucy said, still listening to the little voice inside her head. "Or maybe that's just you."

The woman sucked in her breath; the stag backed away, eyes keen on its mistress. Lucy did not retreat. She took a step, overcome, as though she could hear her soul humming, as though the world was in her veins, alive and strong. Her heart, full to burst—and she thought of Barnabus, Henry, Miss Lindsay. People who cared for her. People *she* cared for, in ways she had not known possible.

She loved them. She *loved*. And she knew what that was now, even if it was never returned. Even if one day, it all fell away.

The woman flinched, staring at her. She began to speak, then stopped. Light burned in her eyes, but Lucy did not falter, nor did her heart dim. The woman turned, stopped, and in a muffled voice said, "Go. Leave. You have your freedom. I give you my word."

Lucy blinked, startled. "And Mary."

The woman stiffened, her back still turned. "I have blessed Henry with a gift. I would have returned Mary sooner, but she stopped loving him as she should. She is not worth his heart. He will be hurt, he will be broken. He has loved an ideal for all these years."

"Because of you," Lucy said, and then, softer: "Henry loved the woman before the ideal. Let him find his own way."

The woman's light seemed to dim, her radiance faltering beneath the gloom. Lucy, in a moment of pity, said, "You could leave this place if you're so lonely."

That flawless head turned just a fraction, enough to see the corner of an eye, the curve of a high cheek.

"We all have our homes," she said quietly. "The ability to choose yours is not a gift to take for granted."

The woman plucked a silver bell from the stag's antlers and tossed it at Lucy's feet. A heartbeat later she was perched high on the fine saddle, her composure fixed and utterly regal.

"Give my regards to Barnabus," she said coldly. "The crows, as well."

And then she was gone. Vanished into the forest twilight.

Lucy picked up the bell and shook it. Mary's voice echoed, like an eerie chime. She held it tight after that, steady in her hand—scared somehow of hurting the woman, no matter how odd it was to think of a woman as a bell—and chose a direction to walk in. Voices whispered all around her, and what filled her ears and head tasted like music, a delightful mix of laughter and argument, lilting into a bustle that burst and billowed like bubbles, or birdsong. The queen—the woman—alone. Or not. There were things living in this place, in this entire world, that Lucy imagined she would never understand.

Twisting trees grew before her, and after a moment it seemed a path appeared, grass rimming its edges. Ahead, light. Lucy ran.

She pushed out of the forest into a sunlight that felt like holy fire, bright and hot and clean. She was not beside the pond any longer, but on the meadow across from the old house. She could see Barnabus in the distance, with an ax in his hands. Miss Lindsay and Henry were with him. Above her head, in the branches of the trees, crows began to shout. And after a moment, so did Henry.

The bell in her hand rattled. Lucy released the silver charm, unable to hold it. She instantly felt light-headed—had to close her eyes to keep her balance—and when she opened them, there was a woman on the ground.

Mary. Still in her wedding dress. Looking not one day older.

Again, Henry shouted. Lucy was not able to see the reunion. She staggered, eyes closing. Inside her head, voices, bells, a woman whispering. The dizziness was too much; her muscles melted.

She fell down and did not get up.

LUCY DREAMED. OF WOMEN AND MEN WHO TURNED into crows, and other creatures with burning gold in their eyes; of beings who grew tails like fish, and dragons that breathed fire; dark figures with green shining eyes, and the woman, the queen herself, with a similar gaze, effortlessly regal and unrelenting in her stare.

"Truce," said the woman, in Lucy's dream. "Never ask me why, but between us, a truce. For one who loves."

And Lucy woke up. She was in her bed. Miss Lindsay was seated beside her, as was Barnabus. There were shadows under his eyes, as though he had not slept in days. She wondered, fleetingly, if he might speak to her—if perhaps there were other gifts in her release—but when he picked up her hand and brought it to his mouth with that silent gentle strength, she knew instantly that was not the case.

"Henry?" Lucy breathed. "Mary?"

Miss Lindsay briefly shut her eyes. "Gone. Already gone. Henry wanted to stay to see you wake, but Mary . . ." She stopped, hesitating. "Mary wanted away from this place, immediately. She said to give you her thanks."

Miss Lindsay made the words sound flat, cheap. Barnabus looked unhappy. Lucy did not know what to think. She felt an aching loss for Henry. She wanted to see him, but thought of Mary, twenty years trapped, and knew why the woman had run—and that where she went, so would he. No choice. She was his home.

Miss Lindsay seemed to read her mind—she was good at that, Lucy mused wearily—and said, "For both of us, thank you. From the bottom of our hearts, thank you, always."

"It was her, not me," Lucy pointed out. "She gave us up."

Miss Lindsay looked sideways at Barnabus. "She does that, sometimes."

Lucy shifted, uncomfortable. "What is she?"

"I don't know," said Miss Lindsay. "She is old, though. Her kind always are. So old, they don't have children anymore. Not with each other, anyway."

."She's lonely."

"Tell Henry that."

Lucy held up her hand. "He and Mary have their time now.

Time to make their own way." Time to finish what they had started, if such a thing was possible. To have their honeymoon, their marriage, their life.

Miss Lindsay murmured, "Patience. I told Henry—both of them—to have patience. They've been through so much. Neither is the person the other married. Not anymore." She glanced away, bitterness touching her mouth. "Is it wrong to wonder whether I should be happy for them?"

Lucy closed her eyes, savoring the warmth of Barnabus's hand. "Did you ever marry?"

Silence, long and deep. Finally, Miss Lindsay said, "A woman like me rarely does."

Lucy opened her eyes and gave her a questioning look. The woman sighed. "I'll tell you some other time, perhaps."

Some other time, Lucy thought. *Like how you read minds? Or how sometimes you are a woman, and sometimes a crow?*

Miss Lindsay stared at her, startled, and then laughed out loud. "Yes," she said, still smiling. "Just like that."

But she never did. At least, not for a long while. One morning soon after, she approached Lucy and Barnabus as they were weeding the garden, and said, quite crisply, "I think I will go away for a time. There's a world beyond the wood, you know. I've been here my entire life, already."

"Yes," Lucy said, though she herself had no desire to go elsewhere. Barnabus put down his rake and regarded the older woman thoughtfully, with no small amount of compassion in his steady gaze. He nodded once, finally, and held out his arms. Miss Lindsay fell into them, hugging the young man so tightly, Lucy thought his bones might break. And then Miss Lindsay did the same for her, and she was quite certain that was indeed the case.

"Tend this place for me," whispered Miss Lindsay, her eyes

glowing golden as the sun. "For all of us. We'll be back. And we might bring others. There is so much in this world I have yet to explain to you."

And then, with no shyness or hesitation, she did a shocking thing—stripping off all her clothes, right in front of them, with hardly more than a smile. Golden light covered her body. Feathers black as jet, thick and rich and hot, poured up from her skin and rippled like water. Lucy could not help but gasp; her knees buckled. Barnabus caught her, and she glanced at his face. He did not appear at all surprised by what he was seeing, and there was an appreciation in his gaze that was from the heart.

He nudged Lucy, gestured for her to look again—and she found Miss Lindsay shrinking, narrowing—until she was no longer a woman, but a crow.

A crow who stared at them with golden eyes—cawed once—and leapt into the air, followed by a flock of companions that shrieked and beat their wings in raucous sympathy.

Quite a sight. But it was not the last time Lucy ever witnessed it.

Time passed. Lucy and Barnabus did as Miss Lindsay asked—maintaining the house and land, as well as the cemetery—though they married soon after to keep local tongues from wagging. She kept the name of her birth, since Barnabus had none to give. Lucy Steele. They called their son William, who also, on occasion, exhibited peculiar talents.

And sometimes Lucy would take a book and sit on the edge of the woods, and read out loud. She never knew if the woman, the *Sidhe* queen, was listening, but she liked to think that the trees were, and that through them the immortal could hear another voice, speaking just for her.

It was a good life for Lucy and Barnabus, a happy life. A life together, a grand adventure, and one that lasted many moons, over many secret stories—each as sweet and golden as honey.

MARJORIE M. LIU is an attorney who has lived and worked throughout Asia. She hails from both coasts, but currently resides in the Midwest, where she writes full-time. Her books include the New York Times—*bestselling* Dirk & Steele *series of paranormal romances for Leisure, and her forthcoming* Hunter Kiss *urban fantasies from Ace Books.*

You can discover more at her Web site: www.marjoriemliu.com.

Cat Got Your Tongue?

KATIE MACALISTER

Fans of the Dark Ones have long wondered what was up with Raphael St. John's amber eyes, and his skittishness around members of the Otherworld. Could there be more to him than was strictly human?

CHAPTER ONE

IT WASN'T UNTIL THE SEVENTEENTH CENTURY, THOUGH, THAT life at Fyfe Castle took a dark turn."

"It did?" I glanced around the room. It was pretty dark even though the sun hadn't yet set, shadows seemingly smudged into the vast gray stone walls of the castle. Narrow window slits reluctantly allowed thin rays of Scottish sunlight to shoulder their way into the passage, but provided less illumination than the somewhat tattered electric candles which had been screwed into the stone wall. "Darker than this, you mean?"

The woman leading the way paused to look over her shoulder,

her eyebrows raised. To be honest, I was encouraging her to talk just because her lilting Scottish accent sounded so delicious to my American ears. "Castle Fyfe has always had a dark and mysterious past. But when the seventh laird took ownership, all who lived here learned what fear truly was. He had a terrible temper, did Alec Summerton . . . Sir Alec he was then, later the earl of Seaton."

"That's the ghost you mentioned earlier?" I asked, waggling my eyebrows and tossing a lascivious grin to the man behind me.

Raphael rolled his eyes, and hoisted up the two suitcases, following as Fiona the castle hotelier started up the famed Fyfe staircase.

"Oh, no, the ghost isn't Sir Alec, although some say he does haunt the lower levels of the castle. Mind the ceiling just here, won't you, Mr. St. John? It's been the bane of many a tall man such as yourself. No, it isn't Sir Alec who is the best known ghost here, Mrs. St. John—it's his wife, Lily Summerton."

Raphael ducked to avoid a low beam as we marched up the stone staircase. Although I wasn't as tall as he was, at roughly six feet in height, even I had to bob my head to get through without braining myself. "Don't tell me—she's the Gray Lady?"

"Green, not gray," Fiona answered with a roll of her *r*'s. She paused and gestured vaguely around. "This staircase was built in the early seventeen hundreds, in case you were wondering. It's known throughout Scotland as the finest example of its kind."

"I can see why." I waited until she continued up the stairs before waggling my eyebrows again at my husband. It had been a long train ride up to Scotland, and I was anxious to get to our room. "So, this ghost haunts the room we're staying in? Does she do anything in particular, or just float around and wring her hands while moaning about her lost love?"

"On the contrary—she says nothing, just appears briefly before people, gives them a searching glance, then sighs sadly, as if disappointed, and disappears into nothing."

"Sounds like a typical moody woman," Raphael muttered.

"Hush, male of the species. This is all very fascinating," I said, hoping Fiona would continue.

"Here's your suite." She threw open a modern-looking wooden door and escorted us into a bright room. "This was the laird's private suite. The later lairds, that is. It used to be Lily Summerton's room, in fact. The original laird's room was on the floor below it, but later lairds had their room moved up here after Sir Alec died. When the last Lord Seaton bequeathed the castle to the National Trust, it was decided to make his rooms available to the public. You'll have all the privacy you want, since these are the only rooms we let. The caretaker will be here, though, in case of emergency. His office is just off the tearoom, on the ground floor. The toilet is through that door. This is the sitting room, and to the right is the bedroom. I'll just make sure everything is proper. . . ."

"Wow," I said, wide-eyed as I took in the heady scent of beeswax and antiques. The room was furnished as if the owner of a hundred years past had just stepped out of the room, with a few discreet nods to technology.

"Very nice," Raphael said, setting down the suitcases. "Worthy of a honeymoon?"

"Oh, yes. You think this stuff is real?" I asked in a low voice as I ran my fingers along the back of a rosewood settee upholstered in blue-and-green crushed velvet.

"At the prices they're charging? They'd better be."

"Good thing we decided to leave the kidlet with Roxy, then. I'd hate to see what Zoe could do to this lovely room. Maybe I should just call to check—"

Raphael stopped me before I could pull my cell phone from my purse. "You called half an hour ago, Joy. I can't imagine that even Zoe could get into trouble that quickly."

I raised an eyebrow.

His lips curved in a rueful smile. "Well, all right, I can imagine it, but I'm sure Roxy has her well bribed with all sorts of sweets and promises of visits to the zoo for her to be behaving badly."

"I suppose," I said slowly, quelling maternal worry.

"You're acting more like a worried mum than a blushing bride," my husband said.

"That's because I've been a mother for two years and a bride for less than a day. I know, I know, it's just separation anxiety, and it's perfectly normal. I've already had the lecture from Roxy, Bob. You don't need to fire one up as well."

"Bob?" Fiona emerged from the bedroom, frowning as she glanced at a card in her hand. "Has there been a mistake somewhere? I had you down as Mr. and Mrs. Raphael St. John, here for a honeymoon visit of a week. Is that not right?"

"Yes, it's right," I said, laughing a little as I grabbed my suitcase and took it into the bedroom. I whistled at the sight of the giant four-poster bed, determined to put my worry behind me.

"Bob is a nickname," Raphael told her. "Joy's a bit rattled because it's our first time away from our daughter. She's just two years old."

Fiona tsked and bustled around the room, chattering about children before pausing next to a large double-glazed window. "You asked about the Green Lady, Mrs. St. John. It is indeed here she makes her appearance . . . but not in the room, you understand. It's there, just outside the window, that her tortured face can be seen, as if judging those within the room."

"Oooh! Bob, a tortured ghost!"

Raphael gave me a long-suffering look.

"Do you not believe in ghosts, then, Mr. St. John?" Fiona asked, her voice kind as she patted him on the arm. "Don't be ashamed if you're not a believer. It's the way with many men, I know."

Raphael had difficulty in keeping his expression pleasant. Despite our experiences to the contrary, he clung desperately to the belief that the world had gone temporarily insane, and any minute now life as he previously knew it would regain the upper hand, allowing him to forget that things like ghosties and ghoulies really existed.

"My husband is a bit of a skeptic," I said, taking pity on him. "But I'm dying to know about this tortured ghost. What happened to her? Was she married? Is she one of those bride ghosts who appear to newly married women? I wonder if she'll show up for me, even though Raphael and I have been together for three years."

"About that, I cannot say. But this I can tell you—for a time, Lily and Sir Alec were happy, but she gave him a daughter rather than a son, and it wasn't long before he was casting his eye elsewhere."

"The dog!" I said, sitting on the edge of the bed as Raphael gave me another long-suffering look. He took out his shaving bag and disappeared into the bathroom. "What happened to her?"

"Well, it wasn't long after the birth of her daughter that Lily mysteriously disappeared. Sir Alec gave out that she'd gone to the seaside to recover, but no one believed such a tale. They heard the cries in the night, you see. They heard her sobbing and begging for help, and they knew what had happened."

"Walled up alive?" I asked, a prickle of goose bumps making me rub my arms.

"Like as not. He'd shut her up in the upper room of the black tower—it's gone now, but it stood in the northwest corner of the castle. No one was allowed near it, and Sir Alec claimed Lady Lily took the keys with her, and sealed the only entrance. For two weeks the servants in the castle heard her cries and pleas. For two weeks, she lived, but at last the devil had his way, and she fell silent."

"Oh my god! How horrible! He really was a nasty customer. What an evil thing to do to someone."

"It was indeed. Sometime during the night after she died, he spirited her body away, announcing a fortnight later that she'd drowned herself in the sea. And what did he do then but wed Grizel Adams, a widow from the village he'd been consorting with."

"Callous, murdering bastard," I muttered.

"That he was. On their wedding night, Sir Alec and his new bride lay together in Lily's bed. But they didn't get any sleep."

"Randy little bugger, was he?"

Fiona shook her head. "No, it wasn't the wedding night activities which kept them up—all night the two of them heard horrible scratching sounds, but though Sir Alec had all the lamps lit, nothing could be seen in the room. In the morning though . . ." She smiled.

"What?" I asked, thoroughly engrossed in the story.

"Do you see that window?" she asked, nodding toward it.

"Yeah." I got up and walked over to it. "Lily appeared outside it? She was scratching on the glass?"

"No. Open it up and tell me what you see."

Another little shiver of goose bumps rippled down my flesh as I opened the window and looked down. We were on the third floor of the castle, smack dab in the middle of the wall. "Well, it's a nasty drop. I can't imagine there's any way someone could get up here—there's no ledge, and the closest pipe is about fifteen feet away. Is that what you wanted me to see?"

"Look at the casement."

I squinted at the cream-colored stone. Someone had carved something just beyond the glass. It was upside down and somewhat blurred with age, but the words LILY SUMMERTON were chipped neatly into the casement. "Oh, wow. She carved her name?"

"That she did. And if you can tell me how anyone could do that in this spot, well, I'd certainly like to know."

I looked around the outer edge of the castle wall. Without some sort of a ladder or scaffolding, such a thing would be impossible.

"Very creepy."

"The Green Lady had her revenge, some said," Fiona continued, a prim set to her mouth. "For it was not but a month after Sir Alec married the widow Grizel that they both died when their carriage overturned. Snapped their necks, they did."

"How tragic. Makes you wonder, though, doesn't it?"

"Are you done with your ghost talk?" Raphael asked as he reentered the room.

"Yeah, but you should have stayed to hear it. It's really interesting," I said, giving the carved name one last look before closing the window.

"I'm sure I'll survive. Is it possible to have breakfast in our rooms rather than the restaurant?" he asked Fiona.

"Yes, but your food is bound to be cold by the time it's brought all the way up here," she answered.

He grinned and took the room key from her, herding her toward the door. "We'll survive."

Fiona melted before his grin, and although clearly desirous of telling us more about the castle's history, confined herself to wishing us a pleasant evening. In less time than it took to say the word "honeymoon," Raphael dashed across the room, stripped off his clothes, and pounced on me.

"At last, we are alone," he said with an atrocious French accent.

I blinked up at him a couple of times.

He kissed the tip of my nose, and cocked one eyebrow. "The accent too much for you, sweetheart? You look somewhat stunned."

"Yes, it was awful, and besides, I think your English accent is the sexiest thing on earth. But it's not that. . . ." Loath as I was to pry myself from his arms, I did just that to sit up and look from him to the entrance to the suite. "How did you do that?"

"Do what?" he asked, pulling me back so he could nibble on my neck.

I shivered at the touch, thought about dismissing my confusion, but decided there were more pressing issues. "Bob, you know just how much I've been looking forward to this honeymoon—"

"Oh, yes. I believe the fact that you almost ravished me on the train coming up here brought that to my attention. And you will notice that whereas I objected to our enacting upon our wedding night in the coach of the Edinburgh Express, I am now agreeable to the whole idea, and you may commence with your planned ravishing of my manly self."

"Mmm hmm," I said, squinting at the door to the suite as I judged its distance.

Raphael's face suddenly filled my vision. His lovely amber eyes were narrowed with suspicion. "You are not ravishing me. You've talked of nothing for the last four hours. Why are you not ravishing me? Is it Zoe? Are you still worried—"

"No, it's not the baby. It's . . . well . . . how did you run from the door to the suite all the way in the other room, to here, without me seeing you move? Not to mention taking off your clothes while you were doing it."

Raphael turned to consider the door at which I was pointing. "What are you talking about?"

"I didn't see you move. One minute you were there, smiling your very best smile for Fiona and making her go all swoony, and the next minute you were naked and pouncing on me. I didn't see you move in between the two actions."

"You were just too busy ogling my chest and imagining the many and varied things you'd like to do to me. With whipped cream."

"Do we have any whipped cream?" I asked, distracted for a moment.

He shook his head. "But I'll get some if you want it."

"Well . . ." I didn't have an opportunity to say more. Once again I seemed to be suffering from an odd sort of time loss. As the word left my lips, he was looming over me, his eyes alight with a familiar albeit exciting glint; half a second later the door to the suite slammed shut, his discarded clothes having vanished somewhere along the way.

"Bob? I didn't mean right now. . . . Oh, hell. Honest to Pete, men! Sometimes they're just . . . just . . ."

"Treacherous? Vile? Whoremongering? No, I have it— murderous, evil bastards who deserve to spend eternity in pox-riddled, pustule-filled, eternal, endless torment!" a voice said from the window.

I fell off the bed spinning around to look behind me.

"Oh, dear, did I startle you? I'm so sorry. I just thought I'd take the opportunity while that male is out of the way." A woman, dressed in period Elizabethan garb complete with green-and-gold-patterned flat-fronted corset, long row of beads, and tiny neck ruff, strode forward and grabbed my hand, hauling me to my feet. "So sorry. Not hurt? Excellent. I'm Lily Summerton. I'm so very glad to see you! You have no idea how long I've waited for someone to help me."

"Lily . . . Summerton?" I asked, gazing with openmouthed astonishment. "You're . . . you're . . ."

"The fabled Green Lady of Fyfe Castle, yes," she said, preening just a little as she patted her hair.

"I see. Hello. I'm Joy Randall . . . er . . . Joy St. John. You're . . . a ghost?"

"Yes, of course! I couldn't very well be the Green Lady if I wasn't one, now could I?"

"I suppose not."

"And you're a Beloved."

"Well, kind of. Not really. That is, I am and I'm not," I said hurriedly. "We don't actually mention the whole Beloved thing very much."

"You don't?"

"My husband gets a little bit testy when he's reminded that I was born to be the soul mate of someone else, especially when that someone is a vampire, although why he gets quite so upset is beyond me. Everything worked out wonderfully. I think it's just a territorial male thing, to be honest," I said, giving her a little smile.

She pursed her lips for a moment, looked like she was going to ask a question, then shook her head. "Where *is* your Dark One? That male who was just here certainly isn't he—everyone knows therians can't be Dark Ones—and I desperately need the latter. Could you summon him, please?"

"Er . . ." I glanced toward the door and wondered if I yelled loudly enough, if Raphael would hear me before he left the castle.

"Oh, it won't take long, I assure you," she said with a kind pat of my hands. "A half an hour at most, I promise, and then you can get back to your man. Surely you can see your way clear to helping me?"

"I'm not quite sure what it is you want me to do," I said slowly, edging toward the door.

"Oh, didn't I mention that? My memory has been shocking the last few hundred years. It's quite simple, really," she said with a bright smile. "I'd like you to curse my husband to eternal torment. I won't be able to rest until you do so."

CHAPTER TWO

SORRY, SWEETHEART—NO WHIPPED CREAM. THE GIFT SHOP was just closing up, but I did manage to get this before the girl left." Raphael held up a jar of clotted cream. "I know it's not the same, but perhaps you can imagine it's whipped cream. Erm . . . why are you still dressed? Why aren't you waiting for me naked and warm, in bed? And why are you wearing an expression of a woman who is annoyed, rather than one who is about to be pleasured from the top of her adorable head to the tips of her delectable toes?"

"—very nice, although to give the bastard credit, Alec was ahead of time so far as having a privy indoors. He had one in his bedchamber, which admittedly wasn't terribly pleasant on warm summer days, but as I spent so little time in his room . . . Oh. The male is back." Lily emerged from the bathroom, where she had been admiring the plumbing. She turned a cold, hard face to Raphael, her eyes narrowing for a moment. "Have we met? No, that's silly, we couldn't have. Still, you look somewhat familiar. . . ."

"Who the hell is this?" he asked, waving the jar of clotted cream toward her. He checked, and added, "*What* the hell is this?"

"I could swear . . ." She shook her head at herself. "My imagination has been running wild of late. My name is Lily Summerton. You may refer to me as Lady Summerton. This, I take it, is your mortal husband?"

"Lily Summerton?" Raphael repeated, suspicion rife in his voice. "A . . . a . . ."

"A ghost, yes, I'm afraid she is." I slid off the bed and twined my fingers through his.

"Oh, hell, this is Christian's doing, isn't it?" he demanded.

"Is Christian your Dark One?" Lily asked me, ignoring Raphael.

"He's not her Dark One. He's got a perfectly good wife of his own! Who's going to be a widow if he doesn't keep his paws to himself—"

"Bob, calm down. Christian didn't set this up. It's just coincidence that we found a castle that was really and truly haunted."

He turned to me, his eyes a bit wild looking. "You know how I feel about all this sort of thing."

"I know," I said, squeezing his fingers again. "You don't like vampires or ghosts or anything of that ilk. But it seems that Lily has a task that must be performed before she can rest, and she's picked us to do it."

"No," he said, his expression darkening. "This is our honeymoon. We're not going to get involved with any more of your crackpot woo-woo friends."

"Crackpot!" Lily gasped.

"Sweetie, I don't think we have much of a choice," I said, pulling Raphael aside.

He glared at Lily. She glared right back at him, her arms crossed over her chest.

"We certainly do. We'll ring up Allie and have her do whatever it is she does to ghosts to get rid of them. I'll be damned if I let anyone ruin our honeymoon."

"She said she will haunt us if we don't help," I whispered, sending Lily what I hoped was a confident smile. "She said if we don't take care of a little situation concerning her mortal life, she won't give us a moment's peace."

"We'll leave, then," Raphael said loudly, hitching up his glare a notch or two. "We'll find somewhere else to stay."

"I'll find you," Lily answered unconcernedly as she examined her fingernails. "You can't hide from me, you know. No matter where you go, I'll find you. If you won't give me the peace I desire, then so shall you have none."

"Why us?" Raphael roared, seeing, as I knew he would, the inevitability of the situation.

"Your wife is a Beloved. She's the first one to come to Fyfe Castle who had the ability to help me. Now, if you're done wasting time, perhaps we can get under way?" She evidently saw the objection Raphael was about to make because she added quickly, "I have told your wife it will take only a half hour to do my bidding, after which I will happily leave you in peace."

Raphael grumbled a few things to himself, but both Lily and I thought it was best to ignore them.

"We would be happy to help you, but I'm afraid a cursing is out of the question. Not only am I opposed to cursing someone I don't know, but even if I wanted to, I wouldn't know how to go about doing it," I said.

Lily's gaze rested on Raphael for a moment. "A curse can be cast only by someone of dark origins. Most people use demons, but Dark Ones are an acceptable substitute, since they themselves are more or less cursed. Your man seems to get upset when I mention your Dark One. Why is that?"

"It's a long story, but basically, somewhere some wires were crossed because I was born a Beloved to a very nice man named Christian, but Raphael was the man I was meant to end up with." I gave Raphael a kiss on the chin.

His eyes flashed for a moment, before they narrowed again on Lily. "Not to mention the fact that Christian found a woman who wasn't born his Beloved, but she turned out to fill that role, so Joy has nothing whatsoever to do with him."

"Well, how are you going to curse Alec if you don't have a Dark One?" Lily asked, her hands fluttering in an agitated manner. "I must have reparation! I will never find my peace without it!"

"I'm sorry, but a curse is out," I said, feeling bad that we couldn't help the distraught ghost.

"So you might as well just run along and let us enjoy our honeymoon," Raphael said with an absolute dearth of tact.

"Bob!"

"What?"

I nodded toward Lily, who was now pacing back and forth, muttering to herself. "We have to help her."

"Says who?"

"Says me! We were clearly meant to help her. She said herself that we were the only ones who could do it."

Raphael grumbled again.

I put a hand on his sleeve and batted my lashes at him. "I couldn't possibly relax enough to enjoy clotted cream knowing there was a ghost around whom it was in my power to help."

His lips thinned. "You don't play fair, do you?"

"Never have, sweetie."

"Very well." He heaved a heavy sigh and turned back to face Lily. "Right. The cursing aside, what is it you want us to do?"

"He must be destroyed. That is the only way I can have rest," Lily insisted as she continued to pace. "But how to do it, that is the problem. Oh!"

"That sounds hopeful. You thought of something?" I asked.

"I'm a lackwit," she said, slapping her forehead. "I can't believe I didn't think of this first, but it's better, so much better than just a cursing!"

"Oh?" I asked, suddenly wary. "If it's anything involving a demon—"

"No, no, I've given up on the curse idea. I have a much better one! You will destroy the stone!"

"The stone? What stone?" Raphael asked.

She stopped pacing to face us, an earnest expression on her face. "There were three stones bound to Fyfe Castle: the castle stone, representing the castle itself. That was placed into the wall of the foundation, so it will not be destroyed unless the castle is razed. The second was the lady's stone, which signified the lady of the castle. That stone Alec says was lost, but I'm not sure he didn't destroy it himself—he certainly wasn't above such an act to ensure that the women of Fyfe have naught but ill luck. The third stone, the laird's stone, is in the Stone Room. *That* is what you must do."

"Er . . . what, exactly?" I asked, confused.

"Destroy the stone, naturally!" she answered, rubbing her hands together with much pleasure. "It's only fitting! Just as Alec destroyed the lady's stone, thereby damning all ladies of the family, so now must you destroy the laird's stone. It will affect not only Alec, but all his descendants as well—a just punishment, don't you think, for a man who killed his own wife for bearing him a daughter?"

"To be honest, I don't think that's very fair," I said slowly, and to my surprise, Raphael interrupted me.

"We'll do it. Where's this laird's stone kept?"

Lily shrugged. "That I do not know. Alec would never tell me the location of the Stone Room. There was some curse on the men to keep them away from it. . . . You'll have to ask him for that information."

"But—," I started to protest.

Raphael clamped a hand over my mouth, and hustled me out of the room before I could say anything.

"Don't let Alec bully you!" Lily called from the bedroom. "Be firm with him!"

"Why all of a sudden are you so hot and bothered to help her?" I asked a moment later as we hurried down the hall.

"It's like you said—the sooner we help her, the sooner she'll go away and leave us alone to enjoy our clotted creamapalooza. Where did she say we'd find her husband?"

"The long gallery, which is evidently on the ground floor, or the stable yard, or possibly the dining hall. But sweetie, we can't destroy the laird's stone, not if it will affect a bunch of innocent people!"

"Who says it will?" Raphael flashed a quick grin. "Fiona said the family line had died out, so there won't be any descendants to harm, in addition to which, I don't believe at all that a stone has anything to do with people's health and happiness. So we'll just find this stone, drop it into the moat, tell her the job is done, and our way will be clear to enjoying our honeymoon."

"I don't know. I don't think it's going to be a good idea to mess with something so historic," I said.

"You worry too much. Everyone concerned is dead already, aren't they? It's not like there's anything we can do to hurt them now."

I held my tongue, but I wasn't so sure on that subject. Allie, a woman who had made her living summoning and releasing ghosts before she met Christian the sexy vampire, had told me that ghosts could be bound to a spot, but since Lily and assumedly her husband were already stuck at the castle, it didn't seem like breaking a stone would change their status.

"I don't see why she couldn't come with us to find him," Raphael muttered as we hurried down the pinwheel stone staircase.

"She said she doesn't go down where her husband roams. I can't say I blame her, given what he did to her. Have you ever heard of the word 'therian'? As applied toward a person, that is?"

"Therian?" Raphael thought for a moment before shaking his head. "It's Greek for 'wild animal.' I can't imagine it being applied to a person—good Lord!"

A woman's scream rent the night, coming from the floor below us. Raphael dropped my hand and dashed down the stairs. I hurried after him, slipped on the highly polished wooden floor, and ended up falling against him where he stood in the middle of a long hallway, his hands on his hips. Despite the fact that my mother describes me as being built like a brick house, Raphael didn't budge when I slammed into him.

"Who is it?" I asked, collecting myself enough to peer around him.

His indignant snort told me everything I needed to know. A moment later, a woman's scream echoed down the long passage, but this time, it was followed by feminine giggles and, "Stop it! Ye're goin' to make me wet myself if ye keep ticklin' me that way! Alec, stop! Nay, ye mustn't!"

Although the hallway was lit with night-lights at either end, there was sufficient illumination from outside to highlight the two nearly translucent figures that came down the hallway toward us. In the lead was a woman with her skirts hitched up and breasts almost wholly out of her corset, her hair tousled halfway out of her French hood, and bare legs flashing as she barreled down on us. In close pursuit was a bearded man clad in a flapping linen shirt and pair of breeches. "Run from me, will ye, ye lusty vixen? Ye'll not be escapin' me that easily!"

The look on Raphael's face was not welcoming, but it was no cause for the woman racing toward us to shriek loud enough to wake the dead. So to speak.

"Lord bless me!" she gasped as she caught sight of us. She came to an immediate stop, her hands on her cheeks for a moment before squeaking and hurriedly rearranging her breasts back into her corset. "Hsst! Alec! We're havin' visitors!"

"Aye, I see them." The ghost who was evidently Lily's husband cleared his throat, puffed out his chest, and strode toward us in a haughty manner. "I am Lord Summerton. By what right do you come to my home and stare at my wife?"

"I have my own wife to ogle, thank you," Raphael said stiffly. "Perhaps if you kept yours confined rather than let her run the hallways half-naked—"

Sir Alec had been in a stretch of shadow, but as he stopped in front of us, he was lit by both the outside light shining through the window, and the slightly orange glow of a security night-light.

My jaw dropped as I got a good look at Sir Alec. "Holy Moses! Raphael, do you see that?"

"By the saints!" Sir Alec said at the same time, his eyes wide as he stared at Raphael.

"Ooh," breathed the disheveled woman. She looked from one man to the other. " 'Tis like seein' twins!"

"My boy!" Sir Alec shouted, enveloping Raphael in a bear hug.

CHAPTER THREE

ERM . . ." RAPHAEL WAS OBVIOUSLY TOO DISCONCERTED BY THE fact that he was being hugged by an Elizabethan ghost to rally much along conversational lines. "Do I know you?"

"Ye're the very image of me when I was a lad," Sir Alec answered. "Ye can be no other but the spawn of my loins!"

"Didn't you say you had Scottish ancestry?" I asked Raphael as I continued to marvel at the ghost. He had a beard, but it was close-cropped enough to make out the shape of his jaw. He had the same stubborn chin as Raphael, the same strong jaw, wide brow, and brown curly hair. Even their eyes were the same, a tawny amber that I knew could glow with molten heat, or glitter with cold intent.

"Yes, but way back. My mother's family. They weren't named Summerton, though."

"Ye've the look of me! Of course ye're my kin!" Sir Alec crowed, giving Raphael another hug. "Grizel, 'tis one of my descendants, come back to the ancestral home!"

"How d'ye do," the woman answered, bobbing a little curtsy at us. "Pleasure to meet ye."

"You, I take it, are Sir Alec's second wife?" I asked. Grizel nodded, a faint blush visible on her cheeks despite the dim light and her transparency. I eyed her curiously, expecting to see a much harsher woman, the type who wouldn't mind coming between a man and his wife. But this woman was fresh-faced, bearing an air of innocence that made me wonder if Lily had told me every-thing.

"This lovely is Grizel, the light of my heart," Sir Alec said proudly, wrapping his arm around her and hauling her up to his side. "She's not related to ye, though, more's the pity. I only had one brat, and she was off the she-witch who was my first wife."

His expression turned sour as he spoke. Grizel elbowed him, whispering, " 'Tis not fittin' to speak ill of the dead, husband."

Sir Alec suddenly grinned, making my knees wobble for a moment, so similar a sight was it. "That'd be us as well, ye daft hen!"

"Oh, aye," she giggled. "I'm ever forgettin' that."

"She's soft on the eye, but a bit light in the head," Sir Alec said fondly, giving his wife a squeeze to take the sting out of the comment. "Now then, ye'll be wantin' to have a tour of the castle, won't ye? I'll be happy to show it all to ye . . . all but the Stone Room."

"Oh?" Raphael and I exchanged glances. I cleared my throat. "Er . . . why not the Stone Room?"

Sir Alec shot me a sharp look. "The laird's stone is there. The stone was cursed centuries ago, and so long as it's kept in peace, so will be the happiness of the men of Fyfe."

"But we're not from Fyfe," I argued.

"He's the spittin' image of me!" Alec said, nodding toward Raphael. "I cannot allow him into the Stone Room. 'Twould be a great danger."

"How so?" I asked as we started down the hall.

" 'Tis the curse, lass. *The Thane of Fyfe shadowed be, thrice around the stone bound; in its light, the devil can see, and the beast within be found.*"

"What does that mean?" Raphael asked, frowning as he tried to puzzle it out.

"Any man of Fyfe who sets his hands upon the stone will be forever changed," Alec answered with a meaningful look.

"Oh? What about the women?" I asked.

He shrugged. "Only the lady's stone affects them, and even if the laird's stone would, they don't know where the Stone Room is. It's a secret room, ye ken, its location told only to the ruling master of Fyfe and his heir."

"I know where it is," Grizel said suddenly.

"Ye're daft woman. Ye don't."

"I do," she insisted. "I saw you go into it from the privy not long after we were wed. You counted five stones up from the floor, five stones over from the door, and five stones in from the corner. The back wall of the privy swung open, and you disappeared into it. I was going to tease you about it when you came back out, but that was last I saw of you until . . ."

Grizel's smile faded as she looked away, her fingers fretting the material of her skirt.

" 'Tis all right, lass. We died together, and we'll stay together for all eternity," Sir Alec said, his voice gruff as he comforted his wife.

Raphael exchanged another glance with me. I could see he was as hesitant as I was about the whole thing. "I think we'll take a rain check on the tour of the castle, if you don't mind," I told the two ghosts.

Sir Alec looked crestfallen until Raphael told him we were on our honeymoon.

"Oh, then ye'll be wantin' a bit of privacy," he said with a wink. "Grizel and I are still on ours, as well. It's goin' on for five hundred years now, but she's still as saucy as a minx! Ye go and have a wee cuddle with yer wife, and I'll be doin' the same. Come here, ye redheaded Eve!"

"Ye'll naught catch me until I say ye can!" Grizel squealed and leaped away, racing down the hall into the shadows, a grinning Sir Alec in pursuit.

I looked at Raphael. "Are you thinking what I'm thinking?"

"Probably. Where did Fiona say the old laird's quarters were?"

"Somewhere on this floor. I'd guess below our rooms. But Raphael . . ." I bit my lip, hesitant to put into words a worry that had nagged me ever since I'd spoken with Lily.

"You don't want to destroy the stone," Raphael said, trying the door to one of the rooms. It was locked. He moved on to the next one. "I figured you wouldn't."

"No, it's not that. That is, yes, that's part of it—Fiona may have said that there was no family living, but they obviously missed your side of the family."

He shook his head and tried another door. "I told you—my Scottish ancestry is quite small, a great-times-ten grandmother, or something like that. Even if she was someone related to Sir Alec, by now the ancestry has been diluted with good old English stock."

"Sweetie, you look just like him," I said, pointing out the obvious. "No wonder Lady Lily thought she recognized you. I wish she'd told us it was her husband you resembled, but I guess if she hadn't seen him in several hundred years, she probably forgot just what he looked like."

"It doesn't matter. This situation is due to genetic coincidence, nothing more. Ah, this one is open." He stuck his head into a room, reaching around for a light switch. Dim light flooded a room empty of all furniture, but containing several boxes of what appeared to be dry goods for the restaurant located on the main floor. "This looks promising. Where would the privy be, do you think?"

"Lily said there was one connected to the bedroom. You aren't seriously thinking of destroying the stone, are you? I know we told Lily we were going to, but that's before we met Alec and Grizel. He doesn't seem at all like the sort of person to cold-bloodedly murder his wife. Not to mention I'm more than a little bit concerned about what destroying it might do to you."

"I'll be perfectly safe, sweetheart. Do you see anything that looks like a privy?"

With much foreboding, I pointed toward a small alcove off the main room. As privy's went, this one was fairly small, more a tiny little closet with a long open shaft in the center of the floor. A board had been laid across it for safety purposes, which Raphael skirted as he squatted next to the back of the stone wall. "Five up, five in, five over," he murmured to himself as he tapped on stones. One of them made a dullish sound, which turned into a low rumble when he put all his weight into pressing on it. "*Et voilà!* Your secret passage, milady."

The air that swirled out of the passage around us didn't smell foul or unclean, but my nerves were still all on end. "I doubt there are lights down there."

"Stay here," Raphael ordered as he got to his feet. "I'll get a torch from the car."

I used the time it took him to run down to the car and back to form plausible arguments why he shouldn't go into the passage, but they fell on deaf ears.

"I'll be fine," he said firmly, giving me a pat on the behind as he shoved one of the boxes from the main room into the doorway to keep it open. He switched on a powerful flashlight, the light showing dark stone steps eerily leading down to inky blackness.

"I don't suppose you'd consider letting me go first?"

The look he gave me spoke volumes.

"All right, but don't say I didn't warn you when this curse or whatever it is bites you on the butt."

"You're the only one I allow to do that," he said with a leer before doubling over to get through the four-foot-high doorway. "Besides, I don't believe in centuries-old curses."

I grabbed the back of his shirt and followed. "You believe in vampires."

"I would prefer not to."

"And ghosts."

"Again, not by choice."

"And werewolves and imps and all other sorts of things we've seen."

An indignant snort was my answer to that. "I may be forced to believe in vampires and ghosts, but that doesn't mean I buy into every supernatural idea out there. People do not turn into wolves, Joy. It's physically impossible."

"Uh huh. Watch your—ow. Sorry."

Raphael rubbed his forehead where it had hit a low over-hanging stone. The staircase we were on was a miniature version of the grand staircase, a narrow stone spiral that seemed to go on forever. "I think this is the bottom," Raphael said as he moved a few steps forward. The light pooled around an iron-banded wooden door.

"Bob, wait," I said, grabbing his arm as he was about to open the door. "We can't just up and destroy the stone and Sir Alec. It's cruel."

"Cruel? Didn't he starve his wife to death?"

"Yes, but . . . well, after meeting him, I'm not too sure about that. I think we should talk to Lily again. Maybe things weren't quite as she remembered."

His lips were warm on mine as he gave me a swift kiss. "Let's take a look at this famed laird's stone. If it's small enough to move, perhaps we can just hide the thing, and tell Lily it's gone."

"I don't see what good that will do, but it's better than nothing," I grumbled.

He laughed and slid back a solid slab of wood which barred the door, swinging it open. It had suitably creepy squeaking hinges, but nothing rushed out of the room at us when Raphael shone his light inside.

"Rats?" I asked, peering over his shoulder.

"Not that I can see. It's just a small empty room."

And so it was. There was a slight musty odor, but as Raphael said, it was a small empty stone chamber.

Empty except for a plinth, upon which sat a greeny-gray chunk of stone approximately the size and shape of a large wheel of cheese.

"That's gotta be it," I said, eyeing the stone carefully as Raphael shone the line around it.

"I'd say so. Hold this while I see how heavy it is."

"Sweetie—," I started to say, but my words stopped as Raphael reached out to grab the stone. A blinding flash of light startled me into screaming and dropping the flashlight, which promptly went out. I scrabbled around on the floor until I found it again, quickly switching it on. "Oh, my God, what was that? Are you all right?"

I shone the light to where Raphael had been standing, my jaw dropping as I blinked in absolute stupefaction at the thing that stood in his place.

A lion, golden, tawny-eyed, complete with mane, fuzzy ears, and an almost comical expression of utter disbelief, stared back at me.

CHAPTER FOUR

OH MY GOD," I SAID, MY SKIN CRAWLING as I reached out to touch the tip of the lion's nose. His eyes crossed as he followed the movement of my hand. "Oh my God! I knew it! I knew something like this would happen if you tried to destroy the stone! OH MY GOD! You're a *werewolf*!"

The Raphael lion rolled its familiar amber eyes and opened its mouth as if it would speak. All that came out was a guttural grunt.

"All right, then, you're a werelion! Same difference, Bob! Oh, my God, what are we going to do?"

Frustration filled Raphael's feline eyes as he made the same guttural noise a couple more times.

"Don't swear, sweetie. We'll figure something out," I said, patting him on the top of his furry head. "That's what that *beast within* bit from that curse must have meant. That's all fine and well, but I am *not* going to spend my honeymoon with an animal. Let's go find Sir Alec and see what he has to say about this. It's his stone, maybe he knows of a way to break this transformation."

Raphael didn't object when I hefted the stone and marched toward the stairs, although he did give the back of my hand a swift lick with his bristly tongue.

By the time we made our way back to the first-floor hallway where Sir Alec and Grizel had been romping, it was obvious that a shouting match was going on.

"How dare you! I'll go anywhere in this castle that I please, and you cannot stop me!"

"Ye're confined to the upstairs. Grizel and I have the lower floors. That's how it's always been, and that's how it'll ever be!" Sir Alec roared.

Lily didn't appear to be threatened despite the fact she was staring her murderer in the face. "I came down to see that you don't harm that dear Beloved and the one who I see now is some relation of yours, the poor man. And don't you threaten me, you murderous whoreson! You were a horrible husband when you were alive, and you're a worse one now that you're dead! Running around the castle flaunting your trollop in that manner. Have you no shame? No sense of dignity?"

"Now there's a pot callin' the kettle black," Sir Alec yelled. "Ye had yer skirts up for any man who caught yer eye!"

Lily gasped. "Oh! I did not!"

Sir Alec leaned forward, all three of them so obviously focused on the argument they didn't notice our approach. "I've three words to say to that: Sir Roderick Langton."

Lily opened her mouth to protest, but quickly snapped her teeth closed.

"Aye, I thought that would shut ye up," Sir Alec answered with satisfaction. "Ye can't be throwing out accusations about Grizel and me when ye were up to the very same thing with that pasty-faced bastard."

"Roddy wasn't a bastard! He loved me! He wanted to take me away from your cruelties!"

"Cruelties!" snorted Sir Alec.

"I'm sorry to interrupt, but there's a situation I'm going to need your help with," I said, plopping the stone down onto the nearest table.

"Just a minute, lass," Sir Alec told me without glancing our way. "I've taken enough from this she-devil. It's time she face the truth rather than the pack of lies she preferred to believe. Was it cruelty, then, to give ye everything ye wanted? Ye had the finest cloth, jewels, the best of my bloodstock—"

"Trivial things," Lily yelled, waving her hands. "You thought to buy my affections with your gold! I saw through that in an instant, though. I knew what sort of man you were—a murderer, a thief who would steal his own wife's jewels to give to another. *You* drove me to Roddy's arms! You and your damned harlot!"

"I realize that this is a heated subject, but I really do have an emergency on my hands here, and I'd appreciate a little help," I said, but the three ghosts ignored me.

"Ye'll not be talking about my Grizel that way!" Sir Alec shouted back at Lily. "She's worth a whole castle full of the likes of ye, not that ye'd know how a proper wife behaved, lockin' yerself away in the tower as ye did for months on end! And as for yer precious jewels—ye'll be needing to talk to Sir Roderick about them."

Lily gasped again, her eyes blazing. "How dare you impugn his name! He was a saint! A god among men! You were not fit to lick his boots!"

Despite the urgency of the situation with Raphael, I was oddly drawn into the argument. "Wait a sec—did you just say that *Lily* locked herself into the tower? I thought . . . er . . . well, I thought you did that because she had a daughter instead of a son?"

Lily lifted her chin and looked away. Sir Alec shot his first wife a nasty look. "Oh, aye, that's what she wanted everyone to think. But the truth is different from legend, isn't it, Lily? Go on and tell this lass how ye locked yerself in the tower in a fit of temper. Tell her how ye had that ball-less whoreson bringin' ye food and wine on the sly, while ye let everyone think ye were up there starvin'. Ye tell her that, and I'll tell her how Sir Roderick disappeared once he finally got his hands on yer jewels and gold, and how yer own stubbornness kept ye in the tower rather than admit what had happened."

Raphael bumped my hand with his nose.

"Just a sec, sweetie. I think we're finally getting to the truth," I murmured to him.

"He didn't disappear!" Lily bellowed. "You killed him! Just as you killed me!"

"I did nothing of the kind! He strung ye along as long as it took to get the key to yer strongboxes, then he up and left ye to starve to death in yer tower. Ye have no one but yerself to blame!"

Raphael bumped my hand again. Absently, I patted him on his head, relieved to know that my gut instinct about Alec hadn't been far off. But how were we to resolve the situation?

"You killed me!" she repeated, and was about to fly at Sir Alec when Raphael had evidently had enough. He tossed up his head and let loose with a roar that came close to shaking the windows. The three ghosts spun around in unison and stared at Raphael.

"Ah, lad," Sir Alec said, shaking his head. "Ye just had to see the stone, didn't ye? And now ye'll pay the price for yer curiosity."

"We are not amused," I said loudly, leveling a stern look at Sir Alec as I pointed to Raphael. "This is our honeymoon. That is my husband. He is a lion. Which of those three statements does not belong?"

The three ghosts blinked at me.

I took a deep breath. "I want him changed back, and I want him changed back *right now!*"

" 'Tis nothing to do with me." Sir Alec shrugged. "He did it himself. I warned him not to go into the Stone Room."

"You didn't say there was a chance he would be changed into an animal!" I yelled, overcome with frustration. "How the hell did it happen anyway? All he did was pick up the stone!"

"I told ye that's all it would take. The men of Fyfe were cursed long ago, ye ken. Cursed to be therianthropes—to change into animals—when they touch the laird's stone. Yon laddy . . . well, ye can see what happened. He's a very nice-lookin' lion, though, don't ye think, Grizel?"

"Very nice," she agreed quickly. "Just like a great big kitty. Does he purr if you stroke him?"

Raphael growled low in his throat. I patted him again. "Calm down, sweetie. We'll get this figured out." I took a deep breath and skewered Sir Alec with a look that would have scared the crap out of a mortal man. "Given the evidence before us, I'm willing to accept the story about the stone. You have yet, however, to tell me what it is we need to do to get Raphael back."

Sir Alec shrugged. "He must learn how to shift back to human form by himself."

"Well, surely you can give him some help!" I said, clutching my hands together to keep from shaking the annoying ghost. "You must have some experience with this!"

"Nay, none," he said, shaking his head.

"But . . . but . . . it's your stone!"

"Aye, and the men of Fyfe were well warned not to go near it. None of us did," he said with irritating righteousness.

I stared at him in outright surprise. "Do you mean to say that you have this horrible stone in the castle, one that can turn any male family member into an animal if he so much as touches the damned thing, and no one ever did so?"

"Aye, that's what I'm tellin' ye. We had the warning, ye see. We knew that to touch it would bring down the curse upon our heads."

I turned to consider the stone. "Then what are we going to do? If we put it back, will it change Raphael back?"

"I'm afraid not, lass. He's therian, ye see. All of us men of Fyfe are, but only those who touch the stone trigger the change."

I looked at my husband. His eyes peered back at me, filled with a heart-twisting mixture of hope, trust, and sadness. "Don't worry, I won't let you stay this way. We just need to think. . . . There has to be an answer. If there's one thing I've learned the last few years, it's that nothing is absolute."

"We'd help ye if we could," Sir Alec said, pulling Grizel to his side. "But I'm afraid that there's no solution. It's as the curse says: *The Thane of Fyfe shadowed be, thrice around the stone bound; in its light, the devil can see, and the beast within be found.*"

"Thrice around the stone bound," I murmured, eyeing the stone. "I wonder . . . Bob?"

Raphael looked thoughtful for a moment, clearly thinking the same thing I was. His head jerked up and down in an awkward acknowledgment.

"Are you sure?" I asked, my heart weeping at the sight of his eyes, so familiar, so human, bound in a body that was nothing more than a furry prison.

He nodded again.

"Right. Here goes nothing." I picked up the stone, grunting a little at its weight as I lifted it over my head.

"What are ye doin'?" Sir Alec yelled, leaping toward me.

I lowered the stone and took a couple of steps back, just in case he had any funny ideas about trying to snatch it from me. "The curse revolves around the stone. You guys have been protecting it all these centuries, believing it made you happy."

"Aye, it has! So long as the laird's stone is safe, all will be well."

"The laird's stone, the laird's stone," Lily muttered before jabbing a finger in Sir Alec's direction. "Ask him what he's done to the lady's stone!"

Sir Alec looked abashed for a moment.

"He destroyed it, that's what he did!" she crowed. "He

couldn't stand to see me happy, and he destroyed it, damning all women in the family to eternal sorrow!"

"I didn't even know ye, ye daft woman!" Sir Alec answered. "I dropped it down the privy when I was a lad!"

I raised an eyebrow.

He cleared his throat, embarrassment plainly written on his face. " 'Twas an accident. I didn't know it was the lady's stone. I used to play in the passage leading to the Stone Room. I never touched the laird's stone—even then I knew what repercussions that would have—," he said, looking at Raphael. "But the lady's stone was different. It was smaller, and pretty. I used to carry it about with me, and it . . . er . . . well, it was dropped into the privy by mistake."

"A likely tale," Lily snorted.

"What happened after that?" I asked, glancing from the stone in my arms to Raphael.

His eyes pleaded with me to do something.

"What do ye mean?"

"Was there any repercussion for destroying the lady's stone? Did something happen to your mother?"

"Nothing happened to her, although she proper tanned my arse for playing in the privy," he said with a rueful grin as he rubbed his behind.

I smiled at him. "I'm sure you deserved it."

"Aye, but that didn't make it any easier to—nooo!"

I lifted the stone as high over my head as I could, and slammed it back down toward the solid marble floor. A shock wave knocked me back off my feet, against Raphael. We fell to the ground in a tangle of human and lion limbs, the explosion as the stone shattered into a thousand pieces echoing painfully along the hall. Beneath us, the ground trembled for a moment, easing as the horrible sound faded into nothing.

A dense cloud of dust choked the air, making me cough as I pushed my hair out of my face and sat up.

"Bob!" I yelled in delight as I flung myself on a familiar man-shaped form.

"Blessed Virgin, what have ye done?" Sir Alec asked, his figure barely visible in the dense, dusty air. He helped Grizel to her feet, ignoring the nasty look Lily shot him as she rose from where she'd been knocked back.

Sir Alec stood looking at the pile of rubble that was formerly the laird's stone.

"I broke the damned curse," I said, hugging Raphael.

"But . . . but ye have destroyed the stone! Ye've destroyed the happiness of the lairds!"

"You don't deserve happiness, you murdering, adulterous blackguard!" Lily growled as she dusted herself off. She turned to face us, giving a regal nod of her head. "You've done as I asked; you've destroyed the stone. I will be at peace now."

"I hate to say this, but that wasn't why I destroyed it," I said as Raphael helped me up. "You okay, sweetie?"

"Yes, thanks to you." He kissed me, his eyes hot with love and desire.

"Ye broke my stone!" Sir Alec wailed, dropping to his knees before the pile of rubble. "Ye've ruined my chance of happiness!"

"Pfft," I said. "I don't know why someone didn't think of destroying the stone earlier to break the were-kitty curse, but I assume it's because you've had it drummed into your heads that no one must go near it or touch it in order to be happy. Well, I've always been a firm believer in people making their own destinies, and their own happiness. You and Grizel seem to be pretty happy as you are, and nothing can change that."

"She's right, love," Grizel said, putting a hand on her husband's shoulder. "We're still here, and we still have each other. What more could make us happy?"

"Oh, for mercy's sake," Lily said, rolling her eyes as she picked her way across the dirt- and rock-strewn floor. "Now that I have been avenged, I can move on and find Roddy. I have a few questions to put to him about what happened to my jewels. . . ."

Lily's form shimmered as it disappeared into the wall.

"Alec?" Grizel asked, prodding him.

"Eh? Oh, aye, I suppose ye're right," he said, sighing as he brushed dust from his hands and stood up. "But I still think it's a tragedy the stone is gone."

"Cheer up," I said, wrapping my arms around Raphael's waist and biting his chin. "You still have the castle stone, right? One out of three isn't too bad."

"Aye, I suppose. Unless ye'll be wantin' to see that too," he said with a barbed look.

"I swear I'll keep Joy away from any other stones," Raphael promised.

Alec grunted acknowledgment.

Grizel smiled winsomely at her husband. "Come, love. We'll go back to the stable yard, and ye can be the stable lad, and I'll be the goose girl. Ye know how ye love to play stable lad."

A lascivious light dawned in Sir Alec's eyes as he turned away from the stone. "Would ye be the dairy maid instead of the goose girl?"

"Perhaps," Grizel said with a coy arch to her brows, and an encouraging twitch of her skirt.

"Ah, lass, ye do know how to stoke my fire," Sir Alec said, lunging for her. She squealed and took off down the hallway.

Sir Alec started after her, pausing to look back at us. "What are ye waitin' for, lad? It's yer weddin' night, and ye're back to yer manly form. Go pleasure yer wife!"

"That's the smartest thing you've said all night," Raphael said, scooping me up in his arms and carrying me up the stone staircase.

"I agree completely," I said, kissing his jawline. "And since I'm so accommodating, would you like to get the 'I told you so' out of the way now, or later?"

"I'd like to forget the whole blasted evening," he growled, pushing open the door to our suite.

"I'm sure you would, but I have to say—you made a very sexy lion."

"That's all over with now. It won't happen again," he said, setting me on my feet as he locked the door.

"I wonder . . ." I nibbled my lip as I went into the bedroom.

"You wonder what? How long it will take me to have you screaming with ecstasy?"

"No, I know that's a given," I said as he followed me into the room. Before I could say anything else, his clothes were off and he was stalking toward me, a hungry, predatory look in his eyes that left me shivering with delight. "I was going to say I wonder if you coming to Fyfe brought forth previously hidden therianthrope tendencies, but I think I have my answer."

"I am *not* an animal," he growled, the sound starting deep in his chest, rolling outward with a rumble that sounded remarkably like a lion's.

"Oh, I don't know," I said, giggling when he pounced on me, sending us both falling back onto the bed. "I think I might like having the beast within you released."

He growled again, nibbling my neck as he peeled off my shirt.

"What a honeymoon this is going to be," I sighed happily. "I can't wait to see what happens at the end of the week."

"End of the week?" Raphael asked, removing my bra. His eyes lit as he swooped down to nibble various and sundry exposed parts. "What happens at the end of the week?"

"Full moon, sweetie. Full moon!"

Two years after she started writing, Katie MacAlister sold the first of more than thirty books. Her novels have been translated into numerous languages, been recorded as audiobooks, received several awards, and placed on the New York Times, USA Today, *and* Publishers Weekly *bestseller lists. Katie lives in the Pacific Northwest with her husband and dogs, and can often be found lurking around online. You can visit her at www.katiemacalister.com.*

Half of Being Married

Lilith Saintcrow

When a werewolf marries a vampire hunter, the honeymoon can be a killer. . . .

THE WORST MOMENT OF MY LIFE WAS SEEING Kat go over backward, vanishing under the first bloodsucker's bulk. I actually half shifted—claws springing free and fur rippling down my limbs with a familiar itch—and flung myself at the sucker, ignoring the second one I'd been feinting with. Pain bloomed as it clipped me on the side, my ribs scraped and a hot spatter of blood splashed moonlit gravel. I crashed into the thing with a sound like locomotives colliding.

I went down hard, little pieces of rock burning up my back where Kat's fingers had recently brushed. *Kat, dear Sun, Kat—*

The bloodsucker exhaled foulness, its twisted-root face compressing as it champed, yellow foam splattering. Its eyes burned violet. It had probably been female while human, because it went for my chest instead of my throat. The mistake cost it its life.

If those sucking machines can be said to have a life, instead of a twilight hell.

Instinct took over and I tore the thing open, amber claws puncturing unhallowed skin. We've been hunting the bloodsuckers for a long time, and the Sun has blessed us with pieces of Herself in our claws and teeth.

We used to die like flies up against them.

Nowadays, they're still hard to kill. But we've got advantages, and we're trained. Even a pup knows how to take them out—though getting into a pitched battle on the shoulder of a country road in Virginia is *not* my preferred method. I'm more of an urban hunter.

The bloodsucker stiffened, screaming without sound because my claws were buried in its chest. A gout of foul-smelling blackness poured from its open mouth instead, slicking my face and getting in my nose. It stank to high heaven.

The point of a birch stake protruded from its chest, dripping. Stinking ash spread as the blessed wood of a Sun-loving tree poisoned the sucker's metabolism. They run fast and hot, and once they're poisoned, it takes very little for it to spread. Core damage to their circulatory systems causes critical hemorrhage.

The bloodsucker slumped, ash threading through its flesh. The blood turned to grit, I sneezed twice, and Kat's face, stained and grimy, rose like the Sun itself over the sucker's shoulder. She blinked furiously, her blue eyes red-rimmed, and my heart exploded in my chest.

I tried to speak, but the only thing that came out was a sharp yipping sound. When we change even halfway, our mouths aren't meant for speaking.

Kat stared at me, jaw set and eyes flashing through tears of irritation from the dust. It gets on you and just keeps itching as it crumbles finer and finer, cells imploding and tearing themselves apart. Her hair was full of dirt, twigs, and gravel, and she held the stake loosely, professionally, but her other hand was a white-knuckled fist.

The road unreeled behind her, a single lane of pavement under silver wash from the almost-full May moon. Tree branches whispered and chuckled as the breeze rolled up from the creek. The bed-and-breakfast was a quarter of a mile away down a long gravel driveway, the creek running behind it in a ribbon of coolness. Water sounded really good right about now.

A prickling itch receded toward my fingers and toes as the change melted away. My jaw cracked, working, and I spoke as soon as I could. "Kat—"

"What the *hell?*" She was spitting mad, her chin up and her clothes torn all to ribbons. The curve of one pale breast showed through a rip in her shirt, and she was bleeding. "You . . ." For once, Katrina Black, née Jasperson, ran out of words.

I never thought I'd live to see that.

I pointed at the stake. "What the hell's *that?*" A faint jasmine-loaded breeze brushed the bushes. Out here in the sticks, the summer nights are warm and redolent before morning fog rises, and the bed-and-breakfast had whole trellises full of fragrance that had escaped to grow wild.

It was beautiful for honeymoons, but I just wanted to sneeze again. A touch of growl laced itself through my voice, and my face itched like hell. I needed a shower.

She lifted the stake and glanced at it, as if reminding herself what it was. "This is a *stake,*" she said finally, in her special tone of withering disdain reserved for idiots. "I've got lots of spares in case one breaks. You just turned into the Hulk in a fur rug. What the *hell?*"

"I, um . . ." *Well, great. There's never a good time for this.* "Stakes? I suppose you've got holy water and garlic too. No wonder my back went out carrying your luggage." *And no wonder you're sneaking around at night. Hell of a reason for a midnight ramble, Kat.*

That did the trick. She took a deep breath, that maddening slope of breast peering at me, and I checked her for more bleeding. A thin trickle from her temple, another rivulet from her nose, and her shirt was sopping wet with copper-smelling blood on one side. Very low, under the floating ribs on her right.

Merciful Sun, I don't like the look of that.

Then she blew.

"Mitchell Black, what's the goddamn idea? Why didn't you tell me you were a werewolf?"

I winced. "Your pop culture is showing, sweetpea. I'm a Sunrunner." *Not a goddamn "werewolf."* "You never told me you were a vampire hunter. And what was I supposed to do, just lay in bed while you snuck out? On our honeymoon, I might add."

Good thing I followed you, eh? But I knew better than to tack that on.

She put her hands to her hips, drawing herself up, chin rising yet more. She looked dirty, beaten up, and completely kissable. The nostrils of her cute little patrician nose flared and her eyes went incandescent.

I get weak in the knees when she does that. Her lips thinned before she spoke, and the urge to kiss her got overwhelming.

"I'm a Knight of the Argentum Astrum, thank you *very* much, and *you* are in serious trouble. Why the hell didn't you tell—*ulp!*"

I took two steps and grabbed her. It wasn't very graceful, but

I wanted to be sure she was all right. Plus she's just sexy as hell. She tasted like adrenaline, apples, and copper blood, and my fingers explored her side while I kissed her, my free hand cupping her nape. The wound was ragged but not deep.

She shoved me away, and I let her.

"You know, before I marry a guy, I like to know little things like him turning hairy and carnivorous on the full' moon." She hadn't lost track. Dammit.

"I'd kind of like to know if my wife-to-be's a Silver Star, too. Night classes, huh?"

"I *do* have night classes, you jackass." The silver crucifix winked at her throat. "Hunting *sanguinant* is all very well, but the pay isn't shit. I'm filing for divorce."

I winced. "Any chance we can solve this in bed?"

"You're a goddamn werewolf, Mr. Black." She looked magnificent, all tangled and flushed and still breathing heavily. "That qualifies as need-to-know information *before* we tie the knot, in my book!"

"So does a case of stakes and a working knowledge of dowsing to find suckers." I folded my arms, grit working its way into my skin. *I get it. We're not going to talk about why you snuck out on a pretty night like this to go looking for suckers. Sure thing, Kat.*

Moonlight drenched the small clearing and the wind shifted. I heard the car before she did and leapt, knocking her down as headlights swept the curve of the road. The vehicle—sounded like a Ford—downshifted, taking the hill at an even fifty. I heard laughter and smelled exhaust. They were probably heading up to Lover's Leap, near where we'd hiked around yesterday after breakfast to look out over the juicy green valley.

My ears told me we were safe from wandering suckers for the moment, at least, but I didn't want any civilians seeing either of us.

That would only lead to trouble, and I'd had enough trouble tonight to last me awhile.

She waited until the roar of the engine faded into the distance before squirming out from under me. I could have lain there all night. But it was gravel, and she was already torn up.

Hope I didn't hurt you even more, sweetpea. "Did he get you? On the side?"

"I'm *fine*." As stubborn as she ever was after falling down that flight of stairs. She'd sprained an ankle on that one, and refused point-blank to go to the doctor. "It won't even scar if I treat it soon. Get *off* me."

I made it to my feet a little less gracefully than she did. They don't tell you how sore hunting suckers makes you. Even if a Sunrunner has a higher rate of tissue regeneration.

She checked the two smears of fine ash left over from the two bloodsuckers—probably only unhallowed dead, opportunistic things more used to preying on livestock than humans—and dropped to one knee. Her hair, pulled back in a loose knot, fell in strands and straggles. Her nape gleamed with sweat. Her free hand came out of her jacket pocket and she scattered holy water over the writhing smears. "*O quam misericors Deus est,*" she murmured.

O, how merciful God is. The Argentum were optimists. It was, after all, why they were in this line of work. Sunrunners are just born to it.

"I love it when you get all Catholic." I hunched my shoulders, tested the wind. My ears weren't tingling, a good sign. No suckers within smelling distance. I relaxed the rest of the way. "I'm itching all over. Let's go, I'll wash your back." *And take a look at that wound. That's not a good place to get hit. Merciful Sun. She could've been really hurt.*

"You are *so* sleeping in the doghouse, Fido." She hauled herself up with a sigh worthy of my old granny.

Granny would have approved of my Kat. "You don't mean that, sweetpea."

"Bullshit I don't. Come on, I dropped my other stake. Help me find it."

All in all, she took the news that I can change into a timber wolf pretty well. Granny would *definitely* have approved.

TWO MORNINGS LATER I WOKE UP WITH AN *oof!* as Kat landed on me. Hot sun poured through the curtains and turned her hair into gold as it fell over her shoulders. The room was done in antebellum shabby-chic, with lots of froufrous and furbelows. The bed even had mosquito netting, as if any mosquito would have dared to intrude where Miz Evans of the Evans Bed 'n' Breakfast ran her shipshape little rock of down-home graciousness and army-neat order.

The breakfasts were terrific, and Kat loved all the frilly girly stuff. She'd just about gone wild over the gardens, tea cozies, and the way the bed tried to swallow us both whole. The stackable washer and dryer down the hall still held our stinking, torn clothes, soaking out the last bit of bloodsucker smell. We'd washed them four times already.

This morning, though, she bounced on me like a terrier. "Get up, lazybones. Time to read the paper."

I wanted to bury my face in the pillow, but she was just too pretty. Kat's small—only about five-four—but every inch of her is packed with dynamite. She looks like a little blonde ballerina princess, helped along by the hour she spends in dance class pretty much every day, rain or shine. I don't see where she gets the energy, between night classes, day work in the office, and hunting bloodsuckers. She has these big blue eyes and this sharp aristocratic nose, and her mouth is just made for kissing.

So I pulled her down, and I did.

It took a long time before I was close to done, and she shook herself free before I was even halfway there. "Try to keep your mind on business. I'm still mad at you, you know."

"Christ, my heart can't take that." I gave her my best *aw shucks, ma'am* grin. It usually works better when I'm not unshaven and bruised—I get my five o'clock shadow before noon. Just one of the perks of being a Sunrunner. "Don't be mad." *Especially since you didn't tell me you were an Argentum.*

I guess being married involves holding your tongue a lot. No wonder most men think it's so rough.

The smile that spread over her face was worth keeping my big mouth shut. That's my Kat, all fire one minute and softness the next. "I'm not mad, I guess." She was only in a tank top and panties, both candy-cotton pink. Matching the room.

The woman just has no mercy.

"I'm not a field agent, anyway. I'm an intelligence analyst, I track migrations and collate reports. That was my first time staking."

Are you trying to kill me? "Your first time?"

"Well, I did okay." She pushed her hair back. Her knees were on either side of my hips, and her weight on me was incredibly distracting. "Now it's time for you to get up and read the paper. Breakfast's still warm. You want coffee, don't you?"

"Coffee can wait." I got both hands on her shoulders and brought her mouth back down to mine, and things were heading in a very satisfactory direction before she broke away again. "Goddammit, woman. You're going to kill me."

"Maybe," she agreed cheerfully. "But not until after you read the *paper.*"

"Screw the paper." I caught her mouth again and ran my fingers over the slim arches of her ribs, my fingers scraping off green herbal paste dried against the wound. Argentum believe in old-fashioned cures. Mugwort and holy water do wonders for blood-sucker wounds.

I went cold all over, touching it, and she laughed, a particular low husky chuckle that just about turned me inside out before she let me do what I was dying to do each time I saw her.

The sunshine had moved on the bed before I stopped breathing heavy, my face in her hair and the little shudders going through both of us. "Nice," she whispered into my neck. "I like that."

"Me too." *Better each time, actually. I guess waiting for marriage was worth it.* "What do you say we do it again?"

"You're a menace." She shivered again, a delightful little movement. The air-conditioning had kicked on. "Move over, I'm cold."

"Delighted to." Something crackled as I finally got her under the covers and cuddled up against me, her panties gone and her tank top discarded too.

She didn't snuggle nearly long enough before fishing around with one hand and bringing up something I blinked at. It was the county seat's daily, the *Cotton Crossing Register*. "Jesus." I managed a moan. "You just don't quit, do you?"

"A couple of minutes ago you were happy about that." She spread the paper out one-handed, awkwardly. "Take a look."

"I don't want to." I brushed her hair back, the golden floss tangling around my fingers like seaweed. "All that's in there is who tipped whose cow or quilted someone else's corn or something."

"Shows what *you* know, Fido."

"Are you going to keep calling me that?"

"Until you live the other night down, yes. Since you won't read, I'll tell you all about it." She snuggled down, her hip bumping me. "Police blotter says four kids disappeared two nights ago. Their car was found up at Lover's Leap."

"Disappeared? In a town this size?"

"You were the one who wanted a road-trip honeymoon; this town is bigger than the last one you subjected me to. At least it's a county seat. By the way, if our children have tails and floppy ears *you're* going to be making the explanations."

"The change doesn't happen until puberty. Protective coloration. And I liked the idea of pulling over whenever you wanted to act like a teenager at the drive-in." I sighed, settling her head on my shoulder more securely. "Four kids?"

"Remember that car? The one that happened by just after we staked those two *sanguine?*"

"Ford. Four-door. Rounded headlights." *Right after you almost gave me a heart attack by vanishing under a hundred and a half pounds of spitting bloodsucker.* A thin thread of unease worked its way through me.

"Was it? I couldn't see, you were in the way. Anyway, their car was unlocked and just sitting up there, the paper says. What does that tell you?"

"That someone's going to have to explain why they left Daddy's car up on the ridge?"

She nudged me with her hip. "No, idiot. It means there's a nest around here."

"Good God." I hadn't gotten past the two bloodsuckers we'd killed. I'd been too worried about Kat. "You think so?"

"I don't think, I know. Guess why it made not just the blotter this morning, but also the second page."

I didn't want to know. "Why?"

"Because two kids disappeared last week too. Boy and girl, a nice couple. She was a cheerleader; he was the local football star. Want to put even money where they probably disappeared *from?*"

FOR A TOWN OF THIRTY THOUSAND PEOPLE, IT certainly looked like a fifties movie set of the proverbial one-horse burg. Kat outright refused to stay in a place with less than two stoplights. I'm not the only urban creature in our relationship.

Of course, Kat's first stop was the local library, a brick building sandwiched between a feed store and Cotton Crossing's City Hall, such as it was.

Scratch an Argentum Astrum, and you'll find both an overachiever and a great believer in law and order, not to mention a dyed-in-the-wool research nut.

"Shhh." She laid her finger against my lips before turning back to the screen. "Will you be quiet?"

"There's nobody in here." Libraries make me itchy, all that quiet and dust in the air. Librarians always look like they could eat you alive if you make too much noise.

Kat rolled her eyes. The muscle in her shoulders flickered as she moved. "It's the principle of the thing, Mitch."

"You and your principles. How did you get to be a Silver Star?" My leather jacket creaked a little. It was ninety degrees in the shade, but I wasn't about to give up the pocket space. Besides, we weren't going to be strolling around outdoors, and in this part of the country, air-conditioning was the rule rather than the exception.

"They recruited me in high school. My mother was one before she died." She spun the dial on the microfiche machine, pushing a little lever and staring at the screen. "Huh. Interesting."

"I love to hear you say that." I ran my fingers under her hair, touched the back of her neck. She shivered, but not enough to disturb her concentration.

"So what do you shift into?" She moved the lever again, glanced over her shoulder at the bookcases. Checking to make sure nobody heard us, or checking her blindspot like a nervous Argentum?

Nice change of subject, Kat. "Timber wolf. I'm a Sunrunner."

"Loup-garou." She made a note on her ever-present little journalist's pad. The design stamped into the leather cover—a cross inside a circle—made sense now. "Or are you *dents-soleil?* Sunrunner is probably *dents-soleil.* So you're allergic to ash wood."

She'd done her research, all right. The only wonder was that she hadn't noticed before. But we're careful, we Sunrunners. We have to be. "Only if it's introduced under the skin, sweetpea, and I've had my shots. It won't kill me. Just gives me a stuffy nose. Like the dust in here."

"Then go wait outside." She made another note while I stared at the fall of her hair, paleness streaked with pure gold. "You're being a nuisance."

"You're breaking my heart. I'm hungry." My stomach gurgled. She'd been at it for hours. I shifted in the hard wooden chair. Why didn't these places ever have comfortable chairs? *"Really* hungry."

"Whiner. I suppose you want to try that greasy-spoon diner you've been looking at so longingly." She closed her notebook with a snap and turned off the machine. "We might as well. I can't work with you poking at me like this."

"I thought this was a honeymoon."

"It is." She turned in her chair and gave me one of those dazzling smiles. The kind that hits right below the belt and spreads like a supernova. "But we can't just let a nest breed out here, you know. We're in the area, we need to do something about it."

"The population can't support more than a few suckers out here. They're creatures of opportunity." *I'm surprised we're not hearing more about cattle mutilations, actually. Or pigs getting bled out.*

"Look, we killed two last night. Those kids disappeared *afterward.* That's just too much of a coincidence. It's a statistical outlier unless there's a nest out here. A nest will breed if the population starts rising, which it has been—did you *look* at the bed-and-breakfasts around here? This is a town on the edge of being a city. A stubborn nest in this area when the population explodes is a recipe for disaster. We have to do something." Her eyes shone with optimism.

"An analyst and a single Sunrunner against a nest? Talk about a recipe for disaster. We usually hunt in packs, you know. Two Sunrunners to a sucker is about a comfortable margin." My shoulders hunched. If I ran across a lone sucker in the city, I knew my way well enough to get rid of it. It's what I was bred for. A mongoose doesn't need to know what to do when it sees a cobra. It's pure instinct.

But the thought of a nest, with its stink and claustrophobic, sweltering heat, and my Kat in the middle . . . She pushed herself up, scraping the chair back along green linoleum. "I think we'll be all right. We can't just let a nest mushroom out here, Mitch."

Now what could I say to that? I settled for hooking my arm over her shoulders. "I'm hungry. Let's go eat." *We're only here for another night, anyway.*

"I told Mrs. Evans we'd be staying another week." She slid her arm around my waist and did the trick of moving someone twice her size for the door. "We'll hit the fiche again after you have your corn-fried lard. There's some interesting things here. Did you know this town's been here since 1784?"

My Kat. Put an obstacle in her path and she just rolls right over it without noticing.

I was going to have to find some other way of keeping her out of trouble.

THE DINER WAS ON THE MAIN DRAG, A cheerful little place with red-checked curtains in the window and air-conditioning working overtime. Most of the customers were truckers or locals, and no few of them stared when Kat waltzed in the door, with her white cotton tank top and skintight jeans, her hair a bright banner and a thin silver *semanario* jangling on her wrist. They probably hadn't seen anything this good since the local goober queen got inducted.

Kat paged back through her notes. "Kids have been disappearing around here for a while. I've found an average of one disappearance a month for as far back as the newspapers go on microfiche. Which, granted, isn't far, only until about 1932. There was some sort of fire that destroyed old records."

I took another bite of my burger, chewed thoughtfully. Next to her I felt even scruffier than usual. Stubble had broken out along my jaw and my eyes felt sandy after all the dust. My jacket creaked, and my sneakers were almost worn through. The heat was already wet and clinging, a fine sheen of sweat standing out on Kat's skin, and I liked it. With a higher-than-human metabolism fueling denser muscle and bone, heat bleeds. I spent one winter in Maine and almost froze my ass off unless I was wearing my fur.

"Howza food?" The waitress was probably forty but looked more like fifty-five, with aggressively-large hair reeking of Aqua Net and bourbon. "Freshen up yah coffee?"

"It's great. Thank you." My words sounded clipped and unhelpful next to her down-home drawl. We waited until she was gone. "That's a lot of kids missing," I said thoughtfully. "I didn't know they had that many around here."

"I hear they have them in job lots, but still. You'd think someone would say something. But it's on the back pages, never makes a lot of news, and I can't help but think . . ."

"It seems a nice little town." And Cotton Crossing was, quiet in a prosperous way. The Appalachian kitsch mixed nicely with antebellum graciousness, to the tune of columns and Confederate flags as well as public buildings from the New Deal era.

Kat took a mouthful of fries and poked at her French dip. "There's enough grease in this to clog my arteries just *looking* at it." She took a long pull of her orange juice and made a small face, probably reminded of her first Southern iced-tea debacle. They drink it sweet enough to rot teeth down there. "Yes, it's a nice little town. But the media should be all over kids disappearing. And teenagers are statistically higher at risk for—"

"Well hello there, good-lookin'." A heavyset man passing the table tipped his hat to Kat, who smiled and nodded. She gets that a lot.

It was enough to make a man feel territorial. But then Kat turned her baby blues back to me and promptly forgot about John Doe Hick, dropping her voice to a confidential murmur. "It's just *weird*. Do the math, Mitch."

Almost a thousand kids. I know humans are sometimes careless with their pups, something no Sunrunner understands. But this . . . "It's a little more than weird. It's downright ugly." I met the man's eyes as he sauntered past, marking him in memory—brown and brown, plaid shirt over yellowed wifebeater, jeans riding below his paunch, work boots caked with black dirt, John Deere baseball cap. A walking cliché. "I suppose you want to spend the whole afternoon in the library too."

"No, just a couple hours. Then we're going to the courthouse to check out birth and death rates, since this is a county seat." She took a ladylike bite of roast beef. "We'll go back to Mrs. Evans's and crunch some numbers."

"Numbers." I tried not to moan. "Come on, Kat."

"You'll like it. Crunching numbers makes me want to undress you."

I suddenly couldn't wait to get through with lunch.

STICKY JASMINE-LADEN AIR BREATHED AGAINST MY NECK AND back, my T-shirt immediately clinging like Saran Wrap. Kat leaned against the porch railing, framed by trellises full of green leaves and little white star-shaped flowers. Dusk was a purple bruise in the sky, and Kat's white sundress a floating ghost, straps creasing her tender shoulders.

I rested my elbows on the railing next to hers and leaned against her despite the heat. "Hey, pretty lady."

"Hey, Rover." Her smile took the sting out of it. "Look at that."

The garden spilled away in regimented rows, flowers nodding as nightly exhalation came off the mountains and down into the valley cupping Cotton Crossing. From here you could see the dusty curve of the road and Lover's Leap, a crag of sharp rock thrust out from summer growth under the worn-down nub of the mountain. It pointed at the town like an accusing finger.

"Still mad?" I didn't think she was, but with Kat you could never tell. I hadn't even known she'd consider dating me until that night in the bar, when I'd bounced a couple of drunks hassling her and her coworkers. I'd thought she just came in after that with said coworkers, but later she'd poked me in the ribs and told me she came to see *me*.

Guess I'm a lucky man.

"No. But you're still not going to live this one down for a while."

"I'm going to have to find a cute little nickname that rhymes with Argentum."

She shifted, her hip bumping mine. She was barefoot, and holding a tall thin glass that smelled suspiciously like mint julep. "I think more time at the library should help you with that."

I should know better than to open my mouth. "Very funny. I'm still sneezing from the dust this afternoon. And you promised me an undressing."

"Did I?" A mock-serious questioning tone. She twirled the glass in her slim fingers. "That's right, I did crunch some numbers. Once you factor in the disappearances, this place has a crime rate comparable to a much larger and more aggressive city."

"Isn't that odd."

"With the amount of lard in the food I'm surprised it's not higher." She yawned prettily, took another hit off her julep. "If you count the disappearances as murders and factor in the percentage of missing-persons that could be just kids getting itchy feet or even running across normal foul play, there's still a significant statistical outlier."

"I love it when you talk accountant." Under the cloying of jasmine lay her smell; fabric softener, female, and her cedary perfume. I dropped my head a little and leaned in so I could take a deep breath of her instead of the garden. Water chuckled behind the house, the creek a shadow of itself. "So what does that tell you, Kat?" I had the sinking feeling I wasn't going to like her answer.

"It's not just a nest. It's something else." She took another swallow of julep. "Which is terrible news. I should call for reinforcements."

It never even occurred to her to leave the damn thing alone. "Kat. We're on our *honeymoon*."

"You really think we can handle it ourselves?" She stared out at the garden, unseeing, a sharp line between her eyebrows and her mouth pulled down at the corners.

For Christ's sake. Do you always have to throw yourself in headfirst? I swallowed what I wanted to say and decided to go for tact. "Why don't we head out tonight, and once we cross the county line we can call it in to the Argentum? You're on vacation, you know." *I don't like the thought of you getting mixed up in this, even with me for backup.*

I could only classify the wide-eyed look she gave me as shocked. The brownish mint-smelling liquid in her glass sloshed as she straightened and turned to face me head-on, her skirt swishing a little and her baby blues big as plates. "But I've done all the preliminary investigation and made all the contacts. I *can't* leave now."

Christ in a casket. "Kat. It's our honeymoon. I can think of better ways to spend it."

"Like running and hiding?" Her tone suddenly got very sweet, and very soft.

Danger, Will Robinson. Danger. "That's not necessary."

She lifted her glass, took a mouthful, and made a face, wrinkling up her nose. "Sorry." To give her credit, she did sound sorry. "But we can't leave."

I was afraid she was going to say that. "Can you at least call for reinforcements?"

"I'm not sure there are reinforcements to be had. What about you? Can't you call in the Puppy Brigade or something?"

I took a firmer hold on my temper. "I'm not related to anyone out here. I'm not even sure there's any Sunrunners in the area. Those suckers last night were awful incautious." *You might not understand it, sweets, but Sunrunners kill suckers because they're a danger to our pups. Not because they're a danger to humans. We can only take care of ourselves. The Dark Ages taught us that.*

Now wasn't the time for a history lesson, though.

"Then we might be on our own after all." She slid her arm through mine and steered me away from the porch railing. "Let's take a walk. I'm sorry, Mitch. Really."

"Don't worry about it." We stepped down onto the concrete path, and I kept a watch out—her feet were bare.

She took another hit of julep. "I'll call in when we go back upstairs. With any luck someone should be able to come out from the closest real city."

"Sounds like a plan." I almost walked into a rosebush, trying to keep her away from the one on the opposite side. Her skirt caught on a thorny branch and she twitched it free by simply walking forward and ignoring it. "You hungry?"

She made another adorable little face and finished off her drink. "Not so much, lunch was pretty heavy. I wouldn't say no to another one of these, though."

"We can do that." I kept her going down the path. There was a little trellis covered in climbing jasmine, arching over a wide wooden bench. Sitting under the jasmine and maybe getting a little foolish sounded like a good idea.

"I know what you're thinking." Amusement colored her tone; she pulled me to a halt. "Here. You go get me another drink, I'll wait for you on that bench you're aiming for. And when you come back I'll give you a prize."

"What kind of prize?" I subtracted the glass from her unresisting fingers.

"You'll like it. Go get me another funny little mint drink, Mitch. Be nice."

"I like being nice to you." I gave her a chaste kiss on the cheek and headed back for the house. The evening breeze had died down, full night gathering between the trees as the valley tipped under shade. Lover's Leap still glowed, streaks of naked rock throwing back a last gleam before the sun sank below the horizon.

I had just set my foot on the creaking porch step when I heard the snap of branches and Kat's short cry.

Instinct took over. I whirled, and the stink of suckers boiled across my sensitive nose. It's like being hit in the face with a bag of wet cement, that smell, and adrenaline bloomed along my arms and legs as I dropped the glass and launched myself.

One Sunrunner against three suckers is usually bad odds.

HOLD IT HERE." MY HANDS SHOOK, BUT I kept the ice to her forehead. My ears had stopped tingling. *Why didn't I smell them sooner? I don't like this.*

Kat blinked, through a mask of blood. "What the hell?" Her voice had a dozy, sleepy tone I didn't like.

"It bit you. Don't worry," I added in an undertone, "I killed it." I shouldn't have told her. Her eyes got all wide and the remaining color drained out of her face, leaving her chalky except where drying blood painted her skin. A terrific bruise was plumping up on her right cheek, and she'd damn near gotten a dislocated shoulder. The sundress was ruined, covered in mud and guck, and I wasn't sure the trellis would ever be the same.

Miz Evans fluttered. "My oh my." Her steel-colored bun was slightly disarranged, and she smelled of nervous excitement and the high brittle edge of fear, as well as talcum powder and her overwhelming perfume—Tabu, the same stuff my granny used to douse her vacuum-cleaner bag in before her daily cleaning. "The sheriff should be here in a few minutes. Harv said he was right on his way." She waved her plump hands, the jet beads of the chain holding her bifocals to her impressive bosom clicking.

"Did you call Animal Control?" The story was that a stray dog had rampaged through the garden and attacked my lovely bride. It was lame, true, but the best I could do on such short notice.

"Well, Harv and his deputy mostly take care of that around here. Can I get her anything? Poor dear." She was shaking worse than I was.

I must have been wearing a mean face. "More water?" I didn't think Kat needed it, but I had to get the woman out of the room. Kat sucked in a harsh breath, her terrified gaze flying up to mine. She was far too pale, and gasping like she had asthma. The ice in the bag crackled, meeting her fever-heat.

"All right. You just rest, honey." She mimed patting Kat's naked shoulder, just touching the air over the skin. One of the sundress's straps had torn free. Kat crossed her arms over her breasts, hugging herself. Rolling around in the dirt had streaked all over the white cotton, and rose thorns had lacerated a fair bit of her back and shoulders. I couldn't wait to get her into a bathtub and wash the grime off.

First things first, though. I peeled up Kat's lip and checked her teeth. Poked at the gums over the canines with one nail. When she didn't cringe or cry out, I relaxed a little bit. Then I checked her pupils—no vacillation, and her heartbeat was normal, pounding with stress but not stuttering like it would be if the infection had taken hold in her bloodstream.

The first fifteen minutes after a bite are crucial. I picked up the half glass of water left over from Miz Evans's ministrations and whispered a bit of bastard Latin over it, breathed on the surface until it rippled, and held it to Kat's lips. She drank without demur, and there was no scorching where the water met her lips.

Merciful Sun, thank you. That was too goddamn close. "We're leaving. Tomorrow morning. Dawn, if not sooner." I didn't sound like myself. "Talk to me, sweetpea."

"My head hurts." She didn't sound like herself either. Kat blinked, and sense flooded her eyes. A little bit of color came back into her cheeks. "It bit me?"

"It did. I killed it, and you're not showing any signs of infection." She wasn't at a very high risk—the bite was just a glancing scrape of teeth, because I'd torn the fucking thing off her and killed it immediately; her immune system wasn't compromised and the Argentum probably had her on a course of garlic shots as well as the silver treatment to stave off infection. "You're clean, Kat. It's all right." The words cracked halfway.

"You don't sound convinced." Her eyes rolled up into her head and snapped back down. She reached up, pressed her fingers over mine, keeping the ice hard against the lump on her forehead. "Hurts. Need my mugwort."

"In a second." *As soon as I'm sure you're all right.*

"What's our story?" she whispered.

"Stray dog."

Amazingly, a pale grin lit her wan face. Her legs were covered in a mass of scratches and claw marks, blood and mud marked the chintz slipcover underneath her. "That's a good one, Fido."

"Ha ha." I tried to feel relieved and failed miserably. "Sit still."

"I want my mugwort."

"In a second." I heard car wheels crunching gravel, tensed, and made myself relax muscle by muscle. "We have to talk to John Q. Law."

"Crap." She blinked, a bit more sense coming back into her baby blues. "You look *awful.*"

I *felt* halfway to awful, mostly because I'd torn something in my leg. One Sunrunner against three newborn suckheads. The only thing that had saved me was the fact that they hadn't had time to figure out how to really get troublesome. None of them could have turned more than forty-eight hours ago, still in the wet stage of transformation from human into sucking machine.

Which led me down some very interesting mental roads, in between checking Kat's breathing and looking at the blood drying on her face.

An engine cut off outside the bed and breakfast, and for a moment I was horribly aware of how alone we were. We were traveling off-season, and there was nobody in the whole bed-and-breakfast but us. The isolation had seemed charming when we'd arrived.

Now I just felt exposed and more than a little weak-kneed.

Footsteps on the porch. A knock, brief and courteous. Mrs. Evans came bustling out of the kitchen as the screen door opened and a wide, portly gentleman in a Sam Browne belt and dun uniform hove into view. He took off his hat, straggles of loose hair combed across the high dome of his skull, and I restrained the tingling in my arms and legs. I was already hairy enough; I didn't need to change right here to add to the fun. Small, close-set, deep-buried eyes met mine, and I took an immediate dislike to Harv the sheriff.

After all, he stank of bloodsucker. Half-moons of sweat spread under his arms, but the creases in his uniform were still starch-sharp. His skull glistened with sweat.

"Well, there, Miz Evans." A thin rolling voice, reedy enough to be a surprise from such a hefty man, whistled out. "What have we here?"

"Stray dog." Evans set the fresh glass of water down and flapped her doughy hands, jet beads clicking. She edged away from the sheriff, probably noticing the smell on a subconscious level. "Attacked one of my guests out in the garden. Made a ruckus."

"I saw one of your trellises was down." His eyes swung over

to me, damnyankee in my torn and muddy clothes. I suddenly wished I knew if or where I was bleeding. "Well hello, son. How's your lady friend? Needing a rabies shot?"

I was barely prepared for the surge of fury rising to my back teeth. Kat's fingers on mine were fever-hot, the ice was fiery-cold. Between those two scorches the fury hit a wall, was forced back down. "My wife seems to be fine, thank you. She wasn't bitten, just scratched."

"I'll get you some tea." Evans passed a little too close to me, and the smell of talcum powder, bourbon, perfume, and hairspray hit the back of my throat. I swallowed another growl, bent down, and took a deep whiff of Kat, broken stems, mud, cedar perfume, and the iron tang of blood. "You want some tea, honey?"

"Tea would be lovely." Kat's consonants blurred. A little more color came back into her face. The plastic bag crinkled, a streak of cleanness sliding down her cheek where condensation from the bag had started to drip.

"Can you describe the dog, missus?" The sheriff didn't step in past the foyer, leaning in the door to the living room. Instead, his eyes roved the surface of the chairs and settees, the dark and dead iron stove, the fringed lamps and overstuffed furniture. The place had once been a nice antebellum mansion, but it looked like the Victorian era had thrown up in here.

"Brown fur and big teeth." Kat gave him a wide-eyed, tremulous smile full of dewy innocence. "I didn't see much else."

The man's face didn't so much as crack. "Big dog? Little dog?" His narrow gaze cut over to me, flashed back to Kat, and slid back to me, eyes almost lost in folds of flesh.

I've seen that look once or twice, and it always makes my hackles go up.

He knows something.

Well, no shit. Reeking of bloodsucker and sweating like a horse, of *course* he knew something.

"Fairly big. Mitch scared it off." Amazingly, Kat actually fluttered her eyelashes. She slumped back against the chintz, her fingers still clamped to mine. "Were you hurt, sweetheart?"

Anyone who knew her would have winced at the sarcasm in her tone. Sheriff Harv scratched at his forehead, dangling his hat in one beefy hand. "Guess you's both lucky. Dogs is nothing to fool round with." There it was again, the furtive little gleam in his eye when he said "dog."

I hate that.

"Well, guess I'll take a report." Harv palmed a cupful of sweat from his broad forehead and dug deep for what looked like a genuine smile, directed at Kat. "You and your fella there don't go nowhere."

"I don't think I'm in the mood for any rambles." Kat bristled, and I suddenly knew it was in my behalf. My heart got four sizes too big for its anchor inside my ribcage. "Not with so many *dangerous things* on the loose."

The smile dropped off Harv's face so fast I was surprised it didn't shatter on the hardwood—tastefully covered by a rug embroidered with cabbage roses, of all things. "Guess not. Ma'am." He mimed tipping his hat to Miz Evans, who made a small idiotic sound, and left, banging the screen door behind him.

"He'll be back with some paperwork." Evans held two tall sweating glasses of tea I could smell the sugar in. "Here, honey. You need some tea. It fixes all ills."

Kat gave a weak smile as I peeled the ice away from her forehead. "What a nice man." Flat and ironic, and completely for Evans's benefit. "Do I look ready to bolt, Mitch?"

"You look beautiful." I took one of the teas, so Kat didn't have to, and she grabbed for the glass of water, reading my mind.

"You're a good liar." But she smiled. We were bloody, battered, and aching. But we'd gotten off lightly, and I knew it.

I'VE BEEN THINKING." KAT ROLLED OVER, WINCING, AND I suppressed a groan.

"Jesus. Do you have to?" I ached, and the bacon and eggs Evans had whipped up for me sat heavy in my stomach no matter how much of the pitcher of sweet tea I poured down. I was more nauseated than I should have been, my body craving protein to fuel muscle repair. Kat's desire for a salad was met with something made of cucumbers, tomatoes still warm from the sun, and fresh mozzarella in an olive-oily sauce. She liked it, but had eaten very little.

I'd started packing as soon as we hit our suite, stopping only to take bites off the piping-hot plate. Kat had picked at her food and gone to bed.

Packing didn't seem to be so much fun when I looked at the shape of her under the sheet. Still, I kept at it.

"I thought you loved me for my mind." She was smeared with thick green mugwort–and–holy water paste, drying and flaking off now, and the green smell mixed with the rest of her made my entire spine go cold.

Bitten. Second time in as many days she could have been seriously hurt. Goddamn. "Mind's no good without the body to put it in, sweetpea. *Three* suckheads—"

"—acting completely uncharacteristically. Seems like someone wants to stop my research."

The air conditioner droned under the silence that followed.

God damn the woman. "Kat." I struggled for control. "We're leaving at dawn. You can call the Argentum from the next town. We'll stop in a place that has a Starbucks and more than three stoplights, not to mention a decent Italian restaurant. I'll get you drunk on chianti and take advantage of you and we'll wend our way toward Disney World. Florida's nice this time of year."

"I don't *want* to go to Disney World. Do you want to hear what I was thinking about or not?"

I stuffed some T-shirts into my suitcase, higgledy-piggledy. "All right. Fine. But we're leaving tomorrow morning. You'd better get some sleep."

"I didn't sit down on the bench because I had a thought. It struck me there was a pattern to most of the disappearances. In most of the newspaper reports Lover's Leap is mentioned." She moved gingerly, settling herself again with a sigh. "Come over here, Mitch. I'm lonely."

Normally I would have burned up the carpet getting my shaggy ass into bed. Right now I jammed a pair of jeans into the suitcase and remembered the clothes we had soaking in the washer. "Be right there."

"You're being ridiculous. I say we go take a closer look at Lover's Leap tomorrow morning."

You're calling me *ridiculous?* "No way, Kat. Absolutely no way, nohow. *No.*"

"You can stay here if you're scared, Fido. But I want to do some scouting. I'll call in before we go, it shouldn't take someone too long to get here."

"This," I announced into the suitcase, "is not my idea of a good time." My fists ached, wanting to clench. The room was stuffy, even with air-conditioning.

"It'll be daytime. Any *sanguine* is going to be torpid and easy to kill. Anything else is likely to be torpid as well." She yawned.

My shoulders were tight as bridge cables. "No, Kat. That's final."

A charged silence settled into the room, made itself comfortable, and cringed away from Kat's soft, inflexible tone.

"If I hear the words 'that's final' out of your mouth again, Mitchell Black, they *will* be." The sheets rasped as she shifted, irritably. "I didn't marry you so you could tell me what to do. I'm an adult, and I'm a Knight of the Argentum Astrum. You can either help me or you can drive that Jeep of yours back to Las Vegas and find yourself both a divorce and a nice little husky to have puppies with."

I don't think she meant to say that. The nausea under my sternum crested, I swallowed sourness. *Christ, don't fight with her. It's still your goddamn honeymoon.* "I don't want you getting hurt, Kat."

She sighed. "We've done all right so far. And I'll call the Argentum tomorrow morning, as soon as I get up."

I didn't have breath to agree or disagree, my stomach rolling like a ship during a hurricane. I'd've suspected some bad bacon, but any Sunrunner worth his nose doesn't eat spoiled meat. Still, I abandoned my packing and made it to the bed. Laid down next to Kat, who probably considered the matter finished, because she didn't speak, just clicked off the lamp on her side. I lay in the dark, my stomach griping, until I passed out.

SOMETHING WAS WRONG. I SMELLED DIRT AND FOULNESS, and there was something in my eyes. It reeked of death. A scattering of something heavy dripped across my face, wet and silken and laden with decay. Everything was black.

Where's Kat?

Smells. Wet dirt, decaying vegetables, a heavy cologne touching off a chain of association. *All my men wear English Leather or they wear nothing at all.* Something heavy across my legs, my fingers tensed, dirt crumbling wet against my nails.

Kat? I didn't smell her.

The men burying me couldn't have been prepared for the dead body to crackle with shifting bones, sprouting fur and moving in ways their entire experience of reality tells them can't be so. They screamed, one teenage voice breaking with fear and another deeper male tone adding a jangling harmony, as I woke in the flush of the metabolic burn fueling the change. Halfway there I realized what was happening, but it was too late. I'd already killed the boy and was on top of the older man, snarling meat-laden breath into his face, my muzzle spattered with hot blood.

Blood's dangerous when you're in between man and wolf. It can drive you right over the edge into crazy. The wolf knows blood but it takes second place to survival, and a real man won't let his blood-lust carry him too far. But halfway? Well, that's the danger zone.

The night breathed, a complex tapestry of scent. Not cold pavement and garbage like a city, but fragrant rotting woodland full of swamp heat and decaying vegetable matter. We were out in the woods, and they had been burying me in a shallow grave. I could still feel tree roots digging into my flesh.

What the hell? I tried to talk, forgetting about my mouthful of wrongly-shaped teeth and tongue. The noises I made weren't human.

Neither were the noises my captive made. His baseball cap had been knocked off, and he was partly bald, smelling of beer and Lucky Strikes. I'd torn his overalls, slashing with long amber claws.

I finally got my wits about me and slowly shifted back, fur melting away. It was damn hot, and I was in a pair of jeans and nothing else. My knees dug into wet earth. The most pertinent question came tumbling out. "Where is my wife?"

The man gibbered and choked with fear, his glands opening up and pouring chemical terror into the meat. *Dammit.* Nothing sensible would come out of him for a while.

I decided to try to calm him down. "Hey. Why are you trying to bury me?"

Poison, you jackass. And you lapped it up. I've never been the quickest on the uptake, I leave that to Kat. I settle for being the most thorough, most of the time. My fingers tingled and my chest constricted, something foreign burning off through my metabolism and sending a wave of weakness through me. Good thing about being Sunrunner, most poisons run right through us and disperse, defeated by heightened tissue regrowth and our neurological resistances, built to handle the sensory overload of the change.

Bad thing? It hurts like hell, and it makes us cranky.

I didn't smell anything in the meat. Then it hit me again, a wave of sugar-coated nausea, and I cursed, grinding the chubby man down into the dirt.

The tea. Sweet enough to rot all the teeth, and sugar will cover up all *sorts* of things where a canine's concerned.

"OhGawd ohGawd—" A sharp stink wafted up. The man had actually peed himself.

Good Christ. What am I going to do now? I showed my teeth in a wolf's grin and he cried out, trying to backpedal, his legs and arms flailing wildly. I let him go, standing up as he gibbered and moaned.

Just a good ole boy, never meaning no harm. Huh. I bent down, quick fingers working, and found a heavy ring of keys. It would be worth my while to find out who the hell he was and why he was burying bodies for someone, but I had a bigger concern.

Poison meant Evans was involved. Which meant Kat was vulnerable, and in deep trouble. I wrapped my fist in the man's overalls and shirt, hauling him up. "Where's your car, Bubba? Be a nice boy and tell me, and I'll let you live."

I CUT THE ENGINE AND LET THE TRUCK drift, rattling, down the long slope. I was about a mile from Evans's place, and pretty sure she'd know my unwitting benefactor's vehicle. The man was trussed with duct tape and tossed in the back with two toolboxes and various other odd bits, since I didn't want to murder him.

Not yet, anyway.

I got out, my boots crunching on gravel. The moon rose, high and white, casting knife-edged shadows along the ditches and under each little rock in the road. It was still hot-humid-damp, so the roostertail of dust the truck left in the air wouldn't be too visible. Besides, it was night.

But what if you're not just dealing with suckers, Mitch? It was the voice of panic. *Where's Kat? Dammit. What am I going to do?*

I rested my hand on the truck's hood for a moment, metal pinging as it cooled. The goddamn thing smelled like lit diesel farts and drove worse than a walleyed wino. It was loud and probably well-known in this neck of the woods. If I left it by the side of the road, sooner or later someone would find it, and whoever was behind all this would know I wasn't dead.

So I either had to dispose of both Bubba and his truck, or I had to work fast.

Of course, if Kat was already dead . . .

You stop that right now. It's only been a little while. They had just started to bury you. Chances are Kat's still alive, they have to figure out what she knows and if she told anyone.

Still, if Evans had poisoned me, she might not be inclined to keep Kat alive either.

Jesus Christ, Mitch, just get on with it!

In the end I decided to leave the truck by the side of the road. If someone found Bubba taped up in the bed, it wouldn't make a rat's ass worth of difference.

I'm no murderer. But if they hurt even one hair on Kat's head we were going to see just what a pissed-off Sunrunner can do to frail human flesh.

THE RAMBLING ANTEBELLUM HOUSE WAS DARK AND DESERTED. My Jeep sat in the gravel parking lot bordered with tall thin willows on three sides and a sloppy mix of kudzu on the fourth heading toward the road. The creek babbled a little under more willows, a long stone's throw away. It was child's play to force the back door—deadbolts are strong, but wooden doors tend to tear away from them if you apply enough force.

The kitchen was pin-neat and the downstairs was completely tidy as well. I went up the stairs to the second floor, took a hard right, and found the door to our suite open and the entire room looking like a hurricane had hit it.

Kat had put up a good fight. The window was busted all to hell, humid night seeping in as air-conditioning escaped. Grit lay everywhere, the smell of suckers rasping against my instincts. The mirrors were shattered and the mosquito netting over the bed was ripped up, the bed thrashed out of recognition and our luggage scattered around. Chairs were upended, the plush settee in a corner where she had probably tried to barricade herself, to judge by the damage to the wallpaper and plaster. The lightbulbs were all smashed, the ceiling fixture pulled out and dangling by a thread like a loose tooth, the lamps both overturned, their fringes tangled.

Small, my Kat. But packed with dynamite. Birch stakes lay scattered through the room, one driven into the flooring like a straw into a potato.

Damn, girl. If the situation had been otherwise, I might have smiled.

No clues. Just the remnants of a helluva fight. Violence still smoked in the air. Had I been deaf to it all, poisoned by sweet tea?

I made my way back downstairs, moving easily through the darkness. Evans's office was on the other side of the detached kitchen, in a connected outbuilding recent enough to still smell like fresh lumber to my sensitive nose. The lock was better than the deadbolts on the front and back doors, and the door itself was metal. Fortunately the new drywall wasn't nearly so resistant, and I walked right in, ducking to avoid the crossbar of the wall's skeleton, sneezing at clouds of chalky dust.

The office was pin-neat, with a wide tall window that looked out on the garden and a desk littered with paper. I glanced at the door and stopped, my skin chilling and rippling for a moment as I fought off the urge to shift to meet a new threat.

Hanging from the doorknob was a little muslin pouch tied with red ribbon. It stank of death, with a peculiar overtone of horehound candy. The fetish rocked slightly against the door, humming nastily to itself. The sound of its tapping was flabby fingers against a pane of wet glass.

I froze and looked around the office. The air was close, thick, and rank with sorcery. Another step in, and the sorcerer's den might wake up—who knew what little traps were left in here?

Great, Mitch. You idiot. How did you not smell her out? Her perfume, and that talcum powder—just the thing to clog up a sensitive nose. And she was scared, not of me but of the sheriff. Merciful Sun.

Something caught my eye. I bent down a little, peering out the window. When sitting at the desk, Evans would have her back to the wall instead of the door. File cabinets marched along the other wall. The picture window framed gardens, the ribbon of the road, forest, and Lover's Leap, glowing slick and wet under the almost-full moon.

"Holy shit," I breathed, and backed out through the hole in the wall.

Of all the bed-and-breakfasts in Virginia, we had to walk right into one run by a sorcerer. I stared through the Sunrunner-sized hole in the wall at the moonlight flooding over the desktop, a big bad Southern moon drenching everything with dead light. There was probably evidence in that office that would tell me what the hell was going on and why Kat had been taken.

You're dumb, Mitch, but you're not that dumb. You're not a private eye, you're a Sunrunner, and your wife's in trouble. You want to finish this honeymoon, you'll go and get her. You know where.

"Lover's Leap." My voice, flat and furious, took me by surprise. The house creaked and sighed its regular nightly song. Old houses are like that, they hum to themselves at night, the heat of the day leaching out of joints and beams. "Hang on, Kat. I'm coming to get you."

I LOPED ALONGSIDE THE ROAD IN FULL CHANGE, my pads silent on the forest floor. The burn of light on shifting textures of fur ran along my nerve endings, the night exploding like champagne on the back of my throat. There was a thread of *wrong* along the road, a scent that shouldn't be, well-traveled, like the passage of a predator at the edge of a herd. It raised my hackles and gave speed to my legs, the wolf's joy at its freedom matching my urgency.

Kat, honey, just hold on. I'm on my way.

A Sunrunner can cover a lot of ground on four legs, but the moon was lowering in the sky by the time I reached the base of the mountain, where the road took a sharp turn and started winding up to Lover's Leap. I could either cut across the hairpin turns, or I could follow them and lose time, remaining more cautiously hidden.

Kat. I decided to take a direct route up the side of a sharp rocky incline, covered with all sorts of trashwood and clinging bushes, scrub pine and bare rocks. Instinct told me there was a way.

I made very little noise, scrabbling through undergrowth and using the rocks as takeoff pads. I'm no mountain goat, but a wolf's hardly the worst animal when it comes to getting up a hill. The faster you go, the easier it is to balance, like a tightrope. Each time I crossed the dusty ribbon of the road fresh urgency pounded behind my heart, each beat saying her name. *Kat. Kat. Kat.*

The last sharp turn unreeled on my right as I bounded from rock to rock, twisting in midair to land splayed on an outcropping. On my left was a widening semicircle of gravel, the parking area for Lover's Leap. Instinct drove me into shadow at the far end, avoiding the bright glare of exposure. I nosed around the edges of the lot, trying to catch something of that thread of *wrong*.

Nothing. The night was still, except for frogs singing somewhere down in the valley and a raccoon bumbling along a ways away, the soft passionless talk of owls sometimes filtering through.

This was the only clue I had, and it was a bust.

Something has to be here. It has to be. Look harder. Look again.

I stilled myself, watching the wide field of pebbles, stamped dirt, and moonshine. Heard the far-off thudding of an engine laboring through the turns. Someone was coming.

I decided to chance it and worked as far toward the edge as I could, nose to the ground. I slunk out into the light, tail held protectively low to keep my profile small, and stepped into the full force of the wind from the valley, the exhalation off the mountain changing to an inhale. Every sense strained, watching, waiting. Little points of light in the valley was the town, stars come to earth.

The knocking engine grew closer. It wasn't Bubba's truck, but every instinct screamed for me to get back under cover.

A stray draft touched my nose, teasing with the decaying tang of bloodsuckers. I stiffened, easing out past the rickety rotting wooden fence meant to keep idiots from taking a plunge. My front paws placed themselves delicately, testing the ground before I shifted my weight.

The draft came again, and I dropped my nose. It wafted up from somewhere below, foul death-reek, bloating flesh and old rotting blood. It was a fermenting smell, hot and juicy.

A nest.

I hesitated. The rock face wasn't quite sheer here, bulging and curving to point an accusing finger toward the town. The change melted away as I lay flat on my belly and swung my legs out over the drop, furry toes lengthening and finding crevices.

This isn't going to work.

Never mind. You have to make it work. Besides, the smell was close. Close enough to make the fur rippling up my back stand on end in hard bristles, a mane of adrenaline-laden fear.

The knocking engine eased closer, gunning, brakes squealing on the turns. Someone was going fast. I hesitated. My questing right foot stretched for a hold and found only emptiness.

What the hell? Meaty warmth caressed my bare hairy foot, caught between wolf and man. Bones crackled as I shifted, trying to find a better shape, fingers jammed in crevices and my other leg twisted awkwardly, anchoring me to the cliff face.

The thought of a nest here, just under the surface of a high school makeout spot, turned me cold. The thought of Kat, maybe trapped in the close wet decaying heat, maybe waiting for the suckers to straggle back home and find a predawn snack waiting for them, called bitter bile up into my throat.

I moved my left foot to another hold, bracing myself, clambered down another few feet. My right foot still dangled. I was on the edge of a cave entrance, I thought, and shuddered at the idea of my leg hanging out in front of a sucker.

Another few moments of squirming while the engine roared closer and closer brought a gift—my right foot touched something solid and gritty, and I dropped onto a long low shelf in front of a pitch-black horizontal crack in the face of Lover's Leap. I peered at the shelf and the rock below, my eyes picking out hand-and-footholds. An easy climb for a Sunrunner—or for a bloodsucker powered by stolen life and ravenous hunger, looking for its safe hole to spend the night. A nest like this could go on, hidden, for a long time. Precious few would think to look for it here, or would believe what they found.

The nest was most likely empty, everything that called it home out looking for prey under the moon. I eased into the pitch blackness, miserably compelled. The sorcerer might only have to get Kat up here, easy if she had accomplices, and leave her tied up. A nice little sucker-snack before dawn sent them into torpor.

I couldn't smell her. The reek of suckers was too thick.

I tried to whisper Kat's name, forgetting I was half-changed and making only a little whine. The reek stung my eyes and filled my nose with stinging pain. Two more steps brought me to a stone overhang that might have brained me if I hadn't been warned by the hair-fine sensitivity of the half-changed. I had to go on hands and knees, squirming over a hillock on the rocky floor, a small part of me noting the geological irregularity that would keep daylight from streaming through the entrance.

A foxfire glimmer struck my eyes. The crack widened into a small corridor, one I duck-walked through. Every bad memory in the world was attached to that hideous wet smell. Suckers don't bring their prey back unless it's small and easily portable, but they dye the walls of their nests with pheromones and slick excretions that raise the temperature. I rounded a shallow bend in the corridor, and the floor sloped away underneath me, turning into fine sand. A low unhealthy glow came from chunks of rock daubed with something like lichen, and my hackles rose. The cave was large enough for a goodish-sized nest, and bones swam in the sea of rot-laced sand on the floor. Against the back wall was a drift of jumbled things— clothes, broken pottery shards, glass twinkling, all sorts of crap.

In the middle of the cave, sunk down three-quarters of the way, a hump of black obsidian surfaced. The light touching its face didn't reflect—it fell in, endlessly, dying in the stone's depths. A sharp tang of sorcery cut through the morass of foulness, and I had to blink several times, eyes streaming, before I realized the shadow in front of the obsidian chunk was humanoid, rocking back and forth as it whispered something lost in the susurrus of warmed air whistling through the crack.

I blinked furiously, trying to clear my vision. Kat was nowhere in here.

And Mrs. Evans, her bun neat and tidy as ever and her house-dress dragging on the filthy sand, crouched in front of me, her chanting suddenly rising from a whisper to a keening. The obsidian sparked, a bloody glow rising from its depths, and I suddenly smelled suckers, up-close and personal.

Now is not a good time to wish you'd studied sorcerers a little closer. But Sunrunners don't tangle much with them. We're too busy with suckers most of the time.

Whatever Evans was doing couldn't mean well. And she, of all people, would know where my wife was.

I gathered myself, legs compressing under me and the change shifting me further toward wolf than man. Sand whispered underfoot, and Evans jerked away from whatever spell she was concocting, too late.

I hit her low and hard, hearing a bone snap as I jolted her across the cave, claws scraping in treacly sand. The chanting vanished, swallowed as her teeth clicked together hard enough to take a chunk of tongue out. She was an old woman, and stout, and hellishly strong. Why had I never noticed before?

Because you weren't looking, Mitch. Stupid dog.

I clapped a hand over her mouth and got my knee in her midriff, opening my mouth to snarl. Strands of her gray hair came loose as she heaved and struggled, and I had to change a bit to get a mouth human enough to talk with.

"Where is my wife?" I roared, the words splitting and echoing across the cave. *"You tell me or so help me I will kill you!"*

I still had her mouth clamped closed. How was I going to get information out of her without her mumbling more spells?

Evans shook, her eyes glazed with shock, her leg twisted at an odd angle underneath me. Sweat stood out on her brow, great pearly drops against doughy skin.

I heard, faint and faraway, the knocking of the engine that had followed me up to Lover's Leap. It cut off, suddenly, and other sounds crept into the cave's dense wet gloom.

Little soft padding feet, and a hiss. The obsidian in the middle of the cave chuckled like wet clay tearing apart. I knew that sound—it was the noise suckers made when their prey was close and unaware.

I snapped a glance over my shoulder. Against the foxfire, little pinpricks of light showed—sucker eyes, throwing back only a small point of light since their pupils are so far shrunk. They're all but blind in anything other than almost-darkness, but their heat-sensitivity makes up for it, and a sucker can hear your pulse a mile away.

I heard the faint thud of car doors slamming as they crowded in through the lips of the cave. Some of the pinpricks halted, the shapes slumping as the suckers dropped down to all fours, turning their heads to catch the sound of prey above.

Faint on the wind came a piercing cry, one I'd know anywhere.

"Mitch! Mitchell Black! *Where the hell are you?*"

Kat? I looked down, and the sorcerer's eyes rolled back inside her head. They're tricky beasts, and once a sorcerer's spell goes far enough it completes itself, whether you interrupt them or not.

I rose unsteadily. A good half-dozen suckers swarmed into the cave, sniffing, probably uncertain of what to do. Without the sorcerer's will guiding them, they would mill around for a few seconds before their pack mentality reasserted itself.

More cries from up above. "Mitch! *Mitch goddammit—*" Choked off. Of course, if there were suckers down here there would have to be ones up there, it was one of their favorite hunting grounds. Food delivered right to their door.

This is going to be interesting. Mitch, you dumbass.

No time for thought. I shifted and launched myself toward the cave entrance, for light, for love, for Kat.

———

A GUNSHOT CRACKED PREDAWN HUSH. HARV TOOK HIS foot from
the sucker's neck as its head exploded into ash. "One thing I've always hated about this town." He paused as Kat brought the last
stake down with a convulsive movement. It sank into sucker flesh
like an ax biting deep into wood, and I let up on the thing's throat
as it turned to ash. "It's all the damn vampires."

The sheriff holstered his gun. Dense cotton fog was filling
the valley, creeping in on little cat feet. To one side, a battered
Chevy Caprice painted primer-gray stood with both driver's and
passenger's doors open. Gravel ground into my knees as I slumped,
breathing heavily, staring at the carnage even now dissolving into
dust.

"Are you all right?" Kat dropped her stake and cupped my
face in her hands, examining me. "Mitch? Talk to me. Are you
okay?"

I dunno, sweetpea. Am I? I found my voice, and realized with relief that I was in human form. When had I changed back? I
couldn't tell. I was bone-weary, little scrapes all over me singing
with pain as the grit worked its way ever-finer against my skin,
sandpaper rasping. "What happened?" I coughed hoarsely, hawk-
ing a wad of something dry, spitting toward the edge. False dawn
was coming up, streaks of gray in the east.

Kat let go of me and sat back on her heels, sparing a glance at
the drifts of dust settling in the stillness. "You were asleep, so I
snuck outside to take another look at the garden. Something about
that attack didn't seem quite right to me until I found this." She
dug in her jeans pocket and dragged out a small leather pouch,
humming as it dangled from its strap. Another fetish, probably the
one Evans had used to get the suckers to jump Kat in the garden. "I
heard a car and hid in the kudzu. Some man in a truck drove up,
went into the house, he and Evans came out carrying something

that looked an awful lot like a body. I snuck back into the house to get you, but you were gone. Then Evans came back up and sicced her *sanguinant* on me." A small shrug. "They were confused by the fetish, so after the fight I popped out the window and ran like hell. The truck had disappeared, you were gone, and I had a very bad feeling about it. So I hiked to that *other* bed-and-breakfast—the one you didn't like, remember? I pounded on the door until they opened up and had them call 911. Turns out Harvey here is an Argentum. Isn't that funny?"

"Hilarious." I struggled to process this. Kat was alive, sitting right in front of me, and covered in dirt, blood, mud, guck, and the dried remnants of mugwort paste. She had a scrape on her forehead, her cheek was still glaring purple, and one of her hands was bound with a dirty gauze bandage. Her T-shirt was torn, but she'd tied it together, the knot underneath her breasts, her nipples clearly visible against the thin material.

Harv's wide Sam Browne belt creaked as he lowered himself stiffly to one knee. He still moved pretty well, for an old fat man. "God have mercy on these poor bastuds. I been trying to figure out what it is with Lover's Leap for years. Kids vanish all the time, and somehow this place always seems connected. But these suckers is tricky—I could only kill 'em by one or two. I've known Widder Evans for years, never thought she was the sorceress type."

"She must have learned it from someone," Kat pointed out. "Where were you, Mitch?"

"There's a cave." I swallowed dryly, my throat clicking. "Under the edge there. Something's in it. Evans is too, and some of her suckers. I think I killed her."

A few moments of absolute silence ruled Lover's Leap. Gray light strengthened in the east, and the fog tightened its grip on Cotton Crossing's points of light.

"Well, goddammit." Harv sounded disgusted. "I woulda liked to question her, son. A cave, you say?"

I wasn't thinking of arresting her, you Southern-fried ape. "Right under the edge." My hands went out, curled around Kat's shoulders. She was alive and breathing, and her blue eyes sparkled as they met mine. She looked happy enough to bust. "I'd take a few people in there with you, though. Looks like an active nest, and there's a chunk of what looks like obsidian. Evans was using it for something."

"Harv called in. There will be a few more Argentum out here by late morning. Can you believe they have to drive all the way from Richmond?"

Sweet merciful Sun. She's alive. "I am going to tan your hide," I mumbled. "Out sneaking around at night."

"I should tan *yours,* Fido. Going into a nest alone." But she leaned into my hands, and the next thing I knew she was in my arms, stinking of bloodsucker but under that, warm and alive and my Kat.

"I hate to interrupt." Harv hitched up his belt, his small eyes gleaming in the strengthening light. "But they's some more work to be done here, and you'd best help me do it. Then you best be on your way. I can clean this up with a little help from the Ordah, but I don't want folks noticin' you tangled up in'm."

Christ, I can't wait to get out of this town. I made a muffled noise of assent, and planted a grateful kiss on Kat's dirty hair before helping her to her feet.

MITCH." SHE POKED ME IN THE RIBS. "WAKE up. It's past noon."

I groaned, rolling over and burying my face in the pillow. "Go 'way." Running around changed and half-changed all night right after being poisoned did not make for a happy morning Sunrunner.

She bounced on the edge of the bed, hardly able to contain herself. *Where does she find all that energy?* The motel room windows were dusty, but she'd pulled the shades back and a flood of sunlight poured through to touch the tired carpet. We were twenty miles from Cotton Crossing, as far as I could drive without passing out and veering us off the road, and the motel was that peculiar Southern roadside type that took cash and didn't ask any questions when a dirty man came in at dawn looking for a room.

"I just called Harv. He's really a very nice man. He had some news."

Sweet merciful Sun. "Didn't we agree—"

"—that I'm not going be involved in that investigation anymore, yes, I know, *ad nauseam, ad infinitum.* I just wanted to check in. Did you know there was an old legend about Lover's Leap?"

I don't want to hear it. "Mrph." I tried plugging my ears with the pillow, but she wrestled it away. I didn't fight too hard—she was probably tired too, bruised and aching.

Yeah. Like that would slow *her* down.

"Seems a Confederate bride got news of her young man's death and threw herself off. After that, kids started scaring each other half to death with stories about Bloody Mary Evans. Mrs. Evans was her direct descendant." She shook my shoulder, but gently. "Try to act interested, at least. There's another legend too, an older one."

"Yeah?" I pried an eyelid open, mostly for the joy of looking at her. She was still bruised, dried mugwort paste daubed on her swollen cheek and gashed forehead. Her hair was still wet from the shower, and she wore one of my button-down shirts. It came down almost to her knees.

Damn, she's gorgeous. Did I mention the woman just has no mercy?

"The local Algonquians had a legend about Lover's Leap. They called it something that translates out to 'hungry rock.' The legend says it was once a stone belonging to one of their shamans, but the shaman got bit by a beast and died. Only he didn't stay dead, his spirit went into the rock and got bigger and bigger and made most of the tribe vanish. This was right after the white man got here, so scholars thought it was a story about smallpox. Only—"

"Hungry rock. That makes sense." I shivered, suddenly fully awake. "Ugh."

"Whatever's in that cave, the Argentum will take care of. There's just one thing that worries me." Her eyebrows drew together, and I saw trouble on the horizon.

"Oh, no. No. Come on, Kat. Harv told us to get out and stay out. He won't be able to help us if law enforcement gets wind of Evans's body."

"Please." She gave the notion short shrift. "He *is* the law enforcement around there. He could really use a hand, though. He's getting old, and he needs an apprentice. Speaking of apprentice, that's what bothers me."

I laced my fingers behind my head and looked at her. Her hair glowed in the reflected sunlight, and even in a cheap motel room she was the best damn thing I'd ever seen. "What, sweetpea?"

"Just where *did* Evans learn sorcery? Harv knew she was a little eccentric, but he swears there wasn't a sorcerer in town for a good fifty years. He says he would have known, and I believe him. *And* the guy you left tied up in his pickup is nowhere to be found."

I groaned again. "No more mysteries. We killed the bad guy and we're both still breathing. Chalk it up to a win and leave it *alone*."

"I don't know. It just bothers me." But she smiled, and leaned down, her hair falling in my face. "You came all the way out there to rescue me, didn't you?"

Of course I did. "Yep."

"My hero." Her mouth met mine, and things were progressing very satisfactorily for a long while until she broke away for some breath. "But I'm picking the next hotel, Mitch. And you're still in the doghouse."

Half of being married, I guess, is knowing when to keep your mouth shut. The other half is probably knowing when to open it. Which for any reasonable man is close to *never,* when it comes to women.

So I settled for diplomacy, us being on our honeymoon and all. "Sure thing, sweetpea. Now kiss me again."

And she did.

I'm a lucky man.

LILITH SAINTCROW is best known for her Dante Valentine series, featuring a trigger-happy Necromance and lots of demons. She lives in Vancouver, Washington, with her husband, three children, four cats, and various other strays. You can find Lili online at www.lilithsaintcrow.com.

A Wulf in Groom's Clothing

RONDA THOMPSON

The Wulf name is cursed. True passion rouses and releases the beast in males of the bloodline, but can facing a worst enemy—even the one lurking within—cast out the spirit?

LAURA WULF WAS A CITY GIRL ALL THE way. She knew her husband of five hours enjoyed monthly trips into the woods. Sam liked to fish, hunt, and do whatever it was that men did when they became one with nature, but Laura had never wanted to stay anywhere there wasn't an outlet for her blow-dryer and a Starbucks on the corner.

That was something she had failed to mention to Sam during their eight-month whirlwind courtship. Laura had, in fact, alluded to the opposite. Sam believed she loved the great outdoors as much as he did. How could she fool him for a whole week?

"What do you think of our love nest, Mrs. Wulf?"

The cabin resembled some type of nest, all right; Laura just didn't see "fantastic honeymoon location" written all over it. There were lights on, however, so true his word, there really was electricity. A faint scent of pine mixed with Lemon Pledge hung in the air, suggesting that Sam had tried to tidy up in preparation for their stay.

But the place was small, a little run-down looking, and there were plaid drapes on the windows. The walls were paneled in pine and the floors were old hardwood, scuffed and in need of a good varnish. But the wood in the cabin wasn't really the problem for her. It was the woods outside.

"I know you deserve better, but with our work schedules and the cost of the wedding, it's the best I can do for now, baby."

One glance into Sam's big brown puppy dog eyes almost made Laura forget about the plaid drapes and the even scarier décor of the rugged outdoors beyond the windows. Maybe this wasn't the honeymoon she'd always dreamed of having, but they were together. They were married. That should be all that mattered.

"It's not that bad," she lied. "And you're right. It's definitely private."

Sam pulled her into his arms. "We're going to have a fantastic time here. Who in their right mind doesn't like a peaceful week in the woods?"

Goldilocks didn't like her short jaunt into the woods. Neither did Little Red Riding Hood. Hansel and Gretel . . . The list went on and on. It struck Laura that from a young age children were taught to distrust the woods. Bad things happened there.

"It's really kind of charming," she forced herself to say, and tried harder to make herself believe. Glancing around, she noticed the bunk beds. Bunk beds? It was their honeymoon! Nodding toward the beds, Laura asked, "Do I get to be on top or bottom?"

Nuzzling her neck, he answered, "Baby, you can have whatever position you want."

Now he was talking. There was at least one sport Laura didn't mind getting sweaty while doing with her sexy husband. But first she wanted to prepare for her wedding night. "I'm taking a shower."

"Bathroom's in there." Sam nodded toward the only door in the cabin besides the front one. "I'll put two bunks together and make one bed for us. It'll be romantic. You'll see."

Romantic? Laura had reservations but she grabbed her overnight bag and headed for the bathroom. She switched on the light, pleased to see a plug for her blow-dryer. Maybe five days in the woods, away from the city and their hectic job schedules, would be more romantic than she could currently wrap her brain around.

They both did need downtime after their whirlwind courtship and the stress of planning a wedding. Some thought their decision to marry was too hasty, but Laura didn't have a single doubt she'd done the right thing by marrying Sam Wulf. It had been love at first sight, made stronger when she got to know him over the past few months.

Besides being absolutely gorgeous, Sam was also considerate, sensitive, and one hell of a lover. He was almost too good to be true. And he was hers. That thought made her smile, even if the bathroom wasn't much larger than a broom closet.

The water was thankfully warm and not the same ugly brown shade as the plaid drapes in the other room. Laura soaped herself with sensuous-smelling shower gel. The smell of lavender calmed her. There were no wedding-night jitters, just an antsy feeling about being stuck in the woods for a week. She and Sam couldn't spend all of their time in bed. What else were they going to do?

Knowing her husband, things that involved lots of physical

exertion, not only indoors but outdoors, as well. Sam owned a landscaping business, which was how Laura had met him. She'd hired him and his crew to spruce up a few properties she planned to flip in her private real estate practice. The first time he'd shown up at a fixer-upper to discuss the bid, Sam had the job. He was worth any price just to see if he'd take off his shirt while he worked. He had, and Laura spent far too much time at the property just watching him labor in the hot sun.

One thing led to another and they'd started going out eight months ago. Now she was Mrs. Sam Wulf. And Laura couldn't be happier. The shower suddenly turned cold, causing her to squeal. Okay, she could be a little happier. Laura could be somewhere else on her honeymoon.

"You all right in there?" Sam called through the door.

Quickly turning off the water, which didn't have much pressure in the first place, she answered, "The water turned cold!"

"Small water heater. You'll have to take quick showers while we're here."

Quick showers? Small water heater? Bunk beds? "I can do this," she vowed, stepping from the shower and grabbing up a fluffy towel.

"Need help drying off?"

"No you don't." Laura laughed. "I'm surprising you with this naughty negligee even if I only have it on for five minutes. You're supposed to be creating a romantic atmosphere."

"Just waiting for you to complete the picture. I'm ready, baby. More than ready."

That got her blood pumping again. Laura dried off, ran a brush through her hair, slipped into an indecent black sheer negligée, matching tiny thong underwear, and high-heeled black slippers. Switching off the overhead light, she opened the door.

In the short time Laura had been in the shower, Sam transformed the small cabin. Several candles were lit and placed around the room. Two large windows were thrown open, allowing the silvery light from a full moon to shine in upon the bunks he'd put together. Her husband was already in bed, bathed in a soft glow that highlighted his tawny muscles and hid his face in shadows.

"Wow," she whispered.

"Wow yourself," came his response from bed. "Get over here, woman. I plan to ravish you."

The way Sam nearly growled the words sent a shot of pure lust racing through her. Laura moved on wobbly legs to the bed. It wasn't that she was unskilled in walking in three-inch heels; to the contrary, the stiletto points kept getting caught in the cracks of the floor. Halfway to the bed, she kicked them off. Sam laughed softly.

"I should have warned you about bringing high heels of any sort to the woods. You did bring a pair of sensible shoes to hike around in, right?"

Hike around? The question drew her up short. Laura had brought a darling pair of denim flats she should be able to stroll outside wearing, but she'd pictured any walking they might do more in the way of short moonlit strolls a few feet from the cabin and back. Just as she feared, Sam had other ideas for them.

"Yes," she answered. "I brought woods-appropriate attire."

"I like what you're wearing right now, even if you're not going to be wearing it for long." He patted the bed. "Hurry up or I'm coming to get you."

Worry over the hiking remark faded. It was her wedding night. She continued toward the bed, moving with a sensuous sway to her hips the heels hadn't allowed her to carry off. Laura had almost reached the bed when something sharp jabbed the bottom of her foot. The sting made her cry out. A second later Sam was there, scooping her up in his arms.

"What happened?" he asked, carrying her toward the bed.

"I think I got a splinter in my foot!"

After being gently lowered to the mattress, Sam bent beside her. "Let me see."

Laura doubted he could see much of anything in the soft glow of the candles. His warm hands cradling her foot soothed the sting though. As big and brawny as Sam was, he had a tender touch. Reaching forward, Laura ran a hand through her groom's thick blond hair. She loved Sam's shoulder-length curls.

"It's just a little splinter," he said. "I can pull it out without tweezers. Ready?"

She wondered how her groom could see a little splinter in her foot much less pull it out when he did the deed. "Ouch!"

"I'll kiss it and make it better," he promised.

Although foot fetishes were not her forte, when Sam nibbled on her toes, Laura reconsidered her opinion. He worked his way up to her ankle, then higher until she forgot about the splinter. His hands slid up her legs beneath her sheer nightgown, pulling the nearly nonexistent panties over her hips and down her legs.

"You smell good," he whispered huskily. "Your skin is so soft. You're beautiful."

Although Laura knew she was attractive, Sam made her feel like a goddess. She loved the way he worshiped her. Slowly, he pushed the sheer nightgown up her thighs, gathering it around her waist. As he nibbled at the inside of her thigh, she moaned softly, her eyes half-closed in anticipation of the pleasures to come. The silvery moonlight spilling in from the open windows showered Sam in floating moonbeams . . . but wait, those weren't moonbeams, they were bugs!

Jerking upright, Laura swatted at one of the insects, slapping Sam on the head.

"Hey." He pulled back. "Why'd you hit me?"

"There are giant insects in here!" Laura snapped her legs closed and jumped off the bed, nearly knocking Sam over in her haste to get away from the swarm.

"They're just mosquitoes, Laura," he gently chided. "Go into the bathroom and spray yourself with bug dope while I shoo them out and close the windows. The repellent is in the medicine cabinet. It was probably the smell of your perfume that attracted them to begin with."

So much for smelling good in the woods. Laura made a mad dash for the bathroom and closed the door behind her. She turned on the light, afraid the room would also be full of bugs, but the mosquitoes were obviously as claustrophobic as she was. Just as Sam said, the repellent was in the medicine cabinet. She sprayed herself down and cracked the door.

"Are they gone?"

Sam moved around the cabin lighting more candles. "I think I got most of them out," he said. "I'm putting a few citronella candles around the bed. The scent should keep them away."

The candles smelled about as sexy as the repellent Laura had doused herself in. She walked out of the bathroom, careful not to shuffle her bare feet lest she get another splinter. "Maybe we can wait to start the actual honeymoon until tomorrow night."

"Nonsense." Sam placed one more burning candle on the floor and moved toward her. "I want to make love to my bride. It's tradition."

So far, nothing about their wedding night was traditional. "Making love together isn't anything new to either of us. I smell bad. There are bugs in the room. Let's call it a night and try again tomorrow."

He shook his head and pulled her into his arms. "It is new, Laura. It's the first time we make love as husband and wife. We seal the vows we made to one another earlier by coming together as one tonight."

Her eyes watered. Sam's words were romantic, but it was the candle aroma that made Laura tear up. She had wanted tonight to be perfect . . . well, as perfect as it could have been given their location, but so far, everything had gone wrong. Regardless, Laura wouldn't deny her new husband his marital rights. She'd certainly never denied him the same rights before the wedding. An idea occurred to her. Taking Sam's hand, she led him into the bathroom.

After pulling the sheer gown over her head, Laura turned on the shower. "Okay, hot stuff, you've got about ten minutes before the water turns cold."

SAM SAT IN THE MOONLIGHT SPILLING IN FROM the windows, watching Laura sleep. With her porcelain skin, her midnight dark hair, and sparkling blue eyes, she was a knockout. He'd fallen in love with his wife on sight—had come to love her more during the past months. She was funny, sassy, and sophisticated. Laura was supposed to be The One, so why didn't he feel any different inside?

Glancing out into the night, Sam still saw things no human could see. His hearing allowed him to catch the slight snap of a branch as a night creature scurried through the brush. The affliction Laura had unleashed upon him should have been cured tonight. He'd met the woman meant for him. He'd married her and consummated their wedding night. What had happened? Why was he still cursed?

"Sam?" Laura mumbled sleepily.

He smoothed a velvet soft curl from her face. "I'm here."

"The bedsprings are cutting into my back."

After grabbing a couple of pillows, Sam tried to make Laura more comfortable. He stared down at her and felt miserable. He'd lied to his new wife, and about more than just the honeymoon location. Sam had plenty of money. He could have taken his bride on a romantic cruise. Hell, he could have taken her to Paris, but the bane of his ancestors kept him a prisoner of the woods and the full moon.

If the curse was not broken as the poem handed down for centuries suggested it should be, Sam needed to be in surroundings where he could blend. He'd have to hide the truth from the one woman he wanted to have no secrets from.

Already the change threatened him. The beast prowled beneath his skin, ready to break free. Sam must leave his bride's side and venture to the woods where it would claim him. Glancing down once more at Laura, he leaned close and kissed her lightly upon the forehead.

"I'm so sorry, baby."

Rising, he walked to the door, eased it open and slipped outside. The smell of damp dirt, overripe vegetation, and fresh air filled his nostrils. The forest beckoned him, as did the full moon that hung suspended in the night sky. He followed the call, moving slowly at first before he speeded his journey to embrace the beast. Sam raced the shadows, jumping fallen logs, oblivious of the pine needles and small pebbles beneath his bare feet.

Although the scourge of his forefathers had fallen upon him, he'd found a gift in a punishment tied to his name. Never did Sam feel so free as when he was one with the night. He'd adjusted to the pain of transformation over the past months and now fully embraced the change. It came to him easily, running on two legs one moment and then on four the next.

He was accepted here, among the other creatures of the night. But Sam wanted to be accepted by his wife, as well, and he wasn't sure how Laura would react to the truth. Maybe tonight was just a fluke and tomorrow night he'd resist the lure of a full moon. As much as he loved his freedom, his love for Laura was stronger. As much as he embraced the beast within him, for her, he would forsake it.

Rational thought became harder to maintain as he made the transformation. The joy of complete freedom found him, and still his mind was shackled by worry. If the curse was not broken by tomorrow night, what in the hell was he going to tell his wife?

AN ACHING BACK WOKE LAURA. THE METAL BEDSPRINGS beneath the thin mattress seemed to have fused to her spine. A string of choice words came to mind, then she remembered. This was her honeymoon. She was Mrs. Sam Wulf. Smiling, Laura turned to other side of the bed. Her husband was missing. The sound of running water and the closed bathroom door located him. Sam was in the shower.

Struggling to a sitting position, she glanced around the small cabin, hoping it would somehow look better in the light of day. The kitchenette with its outdated countertops held one bright spot. A coffeemaker. And the pot was full. Laura threw back the thin quilt covering her and rose. She'd dressed in more woods-friendly pajamas once she and Sam had made a lukewarm shower steamy.

With socks on her feet, she walked to the kitchenette. Laura located a cup and poured a dose of morning courage. What horrors would Sam have in store for her today? Glancing out the double windows over the bed revealed a rugged mountain scene and lots of sunshine. It looked like a gorgeous day. Dammit.

The bathroom door opened. Sam walked out wearing a towel. His sun-streaked hair was slicked back from his masculine features. A sexy morning shadow shaded his strong jawline. Droplets clung to his muscled chest. She sighed. Talk about gorgeous.

"Did you sleep all right, baby?"

Despite the thin, lumpy mattress and the hard metal bedsprings, Laura had slept well once she'd settled against Sam's warmth, snuggled safely in his arms. "Like a log," she answered, thinking it sounded like a woodsy response.

He flashed a lopsided grin. "You look mighty sexy in those flannel pajamas."

As a rule, Laura didn't do flannel. Sam had warned her that it got cold at night in the mountains, even during the summer months. Executing a modeling pivot, she said, "Get used to them. You've seen the last of the sexy stuff. Now that we're married, you'll see the monster I've kept hidden all these months."

Her teasing failed to get the expected smile from Sam. He glanced away, hefting his suitcase onto the bed.

Laura joined him. "You do know I was kidding, right?"

"Of course I do," he answered, digging for clothing. "I thought we'd walk down to the lake, catch a few trout for dinner. How does that sound?"

She was glad Sam had his head stuck in a suitcase so he couldn't see her blanch. Fishing? Walking? They'd have to actually go into the woods to reach the lake, right?

"Can't we drive to the lake?"

He shook his head. "We'll have to hike through some pretty rough terrain to reach the lake, but it shouldn't take us more than an hour if we get going." Pulling a shirt over his head, he added, "Be sure to spray yourself with repellent again before we leave."

The fake smile on her face could last only so long. Laura grabbed her suitcase and rolled it into the tiny bathroom. She should have come clean with Sam a long time ago about her fear of the woods. She'd gone along with the lie about liking the outdoors at first because she knew Sam was a woodsy kind of guy. She hadn't wanted to ruin her chances with him just because they were different in that regard. For months Laura had worried about making excuses if he invited her to the cabin, but Sam hadn't invited her. Why? And why was she just now wondering why?

"Coming, Laura? I've got everything we need. The fish bite better in the morning!"

Glancing at herself in the mirror, Laura straightened her shoulders, "I can do this," she repeated.

SAM WAS NEARLY ONE HUNDRED PERCENT CERTAIN LAURA had never been hiking about ten minutes into their walk. Although her shoes were cute, they weren't meant for serious exercise, and he'd taken an easier route to the lake the moment he saw them. When they'd first met, his new wife had indicated that she liked the outdoors.

It had worried him at the time, waiting for Laura to insist on visiting the cabin with him on his monthly trips. But Laura had never asked to go along. Now he knew why. Her reaction to the cabin last night and to the bugs assured Sam she'd never spent a day of her life in the woods.

"Are we almost there?" Laura huffed beside him. The way she gawked around as they walked, Sam figured she'd trip and break her pretty neck.

"Not far," he assured her. "Laura, are you enjoying yourself?"

"Sure," she answered, stumbling over a fallen branch. She caught herself and smiled at him. "As you said last night, who doesn't like the woods?"

His wife didn't. Laura hadn't been viewing her surroundings as if awestruck by the beauty of the mountains. She was terrified. He sensed her fear with his animal instincts. Sam took her hand in his. "You have nothing to be afraid of, Laura."

She wet her tempting lips. "You mean there's no bears or wild animals around here?"

Lying to her about the possible dangers would be irresponsible. "There are all kinds of wild animals in the woods," he explained. "And yes, there are bears, although most of the time they stay higher in the mountains. As long as we don't leave food outside, they shouldn't bother us. It's wise to be alert to our surroundings, but being afraid defeats the whole purpose of enjoying nature."

The tension he felt radiating from Laura lessened somewhat. She trusted Sam to protect her, and he would, with his life, but Laura needed to learn to trust her own instincts, as well.

"I've taken this path to the lake many times so I'm familiar with it, but if I wasn't, I'd have brought along torn strips of cloth and marked my trail so I could easily find my way back to the cabin in case I lost my sense of direction."

"That's a good idea," Laura said. "What about animals? How would you deal with them?"

Sam adjusted the poles and tackle box he held in one hand. "Most of the time, it isn't a problem. Wild animals, as a rule, don't like to be around people. They'd rather stay out of sight. Only a sick or starving animal or one protecting their young would attack a human."

Laura snapped her head around to look at him. "So surely in all these glorious woods there's at least a few of those."

It appeared he wasn't getting through to his wife. Sam had meant to ease her worries, not increase them. He stopped, pulling Laura around to face him. "Do you want to go back? We can just hang around the cabin today if you'd feel more comfortable."

Her beautiful blue eyes brightened. Then she frowned. "But you want to fish." Straightening her shoulders, she answered, "No, I want to go on. Maybe I'll like fishing."

"I thought you had fished before."

A blush bloomed in her cheeks. "Well, not for a long time. I've forgotten everything I once knew about fishing."

She'd never been fishing, he strongly suspected. Sam didn't mind if his bride had led him to believe she liked the great outdoors, when it was obvious she knew next to nothing about it. A little white lie was nothing compared with what he hadn't told her.

The curse was supposed to be broken. He had hoped it would be something he never had to confess. How did a man tell his wife, a woman who was obviously terrified of wild animals, that she had married one?

"Is something wrong, Sam?"

He realized he stood staring down at her while his thoughts raced. Sam shook his head. "No. Let's go fishing."

WHAT HAD POSSESSED LAURA TO BELIEVE FOR ONE second that she might enjoy fishing? Sam's tackle box was filled with stinky smelling stuff, ugly wiggly plastic worms and bright metal little fish with hooks in them.

"I'll bait your hook," Sam said, and she could have kissed him for not expecting she'd know how to do such a thing herself, or even want to. She wrinkled her nose as he dug into a jar of what appeared to be red squishy caviar. He put one of the eggs on her hook, then placed a red-and-white plastic ball on the fishing line.

He cast out a little ways and handed her the pole. "Trout like salmon eggs. Watch the bobber, and if it suddenly jerks or goes under, pull your rod up and reel it in."

Huh? "Okay," she said as if she had a clue what he'd just instructed her to do. Laura watched the bobber. It moved, so she jerked her pole.

"That's just the current," Sam said. "You'll know the difference when you feel a tug on your line or the bobber actually goes under."

"I know that," she fibbed. "I just wanted to reposition the bobber thingy." *That sounded lame.*

"If you'd like, sit on that rock and make yourself more comfortable while you wait. Fishing takes patience."

Could a rock be comfortable? And if she sat on one, wouldn't she get the rear of her cute shorts dirty? "I think I'll just stand," Laura decided.

"Okay, suit yourself." Sam walked toward the rock with his baited pole. He cast out before settling on the rock. Her rugged outdoor man looked at home in his surroundings. He was obviously relaxed while Laura worried about what she would do if she actually managed to catch a fish on her line.

Thirty minutes later it wasn't such a worry. "Are you sure there are fish in this lake?" she called to Sam.

"I always catch a mess of fish while I'm here. Nothing tastes better than freshly fried trout."

Laura didn't care for fish. She liked crab and lobster, but had always turned her nose up at anything else. If Sam caught a fish, she vowed to eat it, though. She'd misled Sam when they first met. Now might be a good time to come clean with him.

"Sam, I need to tell you something."

He glanced at her and lifted a brow.

Meeting his trusting puppy dog eyes proved difficult. She stared at the ground instead. "I wasn't completely honest with you when we first met. I'm not the outdoorsy type, Sam. I only pretended be that kind of girl because I figured a woman who shared your interests would appeal to you the most. I wanted you to like me as much as I liked you."

Suddenly Sam stood before her. He took the pole from her hand and laid it on the ground. Lifting her chin, he forced her to look at him. "Usually, I am more attracted to women who share my love of the outdoors, but there was nothing usual about the way I felt the first time I saw you. All I could do was stare—think about how beautiful you are, and smart and funny. I knew you were the woman I'd been waiting for all my life."

Tears pricked Laura's eyes, and the reaction had nothing to do with the smell of repellant she'd sprayed down with before they left the cabin. Sam was the sweetest man. Men like her husband were few and far between. They were all but extinct.

"You're not disappointed with me?" she asked. "You're not mad that I haven't been completely honest with you?"

His warm fingers moved up her face to wipe the tears away. "It was just a little white lie. Sure, I'd love it if you wanted to take off with me and come up here, hang out and relax, but if it's not your thing, I understand. Just because it's one of mine doesn't mean you have to pretend to like something that you don't."

Her heart flip-flopped inside her chest. "I've married Prince Charming." Laura raised on tiptoes and kissed him on the mouth. When he didn't respond, she pulled back to look at him. His eyes were haunted. "What is it, Sam? What's wrong?"

He glanced away. "I haven't been honest with you about everything, either. . . ."

She waited for Sam to continue, but suddenly her fishing pole shot forward on the ground. Sam broke away and bounded after it. He grabbed the pole.

"Come here, Laura. You're going to catch your first fish!"

SETTLED IN SAM'S ARMS LATER THAT NIGHT, LAURA didn't mind the lumpy mattress and the hard metal bedsprings. They'd eaten the fish she'd caught earlier and that was pretty good, but not nearly so good as the sex that followed dinner. Who'd have thought Laura Wulf was a fisherman? Certainly not her.

Sam's slow, steady breathing told her he'd fallen asleep. They were both tired after their hike to the lake and back, not to mention their long lovemaking session. On the way home from the lake, Laura had taken the time to really look at her surroundings and appreciate the woods instead of worrying about what might come charging out of them to eat her up.

Maybe she could learn to like the great outdoors. It would please Sam, and although he said it wasn't important to him, it was important to Laura. She didn't want anything standing between time they might spend together. The cabin could be remodeled. She did it all the time in her real estate practice. The first order of business would be a comfortable bed. One that didn't have a big crack down the middle she kept getting stuck in during the night.

Laura drifted to sleep envisioning the changes she would make. Something woke her later—the sound of the door closing softly. She turned to Sam, but he was missing. Sitting, she listened.

"Sam?"

No answer.

Moonlight spilled in from the windows, allowing her to see that the bathroom door was open, the light off. Sam wasn't in the cabin. Scooting to the top of the bed, she glanced outside. Her husband stood staring up at a full moon. He was naked!

"What in the world is he doing?" Laura mumbled.

For a moment, she wondered if he might be sleepwalking, although she'd never known him to, nor had Sam ever said that he was prone to the affliction. But he seemed awake as she continued to watch him. He walked toward the thick trees at the edge of the clearing. Then he began to run. Naked. Barefoot. Away from the cabin.

Her momentary amusement over Sam's actions quickly disappeared. Laura was afraid. Not for herself this time, but for Sam. What he was doing had to be dangerous even if he was at home in the woods. She rose and grabbed a terry cloth robe she'd brought to keep warm. After locating her shoes and slipping into them, Laura did something only a day ago she could never imagine herself doing. She went outside in the dead of night.

"Sam!" she called, but her husband was nowhere in sight. Now what to do? Should Laura go after him? Did she have the courage? The trees looked like tall monsters in the moonlight, branches shaped like claws waiting to grab her if she came too close.

There were animals out there, Sam had told her earlier. So why would he run into the woods, into danger? A horrible thought occurred. Was Sam a little weird? One card short of a full deck? Laura had trouble believing that. Sam was perfect. Too perfect, she'd often thought.

"He's not crazy or weird," she chided herself. There had to be a logical explanation for her husband sneaking out of the cabin in the dead of night to run naked through the woods. Now Laura just had to find out what it was.

———

SAM HAD TAKEN HIS WOLF FORM. AT ONE time, he'd read that the cursed Wulf men couldn't control their thoughts or actions when they transformed. Along with the poem composed by the first Wulf cursed, so faded now it was nearly indistinguishable, were letters handed down from generation to generation, explaining certain aspects of the transformation.

Where had Sam gone wrong in the translation of the poem, that is, what little remained of it? Love was supposed to be the curse but it was also supposed to be the key. Since it was said former Wulfs had broken the curse throughout the centuries by marrying their soul mates, Sam had assumed that was all there was to it. He was obviously wrong.

Unless Laura wasn't his soul mate. Sam shied away from that thought. If she wasn't, he didn't care, he loved her. He'd stay with his wife even if it meant he would remain cursed for the rest of his life. But would Laura stay with him?

Through the trees, his sharpened vision caught the glow of a small light. A flashlight, he realized a moment later. Creeping from his hiding place, the wolf skirted the trees until he reached the light. What he saw surprised him. It was Laura. She wore her ratty terry cloth robe, and every so often, she stopped to flag a tree with a piece of toilet paper, marking her trail. Sam felt immensely proud of her at that moment. He realized how much his wife truly loved him.

She'd admitted to being afraid of the woods earlier, yet here she was, out searching for him. Or he had to assume that was the reason Laura had faced her fears, putting herself in danger. Sam wanted to go to her, wrap her in his arms and tell her how special she was . . . but he couldn't. If Laura saw him in wolf form, she'd be scared to death. At the same time, she needed to return to the cabin.

Since Sam couldn't change at will, he'd have to wait until morning to think of a suitable lie to tell Laura. For now, he wanted her safe. He knew how to send her running for home, even if he didn't like what he must do. Gathering all the misery he felt over deceiving the woman he loved, and the possibility of losing her, Sam released his feelings in the form of an eerie howl.

LAURA FROZE IN HER TRACKS. THE HAIR ON the back of her neck bristled. Her heart rose in her throat. That sound was from a wolf. Were there wolves in the woods anymore? She'd heard they were all but extinct except in places like Yellowstone. It was a wolf . . . unless it was something worse. Maybe it was Bigfoot. No one knew if they howled or what because they supposedly didn't exist.

Every scary creature she'd seen in movies, on television or heard about during junior high slumber parties jumped to the forefront of her mind. Trolls. Swamp Thing. Those creepy flying monkeys from *The Wizard Of Oz*. Frankenstein. Mummies. Vampires. Werewolves. The last thought stuck in her mind. A werewolf would howl, wouldn't it?

"Get a grip, Laura," she whispered, although the flashlight in her hand shook, mocking her attempt to be something other than what she was, which was terrified.

The howl sounded again. Laura jumped. She swore it was closer. Rational thought fled. She ran, disregarding the careful path she had made for herself. It didn't matter. The creature was on her heels and all she could do was try to escape.

There was a stitch in her side by the time the cabin came into view. Laura was never so happy to see anything in her life. She rushed to the cabin, slipped inside, closed and locked the door.

"Sam?" she called in the darkness. "Sam, please be here."

But he wasn't. Her new husband was out dancing naked in the

woods or something equally crazy while a wild animal chased his wife. Laura turned on the overhead light and pulled the ugly plaid drapes closed over the windows. She settled down to wait. Sam had a lot of explaining to do when he returned.

Although too worried to sleep, Laura managed to doze lightly throughout the night. She woke with a start. Sam stared down at her. The expression of love in his eyes nearly melted her. Then she remembered. Scrambling up, she asked, "Where were you last night?"

Sam pulled back from her and glanced away. "I went for a run."

"Naked?"

His gaze snapped back to her. "You saw me?"

"Yes. I woke when you left, looked out the window and saw you standing naked in the moonlight. Then you took off into the woods."

He scrubbed a hand over his face. "You shouldn't have come after me. That was dangerous."

Wrinkling her brow, she asked, "How did you know I came after you?"

Sam rose, presenting her with his tanned broad back. He wore a pair of jeans slung low on his hips and no shirt. "Because I know you, and against your better judgment you would have done something like that."

Despite the nice view, Laura wouldn't be distracted from the conversation. "If you know that about me you know me better than I know myself," she assured him. "But I was worried about you. There's a wolf in the woods. I heard it howling last night. I think it chased me all the way to the cabin."

When he turned, she had an even nicer view of his broad bare chest. "And you were afraid."

She forced her gaze to lift. "Of course I was afraid. I was terrified the thing would eat me."

He sat beside her again, taking her cold hands into his warms ones. "What if I told you that you didn't have to be afraid of the wolf? That it would never hurt you?"

Sam looked perfectly serious. Was he also perfectly crazy? "How can you be certain of that?"

"I've seen the wolf before. He won't harm a human. At least not unless he's threatened."

The feel of Sam's strong hands holding hers had a calming effect. "Is the wolf someone's pet around here?"

"I suppose you could say that."

"Then he's domesticated?"

"As domesticated as a wolf can be."

Now she understood. "He's like a dog?"

Sam flinched. "Well, no, he's not like a dog. He's a wolf."

Laura wasn't even sure she liked dogs. She was fairly certain she didn't like wolves. "None of this explains exactly what you were doing running around naked last night."

Releasing her hands, Sam rose and went into the kitchenette. He poured himself a cup of coffee. "I like to run around naked at night. It's a rush."

How could running around naked in mosquito-infested woods be a rush? Laura was afraid it went much deeper, and much darker. "Sam, are you an exhibitionist?"

He nearly spewed the sip of coffee he'd just taken. "Hell no, Laura. An exhibitionist likes people to see them naked. If I wanted that, I wouldn't run naked in an isolated area in the dead of night."

That was a relief. "Well, I can see where you might want to be," Laura admitted. "You have a pretty impressive package."

His laugh broke the tension between them. Sam returned to her, leaned in close and nibbled her earlobe. "Your flannel pajamas are really starting to turn me on."

Her husband was still the man she fell in love with, even if Laura had discovered a peculiar quirk about him. He'd discovered things he didn't know about her too. Maybe eight months wasn't long to get to know someone, but Laura was still certain she'd done the right thing by marrying Sam. Their love needed reaffirming after a stormy night. She knew the perfect way. Exposing a glimpse of flannel by opening her ratty robe, she winked at him.

"Come back to bed. It was a long night without you."

THEY'D SPENT MOST OF THE DAY IN BED, enjoying one another, laughing, teasing, but night had fallen and Sam worried about sneaking out without waking Laura again. He also wondered if the curse might be broken now so he wouldn't have to run away. If it wasn't, the cycle ended for him tomorrow. But it only ended until the next one. Could he manage to deceive Laura for the rest of their lives? Sam didn't want to. Maybe after they'd been married for a while, Laura could accept the truth.

Snuggled beside him, his wife said, "Something just occurred to me."

He kissed the top of her head. "What's that?"

"I'm afraid of a wolf and my last name is now Wulf."

It had taken her a while to make that connection. The curse cast centuries ago had been tied to the Wulf name. Over the years, its power had faded and now it was a rare occurrence for the curse to resurface. But Sam was proof it still existed. His parents recognized the signs early and prepared him for the transformation that true love would bring. Something Sam might have to do for his own sons someday. Another secret he'd kept from Laura.

Since he'd honestly believed the curse would be broken for him on their wedding night, Sam decided on a wait-and-see approach concerning his children. No need to worry Laura unnecessarily.

"See, you shouldn't be afraid of him. You're practically related," he finally responded.

She giggled and snuggled closer. "You've worn me out. I'm going to sleep like the dead tonight."

He hoped so. If nothing had changed for him, Sam must leave her soon. What else could break the curse if simply finding his soul mate and marrying her wasn't the answer? There had been something said about a man facing his greatest enemy. As far as Sam knew, he didn't have any enemies. Could the verse be an archaic way of saying a man must face his greatest fear? Losing Laura was his greatest fear. The only way to face that was to tell her the truth.

If he did, Laura, terrified of the woods and the creatures that dwelled within them, would want to be as far away from her new husband as possible. Unless he taught her that not all creatures were to be feared. There was a way Sam might prove that to Laura. But she wasn't going to like it.

THE CABIN WAS FREEZING. EVEN LAURA'S FLANNEL PAJAMAS weren't cutting the mustard tonight. She scooted past the crack that resulted from pushing two bunks together in search of Sam's warmth. Not only was the warmth absent, so was her husband. It was still dark. Light failed to penetrate the ugly drapes she'd pulled closed before they went to bed. But she did see a sliver of moonlight coming from the open door.

"Sam?" she called, hoping he was somewhere in the cabin.

No answer.

"Good grief." Laura threw back the covers. "If you must run

naked in the woods at night, you could at least close the door behind you!"

Although complaining did no good, it made her feel better.
She was about to get out of bed when she spotted it. A shadow to
her left. A set of glowing eyes. A scream rose in her throat. She bit
it back, afraid the response might spur an attack from the animal.

When her eyes adjusted to the darkness, Laura realized the
shadow was that of a wolf. It must be the same one she'd seen the
night before—the one Sam told her wouldn't harm a human. But
her husband wasn't around to chase it back outside where it belonged.

"Nice wolf," she said. "Go back outside now."

The wolf rose and moved toward her. Laura rolled off the
other side of the bed and made a mad dash for the door. Adrenaline pumping, she actually made it and ran outside, pulling the
door shut behind her.

"Ah-ha!" she yelled. "Tricked you, didn't I?"

Her cockiness lasted only a second. It was cold outside. The
car was locked and the keys were inside the cabin. The only choice
Laura had was to go in search of Sam. She knew it wasn't a good
idea to traipse off into the woods without a flashlight or anything
to mark her trail, but she had to at least look. Maybe Sam wasn't
far from the cabin.

Taking off in the direction she'd seen Sam run the night before, Laura tried to keep a level head. The full moon lit her way,
but it also outlined the trees. They still looked scary. Her breath
steamed on the night air and her socks were wet because of the
thick dew on the ground. Behind her, the wolf continued to
howl, almost as if warning Laura to return.

"Yeah, come back so I can eat you," she said with a snort.
"Sam!"

No answer.

As she moved farther into the trees, the silence around her should have been comforting; instead it made her feel as if she'd fallen off the face of the earth. How could Sam stand to run around naked in the cold at night? Laura was freezing. She blew on her hands and would have stomped her feet if she wasn't afraid she'd step on something and injure herself.

The farther she walked, the more disoriented Laura became. She had no idea which direction she was headed. Her voice was hoarse from calling for Sam. Panic threatened to take over. Laura sat on a fallen log and took deep calming breaths. Rubbing her arms to keep warm, she called for Sam again. Again, no answer.

Although she wasn't woods smart, she sensed her best action now would be to return to the cabin. Maybe if she opened the door again, the wolf would run outside. For all Laura knew Sam had already returned and dealt with the animal.

Now, to find her way back. Laura rose and trudged in the opposite direction she'd been headed. She walked for what seemed an eternity before she heard a familiar sound. The wolf howling.

She nearly cried. At least now she had something to guide her back to the cabin. Her steps were more certain as she followed the wolf's howls. The cabin came into view. Her knees almost buckled with relief. But she still had a problem. Sam had obviously not returned and the wolf was still trapped inside her home.

Her hands trembled as she wrapped them around the door handle of the cabin. She flung it wide and flattened herself against the outside wall.

"Come out of there, wolf!" she demanded. "I'm not sharing my home with you."

The animal bounded outside, headed for the trees. Laura raced into the cabin, closed and locked the door. She stood with her heart hammering, breathing deep in an effort to calm herself. She was home. She was safe. But where in the hell was Sam? Pushing away from the door, Laura went into the bathroom. She was still freezing and even a ten-minute hot shower would warm her up. If Sam returned while she showered, he could use the spare key he'd told her was under the welcome mat outside.

Just as she hoped, the shower got her blood pumping again. Laura avoided the sensuous-smelling shower gel. Sam had told her it attracted bugs. Once she climbed out, she dried and put a towel around her wet hair. After moving back into the bedroom and switching on lights, she frowned at the thought of wearing flannel pajamas.

Instead she dug a sexy short nightgown and matching robe from the cabin's old dresser. It wasn't that she dressed to please Sam when he returned. Laura just needed to feel feminine. Besides, a woman should look good while yelling at her husband for the first time.

THE NIGHT WAS PURE AGONY. SAM COULDN'T LOSE himself to the beast and run free. His plan to show Laura the wolf within him wouldn't harm her had backfired. He never anticipated that Laura would run out into the night, locking him inside. He'd hurled his body against the big windows over the bed several times. Damn the double-paned glass he'd had installed to keep the cabin warmer. His throat was hoarse from howling, hoping if Laura strayed too far from the cabin looking for him, he could guide her back.

Not only had his city bride found her way back, she'd ordered him from the cabin. Sam was proud as hell of her, but after last night, he knew he must tell Laura the truth. She was tougher than he'd given her credit for. He had to be as brave. Even if he lost her forever.

He entered the cabin naked and dirty from being out of doors. Laura was perched on the bed drinking coffee. She looked like cotton candy in a pink slinky gown and robe.

"The toilet isn't working," were her first words.

Sam grabbed a pair of pajama bottoms from his suitcase and slipped into them. "I'll have a look at it after we talk."

"You'll have a look at it now," she corrected him. "I need to go, and I won't if I can't flush the toilet."

Walking to where she sat, Sam stared down at Laura. "What I have to tell you is more important than a broken toilet."

She crossed her long legs. "That might depend on how bad one of us needs to go."

His talk with Laura would have to wait. "Okay, I'll fix it."

It took him only a moment to figure out the chain to the float had simply come loose. Sam corrected the problem, washed his face and hands and quickly brushed his teeth. He came out of the bathroom.

"It's working now."

She rose and glided toward him in a flutter of pink silk. When Laura reached his side, she handed him her coffee cup. "You might want to fortify yourself. I'm getting ready to yell at you."

He took a sip. "Thanks for the warning."

Carrying Laura's coffee cup to the bed, he placed the cup on a nightstand and took a seat. Laura emerged a moment later. Sam noticed the high heeled slippers she wore. They made her legs look a mile long.

"I see you've learned to navigate the cracks," he said.

"You'd be surprised what a girl can learn when she has a husband who doesn't stay home at night."

Laura got her jabs in where she could. She wasn't the type to let a man walk all over her. His wife was funny, smart, and sophisticated.

She was the best thing that had ever happened to him, even if a curse came with loving her. And Sam was about to lose her.

"That's what I wanted to talk to you about," he said.

She made an adorable snorting noise. "Really? What a coincidence. That's what I wanted to talk to you about too."

Although Sam longed to make love to her, he couldn't keep deceiving his wife. "I need to confess something to you."

Her sarcastic smile faded. "You have some deep dark secret, don't you, Sam?"

He'd add intuitive to his list of wonderful character traits Laura possessed. "Yes."

Sighing, she walked to the bed and sat beside him. "You belong to some weird cult who get together naked in the woods and chant and dance around, right?"

If only it were that simple. There wasn't an easy way to tell her about his problem, so he might as well be blunt. "I'm a werewolf, baby."

The only response he got from Laura was the slight widening of her big baby blues. A moment later she laughed. "Good try. What's really going on?"

Sam wished he could laugh as well, pretend what he'd said was ludicrous. He took her hands in his. "I'm cursed. I thought marrying you, my soul mate, would free me, but it didn't. I had hoped I'd never have to tell you my secret. The wolf in the woods. The wolf in the cabin last night. That was me."

She sat as if shocked for a moment, and then Laura wrestled her hand from his. She stood, glaring down at him. "This isn't funny, Sam!"

No, it wasn't funny. It was horrible . . . at least seeing Laura's reaction was. The curse in itself wasn't so bad. "It's true, Laura."

Turning her back, she ran her fingers through her hair. When she faced him again, her expression was surprisingly calm. Very slowly, Laura asked, "Do have medication you're supposed to be taking in your suitcase? Should I get it for you?"

Laura didn't believe him. She thought he needed medication. Sam would as soon tell her that he was kidding and get back to their honeymoon. But he couldn't. He'd deceived his wife long enough. "I wish I could take a pill and make this go away, baby, but I can't. Since marrying you and consummating our vows on our wedding night didn't break the curse like I thought it would, I'm stuck with it."

Her hand went to her heart. She joined him on the bed. "You're telling me that you're a werewolf. You're not joking. You're perfectly serious. Do you know how crazy that sounds?"

Now that he'd told Laura his secret, Sam was determined to make her believe him. "When you were in here with the wolf last night, you said, "Nice wolf," and then you told me to go outside. Instead I moved toward you. You rolled off the other side of the bed, made a mad dash for the door and shut me inside. When you returned, you ordered me out. If I wasn't the wolf, how would I know that?"

Her brows drew together. Laura narrowed her eyes. "Were you here all along? Were you hiding while I was being scared out my wits?"

Sam rose, needing to stretch his legs. "I would never hide while you were frightened. I hoped you would see the wolf wouldn't harm you, but you didn't give me a chance to prove that. I'm hoarse today from howling so you could find your way back to the cabin. I was terrified something might happen to you."

Laura swallowed loudly. Her eyes watered. He was finally getting through to her. "You're not joking. You really are a werewolf."

A bevy of emotions crossed her face. Horror. Sadness. Everything but acceptance. Sam stood over her. "I know this is hard for you to comprehend, to believe, but—"

"No," she interrupted, looking down at her folded hands. "Surprisingly, it isn't hard for me to believe. If somewhere in my subconscious I've held on to all the things that frightened me as a child, it must mean that deep inside, I believe in the existence of witches and talking bears and monkeys that fly." She lifted her eyes to him again. "So, you're cursed."

Sam shrugged.

"And marrying me was supposed to free you but it didn't? Is that the only reason you married me? Because in order to break your curse you thought you had to get married?"

The pain in her eyes cut Sam to the quick. He bent before her. "I married you because I love you, Laura. Love sets the curse into motion. The minute I came face-to-face with you, it came upon me. I knew you were the one."

Laura shook her head. A tear rolled down her pale cheek. "But I must not be the one. You said it wasn't broken. Maybe there's another woman out there somewhere who can help you."

Wiping away her tears, Sam assured her, "I don't want another woman, Laura. I only want you. If you still want me, I don't care if I'm cursed for the rest of my life. If you can live with me the way I am, I can live with myself."

As he'd done a moment earlier, Laura now brushed away Sam's tears. "In two days I've learned a lot about myself. I've learned I can survive in the woods if I use my head. I've learned I can stand up to what frightens me. I suppose I can live without you, Sam. But I don't want to. I love you. For better or for worse, remember?"

Her words were sweeter to him than the vows they'd spoken

only two days ago. Sam was humbled by his wife's unconditional love. By her acceptance and her courage. He should have told Laura from the start. He should have trusted her and trusted in himself to have chosen exactly the right woman. But there were still things he hadn't told his wife.

"Our sons might also carry the curse, Laura. It rarely surfaces these days, but I'm proof that it can still happen."

She frowned. "Will we know?"

He nodded. "My parents knew from the time I was a toddler. They helped prepare me."

Laura took his hand and pulled Sam up on the bed beside her. "Now I understand the look of hope in their eyes at our wedding. It was so intense. They were hoping for more than a happy future for us. They were hoping I could set you free of the curse I brought down upon you. And I've failed them. Failed you."

His wife wasn't to blame. Sam wouldn't allow her to feel guilt. "I can live with the curse. It's really not so bad. I love the freedom, but I would sacrifice that for you. I would sacrifice anything for you."

More tears fell down her cheeks, but she smiled at him through them. "We'll be all right, won't we, Sam?"

Taking her in his arms, Sam answered, "We'll be fine. I'll make sure of that."

He bent to kiss her but was suddenly knocked backward on the bed. His mouth flew open. A bright blue light spilled out. An apparition poured from him, stealing his breath. Above him, the form took shape. The shape of a glowing wolf.

Laura's shrill scream split the silence. The wolf shadow flinched. She kept screaming until the spirit leapt at her. Mouth open wide, the wolf lost shape and poured into her mouth. Sam could barely breathe, but he lunged for the spirit. He was too late.

It disappeared down Laura's throat. She swallowed with a loud gulp.

"Oh no!" Sam shook her. "No!"

A soft belch left her lips. Her eyes still wide, she asked, "What the hell just happened to me?"

Sam pulled her close. "The wolf spirit left me. The curse is broken, but now it's inside you."

She pushed him back, eyes still huge. "Is that supposed to happen? I mean, have you ever heard of it doing that?"

He shook his head. "I've never read anything about it, but wait, I do recall reading something about the spirit entering other bodies."

Her bottom lip trembled. "Are you telling me now I'm a werewolf?"

Sam didn't know what to tell her. He'd never read much about the spirit possessing someone besides a male Wulf. There was a reference to it in some old writings. He'd have to find the reference again and study it. There had to be a way to call the spirit from an unwilling host. Like an exorcism. "It's only temporary," he assured her. "I'll figure out how to get rid of it."

She threw her hands up. "Great. I'm a woman. One curse a month and now I have another. I don't even like the woods, but I'll have to go running around in them during a full moon."

Having never considered the curse to be much of a curse, but sometimes a gift, Sam wasn't certain how to comfort her. He pulled his wife back into his arms. "At least now you know the scariest thing in the woods will be you."

Her eyes brimming with tears, she hiccupped. "I suppose you're right about that. I'll be like the queen of the woods until we figure out how to get rid of this spirit inside me, right?"

Sam had to give her some assurances. He was surprised she

handled the situation as well as she had. "Other animals and even people won't mess with a wolf."

Laura pulled away, walked to the window and glanced outside. "We'll have to still come up here every month, but now for me instead of you."

"I'll take care of you, Laura," Sam promised. "It isn't so much of a curse as an inconvenience at times. It's a good way for you to learn to like the great outdoors. I already know the ropes, so I can prepare you for the change. And someday, we may both need to prepare our children."

Her voice shook when she asked, "Is it going to happen tonight, Sam?"

He walked up behind her. "No. It won't happen until the next full moon. The rest of the honeymoon is just for us. For talking and laughing and loving."

"That, I can handle," she said. "We can handle anything, right, as long as we're together?"

His heart came close to bursting with joy. He had chosen the right woman. He loved Laura, but he'd misjudged her. He should have trusted her to be strong enough to handle the truth. "As long as we're together," he agreed, turning her to face him so he could kiss her.

Laura stopped him. "You said earlier that you would do anything for me." She nodded at the windows over the bed. "Those drapes have to go. And I want the floors redone and the bathroom made larger. If we're spending a few days a month here, we're going to make it a real luxury hideaway."

Her request was a simple one, all things considered. "Whatever you want, baby."

Pulling his face close to hers, she said, "What I want at the moment is for my husband to make love to me. Then I want you to tell me everything you know about this curse you've passed to me. What happens, how you feel when it happens, how I'm going to feel, and as soon as we get home, we're digging for answers on how to exorcise the thing."

Sam felt certain there was a way. He planned to talk Laura into experiencing at least once, the freedom of being a wolf. It should do wonders for her confidence in dealing with the great outdoors. Simply because he was no longer forced to spend time at the cabin, didn't mean Sam didn't want to continue to visit their little hideaway. It was a place they would someday bring their children. It was part of their future. And now more than ever, he knew they would be together always, regardless of what life threw in their paths.

"Anything for you, Laura," Sam said before claiming her lips.

New York Times *and* USA Today—*bestselling author Ronda Thompson is best known for her popular* Wild Wulfs of London *series. Her most recent release is* Confessions of a Werewolf Supermodel. *For the latest news, visit Ronda at www.rondathompson.com.*